THE SICILIAN AFFAIR

To escort a small boy to Sicily hardly seemed to Laurie Grant to be taking her life in her hands. Yet that is exactly what she did when she found herself responsible not only for her original charge but for his friend – a little girl, missing, believed kidnapped, whom a number of ruthless characters were out to destroy.

With her fiancé, Stewart Noble, far away in New York and involved in the insurance end of this same kidnapping, Laurie had to think and act for herself. To save the children, she is forced to tangle with the FBI, the Mafia, and the strange and mysterious island of Sicily itself. Fortunately the spirited red-headed Scots girl who has appeared in May Mackintosh's two previous romantic suspense novels is equal to all of them, even including the attractive yet sinister American to whom the kidnapped child is touchingly devoted, and the distinguished archaeologist whose interests extend beyond digging up the past.

Against a background of Sicilian customs and spectacular scenery, May Mackintosh unfolds an original and exciting tale.

The
Sicilian Affair

MAY MACKINTOSH

COLLINS

ST JAMES'S PLACE, LONDON

1974

William Collins Sons & Co Ltd
London · Glasgow · Sydney · Auckland
Toronto · Johannesburg

First published 1974
© May Mackintosh 1974

ISBN 0 00 221890 9

Set in Monotype Imprint
Made and printed in Great Britain by
William Collins Sons & Co Ltd Glasgow

For Lena and Esther Forte
who taught me to appreciate
the bouquet of Italy

AUTHOR'S NOTE

I should like to express my gratitude to Captain Antonio M. Gareze for his assistance in connection with the layout and technical details of Il Baglietto 16.50.

I should also like to make clear that any similarity or apparent connection between the characters in this story and actual persons, whether alive or dead, is purely coincidental.

M.M.

Chapter 1

What kind of person am I? Do other people also attract trouble like a magnet?

I do not know the answers to those questions, but I would say that Dukes' Hotel is the last place in the world where one would expect the seeds of adventure, misery and death to be sown.

The silly thing is that at the beginning I did not even mind being alone in London. In fact, it seemed an agreeable little adventure to have those few solitary days and to follow them up with about two weeks on my own in Sicily.

Probably at the back of my mind was the childish idea that, while he was in New York, my fiancé, Stewart Noble, would miss me frantically and that our subsequent reunion in Taormina would show him what his latest case had cost in terms of our postponed honeymoon.

I was certainly not miserable. By now, postponed honeymoons were practically a way of life for us. There had been times when I had gone almost mad with worry and disappointment when Stewart's cases had cropped up just in time to put off our marital arrangements. The torment of wondering if he was lukewarm about the marriage had made me, on occasions, cruel and unreasonable. Often I wanted to shock him, surprise him into an admission of reluctance, but he always grinned and I knew that everything was right between us. Invariably I ended up by determining, like now, to make the best of the situation.

Mentally I saw myself, tanned and glowing with health, meeting him at the airport at Catania. This was particularly silly since, being a redhead, a tan is something to be avoided like the plague.

For many people, I understand, warning bells ring in their

heads when the unexpected is about to happen. Maybe I was too busy enjoying everything about the hotel and, at first, about my friends, to hear them.

From the moment of my arrival, I had been entranced.

My home is in Zürich and I had been long enough away from Britain to find London inexpressibly charming. The small cobbled courtyard off St James's Place was straight out of Dickens. The gas lamps shining above the broad flower-boxes and the serenity of the hotel with its eighteenth-century Wilkins engravings delighted me. I loved Harry, the smiling Scottish hall porter, and Erol, the handsome young Turk in the bar, and I doted on the Duke of Leeds suite, particularly on its small cream and coral kitchen.

But, in less than an hour, Arlene Curzon spoiled it for me with her vague, foolish talk of the Mafia, though I was irritated rather than disturbed.

She poked at the *escargots à la Languedocienne*. Her face had the sallow look it gets when she has been slimming.

'I'm not at all sure that it is a good idea that you should stay all alone at the villa, Laurie,' she said doubtfully. 'The Mafia, you know . . .' Her voice trailed off. 'One hears such dreadful things about them . . . murders and kidnappings and . . . dreadful things . . .'

Tom Curzon frowned.

'If there were a war on, Arlene,' I said cheerfully, 'you would be arrested for spreading alarm and despondency. Cheer up. I have no intention of getting myself either murdered or kidnapped. Besides,' I added tranquilly, 'that's Stewart's field. I keep off his territory.'

Tom Curzon smiled his slow, sweet smile.

'You make my eminently respectable young friend sound like a combination of Crippen and Al Capone.'

He looked like a benevolent owl rather than one of England's most famous QC's, but when his eyes lost their vagueness, it was easy to see why he was feared.

He put out his hand and touched my cheek. 'Forget Arlene's nonsense about the Mafia, Laurie. Take a case of Ambre

8

Solaire with you and lie in the sun until Stewart gets there. I wish we could join you. In May, Taormina is perfect. Pity you won't see any performances in the Greek theatre.'

He picked delicately at the *suprême de volaille*. 'The only conspiracy you need concern yourself with is one that keeps Stewart flat on his back in the sun until the end of the month. I thought he sounded tired when I spoke to him on the telephone. Pity. Always drives himself too hard. Pity.' He hesitated. 'I suppose you wouldn't consider getting married while you're in Sicily?'

My head-shake was a very decided negative.

Arlene's hair was like pale silk against the background of dark green walls. Her hazel eyes had a slightly malicious glitter as she probed for the precise reason for Stewart's absence.

'Business in New York,' I said succinctly, concentrating on the curry-flavoured cream flamed in whisky.

My non-explanation was accepted by Tom Curzon with his usual air of amiable indifference, but obviously Arlene was not satisfied. The atmosphere in the St James's Room had lost a little of its tranquillity. I cursed all curious women.

'Laurie Grant,' she said accusingly, 'you're hiding something. Be a darling and tell me. Tom,' she added plaintively, 'tells me nothing. Stewart is after some crook, isn't he? It must be something really big when he puts your wedding off. It's some big case, isn't it?'

I smiled at her over the rim of my wine glass and, as I denied it, I had not even the slightest twinge of conscience. Sadly, I have to admit that I am learning not to trust anybody. It gets easier all the time.

'Just dreary routine.' I heard the lightness of my voice and, for good measure, I shook my head in smiling disclaimer of any drama in our lives. Stewart would have been proud of me.

Drama? Where did it begin?

Did it start because I came alone to Dukes' Hotel? Was it simply because it was the beginning of May?

Or was it because on a day five years ago, Arlene, her back very stiff, walked along a Harley Street that was fresh and cool and smelled deliciously of spring flowers, after the gynæcologist had told her that she would never bear a child?

Did it start on the morning that Casilda Biagotti got out of her bath in her villa in Catania, looked discontentedly at the reflection of her long naked body and decided to slim?

Was it because, eight years ago, a child screamed in fear and agony and then was silent?

How much of it was due to the fact that, in Genoa, a man called Masouri tried to make a quick fortune by dealing in inferior olive oil?

Did it begin when Eric Dalton bent to kiss his bride and recalled with a wince of pain how much her diamond hoop had cost him?

Was it, in fact, triggered off by Al Scott when he fell in love and closed his art show?

Was the man called August the catalyst? Or Stewart? Or I?

Just dreary routine, I said, but under the table, superstitiously, I crossed the fingers of my left hand, remembering with a faint cold prickle of apprehension how often my fiancé's job had led him into danger.

New York seemed very far away then. Stewart is not only a director of the World Metropolitan Insurance Company, which has its main offices in Zürich, but is in charge of the claims adjustment department. In the latter capacity, he sometimes finds himself in strange places and, not infrequently, in dangerous company.

My function is simply to act as his Girl Friday, but what was created as a temporary position for me pending our marriage keeps going on and on.

'Pity you had to postpone the Sicilian honeymoon, but at least you'll have a holiday, Laurie,' said Tom Curzon in his kind, aristocratic voice. 'A pretty little thing like you shouldn't be left too long on your own. Can't blame the chaps if they try to poach.'

'Tom, you're an idiot.' Arlene's tone was indulgent. 'Five minutes after meeting any man, Laurie is guaranteed to be talking about Stewart in that special voice which is as good as a red light to a normally intelligent being. No wonder Stewart went off quite happily. He knows that – bless her! – she's strictly a one-man woman. But if he thinks he can get away with postponing a wedding again, he's mad.'

'Ha! Wait till she meets those Sicilians. The women are nothing to boast about, but the men . . . ! It's a genetic mystery to me how, in the south at least, they have managed to hang on to the marvellous profiles and striking blue eyes of their Greek ancestors, while the women are usually dark-haired, dark-eyed and pretty stodgy. A bit unfair, I would say.'

'No temptation at all,' said Arlene serenely. She seemed to have forgotten her misgivings about the Mafia. 'She's got her own Greek god in her beloved. At any rate, she'll probably be without him for only a very short time. I'd like to see the Sicilian who can match Stewart's buttery curls and that yummy profile. Besides, you're not likely to meet a six feet two Sicilian, Laurie.' She sighed elaborately. 'Did you know that I cried for a week when I heard that he was going to marry you? I've always wanted him.'

'What about me?' asked Tom indignantly.

'Don't be old-fashioned, darling. Monogamy is terribly dated. I would have kept you on too.'

Deliberately I helped to keep the flippant conversation going, thankful that Arlene showed no signs of returning to her awkward questions about Stewart's objectives in New York.

It certainly was not a secret mission, but WMI preferred to be discreet about their clients' affairs and a matter of 600,000 dollars, while not solely their responsibility, required delicate handling.

My account of the redecoration of Stewart's Zürich apartment kept Arlene's mind off the question of large insurance claims. Tom Curzon regarded me across the table with the inscrutable benevolence of an ally.

I was not sorry to see them go at the end of the evening.

I felt, too late, that I had been a little hasty in arranging to meet Arlene at ten o'clock the following morning in the Hans Buttery at Harrods.

Originally, in Zürich, a last-minute chat had seemed a good idea to fill in an hour before leaving for Heathrow and my plane for Rome. The suggestion had not come from me. Stewart had not fully understood that, previous to our meeting, I had been so long on my own that loneliness held no terrors for me. He had pressed me to see the Curzons and I had no real objections.

It was, we both felt, the least I could do. They had loaned us their villa at Taormina for the whole of May for our honeymoon and been typically generous in arranging for maid service and even for transport for us while we were on the island. The fat bundle which Arlene had sent to Zürich had included entrancing photographs of the villa and beach; of Bruna, the maid; of a white Citroën SM; and lengthy lists of the arrangements for our comfort.

She had that almost unthinking kindness of the very rich which seemed to me to spring more from good manners than from the heart, but at least the end product was highly satisfactory as far as I was concerned.

About ten days ago, complications had arisen. Tom Curzon had telephoned, sounding worried and harassed. He and Arlene had no children, but their large house at Sunningdale was usually spilling over with dogs and the children of their friends, who seemed to have no conscience about dumping their offspring at Suncrest before taking off for Sardinia, the Bahamas or St Moritz.

This time they were looking after Professor Biagotti's son, a twelve-year-old Sicilian whose mother had deposited him with Arlene and Tom three months ago, before entering Dr Leon's Clinic in Rome for the latest slimming régime. A slip in the Via Veneto, resulting in two broken ankles, made her return for her son impossible. Tom Curzon had resigned himself to escorting the boy back to Catania, but then he had been briefed to defend Masouri in the olive oil fraud case. Italy was one country the Curzons wished to stay out of until the trial was over.

Significantly, it did not seem to occur to anybody that the father might collect the boy. That worried me.

What could Stewart say? Of course we would travel via London and hand the boy over to Professor Biagotti at Catania. I had been practically speechless with indignation. *Anybody* . . . on *any* part of our honeymoon journey was unthinkable! Maybe I agreed feebly that it was no trouble because I felt in my bones that once again there would be no wedding bells.

It was certainly no real trouble then but it became one because the Dalton kidnapping case had dragged on for almost three months and Corinne Dalton had finally lodged her claim for 600,000 dollars, half of which was due to be met by WMI and the other half by Lloyd's.

Wedding or no, Stewart had to get himself to New York as quickly as possible and advise his fellow directors as to whether the company should settle the claim immediately, or if they had legal or reasonable grounds for postponing a decision until it had been definitely established whether the child was alive or dead. I sighed and agreed that the atmosphere would not be quite right for a wedding. Mine, I was determined, would not be any slapdash, hurried affair.

Normally I would have gone with him to New York, but it would have been embarrassing in the face of all the Curzons' arrangements to have cancelled the Sicilian holiday. So I found myself committed to going on alone to Sicily, with the expectation that Stewart would be no more than a further week or so in America and would join me in Taormina as soon as possible.

Unfortunately I was now also committed to escorting the boy and I was not looking forward to that.

Tom Curzon was to bring him to Heathrow, where my responsibilities would begin.

Now, at seven o'clock in the morning of my last day in London, I cursed the easy-going side of my nature that had saddled me also with Arlene Curzon's shallow brittleness for a precious hour.

I had opened the curtains, so I awoke to a room awash with pale sunlight. I knew that I would sleep no more.

Even a leisurely bath and some hilarious experimenting with

make-up still left me booted and spurred at a ridiculously early hour. My luggage was already at Heathrow; my nightdress and toilet equipment went into an outsize white leather handbag, which acted as an overnight case; I wrote a brief note to Stewart.

Now I was impatient to get away.

When I had settled my bill, Harry gave me his wide, friendly grin and said cheerfully, 'You're a day late, Miss. Yesterday was the first of May. You could have washed your face in the early morning dew in Green Park. Lucky you don't need it!'

'I'll settle for a brisk walk there. Maybe that will have the same effect. At least, I'll get a look at Buckingham Palace. It doesn't seem legal to come to London and not have a look at it.'

There were few strollers. It was too early for those. The hurrying, urgent figures were bound for offices and shops and the faces had the absorbed look of people reaching eagerly for their burdens.

Impatiently I stepped from the path, glad to feel the spring of the grass under my feet. I wondered briefly if the coldness against my ankles was indeed Harry's beauty-endowing May dew and smiled at the fancy.

A red ball came bounding over the turf towards me and, almost instinctively, I bent, caught it expertly and lobbed it in a slow, easy arc in the direction of a small girl.

She was probably eight or nine years old with the beautifully erect spine and coltish grace of the very young. I had a vague impression of a vivid, rather pale face, dominated by large, sparkling, intelligent eyes and a mop of dark curls that bobbed as she ran. The blazing happiness in the small features caught and held my attention.

She was almost within touching distance when a muffled thud and a sharp click to our left swivelled both our heads sharply in that direction.

Crouched on one knee a few feet away was a press photographer who was already lowering his camera and grinning with an engaging mixture of brashness and friendliness. Against my will, I found myself grinning back, liking the gleam of crisp dark hair and white teeth and the general effect of clean, animal strength.

Probably he was no more than a couple of years younger than my twenty-seven years, so I was considerably startled when he got quickly to his feet, dusted the knees of his trousers and said gaily, 'This is the time for it – a picture of a swan with her cygnets in tow or lambs in a flower-strewn meadow cavorting around the ewe.' He groaned comically. 'The corn is eternally green. This will be much better . . . you and your little girl, forever immortalized as Modern Motherhood.' With exaggerated humility, he pulled an imaginary forelock. 'With any luck, I'll see you in today's *Evening Bulletin*.'

Like a modern and faintly impertinent young Galahad, he swung rapidly along the path, leaving me with, I am sure, my mouth open, while my brain did rapid calculations and came up with the rueful conclusion that it *was* biologically possible for me to be the mother of an eight-year-old.

Meanwhile, ball and child had disappeared beyond a clump of laurel bushes.

For a moment, helplessly, my eyes followed Galahad's progress, then I shrugged and made for the nearest bench and at least the tenth re-reading of my fiancé's letter. The thin airmail sheets fluttered in the slight breeze and I clutched them firmly, spreading them against the fine yellow linen of my skirt.

'. . . the Commodore is very comfortable and I enjoy having breakfast in their Coffee Room, but American hospitality is so lavish that I have had no other meals in the hotel.

So far, I have resisted Tim and Verna's invitations to stay with them, but they have both been wonderfully helpful. They seem to know everybody in New York, including – heaven be praised! – the Daltons, though they are not their favourite people.

Corinne Dalton is exactly like her photographs . . . a glacial English beauty, with silver-gilt hair, eyes like blue marbles, a statuesque figure and the kind of perfect features that you can't remember two minutes after you've stopped looking at her. She has retreated behind a mask of sorrow (sic!) which makes it difficult to talk to her about the kidnapping.

Her husband, Eric, on the other hand, never seems to do anything else. If her training as a singer has given her control, he shows enough temperament for twelve prima donnas. He talks like a consummate ass, but he certainly doesn't look like one. He's a big husky fellow who didn't start out with good looks and hasn't acquired them, but that pockmarked complexion and battered face doesn't seem to deter the ladies. They flock round him and I get the impression that it is not his reputation as a very successful playwright that attracts them. Whatever it is, he has multiplied the effect a hundredfold simply by being the grief-stricken father of that missing child. Besides, he has a quite remarkable pair of brilliant blue eyes which he uses like a ham actor and the women almost sob aloud.

I believe his play in London, *Small Wonder*, is a complete sell-out for the season. Since attendances jumped suddenly after their child disappeared, you'll understand that at times I feel like throwing up . . .'

A breeze snatched at the page and sent it dancing and skidding along the path. In a panic, I raced after it and caught it just before it could be impaled on a long stick held by a park attendant.

When I glanced at my watch, I saw that I had barely time to get to Harrods for my appointment.

The letter was thrust into my bag and I hurried for a taxi.

Then, after all, I had to wait for Arlene and had just seated myself resignedly in one of the big armchairs outside the passage leading to the Hans Buttery when she stepped out of the lift.

She looked very chic and assured in her cinnamon tweeds and spring furs and several heads turned to watch her progress towards me. Those famous eyelashes fluttered like a royal hand-wave in the direction of the plaudits of the crowd.

My lips twitched in amusement until I noticed the forlorn little figure tagging at her heels.

'Come *on!*' Arlene fluted impatiently. 'We'll have scarcely any time at all to talk.' The hazel eyes looked at me reproachfully.

Amusement glinted deep in the child's dark eyes. For a moment his gaze met mine with adult understanding, and then once more he was a weary, small boy, politely trailing after two tiresome females.

Arlene's words came drifting over her shoulder on a wave of Guerlain.

'It's tiresome for you, darling, but Tom had to alter the arrangements. Something about a long telephone call from Italy in connection with the Masouri case. God knows who is guilty. It's all so complicated. We might all have been *poisoned* by that inferior olive oil. I *do* hope Masouri isn't guilty – so awkward for Tom if he is. Where was I? Oh yes! Tom expects another call, so couldn't get out to Heathrow.' She pointed dramatically at the boy whose face automatically went blank. 'So, there he is – your responsibility now, darling.'

Why does she invite these children? I thought in distress. She treats them as though they were animated dolls. She is not usually unkind. Maybe she has something on her mind.

Perhaps the sympathy I felt for the boy warmed my smile. His lips curved politely.

'Mrs Curzon is so excited that she has forgotten to introduce us. I'm Miss Grant and I am glad I am having your company. We'll enjoy the trip.'

His smile was charming. He slid from his chair and bowed with old-fashioned formality. 'I'm Mario Biagotti. Thank you for having me.'

He climbed back and sat with his hands neatly clasped in his lap, prepared to endure the adult conversation. Thanks to an Anglo-Italian mother, his English was perfect.

Arlene pushed impatiently at her coffee cup. She gave me a troubled glance and then went on.

'Did you know that Tom had a long talk with Stewart this morning?'

'*Stewart* . . . to New York . . .?'

I almost choked in my excitement. My cup rattled in the saucer.

'Don't expect me to tell you anything about it.' Her tone was pettish. 'Tom was quite cross when I went into the study while he was on the telephone.' Her eyes widened innocently. 'How could I possibly know that it was *business*?' Her voice sharpened. 'Do you know whose birth Tom was tracing for him in Somerset House?'

'I haven't the faintest idea and I don't mean to find out. If Stewart wants me to know, he will tell me.'

I hoped I sounded more serene than I felt. Ruefully I recognized that the quick stab of feeling had been something akin to jealousy. Surely Stewart could have telephoned me also? A moment later, I remembered my early departure from Dukes'. Probably the telephone had been ringing there while I had been mooning around Green Park.

I had a curious feeling that Mario had moved closer to me, as though in sympathy, but the great, dark, unplumbed eyes simply looked unblinkingly into mine.

Arlene shrugged prettily, but it was obvious that she was provoked.

'Some dreary law case, I suppose, but I had no idea that Tom and Stewart had a case in common. It can't be anything very important, for I do know that the olive oil fraud case is top of the list just now, but – ' she smiled sweetly in Mario's direction, as if to take the sting out of her words – 'these Italian cases can have such dreadful ramifications . . . the Mafia, and all that sort of thing.' She looked vague. 'Do keep away from the Mafia, dear, while you are in Sicily. I believe quite dreadful things happen there.' She seemed quite unconscious of the repetitiveness of the phrase.

Horrified, I stole a quick glance at Mario and surprised on the small, pale face a look that could only be incredulous delight. He looked at me solemnly and one enormous eye closed for a second in a swift, gay wink. I managed to stop myself from winking back.

At least her phobia about the Mafia kept her from enquiring

too closely into Stewart's affairs and mine. It was all very well to be philosophical with Stewart about putting off the wedding, but it would have been humiliating to have found myself being defensive about it. That particular subject was a bit like an aching tooth – best not to explore it. Lots of weddings were postponed every day without the romance crumbling. We were both simply being sensible about an inconvenient business commitment. It was absurd to think that either of us was being *too* sensible.

Determinedly, I concentrated on my companions.

A young shop assistant, holding a square package, crossed to our table. The colour in her cheeks was high as if she had been hurrying. She made straight for Mario.

'Master Biagotti?'

'Yes.' Now he was any small boy, alert and curious.

She handed him the parcel. 'With Mr Curzon's compliments. He told me to tell you that he chose it himself and that he hopes you'll like it.' She paused uncertainly and her brow creased as if she were trying to recall a lesson. 'Oh, yes! And I was to tell you that . . . that . . . *truth shall be thy warrant*. Have I got it right? He was very particular that I got it right.'

The boy smiled shyly. 'Sir Walter Raleigh wrote that. I understand. Thank you.'

His eyes were shining and he kept the package close to the leg of his chair as though it were something very precious.

Surely I was mistaken? That could not have been the quick glint of tears in Arlene's eyes? The false eyelashes fluttered energetically for a moment and she was the cool, poised Arlene that everybody knew. The slim gloved fingers fumbled in her purse. 'Pay the bill at the cash desk, darling,' she said to Mario, 'and then we must go.'

Her eyes followed his slight figure with bland, meaningless, social pleasantness. The corrosive bitterness in her voice startled me. 'There goes one of the most delightful of our underprivileged children. Tom and I differ about how we should treat them. He is all for giving them lots of outward evidence of the affection that their parents either don't feel or are too busy to show them. I think that makes the return to their arid lives infinitely worse. Mine is the cool approach.' Her tone was sardonic. 'Sometimes I think we'll adopt half-a-dozen, and let these poor little rich children fend for themselves. His parents are dillies – a figure-mad mother and an absent-minded professor for a father. Take my advice, darling – don't let Mario steal your heart on the journey. You'll be left at the end like a superannuated Nanny. It happens to me all the time.'

When Mario came back with her change, he stood silently beside her for a moment, but she kept her head down and fumbled blindly in the depths of her handbag.

'Mama said it is always necessary to say "Thank you" to your hostess at the end of a visit.' His voice broke slightly, but he went sturdily on in his old-man's accents. 'But it wasn't really a visit and you aren't my hostess. You're . . . my friend.'

His clumsy kiss landed just below her right ear.

Her hand flew to the spot in a curiously protective gesture, but she simply said unemotionally, 'You've been a good boy. Uncle Tom and I will be in Taormina by the middle of June. Don't get up to any mischief.'

The last I saw of her was a slim, elegant figure stepping into her car. Mario's eyes followed her with a hungry look. When the car had disappeared in the Knightsbridge traffic, he gave a quiet sigh and said with that disconcertingly adult air, 'Shall I call a taxi now, Miss Grant?'

At Heathrow, much to the amusement of the airport officials, he was pathetically efficient, checking that our luggage was on the Rome plane and booked through to Catania, but he was all boy when I bought him a bundle of comics and a bag of sweets. These he negotiated carefully, while making sure that Tom Curzon's gift was never for a moment out of his grasp.

When the plane was airborne and we had unfastened our seat-belts, he drew a long breath, looked longingly at his parcel and said, 'May I?'

Just then, an air hostess put our lunch trays before us. Her smile became slightly fixed at the disappointment on both our faces. I had made no effort to conceal my curiosity, so Mario and I exchanged rueful smiles and I carefully tucked the heavy package under his seat while we ate.

He was surprisingly easy to talk to, rather like having a conversation with a pedantic adult.

While we worked our way steadily through the shrimp salad and charlotte russe, I said carefully, 'Sometimes my fiancé, Mr Noble, and I have private conversations that we don't repeat to other people, so if Mr Curzon and you have secrets, I'll understand. But I am curious about the message the shop girl gave you – the one about "truth shall be thy warrant". I like that. Is it a secret?'

'Not at all. Mr Curzon and I used to have long talks.' He raised limpid eyes to mine. 'I like talking and Mr Curzon always seemed to find time to *discuss* things. Most people don't like to discuss. They just want to tell you. Well – ' he stole a cautious look at me to see how I was taking the conversation – 'I *admire* Mr Curzon. He doesn't talk a lot, but he listens and thinks about what you say. He said that was because he served the law and you couldn't have justice unless you knew all the *facts*.'

I had a vivid mental picture of the lonely little boy and the lonely, bumbling man taking comfort from each other and my throat tightened.

'A few days ago we were talking about the invasion of privacy.' His mouth thinned in disapproval. 'In America, your telephone and your apartment can be "bugged". I said that I thought that was terrible, especially since now it is happening in other countries.'

'I know. I don't like that either.'

'But Mr Curzon explained to me that nowadays the individual had to be prepared to sacrifice some of his rights for the sake of the good of the majority.'

I tried not to smile at the earnestness of the young philosopher.

'That was when Mr Curzon gave me Sir Walter Raleigh's

poems to read and he marked one specially for me.' He quoted in his high, childish voice:

'Go, soul, the body's guest,
Upon a thankless errand;
Fear not to touch the best,
The truth shall be thy warrant.'

He ducked his head in sudden shyness. 'I told Mr Curzon that I wanted to serve the law like him, but that I didn't like interfering with people. That was when he said that about truth.' He kicked the parcel below his seat gently with his heel. 'I just can't think what this can be. Can you?'

'No, but we'll soon find out.'

I signalled to the air hostess to collect the trays and helped Mario, in the confined space, to remove the string and wrapping.

Below us, the majestic Alps raised their snow-capped heads in vain. Since leaving London, neither of us had done more than glance casually at the patchwork quilt that was France or at the slow drift of cotton-wool clouds past the portholes. Now we bent in absorbed attention above the package.

Cushioned in the plain cardboard box was a brown vinyl attaché case with a label attached to the handle.

Slowly I read the inscription aloud: 'The Junior CASMS.' I raised a bewildered face to Mario. 'What on earth is that?'

He was scarlet with pleasure. In a voice choking with excitement, he stammered, 'I can't believe it! Mr Curzon is the *best* man. It's a Computer-controlled Area Sterilization Multi-sensor System! Of course, this won't have a real computer, but I bet it works. I just bet it *works*.'

Quickly he raised the lid of the case to reveal a compact assortment of small metal objects. Each item was stamped with the letters CASMS. Tucked into a double elastic band on the inner lid was a manual of instructions. He touched the book swiftly as if verifying its existence, then ran a thin brown hand gently over the array of metal.

I thought that never before had I seen such absorbed happiness in a child's face.

Case and contents had a solidity and finish that one would not have expected to find in a child's toy.

'It looks expensive,' I said slowly, noting the reinforced corners on the case, the planned comfort of the spring-loaded handle and the secure look about the twin gilt locks.

Mario shrugged slightly, clearly accepting the costliness of the gift with the unthinking air of one long used to expensive presents.

'And it doesn't look as if it is meant for a child.'

'Oh, it isn't meant for a *child*,' pronounced the twelve-year-old scornfully. 'This isn't a *child's* toy. It's meant for young students. I wouldn't be at all surprised if they had sets like this at Sandhurst,' he continued wisely. 'They are almost sure to have them at West Point.'

The tip of a pink tongue flicked anxiously to his upper lip in childish concentration as he cautiously lifted out a tray to reveal a complicated mass of coiled cable and metal rods.

'But what does it *do*? It doesn't look very interesting to me.'

'It isn't meant to be *interesting*.' His tone was severe. 'It's meant to be *useful*.'

He put the tray back carefully and shut the case, snapping the locks with a force that stiffened the stewardess's smile.

Below us was the blue curl of the Mediterranean breaking on the Italian shore. Vainly I tried to identify the seven hills on which the honey-coloured pile of Rome was perched. Quite clearly, Mario was not interested in the terra-cotta and green landscape running behind us like a carpet being pulled from beneath our feet.

As I parcelled the attaché case and verified that his seat-belt was secure, he chattered in the quick, clipped accents that revealed his excitement. For him, the glory that is ancient Rome was a meaningless huddle of bricks and mortar, quite eclipsed by the modern miracle of destruction which had flowered murderously in Vietnam.

He explained this carefully as the plane circled above the

Fiumicino airport and the passengers in the plane made the small, impatient rustlings and shiftings that always precede a landing.

The thump of the landing-wheels going down jerked Mario's voice up an octave.

'The Americans used these devices for electronic eaves-dropping on the Vietnam battlefield.'

I looked in incredulous amazement at the girlish mouth talking as I would have expected a military engineer to talk.

'They used hundreds and hundreds of small, self-contained "bugging" devices which were dropped by aircraft or troops and helped the Americans to do large-scale surveillance work.'

He stumbled childishly over the word 'surveillance'. That gave me the courage to straighten his tie. He wriggled impatiently and continued, stretching his toes to make sure that the precious parcel was safely under his seat.

'They work on vibrations, you know. I mean, they pick up movements of men or vehicles. Some of them in Vietnam were sensitive to the heat given off by the soldiers' bodies or by their vehicles. I just can't wait to read the manual and see if I've got any of those.' He gave a crowing, naughty boy's laugh. 'Have you heard of the BO "bug"?'

'No. All this is news to me.'

'Well, that's the "bug" that can sense human body odour from a distance of fifty feet. Isn't that *something*? Imagine a "bug" that *smells* the enemy!' His brow crinkled anxiously. 'Of course, the real thing needs a mobile computer, maybe miles away, to interpret the information. I wonder how my set will do it. What do you think, Miss Grant? After all, it has to *work*. It isn't just for *looking* at.'

He broke off to look at me closely. 'Do you know that you're awfully pretty? I think you have the biggest eyes I've ever seen. What do you call that colour of hair? Auburn?'

I nodded and concentrated on applying my lipstick. 'You must tell me more about the CASMS – have I got the initials right? – and I'm quite sure that Mr Curzon wouldn't dream of

24

giving you a set that didn't work.' Fervently I hoped that it would *not* work.

I glanced at the intent little face whose childish features were at such variance with his grown-up talk. 'My brain reels when I think of the possibilities of such a collection. A bit dangerous, don't you think?' We exchanged uneasy looks. 'No wonder Mr Curzon warned you that "truth shall be thy warrant". I'm not too sure about the ethics of such a set. Do you understand what I mean, Mario?'

'Of course!' The plane bumped gently down on the runway. 'I know it's not right to listen in to private conversations. I wouldn't do that, Miss Grant.' He looked gloomy. 'Even if I wanted to, I won't get the chance. My father doesn't do much talking. He's always writing or reading. Did you know that he is Professor of Oriental Languages at the University?' I nodded. 'But just now he has a big excitement on about a seventeenth-century Sanskrit manuscript.' He made a grimace of distaste. 'Who would want to listen in to anything about that?'

'Isn't there anybody else at home?'

'Oh, yes. There's Melina. She's – what do you call it in English? – the housekeeper. She's a horrible, fat old thing who steals from us all the time, but Mama doesn't care, so why should I worry about what she takes?' He shrugged philosophically. A longing expression came into his eyes. 'Do you think a "bug" would work from Taormina to Catania?'

'I don't think so, but I don't really know much about these gadgets. We could try. If you like, I'll take one with me and fix it up. You can telephone me and tell me if you are getting anything.' I felt slightly ridiculous and rather guilty about encouraging him to believe that a toy might be effective at such a range. Flippantly I added, 'Our signal could be "Bye baby buntin', Father's gone a-huntin'." '

Rather drearily, I reflected that the conversation was very different from what Stewart and I should have been having.

'What's that?'

'An old English nursery rhyme, but – ' the guilt deepened as

I looked at his eager face – 'I honestly don't think it will work. The range would be too great. Remember that it *is* a toy. It does have limitations.'

For a moment he looked crestfallen, then, as he fumbled with the buckle of his seat-belt, his face crinkled up with laughter. 'Uncle Tom won't tell Aunt Arlene that it has limitations, so at least she'll be relieved to think that we have a good defence against the Mafia!'

Chapter 2

Fiumicino airport was larger and uglier than I had remembered, nor was the Leonardo da Vinci much better, but Mario, undeterred, kept a businesslike eye on the board announcing movements of aircraft.

He could have found his way to China unaided, I told myself wryly and for a moment the spectre of my own childhood peered over my shoulder. Indifferent, remote parents certainly seemed to breed self-reliant offspring.

I looked doubtfully at the small, pale face. Beneath the dark mop of hair, the forehead still bulged childishly, but the brooding calm of the expression was disturbingly adult.

'I'm not sure,' I said carefully, 'but I believe there are at least five flights a day from Rome to Catania. Maybe I could arrange transfers. It might mean staying overnight in Rome, but I am sure I could telephone your father and I don't think he would disapprove. You might have a few hours at the Clinic. What do you think?'

His gaze was uncomfortably direct. 'It's kind of you to think of it, Miss Grant, but I imagine that Mama would prefer that I went straight to Catania.' His voice was matter of fact, but there was an ironic twist to the childish lips. 'Once I heard her say that children and calories were necessary evils – only endurable when strictly rationed.' He sighed. 'I like watching you eat, Miss Grant.'

I laughed. 'You've seen my efforts with a plane lunch. Wait till you see me tackling a dinner! I am afraid I have a very healthy appetite, so I can't expect to have your Mama's lovely, slim figure,' I added placatingly.

'It isn't a lovely figure – she's skinny,' he said positively. I blushed faintly under the long, considering gaze. 'You're just right.'

Hastily I leaned forward on the leather bench and studied the times of departure on the board.

'We are lucky to be in time to catch the quick connection. This means that we will be in Catania long before dark. I'll be able to see something of the coast. We'll be moving soon,' I announced cheerfully. 'This is my first visit to Sicily, so I'm excited about it, but I certainly hope Etna behaves itself while I am there.'

'You don't need to worry,' he said comfortingly. 'It has been nearly fifty years since there has been any serious eruption, though you'll see signs of activity every day from Taormina. Catania is of greater commercial importance now than the capital Palermo, in spite of the fact that it was destroyed several times by eruptions and earthquakes.'

Like a miniature professor, he poured forth statistics and general information about the town.

'I hope,' he concluded with grave courtesy, 'that you'll allow me to show you the park of the Villa Bellini and Monteverdi's Bellini monument with the figures that symbolize the composer's four operas?' His tone warmed. 'There are lovely ponds for the swans and dear little houses for them in the middle of the water.'

'When I see your father tonight, I'll make an arrangement to call on you. Perhaps on Friday?'

He nodded eagerly, then said briskly, 'There will be an announcement soon. Our flight has been flashed on the board.'

When we crossed to the plane in the blinding glare of the Italian sun, his hand in mine seemed trying to communicate reassurance, as if reminding me that he was in his homeland and among familiar things.

Aboard, it was he who insisted that I take a window seat on the starboard side, so that my first sight of Catania when we swooped down from the blazing arc of the sky was of a compact modern town poised on the shores of the Mediterranean at the furthermost point of a fertile valley running between the green folds of mountains. On the right, the snowy cone of Etna stretched skywards in serene beauty, a majestic pyramid that dominated the landscape.

I thought fleetingly of Stewart, really resenting for the first time that I could not share the moment with him.

When the formalities at Fontanarossa airport had been completed, we stood for a moment in the milling crowd, looking around us.

Once Mario darted after a tall, stooped man with a silvery, leonine head, but came back dragging his feet and looking disappointed. His quick eyes saw the uniformed young man holding aloft the piece of cardboard, inscribed MISS GRANT. Tom Curzon had arranged for a driver to meet me with the car and take me to the Villa Noto at Taormina.

My luggage had been stowed in the boot and Mario and I had chatted uneasily to each other for fully half an hour before we were forced to recognize that Professor Biagotti had not come to the airport.

Carefully I avoided looking at the boy's stricken face and ignored the growing impatience of the driver.

'Your father has probably got tied up with some students. We'll drive to your house now. Perhaps he'll be there before us.'

Deliberately I chattered as we drove slightly north of the town, along the romantic Riviera dei Ciclopi where a long row of beautiful villas stretched along the coast, the black rocks of lava forming a strange contrast to the white houses and the startling blue of the sea. Between the road and the water were extensive lemon groves where blossom and fruit grew together among the jade of the leaves. I could scarcely believe my eyes. Great wafts of tangy perfume drifted into the car and Mario roused himself to point out the rocky portion of the beach where Etna had once hurled its rocks of lava in savage anger and given rise to the legend of Odysseus's encounter with the one-eyed giant.

'The other side of Catania is very flat,' Mario explained, 'but this part of the Golden Ribbon route, from that bay, which is called Porto Ulisse, to Cape Mulini and on to Santa Maria La Scala, which is quite near Acireale, is interesting. Lots of cliffs and promontories and mysterious caverns, all formed from lava.' He looked longingly at the vividly blue sea. 'Will you come some time and bathe in one of the little coves here?'

'Of course.' But my eyes were on the great shoulder of Etna and the sweet slope of the hillside, covered with olive trees and fruit orchards.

'Further on, the mountains come right down to the road that goes to Taormina, but there is no need to be afraid. It is quite safe,' he added consolingly.

Rather to my surprise, we moved away from the line of sumptuous villas, driving in a long arc which appeared to take us back to the edge of the town.

The car crept along the narrow crowding streets of what was obviously an old residential area. Tall, gloomy terra-cotta-coloured houses, stiff with dignity, lined the pavements, their secretive, withdrawn look enhanced rather than relieved by the delicate tracery of tiers of wrought-iron balconies.

'How lovely!' I exclaimed.

'That's the Spanish influence,' said Mario indifferently. 'Spain ruled Sicily for more than three hundred years, so you see balconies everywhere. Papa says that they are the social centre of life for most Sicilians. They are the extra room for the poor; the gossip post and the watching post. Only in the towns, of course.'

'What do you mean?'

'Well, you won't find them in the country, for two reasons. First of all, in the country there is nothing to watch. The second reason is that there aren't very many houses in the country and practically no villages in Sicily.'

'I didn't know that.'

'No. Most Sicilians live in the towns and many of them have to travel many miles to their work.'

The car turned into a shadowy street which was slightly wider than the others and where the houses had a more imposing, though faintly seedy, air. Eighteen-century baroque, I decided, looking at the ornamental stone supports for the balconies and the elaborate carving on the heavy doors which gave directly on to the street.

When we drew up, Mario said, 'We're on the wrong side of the road. There's our house' and pointed to a great mass of crumbling, honey-coloured stone. 'That's the Villa Casilda. It is named after Mama.'

The street was very quiet in the gentle evening light and I felt vaguely depressed as the driver deposited Mario's case in front of the massive door. The heavy iron head of a lion snarled at us from the middle of the upper panel. Mario's hand was stretched upwards towards the ring in the lion's mouth when we heard the slap of feet on the far side of the door and then the prolonged screech of a bolt being drawn.

When the door swung inwards, it was so dark in the hall that it was a few seconds before I made out the round outline of the old peasant woman who stood glaring out at us with undisguised hostility. She was enormously fat, with small, hot, black eyes, set deep in a lined, leathery face. The tiny mouth looked bad-tempered and intolerant and she smelled unpleasantly of garlic and sweat.

The dark eyes raked my face and turned with sharp dislike on Mario. The layers of black garments and the two bulging bags which she dropped on the tiled floor said unmistakably that she had been on the point of departure.

While I am fluent in Italian, I could make nothing of the searing stream of Sicilian dialect directed at Mario. Obviously she was very angry. Her voice got louder and coarser as she spat out the torrent of words. I took one protective step towards him, but he stopped me with a small, dignified gesture.

His tone had an icy ring of authority which brought the hot blood up into the bitter old face. She took an uncertain step backwards towards her bags. A cabbage rolled out from one of them and Mario kicked it contemptuously into the street.

I heard the driver on the other side of the road laugh.

There was a rapid exchange of question and answer and finally the old woman stalked towards the rear of the house with a last malevolent look in my direction.

There was a glint of tears in Mario's eyes as he turned to drag his case in from the street. Hastily I lifted it and deposited it just beyond the two bags.

He ushered me into a dusty room on the left, saying apologetically, 'I'm sorry Melina was so rude. She is a peasant with no manners. She hates me, but it's mutual,' he added prosaically. 'Now she could kill me because she was just leaving for a week's holiday at her native place in the Madonie Mountains.'

His brow puckered anxiously. 'She tells me that my father is in Rome. Evidently, he mistook the dates and didn't expect me for another week.' He gave a faint, tolerant smile. 'He is very absent-minded, but Melina assures me that he remembered to give her a holiday. She was afraid that I had spoiled things.' His lips curled contemptuously.' I told her to make us some coffee and then be off. I don't need her. I don't need anybody,' he added sturdily, but I saw the thin line of white round his lips.

I looked at him with dismay. 'But you can't stay here alone,' I protested and wondered frantically what was the best thing to do.

'There is nothing worth stealing in this house,' he said practically. 'Melina has seen to that and my parents wouldn't notice if she stole the foundation stones. I don't expect a visit from burglars and certainly nobody is interested in stealing *me*.'

The gallant smile almost broke my heart and a slow, savage anger began to burn in me, a blind, undirected rage that must have shown in my face, for Mario said soothingly, 'Don't worry, Miss Grant. I'll manage.' His face crinkled in a smile. 'At least, I can cook as well as Melina.'

'How are you at cooking for two?' I was looking round the room for a telephone, but I saw the slow flush and the swift dawning of incredulous joy. 'Frankly, I'm not as brave as you are about living alone, so this is a piece of luck for me. May I have the pleasure of your company at Taormina?'

He shot out of the chair like a rocket and made for the door. 'The telephone is upstairs in Mama's bedroom.'

Selfish creature! I thought furiously.

'I'll phone Rome now, but I know it will be all right. I'm a burden to them,' he added seriously, 'so they will both be glad.'

The clatter of his feet on the tiled stairs had a joyous ring which upset me so much that I scowled at the old woman when she placed a tray on a table at my elbow.

I had finished my second cup of coffee when Mario put his head round the door and announced breathlessly, 'I've spoken to Mama and at first she was annoyed, though why she should be annoyed with *me*, I don't know. She said to thank you and she is grateful and will write to you. I've packed another case. Was that all right?' The anxious note was back in his voice.

I nodded, inwardly cursing all adults who unthinkingly forced on children the first lessons in worrying.

'The driver is in the kitchen finishing his coffee. We can leave whenever you are ready. I'm taking my fishing gear. I'll show you how to fish underwater. It's marvellous and I'm super at it,' he added modestly.

When I went out into the hall, I stood for a moment looking around, trying to picture a solitary small boy in that environment.

The tiles on the floor and the wide stairway were old and beautiful, but dingy as though they had not been thoroughly cleaned for a long time. A silver tray on which were half a dozen visiting cards lay on the marble-topped table and, on either side of it were two small gilt chairs with hard red brocade seats that looked as if no one had ever sat on them. The place had a faintly musty, unpleasant smell. Obviously I thought, no one has ever loved this house, at least not for a very long time.

In the mirror, I caught a glimpse of my angry eyes, wide with disapproval and, as I heard Mario clattering down from the dimness of the upper floor, I schooled my expression.

For the first time, I understood the Curzons' pleasure in entertaining their young friends and wondered how I could ever have thought of Arlene as shallow. Something deep and primitive stirred in me and I put my hand on Mario's bony shoulder with a force that tilted his face up to me enquiringly.

While I stood on the pavement watching him officiously supervising the stowing of his cases, something of the charm and peace of the neighbourhood reached me. Although I knew very well that nothing of seventeenth-century Catania had survived the corroding lava and engulfing earthquakes, the place evoked pictures of wealthy Sicilian ladies being handed into their carriages to go jolting over the cobblestones in order to drink a glass of Marsala in the shuttered coolness of their friends' salons.

The sudden blast of a motor-horn brought me sharply back to the twentieth century. A red Lancia skidded to a halt in line with the Citroën SM. Across the gleaming white bonnet I saw a grinning, delighted face.

'Jumping Jehosephat! I can hardly believe my eyes! I was driving past the top of the street when I saw you on the side-walk and I told myself that there's just one little girl with hair the colour of copper beech leaves and a pocket Venus figure.' He was out of the car in a trice and pumping my hand with un-disguised affection. 'Laurie, I'm so pleased to see you that I could eat you up! What on earth are you doing in Catania?'

I was aware of Mario standing stiffly erect by my side and of his unease.

Hurriedly, I introduced them.

'Mario, this is Professor Stein from Northwestern University, Chicago. He is a very famous archaeologist and a dear friend.'

When I had completed the introductions, the two males measured each other and I could almost feel the atmosphere snapping.

Gregory Stein listened attentively when I told him about my postponed marriage and what had happened since Stewart had gone to America.

I had always thought of him as middle-aged, but now with the last of the sunlight shining on the crisp brown hair and giving a golden cast to his sunburned features, I realized that he was no more than forty and a very attractive man. The lean, hard look had come from years spent in the open at the excavations which took him mainly to Greece and Italy. When the direct, considering gaze of the grey eyes lingered on my face, I felt ridiculously pleased that my yellow suit was still crisp and fresh and that I had the stamina of a Shetland pony.

'But what on earth are *you* doing here?' I could hear the pleasure in my voice and I could hardly explain to him that it was sheer relief at meeting a friend on whom I could unload my growing anxiety about Mario.

'Mainly diggings, of course. I'm on my way to visit a fellow archaeologist – a Sicilian, whom I met at a conference in Iran a couple of years ago.' He aimed a playful punch at Mario's small chin. 'Sorry, old fellow, but I'm not too keen on Catania. Too modern. I'm living on a boat at Trapani. Bring Miss Grant along and we'll do a bit of sailing. It's the *Più Tardi*, but be sure to let me know when to expect you.'

Mario laughed delightedly. 'That isn't a Sicilian name, sir.'

'I know, young fellow. I'm not strong on saints and I belong to the school of thought that believes most folk are in too much of a hurry. I didn't name the *Later*, but I sure like what it suggests.' He threw his arms wide in an expansive gesture that embraced us both. 'Come loaf with me!'

'We will, Gregory,' I assured him. I handed him one of Arlene's Sicilian cards. 'That will give you our address and telephone number. It's good to know you are not so very far away. If I have problems with Mario, I'll bring him along and you can keel-haul him!'

His farewell kiss landed, not, as I expected, on my proffered cheek, but warmly and disturbingly on my mouth. Startled, I tried to draw back, but he held me firmly.

Stonily Mario watched us both.

When the Lancia roared off, I had a queer little desolate feeling, but Mario's excited chatter soon dispelled it.

The shadows were lengthening along the quiet street and the boy's shoulders had a tired droop. As we climbed into the car, I hoped fervently that everything would be in order at the Villa Noto. It had been a long day and the thought of bed was fast becoming akin to the tortures of Tantalus.

As the light failed, the mountains seemed to loom above us in menacing fashion. The black ribbon of the road hissed beneath our wheels with a sound that rang sweetly in my ears. I scarcely listened to Mario's dutiful explanations of the route, uttered in a polite monotone that presently died away as his weight slid heavily into the curve of my arm.

Occasionally, as we sped past crowding buildings golden with lights, the driver would call out a name, Acitrezza and later, Acireale. There I could smell water and the headlights picked out some beautiful baroque work among its houses. High in the darkness on our left flames from Etna glowed softly and my startled movement jerked Mario into wakefulness.

He followed the direction of my gaze and patted my hand with a paternal solicitude that made me smile in the dimness of the car.

'Nothing to worry about,' he said cheerfully. 'You'll see that most nights. The tourists love it and we Sicilians don't mind as long as Etna doesn't get any fancy ideas and decide to show off. Those aren't really flames. It is simply the glow from the molten lava. As long as Polyphemus's single eye doesn't get really inflamed, we are all right.' He laughed with genuine amusement and settled back into the curve of my arm with a confidence which pleased me.

The car seemed to wheel away from the sea, but when we got to Giardini and took the zigzag road up to Taormina, I heard the waves breaking far below us and the lonely cry of a bird mourning for a lost mate. Lights twinkled like hundreds of jewels from the ledge on which the old town rested and outlined the Corso Umberto which was stretched like a hammock from the Greek Theatre to the lower edge of the town.

The car plunged in a series of dizzying rushes that brought us to the beach of Mazzarò and the Villa Noto.

Somewhat to my relief, there were the pale outlines of other houses fairly close at hand and bursts of laughter that made the night seem friendly and gay and not alien at all.

We entered from the back of the villa, moving through the darkness of a garden that smelled delicately of hyacinths and bee orchids. The driver went ahead, turning on lights in a narrow passage that skirted what was apparently the kitchen and which widened out to a small, square, tiled hall. The white and green tiles were fresh and attractive in the amber light from the lamps and my spirits rose as I saw evidence of Arlene's lavishness and good taste.

When the driver had gone, we stood for a moment in the hall, smiling at each other like old friends who had reached a common goal and I was unreservedly glad that the boy was with me.

Of the maid, Bruna, there was, of course, no sign. She would long since have given me up and gone home, but in the kitchen we found a tray under a snowy white napkin. There was a simple meal for one – cold ham, green salad and a small carafe of wine. Mario ate everything almost automatically while I explored the upper floor.

The room and adjoining bathroom at the left of the staircase was obviously intended for me. There were small tight bunches of flowers in jars on the bedside table and on an ivory-painted chest that served as a dressing table. It was a charming and comfortable room, more English than Italian in style, with a polished wooden floor and ivory furniture against matt-white walls. There were windows on two sides, covered now with long, lettuce-green linen curtains.

When I twitched one aside to look out, the reflection of my own face stared back at me from the blackness of the glass, but I could hear the soporific rise and fall of the sea and smell the pleasing sharpness of salt in the air. There were no blankets on the double bed, but the pink linen sheets held the fragrance of thyme.

The two adjoining rooms had the same feeling of freshness and cleanliness. I chose the one above the front door for Mario, simply because the sheets were already on the bed and the thought of preparing a room seemed now to be more than I could endure.

He seemed as anxious as I was to get to sleep, but just before I left him, he looked at me in a puzzled way and asked, 'Are all British people fond of children?'

I hardened my heart against the pathos of the question and

said as lightly as I could, 'Not all, Mario, but I'm certainly fond of you.'

He turned towards the bed with a tiny, satisfied sigh.

Sleep came to me, as I am sure it did to him, like a velvety curtain, instantly blotting out the happenings and sensations of the long day. I was wrapped so closely in it, sunk so deep in it, that there was no thought even of Stewart nor of the thousands of heaving, watery miles that separated us.

I slept, sweetly and restfully, somewhere far off in a place without a name, but to which I clung resentfully when the harsh ringing of the telephone bell tried to call me back. I was drunk with sleep when I struggled up on the pink pillows and fumbled in the darkness for the light switch.

I blinked at the hands of my travelling clock, trying to focus and to interpret the message on the clock face. One-thirty! Who could be telephoning at such an hour?

The shrill sound of the bell went on and on. I heard the soft opening of Mario's door and somewhere the click of a light switch.

Of course! Stewart was phoning! I told myself happily and cursed the clumsiness of my fingers on my dressing-robe girdle. Naturally he would want to talk to me on this special night.

I flew to the top of the stairs, shooting upwards to full awareness like a deep sea diver surfacing on the waves. Mario's face, bewildered and vaguely alarmed, peered round the jamb of his door.

'Go back to bed, dear,' I said quickly. 'It may be a wrong number.'

He nodded as if completely satisfied and his door closed quietly.

Don't stop ringing! I prayed, as I sped towards the salon. I couldn't bear it if we were cut off.

But the bell went on and on as if it would never stop.

When I lifted the receiver, I said foolishly and happily into the mouthpiece, 'Stewart!'

An impersonal voice said politely, 'Hold on, please! I have a call from London for you.'

And it was Arlene's voice, not Stewart's, that came over the wire, but a voice so shrill, so reedy and so charged with anxiety that at first I did not recognize it.

'Laurie?' The voice said. 'I simply had to telephone you. You are wanted by the police!'

Chapter 3

I laughed.

Probably it was release from tension that sent my laughter soaring upwards in a great joyous whoop that had an edge of hysteria to it. One part of my mind registered the hysteria and disapproved.

Arlene heard it too, for she said sharply, 'Don't be a fool, Laurie. This is serious. This call is costing me a fortune, so listen!'

It was then the wave of panic started, low down in my chest and sweeping upwards to my throat, so that I could not have uttered a word even if I had tried.

Of course the police did not want me because I had stolen somebody's wallet, or robbed a bank, or decamped without paying my bill at Dukes'. The police looked for people whose relatives were ill, had been injured . . . had died!

The blood in my head thundered *Stewart!* so loudly that I missed the beginning of what Arlene was saying.

'. . . saw the late edition of the newspaper in the hairdresser's, while I was under the drier. There was a simply enormous caption above the photograph. Just a minute. It says WHO IS THIS WOMAN? There's a picture of you, playing with a little girl in a park. Did you say anything, Laurie? Well, of course I recognized you though nobody else would. Your face is hidden, but I'd know that linen suit anywhere. I'll post the cutting to you in the morning . . . you won't get London evening papers in Taormina . . . but the gist of it is that Scotland Yard wants to interview the woman in the photograph. Of course they don't actually *say* anything but they might as well have shouted it from the housetops. The little girl is Pia Dalton and obviously they think you've kidnapped her.'

I laughed again, but this time the sound was different.

Scotland Yard could accuse me of murdering Rasputin! I didn't care. Stewart was all right!

'Laurie!' There was no mistaking the anger in Arlene's voice. 'You are not behaving in a very responsible fashion. I've been sick with worry and all you do is laugh. It isn't good enough.'

'Sorry, Arlene, but it is so absurd that I can't help laughing. I thought it was bad news about Stewart.'

'That's just the problem.' Arlene's tone was grim. 'Maybe it *is* bad news, not about Stewart, but *for* Stewart. He is a bit like Tom in that respect . . . you know, Caesar's wife . . .' Her tone sharpened. 'Isn't WMI handling the insurance for the Dalton case?'

'Yee–es. I see what you mean. But at least the photograph proves that Stewart was right about not rushing to pay out. It's wonderful that the child is alive. Now that Scotland Yard knows that the little girl is in London, surely it shouldn't be too difficult to find her?'

There was what sounded like an exasperated sigh in my ear. 'They are convinced she is already out of the country. The newspaper report says so and – ' there was a sick note in Arlene's voice – 'they think you may have tried to disguise the child. They go all round the houses to say so, but their meaning is clear. They are looking for you and *possibly* for a boy. Isn't it provoking? It is a pity you didn't think of dumping Mario at the Clinic in Rome, but thank God he is off your hands now.'

I couldn't help it. I simply had to laugh, as I thought of Mario asleep upstairs.

This time, I thought Arlene was going to hang up. I said hastily, 'What does Tom say?'

'That's just the problem, I can't ask him. He had to go to Genoa about the Masouri case after all, and will be away for at least a week. By good luck, Thompson, his clerk, has lumbago and couldn't go, so I got in touch with him. He is a clam, so that's all right. He found out that it was sheer chance that the child was recognized when some young cub of a reporter was examining the proofs. His advice is to do nothing at all . . . just keep quiet and hope that the Yard will get the child back in the next few days and they'll feel so foolish about the stramash about the unknown female kidnapper that they'll quietly bury the matter. He does think, however, that you should get in touch with Stewart *at once*.'

'Of course I will and I am sorry you have been so worried. I happened to be around when a young photographer was snapping the child. That's all. Incidentally, she looked very happy so I'll probably go down in history as "the Kidnapper with the Heart of Gold".'

The silence at the other end of the telephone was definitely disapproving.

I blundered on, 'Honestly, I am grateful, Arlene. I know how awful it is for a breath of scandal to touch a QC and his wife, so it is heroic of you even to make this call, never mind keep quiet about who I am and where I am.'

I had a sudden, horrifying thought. *I'm in their house. The so-called kidnapper is in the home of one of England's most eminent QC's!*

I swallowed feebly.

'I'll put in a call now for Stewart. He'll know what to do.'

She must have heard the distress in my voice for she said with a return to her usual kind drawl, 'Go back to bed, Laurie, and don't worry. Try to sit tight for a week until Tom or Stewart gets back. They'll know what to do. Don't offer your head on a charger to Scotland Yard. The Press will really make a Roman holiday of a very simple mistake. I'll let you know if anything new turns up, and do let me know what Stewart advises.'

The click as she hung up the receiver seemed to clear my mind finally of the fog of sleep.

The fact that she had not asked about Mario brought home to me how deeply disturbed Arlene was over the tragi-comic series of events. She had always made a fetish of discretion, but now it seemed to me to be carrying things too far to blame me, as she appeared to be doing, for a perfectly innocent involvement in a sensational case.

Whether she would worry more or less if she knew that Mario was still with me, I could not decide, nor why I had not taken time to tell her that he was in the Villa Noto at this moment.

Impatiently I shrugged these thoughts aside. The most important thing was to speak to Stewart, or rather to lodge a call and hope that the transatlantic lines were not busy.

I sat for a few moments in the pleasant pink and white salon, trying to work out how my chance encounter with the Dalton child could possibly affect Stewart and I could almost hear his incisive voice dismissing Arlene's attitude as alarmist and absurd.

Two months ago, when the girl had disappeared in New York, I had been in Zürich and . . . oh! the whole affair was too ridiculous to be worth worrying about.

That absurd photograph had at least achieved a number of good things – it must have filled the Daltons with supreme happiness to know that their little girl was alive and well; it had pinpointed for Scotland Yard an area in London where they could search for the kidnappers; and it was no longer necessary for Stewart to remain in New York.

The last thought sent me winging up the stairs to get the telephone number of the Commodore Hotel.

As I scrabbled in my handbag for my little leather diary, Stewart's face looked out at me from the crocodile travelling frame on the bedside table. The photograph had been taken for inclusion in a WMI booklet and showed what I called his 'public' face. It was undeniably an arresting face. What I did not like about it was that the blue eyes looked coldly out at the observer as if the man behind them had few illusions about human nature and the mouth seemed hard and uncompromising. I certainly had no illusions about my beloved. I knew very well that his reputation for ruthlessness had been earned, but I also knew that if he was unwavering in his pursuit of truth and justice, he was also a compassionate man.

Now I looked at the tiny laughter lines fanning out from the corners of his eyes and felt comforted as I thought of how he would smile at my predicament.

When I had given the New York number to the operator, I curled up on the big settee to wait.

It was fully ten minutes before the telephone rang and I had lifted the receiver before the second ring had been completed.

'I'm sorry, but there is a seven hour delay on all trans-atlantic calls. I will keep you informed if the position changes.' The voice was pleasant, but impersonal.

'But . . . but . . .' My dismay must have been very noticeable, for there was a little more warmth in the telephonist's voice. 'Surely this is very unusual?' I protested.

'I'm sorry. I'll keep trying. The trouble is technical so it is possible that some of the lines could be available soon. I'll let you know.'

Clearly, there was no point in sitting staring at the telephone. It was possible that I might not be able to talk to Stewart before nine o'clock in the morning.

What time would it be in New York now? I struggled with the calculation, knowing that if I had had the wit to ask the operator, she could have supplied the information at once. I came to the conclusion that it would be early afternoon and that Stewart was practically certain to be out of the hotel.

Making a determined effort to free my mind of the Pia complications, I concentrated on figuring out what Stewart would do. Having missed me in London, he would try to get in touch with me late this evening or at any rate in the morning. Probably the simplest and best course would be to leave the telephoning to him.

I lifted the receiver and cancelled my New York call, but told the operator that I would be immediately available for incoming calls. Stewart would telephone very soon or not for many hours.

I was halfway up the stairs before it dawned on me that if I couldn't telephone him, he was equally cut off from me.

I had a sudden, hilarious picture of dozens of little men sitting on the bed of the Atlantic patiently fastening the severed ends of a cable together with enormous rolls of Sellotape, but my smile was a feeble effort.

Slowly I climbed the stairs and got back into bed with the dismal conviction that I would have a sleepless, miserable night.

Hopefully, I left my bedroom door open so that I would hear the first tinkle of the telephone, but the door might as well have been bolted and barred. Almost at once I was in a deep, dreamless sleep and did not waken until shortly after eight o'clock when Mario's cheerful whistle rang through the house and the goodly smell of coffee drifted upwards from the kitchen.

The morning was clear and sunny and I was charmed to discover that the curtains on the left wall of my bedroom concealed a french window which led on to a wide tiled balcony. This ran right round the upper floor of the house and was suspended at one point practically above the edge of the beach.

High on the right, the snowy slopes of Etna were silhouetted against a cloudless sky, but there was no sign of the activity which had alarmed me the night before.

When I saw how steeply the road climbed up to Taormina, I was grateful for the Citroën SM and felt guilty about my impatience with Arlene. Mario and I, it seemed to me, would not be walking up to the town very often.

I leaned over the front balcony and studied the beach. Immediately I gave a sigh of pure pleasure. It was a world of wet emptiness. Although the Mediterranean was, in fact, tideless, what looked to me like a slack tide had gone out, leaving the sand washed to dark gold and the air smelled of kelp and of moving water. The rumble of the surf against the wet, red rocks and along the sweet curve of the beach was a pleasant growl. Nobody sat under the striped umbrellas or in the brightly painted boats pulled high above the water mark, but I could make out figures breakfasting on the terraces of villas strung out on my left.

Far out, two heads bobbed like rubber balls among the waves. I watched them anxiously and was relieved when I saw the figures reach the shallows almost together and stride over the sand as though making straight for the Villa Noto.

Both were big men with the broad shoulders and tapering torsos of athletes. They had hard brown muscular bodies on which hundreds of drops of water glistened like diamonds. They strode in step like lifeguards in a musical comedy. Behind them, the surf curled and creamed.

They saw me almost simultaneously and the big blond man on my right raised his hand in a friendly greeting.

'Hallo there!' he called, squeezing the water from his hair with the other hand. He had a pleasant, overbred, English voice and a warm, attractive smile. 'You must be Laurie Grant. I'm John Niven. My wife, Liza, and I are your next-door neighbours. This is Al Scott. He lives thataway.' He pointed along the beach.

It is difficult to define personal magnetism, but the other man below me certainly had it, a strong, physical attraction that had little to do with intelligence or good looks, though it speedily became apparent that he had both. He had worldly, merry brown eyes in a dark, finely chiselled face that reminded me vaguely of paintings of Sir Francis Drake or of some swash-buckling pirate joyously urging his victims to walk the plank. His teeth were excellent, very white and strong, between well-defined lips that curled impishly as though at a perpetual joke. It was impossible not to smile back when that lazy, sexy smile lifted the planes of the face in a fascinating rearrangement of shadows and highlights. The eyes twinkled in acknowledgment of a shared joke and even the short, dark beard seemed to bristle with good humour.

I had rarely liked a man more at first glance.

'Ma'am, your servant!' His heels clicked together on the sand and he bowed deeply. Any man who can do that in bathing trunks and not look ridiculous has to be special. He had a deep, pleasant American voice, with the non-accent of the well-bred Ivy League man. Respectfully, I admitted to myself that he had made a conquest.

John Niven laughed. 'Watch this one, Miss Grant,' he warned. 'We call him Casanova. Arlene Curzon asked Liza and me to keep a neighbourly eye on you. I'm taking my duties seriously and warning you against this fellow. We're having cocktails tonight at seven-thirty. Come and join us and you'll see what I mean.'

'I'll be glad to,' I said happily, doing a lightning mental survey of my stock of cocktail dresses. 'First house on my right?'

'Correct!' With a friendly wave, they ploughed through the sand and I went back into the bedroom with a quite absurd feeling of exhilaration. How different the two men were! Thoroughbred and plough-horse!

It looked as if Taormina, even without Stewart, was going to be an interesting place.

When I went downstairs, Mario and Bruna were waiting for me in the kitchen, a large sunny room with walls festooned with strings of garlic cloves and a couple of muslin-wrapped hams, cheek by jowl with squat wicker-covered wine bottles. The room was like an advertisement in a travel poster, but I liked it, just as I liked the rich smell of gently bubbling coffee and the warm, yeasty odour of newly-baked bread.

Mario wore only a brief pair of gaily striped trunks, but they had that incomparable elegance of Continental beach clothes and he looked relaxed and happy. He was seated at a big scrubbed wooden table with a top as thick as a butcher's block. One end was piled lavishly with fruit and vegetables. Obviously, Bruna had already been to the market.

Mario carefully placed the big pottery coffee cup in its saucer. 'Aunt Arlene liked her coffee percolated, so Bruna thinks she is giving you a treat this morning. If you prefer espresso, you will break her heart.' He grinned the small boy's grin that I found so attractive. He slid from behind the table to introduce me to Bruna.

She was a small, slim woman of indeterminate age, with the brown, seamed face of the peasant. She looked kindly and good-natured, though the gentle, equine features had a slightly stupid look as if anything beyond the chores of the house would tax her intelligence. Comfortably, I decided that Mario had enough brain power to supply the three of us.

She smiled and clucked at me approvingly, obviously admiring my white sharkskin sheath. Crowing with delighted laughter, she pointed to my toenails which I had painted a burnished copper to match my hair. Gently, she took my right hand and examined my fingernails, pouring forth a stream of Sicilian which left me smiling inanely. My emerald engagement ring obviously impressed her.

'She thinks you are beautiful,' said Mario, 'but she says that you must not lie in the sun or you will become as wrinkled as a walnut. She has decided that you are a film star and it would be a pity to deny it. She will have great prestige among the other maids.' He shrugged philosophically. 'The important thing is that she likes you. Now she would die for you,' he added in matter-of-fact tones.

When I made a move towards the coffee-pot, she touched my arm humbly with a work-roughened finger and indicated that we were to go out to the balcony facing the sea.

It was very pleasant in the sun-dappled shade of the green and white striped awning. We were sufficiently remote from the main stretch of the beach to preserve a fair measure of privacy, being able to watch the sun worshippers, the bathers and those who messed about in small, gaily painted boats, as if they were actors in a very sophisticated play and we occupied a box in a theatre.

I drank in the colour, warmth and beauty of the scene and decided that within a week on my own, it would bore me to death. Here had been deliberately created a place and an atmosphere in which to live and play and dream, but it was not my place, and it was not my dream. Perhaps I was the type who in the domed forests of Brazil would long to be skiing in Japan.

The small boy looked back at me from the other side of the white wicker table and I had the uncomfortable feeling that he was reading my thoughts.

'When people are friends,' I said firmly, 'they don't have to like the same things. Do you agree?'

'Of course. I don't expect you to spend all your time on the beach with me.' I was ashamed of his percipience. He threw his arms out in an expansive gesture. 'There are children in many of the villas. That is one reason why I have always liked staying here with Aunt Arlene. Here, I am never lonely.' He looked at me gravely. 'I hope it will be so for you too.'

48

For one dreadful moment, I thought that he knew all about my arid childhood and the chilling solitariness that had been my lot for years. I pulled the thought of Stewart around me like a protective cloak and the sun was warm again.

I stood up and Mario got to his feet.

'One of our English writers, a man called Hazlitt, wrote that he liked to go on a journey but he liked to go by himself. I feel that way about exploring a place for the first time – I like to do it alone. Will you be all right?'

'Of course.' But he lingered, rubbing the sole of one bare foot over the other in a rhythmic, contemplative way.

'You have a problem?'

'Yes. Money.' He smiled at my startled expression. 'My father forgot to send me any for the last month when I was with Uncle Tom and there was none at the Villa Casilda. I looked.' He gave me the level, adult glance that I found disconcerting. 'On the beach with the other children, my poverty will be an embarrassment. There is a matter of ices and replacements for my snorkel kit.'

'Of course,' I said hastily. 'I should have thought of that. Come upstairs and I'll get my handbag.'

When I gave him the lire, he thanked me with a small tight smile, but I could sense the humiliation underneath.

'I'll pay you back,' he said stiffly.

From the upper window I watched him running across the sand and wondered irritably why Stewart did not telephone.

At eleven o'clock, tired of waiting, I climbed into the Citroën and drove slowly between the pink banks of pelargonia out on to the state highway. The car purred sweetly up the stiff gradients and held the road well on the sharp corners. The small nagging sense of depression went away, but, buried deep, was the shameful thought that Stewart would telephone while I was up in the old town. He would be hurt and angry that I was not there to speak to him and that thought comforted my injured pride.

But it was hard to hang on to ill-natured thoughts on such a morning.

The green hill on which Taormina was situated rose almost perpendicularly from a sea like milky jade. When I was almost opposite the point of Capo Taormino and had left the highway for the Via Pirandello, the road was so steep and there were so many sharp twists and turns that I had to concentrate on my driving. Nothing, however, could make me oblivious of the heady, resinous air, the velvety greenness of the landscape or the vivid scarlets, pinks and whites of the flowers which seemed to bloom everywhere.

When the Via Pirandello widened into a small square I eased the car forward, looking for a parking space. On the right was what was obviously a bus station and I quickly accelerated when I saw an empty space.

The offices of the tourist organization occupied what, thanks to Fodor, I knew was the Corvaja, or Parliament House. The beautiful, dignified old building with its crenellated Arab tower dated from the time when it had been the seat of the Sicilian Parliament in 1410. Just below the town would be the famous architectural treasure of the Greek theatre. My spirits soared. Here, I decided, there was no danger of boredom.

Arlene had left a supply of maps and, among them, I found one of Taormina. Apparently, I was at the top of the well-known Corso Umberto. I looked incredulously at the narrow opening where a bus was inching its way downwards while people flattened themselves good-naturedly against shop windows or squeezed into doorways.

The street was a tunnel of coolness and drifting sunlight which laid lozenges of gold on the heads and shoulders of the strollers.

Cobbled alleys, spilling with flowers, led to steep flights of steps which seemed to follow no set design. Some led up, some down, as though the town were built on many levels. Old houses, drenched in bougainvillaea, gazed serenely out from behind old gateways and the many churches told of a past when religion had been the mainspring of the people.

I stopped counting the numbers of small shops that edged the street. They were filled to overflowing with ceramics, beautiful embroideries, continental silver goods, hand crocheted suits and coats and beach hats. Fascinated, I wandered from one side of the twisting street to the other, caught, and happy to be so, in the tourist trap. Mario, I felt sure, would curl a lip at the colour, gaiety and profusion of goods, so I made the most of my freedom.

Near the Piazza IX Aprile was a small, beautifully appointed shop which would have done credit to New Bond Street. Inside, it was cool and dim and behind the two short counters were pyramids of the most beautifully fashioned marzipan fruits I had ever seen. Realistic bananas, apples, oranges, lemons and grapes were piled in exquisite miniature Sicilian painted carts. I chose two carts and a selection of fruits and ordered a parcel to be sent to Arlene and one to Zürich, but my pleasure was diminished because there was no one to share it with me.

Feeling a little sorry for myself, I went back to the little paved square, backed by cafés, chose a table at the edge of the pavement and ordered an espresso.

Beyond the balustrade, the Mediterranean was unbelievably blue, like taut silk, and, to the right, framed in the line of the lower hills, the snowy outline of Etna glittered.

Across the belvedere, Al Scott bent his handsome head to talk to a tall, blonde girl in a green cotton frock. I watched them with interest. He was close enough for me to see the gleam of his teeth and the suggestion of a dimple close to the corner of his mouth. His air of casual elegance made the men in the vicinity look sloppy and untidy. I suspected that while the startlingly white open-necked shirt, navy blazer and white slacks had come from Fifth Avenue, he would have looked just as immaculate in a fisherman's jersey and cotton jeans. Remembering the lean hardness of his body in the bathing trunks, I was in no danger of thinking him a fop.

Frankly I acknowledged to myself that he fascinated me and I watched with a good deal of pleasure the way the muscles in his brown face lifted and rippled with laughter. His eyes were hidden behind dark glasses, but his hands wove expressive patterns in the air, so that one had no sensation of being cut off from the thoughts of the speaker.

I sipped my coffee and openly studied the girl. The cotton frock could have come from a chain store or been run up by a local dressmaker, but she did not need couture clothes to show off her slim, rounded shape. She was tall and graceful with a hint of maturity in the high-breasted figure. Probably about thirty, I decided, and pretty, but not spectacular. The heavy strands of blonde hair had been cut in an unfashionable page-boy style, but it suited her and gave a certain strength to the pointed chin and the rather uncertain mouth. A strain of weakness there, I thought.

She tapped her sunglasses against her thigh and swung round for a moment so that I saw her profile raised to Al Scott's. The light grey eyes had a frankly adoring look. Whatever the debonair American felt, there was no doubt that she was deeply in love with him.

Probably he missed that look for his head was turned in my direction and his hand went up in a quick, friendly salute. He put a hand under the girl's arm and guided her across to my table.

Close up, he was even more attractive than he had seemed on the beach. He had a social ease of manner which I greatly admired. He greeted me with a warmth which seemed natural and genuine and made the necessary introductions very suavely as he settled the blonde girl opposite me at the café table.

'This is Miss Susan Bradford. Isn't that a ridiculous name for an Irish girl to have? Be kind to her, for she has the bad fortune to be my secretary and since I don't know my own mind for two consecutive minutes, it's the devil of a job.'

She had a lovely smile, warm and gentle, though at close quarters I could see unexpected lines of strain round the mouth and eyes, as though she had been under pressure for a very long time.

'He is trying to make me sound important,' she protested. 'My typing is terrible. I always suspect that he does it again when I'm not around.' She looked at me frankly. 'My real job is looking after Mr Scott's daughter and the truth of that is that it is a joy, not a job.'

I was curious. Was there a Mrs Scott?

The girl laughed a little self-consciously. 'I probably sound like a doting parent, but I've looked after her for many years.'

'Vira,' said Al Scott lazily, twirling his campari round in the glass. 'V-I-R-A, short for Elvira. The full name is too heavy for a little girl, I think.'

'I hope she isn't too little,' I said. 'Mario is hungry for companionship.'

'You have a son?' He looked startled.

'No.' It was too much trouble to explain. 'I'm looking after him while his parents are in Rome.' I glanced at my watch. 'I must be getting back, or he may feel neglected. Besides,' I added, 'I'm expecting a telephone call from my fiancé.'

He got instantly to his feet. 'Then we must not keep you, but I had hoped that you might have joined us for lunch. Miss Bradford and I are lunching at the San Domenico Palace. It was an old monastery founded in 1430. The cloisters and monks' cells are still there as modern rooms. That sort of place always impresses Americans.' He laughed with charming self-mockery. 'Probably I enjoy Taormina because I can get my history in a de luxe package.'

He seemed to come to a decision. 'After the Nivens' party this evening, I'd like to take you out to dinner. May I? The place I have in mind is very close to your villa and I have a selfish desire to be the first to show it to you.' He seemed to assume that I would agree for he added, 'Bring a wrap, for we will be dining in the open.'

I was half way up the Corso Umberto before I began to feel guilty and uneasy about the engagement. Had I been too susceptible? And what was I to make of a man who took his secretary out to lunch and, in her presence, arranged to take another woman out to dinner? But the question that I kept resolutely at the back of my mind was the most important one of all. What would Stewart think of my dining alone with a man as attractive as Al Scott?

Chapter 4

Bruna had propped the light blue cablegram against a ceramic ashtray on the hall table.

I expected no more than a loving message and enquiry about my safe arrival, but, with a spasm of happiness, I read, LEAVING NEW YORK. PHONING FROM LONDON. LOVE. It was dated May 2nd, but the typed white ribbon of paper had been carelessly torn and I had no means of verifying the time of despatch.

Probably there were stars in my eyes and I couldn't get Stewart out of my mind, so that I was disgracefully abstracted throughout lunch.

Mario and I ate at a glass-topped table on the terrace, with the perfumes from the small garden between the villa and the beach mingling with the tang from the water.

I sipped my glass of Marsala, only half aware of the hot wind blowing between the Peloritani mountains and the mountains of Calabria and reaching down to the Gulf of Etna. The pastel-tinted villas shimmered in the heat haze. The great sweeps of the olive groves and pine-wooded hills climbed high above the bay of Spisone and Mazzeo and the sweet curve of the Lido di Isola Bella lay like an aquamarine in a setting of emerald.

Dreamily, I thought of Horace's pronouncement that this was where one would wish to live . . . forgotten and forgetting . . . *oblitus* . . . *obliviscendus* . . .

Boring? I must have been mad!

Mario tapped sharply on my glass with a fork. 'Bruna is a good cook,' he said, 'but she knows little about wines, beyond the rough country wine that she drinks. The Marsala is for the evening.' He got down from his chair. 'Now you must drink a dry wine. Papa, I think, would give you one of the wines of Etna, the Ciclopi, or perhaps Uncle Tom has a Regaleali of Caltanissetta.'

In a few moments he was back again, carefully balancing a bottle between his small hands. I was at pains not to smile.

'It is not cold enough,' he said, 'but it will do.'

He sipped with obvious enjoyment the cloudy liquid in his own glass.

'What on earth is that?'

'Milk of almonds . . . a very good thirst-quenching drink for summer. I drink it all the time. But – ' he sounded like a severe adult with a recalcitrant child – 'you are not eating. You must eat.'

I looked in dismay at the mound on my plate. Dreamily I had watched Bruna spooning the dark mass on to the yellow plate. I felt guilty and faintly revolted.

'But what is it?'

'Only *pasta col nero* . . . pasta with black,' he said encouragingly. 'It is spaghetti with a black sauce made from the ink of the cuttlefish. It tastes like meat. Try it. It is good.'

It was surprisingly palatable, but I was not interested in food. I sat patiently through the meal while Mario ate *i bicciolani*, tea cookies, which were, he informed me, a speciality of Taormina and I nibbled at a piece of crystallized jasmine.

His skin was a faint pink and he seemed full of the busy plans that sand and sea appear to invoke in most small boys. I was busy with my own thoughts, so that the stream of his talk made a pleasant obbligato to my conjectures about Stewart. The expression 'my friend' occurred with satisfying frequency in his recital. At least, I thought contentedly, he will not be lonely.

Bruna moved quietly behind us, in her felt slippers, removing plates and swatting angrily at an occasional fly. Our conversation, I assumed, was quite unintelligible to her.

Idly I enquired, 'Is your friend Mr Scott's daughter or Mr Niven's?'

At the sound of the names, Bruna halted and put one brown forefinger across her lips in the universal sign that signifies silence.

A tide of warm colour flooded Mario's face. His hands on the

edge of the table clenched with rage and the stream of cold
Sicilian drew the corners of Bruna's mouth down in woe-
begone fashion and sent her scurrying indoors.

'What was that?' I enquired curiously.

He got down from his chair and gave a little formal bow in
my direction. 'At table, Bruna must only serve food. I told her
so. Forgive me. I do not mean to take your position. I correct
her to help you.'

I knew that there was something more to it than that, but the
heat and the rhythmic surge and suck of the waves were making
me pleasantly sleepy. My eyelids felt heavy.

'I'll get a book and lie in the hammock over there. Mr Noble
may call and I'll be able to hear the telephone from here. Cover
up before you go out on the beach.'

I told Mario of my plans for the evening and his face lit up as
though he felt responsible for my entertainment.

I looked at him doubtfully. 'I suppose Bruna will be going
home when she has given you your meal this evening. How do
you feel about being on your own for a time?'

His patient look struck me like a blow. It said more plainly
than any words could have done: I am always alone.

On an impulse, I drew him close into my arms and buried
my face in the soft hollow between neck and shoulder. Under
my hands, his bones felt as fragile as a bird's.

He said in his matter-of-fact voice, 'You smell of strawberries.'

I laughed and the emotion-charged moment was gone.

The long, golden, heat-drenched hours went softly past
while I dozed, awoke and finally slept the deep, refreshing sleep
of the young.

Once I roused myself to pad across the terrace and look along
the length of the beach.

The children had combined forces to build a large, fortress-
like shelter of sand. They crawled in and out of it like bees in a
honeycomb, so that it was difficult to distinguish individuals or
to count numbers. There were several torsos as pink as Mario's
and, I judged, between twelve and fifteen children in the

group. In such a company, I told myself, he was unlikely to come to any harm.

There were also several adults in the group. The sun glinted on Susan Bradford's bright head. From a distance, her body had the taut, agile look of a young girl. Once Al Scott put his hand on her shoulder and I saw her head come up sharply, as if she had been jerked into movement by an electric current.

I felt vaguely troubled as I went back to settle myself again among the yellow cushions. Poor girl . . . rich man . . . could there be a happy ending? The words of an old song danced in my brain . . . Where is that happy ending?

The silence of the telephone did not worry me. Stewart might even now be in London, but I was quite confident that before the day was over, I would hear from him. The piercing sense of physical loss which had troubled me since his departure would, I felt, lose its intensity. Yet, if I could, I would not bring him back. I had seen the sudden sharp light of exultation in his eyes whenever a job was going well and I would not deny him that.

Since my talk with Arlene, I had not thought again about the Dalton child, but Stewart's return must surely mean that she had been found, or at least soon would be. I tried to imagine what the past months must have been like for her parents and I shivered in the sunlight.

When Mario finally climbed up on to the terrace, stamping his feet on the tiles to shake the sand from between his toes, he gave me a brilliant smile and hurtled into the kitchen, announcing loudly, 'I'm starving.'

He ate his meal at one end of the kitchen table, while I sat opposite him drinking an espresso. At first he was inclined to droop over the dish of what he told me was called *involtini*, a savoury mixture of slices of meat with ham, cheese and breadcrumbs, cooked in tomato sauce, but soon his energy returned and his account of the day's activities and plans for the morrow came tumbling out.

'Mr Scott has a motor-boat. It is called the *Golden Eye*.' His own eyes were bright with excitement. 'He and the lady will go

57

to the Lido di Mortelle at Messina tomorrow. There will be a picnic.' He bit quickly into a prickly pear, scooping the red juice back into his mouth with a sticky forefinger. 'The boat will hold eight or ten children if we squeeze up. May I go?'

Impossible to say no in face of that glow of anticipation.

'Mr Scott must be very fond of children,' I said amusedly, trying to picture that sophisticated gentleman surrounded for an entire day by some of the restless brown bodies I had watched on the beach.

'The lady will help him,' said Mario indifferently. 'Everyone will behave, or he won't take us again,' he added wisely.

'When do you leave?'

'About ten o'clock. He said he specially wanted me to help him to speak Sicilian, but he was just being nice. He speaks it as well as I do. He's had the Golden Dream – that's his villa – for years. I'll take my money belt,' he added thoughtfully. 'I can buy ice-cream at the Lido.'

'We-e-ell . . . I suppose it should be all right. Miss Bradford seems a very sensible person.'

A look akin to embarrassment swept over his face. He kicked the leg of the table with a rhythmic force that set my teeth on edge. With his head bent to watch the swinging foot, his voice came up hesitant and indistinct. 'Do you think it would be all right to try out my "bug" on the *Golden Eye*?' He raised his head eagerly. 'It isn't as if I would be listening to the lady and Mr Scott. It would be all kids' talk. A trial, you know. Maybe it wouldn't work.' But his eyes were desperate with longing.

'I don't think you'll hear any State secrets,' I said lightly, 'but you must ask Mr Scott's permission. I'm sure he won't refuse. Now, I had better get ready or I will be late for the cocktail party.'

But I don't think he heard that, for he was already half way up the stairs.

That manual! I thought resignedly.

When I had finished dressing, I went down to the salon to find him hunched over what looked like a transistor set.

'What on earth is that?' I enquired.

He straightened and brushed a lock of dark hair impatiently back from his brow.

'A recorder . . . must have a receiver, of course. The "bug" works on vibrations which operate this. I do know that it will record for four hours but I don't know the range.'

'Is it yours?'

'Well . . . no. It's my father's. I've no idea why he bought it. I've never seen him using it. But honestly, Miss Grant, he won't mind.'

'I sincerely hope not,' I said, a little grimly.

His eyes travelled over me from head to toe and I felt foolishly pleased at his approving look. The soft green chiffon dress was new and, Stewart had told me, very becoming. When I had worn it for the first time, he had called me Pansy Eyes and, next day, had bought me the bracelet which he said the dress needed.

Now Mario touched the heavy gold and enamel lozenges and said, 'That's beautiful. It looks special.'

'It is Chinese . . . old and quite valuable. I call it my lucky bracelet, for those are the six Chinese gods of good fortune.'

Privately I thought I should have worn it earlier, but now I fastened the safety-catch and smiled as I remembered that I would soon be talking to Stewart again. That was the only good fortune I wanted now.

Before I left the villa, I called the operator and asked to have all incoming calls transferred to the Nivens' number.

Mario walked with me as far as the main road and would have escorted me the short distance to the Nivens' villa, but soon it would be very dark so I persuaded him to go back into the house and close the door before I moved away.

There was the sound of subdued laughter from behind the Nivens' front door and I hesitated for a moment with my finger on the bell, suddenly assailed by the shyness which I thought I had completely conquered.

To my surprise, it was Al Scott who opened the door and drew me inside with an urbanity that set me completely at ease.

There was a bitter, earthy odour from some strange yellow

flowers in a blue vase on the hall table. The air-conditioner sighed like an asthmatic old woman. From the right, the tinkling sound of a piano ran through the eddies of conversation like a silver thread.

For a moment the American stared at me with an admiration so frank that it brought the blood in a hot wave to my cheeks.

It was the best possible preparation for entry to a roomful of strangers.

'This is one butler whose hand you can shake without making Amy Vanderbilt blench,' he said gaily, taking my gold lace stole and wagging an admonitory forefinger at me. 'Pretty, but if the sirocco blows it away, I'll have to give you my jacket. John is charging glasses, so I'm buttling for him.'

With a sure hand under my arm, he guided me into the L-shaped room. I had a quick impression of an amalgam of styles that would probably have made an interior decorator shudder, but the total effect, if startling, was surprisingly pleasing.

Stretched across the room were the familiar and greatly loved Japanese lanterns of my youth. How could I have forgotten them? They swayed with the same fragile grace of twenty years ago. Their colours were unchanged – deep purple, rosy pink, greenish blue, and clear yellow – and on each base rested the familiar slender fluted candle, no thicker than a child's finger.

The salon lights had been extinguished so that the room seemed to float mistily and mysteriously like a scene in a theatre. Strange shadows formed and dissolved in the corners. In an eddy of air, the lanterns swayed with a papery whisper, infinitely strange and sibilant.

I was enchanted. In the dancing light, Al Scott's eyes shone, grave with an almost fearful pleasure. The pressure of his hand on my arm was light and intimate. Shaken, I drew back, alarmed at the bubbling sense of happiness.

Liza Niven hurried towards me. She was small, dark and plump, with rosy cheeks and bright, dark eyes. The scarlet silk of her dress, stretched tightly over the pouter-pigeon chest, gave her the look of a friendly robin.

'How very kind of you to come, Miss Grant,' she said in a sweet, fluting voice. 'We have some dear friends here this evening, but we all love to make one more. Come and meet everybody. I'll guarantee that you won't find a single bore in the room.'

There were probably twenty people there, a civilized crowd that obviously knew the rules of the cocktail party circuit. Regularly, small groups broke up and reformed with new components, as if pebbles had been thrown into a glassy pond and sent out ripples in endless patterns.

I found myself in front of a tall cabinet filled with *objets d'art*. An elderly Sicilian with a patriarchal head brought me an iced Campari.

'I am Michle Spina,' he said in beautifully enunciated English, 'and I am a black sinner, for I envy my neighbour's goods.'

Liza Niven went smilingly away to the far end of the room.

He pointed a wavering finger in the direction of a small wooden frog. 'This is the work of Masanoa the First of Yamada, one of the most famous of Japanese carvers. Its date? About 1750. The patina almost certainly comes from years of constant rubbing against silken garments. I suppose the simplicity of this piece is its main attraction. Only a man who carves in wood could fully appreciate the skill here. Look at the posture! You feel that at any moment those bulging eyes will blink and Mr Frog will jump.'

'It's a netsuke, isn't it?' I asked.

'Yes. They are really sculptures in miniature. Not all are as beautifully made as this one.' The filmy eyes twinkled. 'My revenge is to show John Niven my Vernis Martin fan. It is guaranteed to set him drinking for days.'

He laughed a high, old man's laugh and led me towards the window. 'Come, signorina, and meet a good friend of mine, Giuseppe Fontana. He may be a very great artist, but he is still little Peppino to me.'

Everybody in Europe knew that name. Fontana was a big, florid man who looked as if he would have been at home in the

London Stock Exchange. His booming laugh was like the ringing of a great gong and I saw a thin, sallow little woman in
black put a gently restraining hand on his arm in a familiar,
wifely fashion. The four other members of the group were
listening to him with close attention and, as we approached,
Don Michle signalled to him to continue.

'. . . modern preoccupation with names. They are hot to
possess a Gauguin or a Monet or an Epstein or a Henry Moore.
Pshaw! I do not care a fig about the artist if the work is good.'

'But surely we know about the artists because the work *is*
good?' The speaker was a young woman with a clever, intense
face.

'Not necessarily. Practically every history of sculpture carries
an illustration of "The Knight of Bamberg". Since AD 1230
that work has been speaking for itself. Nobody knows who did
it, and nobody with any sense cares. Last month I went again
to Bamberg to look at it.' The big sensual face seemed to
sharpen. 'Ah! that old timbered courtyard of the palace!
Simplicity does not age. Every time I look at the Knight in the
Gothic Cathedral, so handsome, so romantic, so *kind* – I renew
my youth and remember my ideals. The artist did not need to
carve his name on a fold of the garments, nor on a hoof. Each
time I go, he reaches across more than seven hundred years and
says to me, *Peppino, live like this man!*'

Don Michle said mildly, 'Stop showing off, Peppino. Everybody knows that you are a libertine and have no intention of
reforming. Perhaps Miss Grant will have a refining effect upon
you. She is from Zürich. Maybe she'll be able to do what I have
failed to accomplish – turn your eyes away from other men's
work and persuade you to look at the world around you.'

He patted my arm gently and moved slowly away.

Al Scott's amused voice came from behind me. He had been
moving restlessly round the room, his progress punctuated by
bursts of laughter from the various groups.

'That's a pretty good way of advising us all to "do our own
thing", in today's inelegant phrase, but it doesn't work for me.
Whenever I go to Ghent and see Hubert and Jan van Eyck's

"Adoration of the Lamb", I'm so demoralized that I decide I simply haven't got "a thing" and put my brushes away for months. If I didn't take frequent looks at the work of the masters, I suppose I'd go on happily turning out tenth-rate paintings that would be better left undone.'

'No, Mr Scott!' the dark, intense girl protested. 'When I was in New York at the beginning of April I saw your exhibition. I positively lusted after that snow scene in Central Park – so delicate . . . quite without pretentiousness. Why on earth did you close the exhibition so suddenly? Wasn't it advertised to go on until the end of May?'

'Even bad artists claim the right to be temperamental, Aurelia.' I thought there was a note of reserve in his voice, but when I glanced up, his face was as bland and smiling as usual.

One of the lanterns tilted momentarily in a draught from the terrace and a shadow fell across his face giving it a secretive, brooding look. Scott, I decided, was more than an attractive socialite. But what, exactly?

A group parted obsequiously to let Don Michle rejoin us. He said serenely, 'That pose as a dilettante deceives no one, Signor Scott. I still recall with pleasure a night two years ago when you played your piano concerto, *Con Amore*. Didn't Buttita play it at the Sargent Memorial concert? I thought so. But you must not dissipate your talents. You have not yet decided whether you want to be an artist or a musician. It is time you did.'

He shrugged, smiling faintly.

'Take Freud's advice and toss a coin,' I said helpfully.

He looked at me enquiringly.

'It works – just as Freud says. If Mr Scott feels disappointed when the coin comes down in favour of the musician, he'll know that he secretly longs to be an artist.'

Al Scott laughed and said to the group, 'Now you'll understand why I persuaded Miss Grant to dine with me.' He and Don Michle exchanged pleased looks.

John Niven joined us. He had the sleepy, contented look of a man who had spent a long day in the sun. The big, athletic body and bluff, almost schoolboy, manner did not suggest the collector or connoisseur to me. I could not believe that there was any real depth or sensitivity to the man.

Tentatively I said, 'I'm feeling abashed, Mr Niven. I thought these beach villas would be full of sand and shells and flasks of Coppertone. What a pleasure it has been to see your pictures and your collection!' I gestured in the direction of the display cabinet. 'I'm having a wonderful time and I am very grateful that you invited me.'

'I'm glad, Miss Grant. Liza and I are hoping that we will have the chance to get to know you without quite so many people around, but I promise you that we won't intrude if you crave solitude. Incidentally, my wife is the real collector. I simply take the credit for her good taste. Of course, I do enjoy our bits and pieces and I try to bolster up my ego with Thackeray's belief that next to excellence is the appreciation of it.' He looked beyond my right shoulder and I saw the warmth of his smile. 'Here comes Casanova! I can tell from the look in his eye that he is going to take you away. He had the nerve to tell me that I must not invite you to tomorrow's party. Too exhausting, he says. But it's because he won't be there.'

'Envy will get you nowhere, John,' said the American lightly. 'I'm taking Miss Grant to dinner at the Villa Sant' Andrea. I hope you appreciate how magnanimous I am! Since Taormina is an enduring bastion of the British Empire, I am prepared to recite the list of the English contributions to this area for the last one hundred and fifty years and to take her to a hotel as English as "Greensleeves". Can an American do more?'

'Yes. Bring her and Miss Bradford to lunch tomorrow . . . at about one-thirty.'

Was there the faintest hesitation before he included Susan Bradford in the invitation? If he had noticed, Al Scott gave no sign.

'Sorry . . . Can't . . . Tomorrow I'm the Pied Piper and leading the children out of Taormina to Messina. I'll let you know the ransom fee later.'

John Niven clapped him affectionately on the shoulder. 'I'll be at the *Golden Eye* tomorrow to see you off. Have a good dinner.'

We got ready to leave.

The night was as black as Pharaoh's tomb and stifling with the sirocco from Africa so that I was glad that we did not have to hurtle round the hairpin bends of the miniature Corniche while the slumbrous breath of the Ionian Sea sighed somewhere far below us.

Al Scott handled the car well, all the time talking quietly and easily as if we were old friends.

'John Niven is a good sort,' he said, 'very hospitable and kind, though not exactly an intellectual heavyweight. He's impulsive and inclined to behave like a bull in a china shop at times.' He grimaced slightly. 'I've known him for years, but I can't claim that we are close friends. I suppose we are too dissimilar. My abstemiousness gets on his nerves and I get angry when he drinks too much. Does that sound superior? I don't mean it to be.'

I had the impression that he hesitated. Then he seemed to come to a decision.

He gave me a sharp, sidelong glance before continuing quietly, 'In Sicily, a man needs to keep his wits about him. John Niven is a bit naive, with his eternal parties and open house. No doubt we are all rubbing shoulders with the Mafia, but . . .'

My eyes widened. 'You mean that there were some members there tonight?'

'Of course.' He laughed. 'I saw you talking to at least two of them – a charming young man called Francesco Picciotto, and old Don Michle. People say, but very, very quietly, that Picciotto is *Capo-mafia* of the province and that Don Michle is *Capo dei Capi*, the head of the whole set-up. I like them both.' He shrugged tolerantly. 'In any case, it is not our affair and certainly nothing for you to worry about.'

He began to describe the hotel where we were to dine.

'The villa is like a very beautiful country house,' he said. 'More than a hundred and fifty years ago, the Trewhella family left Cornwall to help build the railways of Sicily and they have been here ever since, preserving unchanged their British nationality and the purity of English taste at its best.'

'Not Ye Olde English Tea Shoppe offering English tea and toast?'

'Heavens, no! Wait till you see the public rooms. There are deeply carved oak-panelled rooms, very restful and quite un-Italian . . . full of English porcelain, Danish silver and good examples of Sicilian art.'

'Does the same family still own it?'

'I suppose so. At one time the family owned considerable estates in the district, but the fortunes of war compelled them, some time in the early 1950's, I think, to convert their country home to its present form. Mrs Manley and Lady Nicholson, daughters of G. and V. Trewhella, were really responsible for this marriage of the glamour of the sub-tropics with the best of English comfort. Note that I promise you glamour!'

He parked the car carefully, well into the side of the road, and handed me out, while I thought how strange it was that I should feel so completely at ease with a man whom I had met for the first time only that morning. Maybe, I thought confusedly, a true sophisticate could tolerate the Mafia and still be a person of integrity.

The tall, wrought-iron gates of the villa opened directly on to the main road to Messina, but once we had stepped beyond them, we were in a world of velvety blackness, full of the small secret sounds of myriads of tiny insects.

Almost immediately we were negotiating endless flights of stone steps still warm from the lion-sun and going deeper and deeper into perfumed darkness. Al Scott's hand under my arm was cool and firm.

Was ever a night so drenched in sweetness? Honeysuckle, the musky tang of bougainvillaea, the evocative pungency of the orange and lemon, waves of thyme crushed beneath our feet, all blended to make a draught as heady as vintage wine.

Then, through a mist of white jasmine, snowily perfect and like the delicate tracery of an oriental screen, we came to the terrace of the villa.

66

In a pool of soft, greenish light, diners sat at tables set under huge umbrella palm trees. The golden shoulders of the women gleamed against the backdrop of sub-tropical plants.

We sat close to the terrace wall, under our tent of palm leaves, savouring the perfection of the night and the setting where, during the day, Al Scott informed me, tiny lizards flashed like green fire.

He had a conference with the head waiter and arranged that the telephone operator should be called and told to transfer any calls for me to the villa. My mind was at rest, so that I was free to enjoy his suave attention and the loveliness of the night.

We ate cannelloni stuffed with creamed spinach, grilled sword-fish with crunchy golden strips of zucchini, and strawberries, cool as Etna's snows, swimming in fresh orange juice.

Opposite me, Al Scott's dark eyes sparkled in the lamplight and I noticed afresh the Mephistophelian upward quirk of his eyebrows and the gaiety of his smile.

His travels seemed to have taken him to the great art centres of the world, so that he talked well about the Prado, the Uffizi Gallery, and the red-brick art centre of Bruges.

I felt dreamy and content, with an almost mindless enjoyment of the talk. He had a gift for making everything seem new and interesting.

I don't know why I asked, 'Has Miss Bradford seen these places?'

There was a tiny pause and he said steadily, 'I don't imagine so, but I have known her for only two years, so perhaps earlier . . .'

I sipped from the glass which he had filled and tried to pin down an inconsistency that was troubling me, but the thought eluded me. Soon Stewart would call, so this was no time for puzzles.

Al Scott leaned forward and put a finger very gently on the corner of my mouth.

'Sometimes, not always,' he said, 'you have the ghost of a dimple there. Waiting for it to appear is fascinating. Have you a fool for a fiancé that he lets another man watch it?'

I looked up quickly at something in the voice. The tone was light and mocking, but I sensed something searching in the question that made me answer evasively. 'The male denizens of Zürich have a reputation for hardheadedness. Maybe he thinks that the dimple will only appear as long as there is trust between us.'

'Trust . . . yes . . . I divorced my wife eight years ago. It is hard to re-learn how to trust.'

He leaned back comfortably, crossing his long legs. There was something definitive in the gesture, as if he wanted me to know that the subject was no longer of interest to him. Yet he looked at me with a faint smile, expecting some comment. The smoke of his cigar made a silvery mist between us.

I thought of Susan Bradford's naked look of love and pitied her. On her own admission she was something less than a secretary, while he was obviously a wealthy man, separated from her by a background of education and culture that was meaningless to her. But now, in the scented Mediterranean night, I realized that the greatest barrier of all was probably his crippling, unsatisfactory marriage. I felt like a Jewish matchmaker who was obliged to confess to failure.

'Why do you look so sad?' he asked suddenly.

And stupidly, foolishly, impulsively, I put my hand over his and said, 'Because I like you very much and I think that you may be missing the boat.'

He was silent so long that I thought I had offended him. In the drifting light, his eyes looked drained of laughter. Very gently he said, 'Perhaps not.'

His hand went into an inner pocket in his jacket and he clicked open a small box. The light above us in the palm tree lit a fire in the heart of the uncut ruby. I gasped and was silent.

'I am going to offer Susan that tomorrow. Wish me luck!'

Then, naturally, the only possible thing to do was to drink champagne and smile at each other, the happy, foolish smiles of people who have discovered that they speak the same language.

When the last of the diners had gone and we were alone under the palms, the liquid-eyed Italian waiter extinguished the lights one by one. His hand hovered over the last switch and I would almost swear that he winked, an impudent Latin gesture that mocked and challenged British reserve.

When Al Scott took me back to the Villa Noto, we heard the first shrill ringing of the telephone. I fumbled with the lock, gave him a frantic, incoherent, dismissive gesture of gratitude and ran to grasp the receiver like a lifeline.

The American left quickly, shutting the door very quietly behind him.

When I closed my eyes, it was as if Stewart were in the room beside me. Naturally, the first few moments were concerned exclusively with the feelings, hopes and fears of Laurie Grant and Stewart Noble, but soon his voice came crisply over the wire . . . his business voice.

'. . . naturally, the photograph was in the New York papers that same day . . . remember the difference in time . . . and caused more of a stir than it could possibly have done in Britain. I certainly didn't recognize you and knew nothing about your connection with the child until I arrived here at Suncrest.'

'Are you upset about it?'

'Good God, no! There is certainly no reason for you to be upset about it. Arlene is inclined to take herself and her position a little too seriously. She loves drama, or she wouldn't go on filling her house with stray children when there is no reason on earth why Tom and she couldn't adopt a couple for themselves. But I don't want to talk about their affairs . . .'

'Did the photograph bring you back to London? If so, bless it!'

'No. I was coming in any case. You know that the nursemaid, Emma Rice, disappeared at the same time as the child, Pia?'

'I didn't know anything about her. I suppose if you had been involved in the affair from the beginning, I would have known all the details. Do you think she kidnapped the girl?'

'I didn't at the beginning. Now . . . well, there are some very puzzling features about this case. The Rice woman seemed to vanish into thin air, so the New York police came to the conclusion that she had been murdered. It is difficult enough to hide a child, but a child *and* a woman . . . !'

'You sound as though you think she is alive. I do hope you are right.'

'I'm sure she is. At the end of the week, she wrote to Mrs Dalton and resigned, as from April 30th. She enclosed a money order for a month's salary in lieu of notice. Note, she gave back a month's salary!'

'*What!*'

'Note! . . . a month's salary . . . not three months'. Obviously, she considered herself still in the Daltons' employ during March and April.'

'But this is fantastic! What on earth are the Daltons saying? They must be overjoyed to know that their little girl is alive and well, and that apparently the nursemaid has been looking after her.'

'They know about the London photograph, but they don't know anything about the Rice woman. The FBI intercepted her letter of resignation. The letter and the money order brought me back to London. The envelope had a London postmark and the money order had been issued at Exton, a very small village . . . really a hamlet . . . in Cornwall. I've been down there already. It didn't take me long to discover that the woman and the child had been living there quietly for the past two months.'

'Living there? You mean that they weren't being *held* there . . . that the Rice woman did, in fact, kidnap the girl?'

'Darling – ' he sounded very weary – 'I don't know, but why would a woman who had looked after a child devotedly for a little over seven years suddenly decide to kidnap her? It doesn't run true to form. I've got to find the answers to all sorts of questions, or wait until the English police find them.'

'What kind of questions, Stewart? I'm afraid I'm stupid tonight, but I am so surprised that my brain doesn't appear to be working.'

'Well, I've got to try to find out who owns the cottage where they have been living. Then I want to know who let it to them –

the owner or a real estate firm? Above all, I want to know who paid the rent?'

'I see . . .'

'At the moment, it looks as if it might have been a chap called Scott . . . Al Scott . . . who seems to have been friendly with the maid for a few years. Significantly, he, too, is no longer at his usual haunts in New York.'

My hand was gripping the receiver so tightly that it is a wonder it did not snap. The pounding in my head was so loud that I felt that Stewart must hear it. I had a vivid mental picture of the American's face, tender, gay, sensitive. It was a cruel coincidence. It could not possibly be the same man.

Stewart's voice sounded strongly in my ear. 'Are you there, darling? I thought we had been cut off. The police are trying to find this man, Scott. I've a feeling he might be the key to this whole affair.'

'But he can't possibly be . . . I mean he's such a nice man. I'm sure he's not a kidnapper.'

There was a long moment of silence. Then Stewart said very quietly, 'I know I'm tired and probably I'm not functioning too well but, my darling Laurie, would you mind explaining what in the name of heaven you are talking about. You sound as though you know this man.'

'Perhaps it is not the same Scott, but I left an American called Al Scott about fifteen minutes ago. I had dinner with him this evening.'

I got frightened as the silence at the other end of the line continued. When he did speak, Stewart's voice was quite expressionless.

'Have you talked to this man about the Dalton case or about my connection with it? Have you spoken about the London photograph?'

'No . . . no . . . oh no! He probably thinks you are a Zürich businessman. I met him only this morning. Arlene's neighbours introduced us. Evidently he has had a villa here for years – seems to be very well known and well liked. Oh, Stewart, he can't be a kidnapper.'

71

'Well, he is not likely to vanish overnight. Just behave naturally with him. Don't talk about me at all and we can only hope that Arlene hasn't chattered about my job to those neighbours you mentioned. It is quite possible that your Al Scott has no connection at all with the man I'm interested in. I can't decide that until I know more about *my* Al Scott. I'll get myself to Taormina as quickly as possible, but it won't be tomorrow. It will probably be two days from now or, at the very most, three. Meanwhile, darling, just lie in the sun and forget about the whole business. I'm inclined to agree with you that the poor blighter is simply unlucky in having a fairly common name.'

'Oh, Stewart, I'm sure of it! I'm quite, quite positive that he is incapable of anything as cruel as kidnapping. He is simply not that kind of person.' But he didn't condemn the Mafia, I told myself miserably.

'Well, we'll know pretty soon. I'll telephone you tomorrow night and perhaps by then the whole business will be over. By this time tomorrow night, Scotland Yard may even have the child. Certainly there is no point in my volunteering the information now that my future wife has met an American called Al Scott in Sicily. So far, there is nothing to connect your nice American with the Daltons, so stop worrying.'

But naturally I continued to worry and when finally I replaced the receiver, I went heavily up the stairs to my bedroom, feeling that I had somehow betrayed my new friend.

I was undressed before I saw the envelope which Mario had propped against the base of my bedside lamp.

He had printed on the front of the envelope in characteristically neat capitals ... NOT FOR KEEPING! PLEASE RETURN TO OWNER IN THE MORNING!!! The envelope was slightly sticky in one corner.

I smiled and drew out the two snapshots and was charmed by the unexpectedness of the poses. Obviously they were commercial photographs taken with a polaroid camera, so that he looked upwards over his left shoulder with a naturalness that an adult would have envied. I do not know whether he had thought of it or if it had been the photographer's suggestion, but he had just finished writing his name in bold, flowing script in the sand.

Smilingly, I turned to the second photograph which I had already guessed would be of his friend. I was so startled that at first I looked at the print with the feeling that someone had played a trick on me.

The pose was similar, but there was a questioning look in the girl's dark eyes as if she were wondering if she had interpreted the photographer's wishes correctly. It was the child whom I had last seen in Green Park.

Printed in the sand was the name PIA.

Chapter 5

Very slowly I slid the photographs back into the envelope.

As far as Al Scott and Susan Bradford were concerned, Mario had spent his pocket money to deadly purpose.

I sat on the edge of the bed and stared bleakly at my face in the mirror on the opposite wall. My eyes looked back at me with an almost frightening intensity. There was surprise and embarrassment in their depths, embarrassment for Al Scott, as though I had caught him out in a social *gaffe* and not in a heartless crime.

Susan Bradford's involvement scarcely registered with me. Probably an accessory after the fact, I decided, remembering the softness of the mouth and the tell-tale lines of strain.

That man, I told myself bitterly, was a persuader of women. I remembered with shame how much I had enjoyed his conversation and restless gaiety. My behaviour had stopped just short of flirting. The desolate feeling that I had lost something valuable persisted. Could a man have his warmth and sympathy, yet be a villain?

Common sense told me that I must ring Stewart immediately, but I sat on, slumped dejectedly, trying to find something to explain a word written in the sand.

There should have been exultation that I had found the child whom the FBI and Scotland Yard had failed to trace after three months of intensive professional search. Instead, there was only this empty feeling and the sudden, wrenching memory of the happiness in his eyes when he had shown me the ring.

How *could* a man of sensitivity become involved in such heartlessness? He had certainly lied about her name. Vira, indeed!

Arlene's vague dread of the Mafia no longer seemed quite so foolishly groundless. Sixteen key figures in the US and Sicilian underworlds had been sent to Filicudi, one of the 'magnificent seven' islands of the Lipari Archipelago, about fifty miles off northern Sicily. There the Mafia bosses had to live in enforced residence under police surveillance. Obviously the ties between the crime-makers in America and Sicily were strong and far-reaching. Stories came back to me of cultured, wealthy men of apparently impeccable backgrounds who had been proved to have been embroiled in the Society's activities.

Had Al Scott also been corrupted by money and power?

The tick of my travelling clock seemed unnaturally loud in the quiet room. It was late. It would be better to let Stewart sleep and call him early in the morning.

As I was pulling the pink sheets high above my shoulders, I had a sudden, chilling thought. If Mario had already shown the photographs to the American, he might be already on his way to the ferry at Messina and *en route* for the mainland.

Bolt upright in the darkness, I considered the possibility with a growing sense of helplessness.

And all the time, one foolish, obstinate corner of my mind refused to accept the reality of Al Scott's guilt.

I could hear Stewart's voice quoting mockingly, 'She liked whate'er she looked on, And her looks went everywhere.'

Anger drove out pity and it was anger I felt next morning when I dressed quickly and went quietly down the stairs so as not to awaken Mario.

It was barely seven-thirty when I put the call through and only minutes before the operator called back and said, 'Mr Stewart Noble is not available. Will you speak to Mrs Thomas Curzon?'

I could picture Arlene lying back among the pillows in the vast gilt bed from which she could look over the Sunningdale golf course.

Her voice was sleepy and slightly cross. 'So sorry, Laurie. You really must slow Stewart up. He looks *driven*. Mary tells me he left without any breakfast this morning. *So* bad for him.'

'Do you know where he is? It's important that I get in touch with him.'

'Oh yes, I know where he is. He has an appointment at eight o'clock at Scotland Yard. Incredible! I thought that positively everything in Britain nowadays operated only between ten a.m. and five p.m. It's *inspiring* to know that the Law never sleeps.'

'Arlene, please don't be flippant now. This is important.'

Her tone was different, kind and thoughtful, when she spoke again. 'What do you want me to do, Laurie? I'm hateful when Tom is away. I don't sleep. Stewart saw the light under my door about two o'clock this morning and came in. He told me that, after he talked with you, he rang Thomson, and he will be seeing him some time this morning. Object? – undeclared. His appointment at the Yard is with Superintendent Lang. So I have two chances of catching up with him if you want me to give him a message.'

'Right,' I said crisply. 'The sooner he gets this news, the better – we have a mutual friend called Scott. The child Stewart is interested in is definitely in Mazzarò.'

Her gasp came clearly over the wire.

When she spoke, discretion and curiosity were struggling for supremacy. 'You mean near the Villa Noto?' Her voice grew faint, but urgent. 'Laurie, darling, do be *very* careful. Do you remember what I said? Well . . . oh! this *is* worrying . . . I'll hang up. I must get in touch with Stewart at once.'

There was a sharp click and I was left staring blankly at the receiver.

Mario was already in the kitchen when the drifting coffee fumes announced that breakfast was being prepared.

Appalled, I halted on the threshold, arrested by the tableau of Mario kneeling on a kitchen chair at the sink while he held Bruna's hand under the running tap. The water that dripped from her left hand was bright red. He was talking to her in a gentle, soothing murmur such as one would use to a frightened child, but the leathery, brown face was quite tranquil.

The long mortadella sausage and the blood-stained knife at the side of the sink told the story.

I pulled the chair away and examined Bruna's hand while I

told Mario where to find my first-aid box. He clattered noisily up the stairs.

There was a diagonal cut about five centimetres long in the fleshy pad of the palm, just below the first three fingers. Fortunately, it was not deep. I pressed the edges of the wound together, under the running water, while I waited for Mario.

I was conscious of Bruna's expression. It was gentle and almost happy and I heard her sniffing softly at my perfume, like an inquisitive puppy. When Mario ran in with the box and the dressing was firmly in place, she beamed at me as though I had done something very brave or clever.

I insisted on pouring her coffee and cutting up the bread and sausage for her breakfast. All the time, her eyes followed me in a wondering way.

Just as we finished eating, Mario said suddenly, 'What did you think of the photographs, Miss Grant? Did you realize that the photographer gave them to me almost immediately after they had been taken? I had only to wait until they dried. Aren't they super?'

'Excellent! What did your friend think of them?' My voice was carefully non-committal. 'Did Mr Scott like them?'

'Oh, none of them has seen them yet. Vira had to go off at once, even before mine had been taken. I asked her not to say anything. It has to be a surprise for her father and Signorina Bradford. May I have them now, please?'

I found I had been holding my breath. I let it go in a short rush. 'I'm sure they will both be *very* surprised.'

Mario looked up sharply at the dryness of my tone.

I was in an agony of indecision.

How could I possibly tell Mario that Al Scott might be a member of the Mafia; that he was certainly a kidnapper; that he was not the girl's father and that her name was not Vira?

It was quite clearly important that the two adults should be left in their state of false security until Stewart and the Scotland Yard or FBI men appeared. It was too much to expect a twelve-year-old not to show by his manner that something was wrong.

On the other hand, if I said nothing at all to him, there was a big risk that an inadvertent remark of his might put Scott on his guard. The mere mention of a photograph would be enough to alarm him.

Bruna was watching me closely, as if she sensed that I was troubled. She spoke sharply to Mario.

He looked aggrieved. 'Bruna says I must not worry you. But I am not doing anything,' he protested. 'Are you worried, Miss Grant?'

'Yes,' I said simply, 'but it is not your fault.' I looked at the curiously adult eyes and came to a decision. 'Mario, you will have to trust me. I can't explain, because it is not my secret, but I promise that you will know all about it by tomorrow night or, at the very latest, the next night. Will you do what I say without asking any questions?'

He nodded, his big eyes searching my face.

'Please go on the trip to Messina as arranged, but don't, under any circumstances, mention the photographs. Meanwhile, I'll keep them safely. Did you show them to Bruna or to anybody else?'

He shook his head.

'Do you think your friend will talk about them?'

His face went that painful scarlet that I had seen before when Bruna had put her finger to her lips. He said stiffly, 'She won't. Most of the time she doesn't volunteer information. You see . . . she is deaf and dumb.'

I stared. His eyes met my appalled glance with great dignity. He waited.

I pressed my fists against my temples. 'Oh, Mario, the poor little girl! Of course I didn't know. How do you talk to her?'

I remembered the quick turn of her head in the Green Park. Obviously, she had felt the vibration when the photographer's knee had thudded to the ground.

'She lip-reads.' He drew a small tattered notebook from his pocket. 'She is teaching me finger language, but I know only five words and a bit of the alphabet.' He looked at me with a terrible enquiry in his eyes. 'May I ask just one question?'

I nodded.

'Would Signor Scott harm her?'

'He might,' I said heavily.

His sigh was barely audible. He came round the table and leaned against my knee. He said earnestly, 'I'll be careful.'

We stared at each other, recognizing that, in less than a minute, we had become fellow conspirators.

Bruna's dressing had come off. I was fixing a fresh one on her hand and taping a bandage round it to hold it in place when the back door opened and a tall woman, wearing the striped overall and large white apron of a maid, came in. She was carrying a letter.

Bruna pointed to her delightedly and said, 'Sylvana . . . Signor Scott.' She bustled about, pouring her a coffee, while I slit the envelope and read the short message.

There was no salutation and the words, written in a bold sprawling hand, seemed to bring Al Scott right into the room.

'Have you ever drunk Veuve Clicquot at 9.30 a.m. on a beach on a glorious May morning? Having just put a ruby on a girl's finger, I can't rise to dissolving a pearl in your champagne, but Susan and I would consider it civil of you if you came just the same.'

It was signed: 'The Rake Reformed.'

I blinked angrily as tears blurred the words. It was upsetting to find my villain behaving like an ordinary, happy man. I pulled myself together. Three pairs of eyes were watching me curiously.

'Signor Scott and Signorina Bradford are going to be married. He wants me to go along to the boat at 9.30 to celebrate their engagement with a glass of champagne.' Mario's eyes widened. 'How do you think your friend will feel about that?'

'She'll be happy,' he said simply. 'Boy! maybe she'll stay here forever.'

I sighed and thought how much simpler life would be if everything were a definite black or white and not the puzzling shades in between. Apparently it had been too much for Mario also. His newborn distrust of Scott had been quite swallowed up in the thought that his friend might become, not merely a summer visitor, but a neighbour.

As we ploughed through the sand towards the *Golden Eye*, he kept darting ahead, then returning dutifully to walk beside me. I wondered uneasily how much of my warning had in fact registered with him. Something still remained to be said on at least one point.

'Mario,' I said finally, 'your friend's name is Vira, but she wrote Pia in the sand. Why was that?'

He raised puzzled eyes to mine. 'I don't know. I was going to ask her this morning. Maybe she would like to be called Pia. Children often do that – give themselves the names they would like to have.' He laughed merrily. 'I used to call myself Turiddu. That's the Sicilian for Salvatore. But I was young then,' he added tolerantly.

'Please don't mention the name Pia to anybody. Will you remember that? It is very important.'

He nodded, looking up at me with a flattering intensity. 'Did you know that your hair looks like a fire, because the sun is shining right on top of it? Nobody else has hair like yours.'

A thought seemed to explode in my brain, so that I halted abruptly and Mario's skipping trot carried him a few paces ahead before he realized that I was not with him. He looked back at me in surprise.

In a few moments, I would be having my first real look at Pia Dalton, but I had blundered badly. She would likewise be having a good look at me.

Would she recognize me as the woman she had seen in the London park and remember that there had been a man with a camera?

Too late I realized that until Stewart and the police officials arrived, I should have kept out of sight. It was much too late to do anything about it now.

As I went forward and congratulated the engaged couple, I felt like Judas, but nobody seemed to notice anything unusual in my manner.

The children were already in the cruiser, drinking Coca-

Cola and calling excitedly to each other. Mario was hauled aboard and none of the children appeared to take the slightest interest in the adults on the beach.

The sun glinted on Susan Bradford's heavy wheatsheaf hair and on the smooth gold of her shoulders. She wore a dazzling white one-piece bathing suit and looked almost drunk with happiness. I looked at the enormous ruby on her left hand and privately christened it the badge of courage.

The Nivens, with their impeccable good manners, kept close to her. John Niven was like a chameleon, assuming the emotions of his immediate companions.

I looked curiously at the tall, good-looking man called Francesco Picciotto, whom an ebullient Al Scott addressed affectionately as 'Ciccio'. I had scarcely noticed him before. Was he really *Capo-mafia* of the province? It was hard to believe. Only the Nivens seemed to be natural and above-board.

The pretty, dark girl whom I had met at the party was there too. She was no more than nineteen years old, and was pretending to weep in heartbroken fashion on the American's chest. Her name was Aurelia Schiera. She waved her champagne glass at me and invited me to join a skin-diving party that afternoon.

'Wait till Susan and I come back and we'll all go,' Al Scott commanded. 'We should be here at about three o'clock.' A horn blared in rage from the cabin cruiser. 'My passengers are becoming impatient. We had better get started.'

He had been in high spirits, pressing champagne upon everyone and behaving as though the hot stretch of sand were an elegant drawing-room. Now, as he took my hand for a moment, he looked suddenly tired and I sensed a certain tension in his voice. 'I have offended you in some way,' he said quietly. 'You are different this morning. I wouldn't offend you for the world.' His eyes were searching. He *was* percipient.

I felt the foolish prick of tears and was saved from disgracing myself only by a staggering, illuminating thought. *He thinks I am jealous!*

Suddenly I felt light-hearted. He doesn't know anything about the London photograph or connect me in any way with

Pia. I gave him a brilliant, meaningless smile and saw him turn away as though he were disappointed.

I walked back along the beach with the Nivens and the three of us swam and floated lazily for about half an hour. Later, it would be very hot, but it was heavenly to let the warm, slow roll of the waves blot out thought and let pure sensation take over for a time.

When I went back to the villa to bathe and dress, the rooms were cool and peaceful. Arlene had indulged her liking for pink and orchid colours, so that the window shades in the salon were of her favourite pink linen. The room had a subdued rosy glow. I sat in the cheerful dimness and thought about villainy and wondered how I would outwit Al Scott. I wondered, too, when Stewart would come and when I would hear from him.

There was always the danger that the kidnappers might leave suddenly. In the light of the engagement, nobody would think that at all strange. The longer I contemplated that thought, the more depressed I became.

I wandered into the kitchen and found Bruna in the act of removing the bandage and dressing. She looked crestfallen, then pointed apologetically to a basin of vegetables. The bleeding had stopped and the cut had closed. I fetched the first-aid box and got out a tube of Nuskin. I signalled that it would sting, then spread the jelly along the line of the wound, but her expression did not alter as the fiery liquid dressing went on. In a moment, she was looking in delighted amazement at her hand, as though I had performed a minor miracle.

Beyond the kitchen window, I could see a tall figure taking the road that led up to Taormina.

Bruna followed the direction of my gaze and said energetically, 'Sylvana . . . Signor Scott.'

She was watching my face as the idea was born and she followed me out of the kitchen as I walked behind the villas in the direction of the Golden Dream. Her voice floated after me on a rising note of agitation and fear.

It was easier than I had dreamed possible to get into his house. There was a garden as short and as flower-filled as that at the Villa Noto. A crazy-paving path, with clumps of camomile growing between the cracks, led up to the kitchen door. I had only to push it and walk in.

The house was as quiet as the garden. Honeysuckle and wistaria peered in at the kitchen window and the warm spicy smell from the cypress hedge seemed to hang in the air. It mingled with the steamy smell of boiling water.

The room seemed familiar and I saw that this was because the lay-out was almost exactly the same as that of the kitchen at the Villa Noto, though the furnishings were different. There was a wide, shallow sink with brass taps, bright blue walls hung with copper pans and a white tiled floor that felt slippery under the feet.

A saucer of water stood on the floor near a cupboard and I wondered if they kept a cat. There was no sign of one and in a cage suspended above the sink a goldfinch sang the same song boringly over and over again.

There was the hiss from a gas-jet and a subdued roar and gurgle from a two-handled zinc pan, like a miniature bath, where water was simmering steadily on the top of the stove.

That stopped me for a minute until I remembered Sylvana's plodding, uphill walk and realized that she must have forgotten to turn off the gas. She wouldn't, couldn't be back soon and the water might well have boiled away before she returned. My hand was out to switch off the jet when I realized that I must not do it.

At least, I promised myself, I'll turn the gas down before I leave.

The lower rooms were of no interest to me. Passports, those magic documents that enabled one to move about freely in Europe, would probably be upstairs in bedrooms along with any other important papers. If Al Scott had a safe, I was sunk.

Upstairs, the layout was also familiar, though there was no upper terrace as in the Villa Noto.

Obviously, the large bedroom on the left was occupied by Susan Bradford. She was a tidy and trusting person. Keeping my mind carefully blank, I began the search. Her diary and two bundles of letters were in the second drawer of a tallboy under a neat pile of underwear. I put them in a gold mesh cord bag which was hanging over a bedknob.

Somehow I felt worse about taking her shopping-bag than I did about stealing her papers.

I felt uneasy as I moved back again to the upper landing, as though unseen eyes were watching me. It was ridiculous to feel afraid in an empty house, but I recognized the dryness in my throat and the stiffness in my neck as blind, unreasoning fear. I had to force myself to go on.

The door facing the stairs was open and it was clearly a man's room. I recognized Al Scott's striped beach robe flung carelessly down on a chair. One slipper was half way under the bed, as though he had dressed in a hurry. The bed had not been made and I frowned at the rumpled sheets and at the blanket draped untidily over the end of the bed. Sylvana, I felt, would be making that bed ten minutes before the master returned.

There was a desk under the window on the left, but every drawer was locked. I found the keys in an empty tobacco jar on the window ledge.

A photograph of Susan Bradford in a silver frame looked disapprovingly down at me as I went through the drawers.

There were too many papers for me to examine. In any case, I was not interested in deeds, or securities, or shares, or chequebooks or bills. If he kept a diary, I did not find it, but I did find two passports and a large, fat manilla envelope which held the papers which he appeared to value. This envelope was foolscap size and looked rubbed and old. The sides and bottom were ready to part under the weight and bulk of the contents. The flap had not been sealed. A hasty glance told me that there was a will, some photographs, letters, a weighty, sealed envelope and some very imposing legal documents.

I thrust the passports and the bulky envelope into the gold net bag and put the keys back in the tobacco jar.

For a moment I stood biting my lips in indecision, cursing myself for my inconvenient streak of honesty and consideration for others.

I had come for the passports, hadn't I? Why didn't I leave now that I had got them? Wasn't my idea of keeping Al Scott on ice until Stewart arrived a good one?

It was no use. Something in me baulked at depriving a man of a document that was practically his lifeline in Europe. I decided that I couldn't do it. Slowly I retrieved the passports from the bag and looked around for a hiding-place. Finally I put them back where I had found them.

The air-conditioning unit gave a noisy belch and I jumped nervously. The uneasy feeling was back and I had to control a panicky impulse to drop the bag and rush out of the house.

I had taken one step towards the open door when I saw a brown snout protruding beyond the jamb. The two needle-pointed ears seemed to materialize out of thin air and the pair of eyes were the coldest, most vicious I had ever seen. Silently, as though gliding on velvet paws, a big brown Dobermann moved into full view and stood quivering with eagerness, blocking the doorway.

The ears went back, the lips lifted and I saw the great white fangs.

Chapter 6

When I was ten years old, I saw a man being killed by a chow.

Seventeen years ago, nobody bothered too much about traumas and a child's terrors. At least, they didn't in our circles. In time I achieved a sort of icy control, a spurious calmness born of the knowledge that nobody understood or would do anything about the terror that held me rigid in bed night after night.

Now, with those unblinking eyes fixed on me, I felt the same sort of despairing detachment.

I knew nothing about Dobermann Pinschers other than that they were killer dogs.

I stood perfectly still.

The dog began to pant. The expression in the eyes did not change.

There was a shuffling noise from the hall. The muscles in the Dobermann's shoulders bunched. In the act of springing, the gathered strength of the hindquarters froze and the big body slewed round as if on oiled wheels.

Above the dog's head, I could see Bruna's wiry figure. She was about two paces away from the doorway, her body in a line with the stairs and her arms straining backwards, rigid with the weight of the basin.

Something feral in her eyes and menacing in the catlike crouch sent the Dobermann skidding round to face her squarely.

Her arms completed the swing. The silvery arc of water, clouded with steam, met the great plunging body in mid-air. The Dobermann seemed to dance above the ground. The savagery of its cries, muffled by the zinc basin, chilled my blood. It tossed the basin off like a maddened bull freeing itself from the cape, and the great tortured leaps seemed to go on endlessly.

I was pressed against the desk when the quivering body

came to rest, thudding to the floor inside the bedroom.

With the fluid swiftness of a black cat, Bruna seized the blanket from the foot of the bed and dropped it over the threshing brown body. Then she was on her knees, pushing and pressing as if to drive the head through the tiles. Under the blanket, the dog's legs moved like pistons that gradually slowed, then stopped.

Even when the twitchings had completely stopped she continued to crouch there, as if locked endlessly in primitive battle.

I went stiffly forward and raised her up and the spell seemed to be broken.

She plucked the blanket from the dog and threw it back over the end of the bed.

The Dobermann lay with its long legs stiffly extended. The lolling tongue and one agonized eye seemed already fixed in death.

Without looking at me, Bruna went to the adjoining bathroom and brought back a bath towel. She mopped up the water from the tiles, making several journeys into the bathroom to wring out the sopping towel.

Tiles and towel would dry quickly in the sub-tropical heat.

When she had finished, she looked carefully round the bedroom, then looked at me in a satisfied way.

The basin had cracked a tile in the hallway, but there was nothing that we could do about that.

At the top of the stairs Bruna took the mesh bag from my hand and tied it to her belt under her apron. She lifted the zinc basin and stood humbly aside to let me precede her down the stairs.

In the kitchen the lighted gas jet still hissed and spat and the bird in the cage sang its boring song.

I turned on the water tap while Bruna filled the basin and put it back on the stove.

The cut in her hand had opened slightly and blood was beginning to ooze from it. I fastened my handkerchief round her hand and thought that she flinched when I touched her.

I remembered to wipe the handles of the basin.

We met nobody on our walk back from the Golden Dream. Most of the villa owners would be dining on their terraces at the front and the maids would be serving them. We might have been alone in the sunny, perfumed world.

Back in the kitchen at the Villa Noto, Bruna loosened the strings and brought the gold mesh bag from under her apron. She stood with it in her hand, her eyes gentle and troubled as though she had just thought of some complication. She thrust it deep into the big black leather bag that travelled with her night and morning.

When she straightened, she pointed vigorously in the direction of the town and I realized that she meant that she would take the bag to her house.

And I had thought her stupid!

It was then I saw a blister the size of a hen's egg on the back of her hand where she had been splashed by the scalding water. I moaned with pity and raced for my first-aid box.

First of all I gave her a sedative and swallowed one myself to give me heart for my task.

When I held her hand under the trickle of water from the tap she did not flinch, but I wept as if my heart would break.

When it was over and the gauze and bandage were in place, I took her upstairs to the unoccupied bedroom and bent and took off her shoes. She recoiled in horror and I had to lift her forcibly on to the bed where she lay stiffly, her eyes bright and un-winking like the eyes of a mother bird in a nest.

Only then did I bend to kiss her gratefully and saw one tear roll slowly down her cheek.

At two o'clock I went back to the bedroom, carrying sand-wiches and the blue bowl of coffee which I knew she enjoyed. She woke immediately and I saw that all was well with her.

Almost immediately, Bruna got ready to leave, but I stopped her and took the big envelope over to the kitchen table. Some of its contents, I felt convinced, would be connected with Pia's kidnapping.

When I had looked at the package before in Scott's bedroom,

the bulky quarto-sized envelope had been at the bottom of the packet, but now it was on top. It had been folded over to allow it to fit into the larger envelope.

I slit it open and tipped the contents on to the kitchen table. There was a tiny whisper of sound. A rubber band, probably rotted by the heat, had snapped. It had secured a man's handkerchief, covered with rusty stains, which had been wrapped round what was obviously a gun.

I had enough sense not to handle it. With the blade of the kitchen knife, I flicked back the corners of the handkerchief. The small pearl-handled gun looked almost dainty, but my flesh crawled and above the package Bruna and I stared at each other.

I tipped the ends of the handkerchief back into position as if, by blotting out the sight of the gun, I could somehow annihilate it.

There was a small brown leather case marked STUDS. The edges of the box were scuffed and the gilt letters had began to fade. It held a single bullet.

The only other thing was a letter-sized envelope. It was sealed and across the flap was scrawled, in a feminine, spidery hand, D. C. SCOFFONE.

I was hesitating about opening it when Bruna made a sharp, restraining gesture.

'Anybody home?' John Niven's voice boomed from the front of the house. He would think nothing of walking straight into the kitchen.

Hurriedly I pushed the handkerchief-wrapped gun, stud box and envelope back into their original packet and went quickly to the front door.

Liza and John Niven were already on the terrace, with the lovely young Sicilian girl, Aurelia Schiera, and her tall friend, Ciccio Picciotto, standing a little uncertainly on the lower step. They looked so carefree and normal that I gave them a dazzling smile which must have been so welcoming that the young couple climbed confidently up to the terrace.

Obviously all of them had already been in the water and they flopped like bronze seals into the terrace chairs.

John Niven pointed to the white caps beyond where a rocky tooth broke the curve of the bay.

'Not suitable or safe for skin-diving,' he pronounced, 'so the committee has changed the agenda. Snorkeling – or you can stretch out in the boat and digest your lunch, Miss Grant. Suit you?'

In her chair Aurelia Schiera stretched her slim arms above her head with the sinuous grace of a sleepy cat. She had strange green eyes. Ciccio Picciotto drew off his sunglasses and concentrated on the taut lines of her breasts with a contained sensuality.

'Don't we wait for the Pied Piper?' I asked lightly.

The Schiera girl laughed. 'Susan won't risk her ruby in the bottom of the bay and she won't take it off.' She looked under her lashes at the boy, 'I know I wouldn't. Besides, she won't want to get her hair wet – not when she has just become engaged.'

'And Al won't leave her?' Liza Niven was amused. 'You don't know our Casanova! A ring, even through his nose, wouldn't change him. You'll see!'

'Liza's right. I'll bet even money that Al won't change his habits in the slightest degree. He'll be along.' John Niven was smilingly confident. 'But we won't wait for him. He'll see us from the beach.'

They waited good-naturedly until I had changed into my bathing suit.

Upstairs, in my darkened bedroom, I stood for a moment before the cheval glass with the wisp of blue jersey in my hand. In the mirror, my body had a faint golden sheen and a young fluid grace. Impersonally and with a strange objectivity, I saw how the rosy-tipped breasts rose high and firm above the tapering rib-cage; the way the hips swelled gently from the narrow waist and the tender curve of the dimpled abdomen. Gravely, my eyes swept up to the dusky hollows above the collar bones and travelled over the firm golden column of the throat.

I gave a harsh, dry sob and sat down heavily on the ottoman at the foot of the bed.

But for Bruna, that body would by now have been a bloody, mutilated mass, with the forces of corruption already at work in it.

Stewart's eyes stared coldly out at me from the photograph on the bedside table. Our eyes met in the mirror, and mine dropped in shame. I sniffed loudly and my chin came up.

When I had dashed cold water on my face, I substituted my best white bathing suit for the blue one. I contoured my face with Bronze-Glo, so that my eyes seemed to sparkle as if I had been on a steady diet of champagne. I looked vivid and rather reckless, but my spine was stiff again and I was ready to face the group.

The sand was so hot that it scorched my feet, so the boy scooped me up and ran to deposit me in the jade shallows. I waded out until the water was a warm bracelet round my waist and heaved myself into the gently rocking boat.

When we were out where the water had changed to a deep sapphire, John Niven anchored and began to sort out the heap of snorkel equipment and rubber fins piled in the bow.

I have always thought the equipment offensively ugly, so when he offered me a set, I waved it away and showed him my nose clip.

'That's dangerous,' he said sharply. 'You'll get happy dreams down there and end up as a mermaid in Neptune's harem if you are not careful.'

'I'll be careful,' I promised.

The two men steadied the boat as I dived over the side.

There is nothing to equal the moment when you open your eyes in the translucent waters of the Ionian Sea and watch the little sea-horses rocking gently and a silver fan of sardines flashing past in military formation. Always it is a new, virgin world, where wisps of strange algae drift and form surrealist designs of infinite variety. There is the deep, relaxing silence and the astonishing range of colours that lulls one into a dangerous forgetfulness.

When the first deadly feeling of euphoria came, I arched to

the surface and lay on my back, breathing deeply through my pinched nostrils.

'Do you do that often?'

I opened my eyes. Aurelia Schiera was watching me from the boat and her glance was curious and respectful. Her snorkel mask dangled from her hand.

'Not as often as I would like,' I said, 'I don't fancy tackling this in Lake Zürich. Besides, I'm vain – I don't want to develop a suffused nose. The nose clip does that.'

I had drifted well beyond the boat. Now I turned over and swam back, watching with pleasure the silver veil of droplets that fell from my arms with each stroke. Thought seemed to have been washed away and only pure sensation was left.

Liza Niven surfaced beside me and had some difficulty in getting her plump little body back into the boat. I helped to heave while Aurelia Schiera tugged and then I hung panting, clutching a rowlock and trying to get my breath back.

There was no sign of the two men. The women chatted amiably. Liza Niven spread her hair out to dry in the sunshine and Aurelia Schiera sprayed her body, stroking the oil on with long, caressing movements. She would be fat by the time she was thirty, but now with her smooth shoulders, small, pear-shaped breasts and tapering legs, she was like a gold figurine from some medieval casket.

She opened those strange green eyes widely when I asked, as casually as I could, 'Is Al Scott a Sicilian?'

'Heavens, no! What made you think that? He speaks Sicilian very well, but he is not native-born.' She shrugged. 'It is difficult to give you examples, but there are small nuances and turns of expression which no Sicilian would use.'

'He's a dyed-in-the-wool American all right,' Liza Niven put in lazily. 'He was born in Treasure Island, Florida. He told me so,' she said firmly, as if that ended the matter.

'What about his parents?'

The Schiera girl turned on her side to stare at me. 'Not Sicilian.' The small smile was secret and almost furtive. I decided that I disliked her. 'Ciccio told me.' For a moment there was a flicker of fear in her eyes as though she had said too much. She shrugged again. 'When a man comes often to the island, people get curious and it is easy to read his story. Signor Scott's is not particularly interesting – a rich American playboy – not quite top-flight artist – not quite top-flight musician – only money.' The contempt was unmistakable.

Remembering the scene that morning on the beach, I allowed some of *my* contempt to show.

She flushed and closed her eyes. She said lazily, 'That dark skin isn't a Mediterranean tan. Probably a touch of the tarbrush.'

Looking at the malicious curve of the small mouth, I wondered how I could ever have thought her good-looking.

I felt more ashamed of the conversation than of anything I had done to him up till then. He had kidnapped a child, lied and kept a savage dog, yet he was a kind, cultivated person. What kind of man was he?

It was a relief to plunge down, down, down . . . When the water turned a deep plum colour, I knew that it was time to surface. I thought how fine it would be to lie beside Stewart on the great silver rock on the distant curve of the lido and then climb slowly up to the old town to drink a little wine and feel the tiredness ease out from the body. I felt my eyes stinging and it had nothing to do with the sea.

In the boat John Niven sat hunched, squinting in the direction of the far end of the beach.

'That's strange,' he said slowly. 'The *Golden Eye* has been in for quite a while. All the kids have gone. I saw our little Tina go into our villa, but there doesn't seem to be any sign of Al or Susan. It looks as if I would have lost that bet.'

My heart began to pound.

He leaned forward. 'Dammit! I'll soon be an old fogey needing glasses. Ciccio, is that Alaimo, the vet?'

'I think it might be.' His tone was concerned. 'Do you know Felice Pegna, the butcher, who has the shop just off the Via Apollo Arcageta?'

John Niven nodded.

'Well, two days ago, he mixed some preservative into the pet food he sells. He didn't mix it well enough and seven cats died from an overdose of benzoic acid. I believe they went into convulsions before they died. If that has happened to Scott's dog, I wouldn't like to be Pegna.'

I wondered if I looked as sick as I felt.

Nobody spoke as we made for the shore, but when we were walking up the beach, Aurelia Schiera said defiantly, 'If that ghastly Dobermann is dead, I won't pretend to be sorry. It wasn't a pet dog. It was a savage brute. I'll never understand why Al had it about the place. You would have thought that with the little girl there, he wouldn't have such a dog, but he brought it here for the first time when he brought his daughter. Strange!'

John Niven said nothing, but his face tightened and he turned away abruptly, walking with long, urgent steps towards the Golden Dream.

I walked slowly up the beach. Mario was sitting cross-legged on the stretch of sand below the villa. I left the others and flopped down beside him. He looked pinched and unhappy.

'What's wrong?' I said anxiously, wondering if he and Pia could have seen the dog.

'Everything.' I had rarely heard a more hopeless note in anybody's voice. My lips twitched in a smile. Obviously, it had nothing to do with the dog. Probably lost his money-belt, I surmised.

'I'm sorry, Miss Grant. It's all my fault, but I didn't mean to do anything wrong.' His eyes met mine steadily. 'Honestly, I meant to ask Signor Scott's permission, and then I simply couldn't.'

'Suppose you tell me just what happened.'

'Well, last night when you went out to the party, I began to think about the "bug". I knew that if the other kids saw me putting it in the boat, they wouldn't leave it alone. So I went along about nine o'clock and put it inside the forward cabin. I thought that would be the best place.' He moistened his lips. 'I meant to tell Signor Scott about it at once and, if he didn't

94

like the idea of the experiment, I would apologize and take the listening device away.'

'Oh, Mario!'

'I know now that I was wrong, but I'm really not sorry, Miss Grant. There was such a fuss about Signorina Bradford's new ring that I didn't get a chance to talk to him until we were well along the coast. I went forward to the cabin when I heard the "bug" clattering down.'

'*Mario!* What did he say?'

'He swore and I could tell that Signorina Bradford was frightened. She said, "I know it's the Daltons, Al. They've found us." Signor Scott didn't say anything at first. Then he said, "Susan, I promise you the whole business will be settled for good very soon. Maybe the time has come when I've got to use that gun." '

Two bathers laughed and splashed each other below us in the bay. Their happy shouts rang clearly through the still air. I shivered with cold and could not find my voice.

'Signorina Bradford began to weep and then she said, "Al, you simply can't do that to Pia. You mustn't. You mustn't. You can pay too high a price for some things." '

'What happened then?'

'I don't know. I went back and sat beside Pia. Everybody thought I was seasick and the boys laughed. Pia was angry, because she could see them laughing. I was glad when it was time to come home.'

I couldn't find the words to reassure him. When I pulled him to his feet, I was clinging to his hand as much as he was to mine.

My guilt about the dog went away.

Chapter 7

Mario's feet dragged as we left the beach and went slowly through the garden towards the villa.

Automatically, he stopped as usual half way along the paved path, reminded of the lime tree by the heady fragrance of its flowers and the flashes of white from its silver-backed leaves. An errant breeze from the Ionian Sea sent the weeping foliage into gentle motion. The *Tilia petiolaris* is narcotic to bees, and Mario, so he had informed me, liked to gather the dozens of small furry bodies to be found drunk on the ground in the evening. It was not, I decided, politic to enquire what he did with them, but now he merely stirred them carefully with a bare toe, risking a sting, sighed and came gloomily away.

Arlene had created a beautiful and unusual garden, with exotic plants which not only survived, but thrived in their Sicilian setting. An Elizabethan lawn of camomile gave off a sweet fragrance at every step; the rich oriental colours of Chinese pinks glowed happily under champagne bubble shrubs; in the borders Fire Emerald gazanias, shading from black to intense emerald green, flowered as fabulously as in their native South Africa.

For Mario and me, the garden bloomed in vain. We sat on the terrace and looked blankly out to where the waves cast a lacy scarf along the edge of the beach.

Mario broke the uneasy silence to say bitterly, 'The worst thing of all is that that "bug" didn't work. I tried the recorder as soon as I got back to see if it had recorded any talk before the "bug" fell off. There wasn't a peep out of it.'

The bewildered unhappiness in his face worried me. Even Tom Curzon had let him down. The elaborate box was only a child's toy.

I got to my feet. 'I need a drink,' I said firmly. 'Sit there and

I'll bring you an almond milk cocktail, sir, guaranteed to raise the spirits.'

For a moment there was a gleam of humour in the dark eyes, but it passed quickly.

There was no sign of Bruna and I busied myself in the kitchen, concocting a drink that would amuse and please Mario. I poured the innocuous mixture of grenadine, almond milk and orange juice into a chilled champagne glass and carried it and my own drink out to the terrace.

We sat like two old topers, each busy with personal problems. I was willing the telephone to ring, secure in the knowledge that Stewart would tell me how to get Pia to safety. While I knew that I ought to be stirring myself, taking some positive action, I was trapped in inertia.

The gentle afternoon light thinned and I had the illusion that it flushed like the uncertain pearly glow in a conch shell.

Would Al Scott dare to harm Pia while there were only the three of them in the villa? Surely even a member of the Mafia would not commit such a blatant crime? A gun used against a little girl would inevitably open a searching enquiry. Surely no one would shoot a child? Scott was not stupid. Wouldn't he stage a simple accident, such as might easily befall a deaf-mute child?

I began to feel sick and put my gin and tonic glass down on the wicker table with a thump which brought Mario's head up alertly.

There was no doubt now about the rosy glow in the air. I sniffed. There was an acrid smell as if someone had spilled hot water in ashes.

Great puffs of dark smoke stained the blue of the sky above Etna. A thread of scarlet crawled down the side of the mountain and presently, as if someone were operating a giant bellows, a spray of flames erupted skywards and fell like a fireworks display towards the ground.

The combination of brilliant blue sky, snow-capped mountain top and scarlet lava made a spectacular picture. I watched it dreamily, only half aware of a nagging uneasiness.

'Pathetic fallacy!' I murmured.

'What's that?'

'Oh – an English figure of speech when nature seems to share your mood.' I waved vaguely in the direction of the mountain. 'You know, like Etna spitting flame just now and you and I sitting here worrying about a gun being used.' I laughed. 'Daft!'

Mario smiled, but it was a poor attempt.

'I don't suppose Signor Scott has even *got* a gun.' He wanted to be reassured.

'No,' I agreed mendaciously, comforting my conscience with the thought that it was literally true. I had his gun and surely members of the Mafia in good standing didn't keep *sets* of guns? 'Stop worrying about Pia. Nothing is going to happen to her.'

'Pia?' The frown was back between his brows and I noticed that the mouth no longer looked childish. Mario seemed to have matured quite a bit since morning. 'Why do *you* call her Pia?'

The telephone bell shrilled from the house.

The rosy glow from Etna seemed to drench me in a magic light. I drew a deep, quivering happy breath. Thank God for Stewart! It was as if a heavy burden rolled from my shoulders.

I fumbled with the screen of the hall door and barked my shins on the leg of the hall table in my hurry to reach the telephone.

When I heard his voice, I closed my eyes as usual, as if, by shutting out the sight of Arlene's house, I could bring him closer to me. Under my bare feet the creamy marble of the door felt cold and silky. I had a terrific feeling of well-being. probably it was only then that I realized how worrying the sense of personal responsibility had been.

'. . . was impossible to get in touch with you earlier. I have been working against time, for I want to come to Taormina tomorrow.'

I drew a deep, thankful breath.

'Are you all right, darling?'

'Of course I am, Stewart, but I *need* you.'

'I know, but it won't be long now. I got your message about

Scott and the child. Just keep calm. He has been floating around the fringes of the Dalton ménage for at least two years. Pia Dalton knows him well and appears to be very fond of him. He left New York in April, almost a month after the maid and the child had disappeared. He's a cool, cool customer. He won't take off anywhere in a hurry, so don't get in a flap.'

'You mean he sent the maid to England?'

'No, I don't mean anything of the kind. There are a lot of loose ends to be tied up. We don't know all the answers, but Scott seems to have been at least an opportunist. Whether he was working with the Daltons or against them, we don't yet know. We – '

'But, Stewart, you can't mean . . . ?'

'Yes. There isn't any doubt at all, in my mind at least, that Corinne and Eric Dalton staged the kidnapping. They paid the rent of the house at Exton. They paid the maid three months' salary in advance. I've got proof of that. The whole affair was handled with incredible clumsiness. The amazing thing is how they got away with it for so long.'

'But why did they do such a terrible thing?'

'For money . . . for 600,000 beautiful dollars . . . for publicity, to help to prop up their sagging careers. Don't misunderstand me – they are both good in their respective fields, but neither is any longer in the top class. In my opinion, Corinne Dalton is a magnificent coloratura soprano. I heard her singing the title rôle in *Lucia* and the title part in Donizetti's *Maria Stuarda*. My God, what a voice! But even I had to admit that she was better five years ago in Gilda's role in *Rigoletto* and the last four records she made have been disappointing. She's only forty-one. She should be good for a very long time, but it is not working out that way. I've been sounding out people who should know why the skids are under her.'

'Drink?'

'No, no. One old musician who has been around the opera stars for a long time put his finger on the trouble – at least, I think so. An unhappy woman sings badly was how he put it.'

'And you think she is trying to comfort herself with money?'

'Yes. Eric Dalton's position is clearer than hers. There is a new vein of cynicism in his plays that the public apparently doesn't like. He is finding it harder to get backers. With money tight all round just now, "angels" will only bet on certainties. But pride also comes into it for both of them. Temperamentally, neither of them seems capable of stepping down gracefully.'

'But to do this to their own child! They must have realized that the child had to come back some time. How on earth were they going to get over that? If they did, what purpose would it really have served?'

Stewart sighed. 'It would take too long to go into it now. I've had difficulty in restraining the American company that holds the policy. Their directors have been howling for the last drop of the Daltons' blood. I've been patiently explaining the difference between attempting to defraud and actually defrauding. I was going to let the Daltons have enough rope to hang themselves, but an over-zealous and damned stupid official in the company blurted out to the Daltons that they were in big trouble.'

'Yes, I see. What are they doing about it?'

'They threatened to clap a suit on the American company if they didn't forthwith produce proof (*a*) that Pia Dalton was in fact alive and (*b*) that she was being concealed somewhere with their knowledge and consent. We'd have to produce the nurse-maid's letter corroborating that this was so and you'll remember that Corinne Dalton didn't lodge her claim until late in April.'

'Oh. Then the onus is on the insurance company to produce the child?'

'Yes. This morning I felt like cutting my throat. That loud-mouth in New York was so cock-a-hoop that he blurted out to the Daltons that he had every reason to believe that the child is in Taormina.'

'Stewart!'

'Yes. It is practically certain that they are either on the island now or on their way there.'

'But where does Al Scott come in?'

'We haven't got that tied up. He has been very friendly with the nursemaid. Incidentally, her name is Emma Susan Bradford Rice and, with that unlikely mouthful, she is Irish. The Daltons seem to have pulled the wool over her eyes very nicely. Probably Scott did likewise. He left New York suddenly early in April and was certainly living in Exton soon after that, but not in the Dalton house.'

There was the dull banging of the screen door and the slap of Mario's feet on the tiles of the hall. He seemed to be in a hurry. I thought I heard an excited giggle.

'One thing, Stewart, I must tell you.'

'What? About what?'

'About Scott. I think he is a member of the Mafia.'

There was a sigh from the other end of the telephone.

'Laurie, it has been said with considerable truth that America, Italy and Sicily have a common problem. It is practically impossible to draw a dividing line between Mafiosi and non-Mafiosi.'

'Well, listen . . .'

'I'll have to ring off now. I'm sorry, but I think I hear Thompson in the hall. This is important. I'll be with you very soon.'

'But, Stewart . . .'

I put the telephone down slowly. The happy, exhilarated feeling had completely evaporated.

Al Scott was standing in the doorway, watching me.

How much had he heard?

I gripped the back of the chair, aware that beyond the windows the swallows were darting and swooping in their nightly forays for insects. Soon they would be gone and, in moments, the blackness of night would press round the villa. I was full of a strange, tense certainty that Al Scott was aware of my fear.

His tan looked yellow as if he were sick. Under the checked shirt, his shoulders looked broad and powerful. I was deeply afraid. He looked hard at me, but it was impossible to tell whether this was a habit suddenly acquired following the death of the Dobermann or if he was making up his mind about something.

I waited, schooling myself to *feel* innocent and slightly puzzled and trying to ignore the chill down my spine.

He had the slight frown of a person wrestling with a problem. Almost detachedly, I noticed that the spectacular good looks were not as much in evidence as usual. He looked strained and tired; his cheeks were hollow, the bones of his temples sharp and the lines of his mouth thin with exhaustion.

The pounding of my heart grew steadier. Suddenly I was uncomfortably aware that I was wearing only a bathing costume. What had seemed suitable on the beach now seemed immodest. I was frantic to get past him, out of the room.

I said shakily, 'I feel like a slut of a housewife who has been caught in her dressing-gown at noon. I've just been talking to my fiancé, so I didn't hear you come in. Let me get a robe and then we can talk. He's coming tomorrow.'

I had surprised him. He said indifferently, 'I hadn't noticed your dress or lack of it. I hope I didn't startle you. Mario let me in at the back door. Until I heard you talking on the telephone, I didn't realize you were here.'

I willed myself to walk steadily past him, not hurrying obviously and keeping my pace on the stairs normally brisk and even.

There is still time to run, I reminded myself as I fastened the belt of my dress, but I knew that I couldn't do it until both the children were safe. All the time, I was wondering frantically how I could get Pia away from him.

When I returned he had switched on the lights in the salon and was standing in the curve of the window, staring into the room. He said surprisingly, 'This is a peaceful room, Laurie. You've got the art of calming the atmosphere. The Golden Dream is all shot to hell.'

'What's wrong?' I was taken aback by the misery of his tone. Rather feebly I asked, 'Will a drink help?'

'A beer would be fine, but don't go for a minute. Everything seems to have gone wrong today.' He moved into the middle of the salon and strode restlessly about the room, occasionally touching an ornament lightly, but I knew that he was not aware of what he was doing. 'While we were at Messina, somebody got into the villa and killed my dog – scalded and strangled it.'

Oh God! Oh God!

'What are the police saying?' I asked carefully.

His look was sardonic. 'In Sicily, not everyone has faith in the police. I, for one, will not be troubling them. Sometimes it is better to solve one's own problems. I expect to do that.'

'What was stolen?' Had my voice a self-conscious ring? He looked at me sharply, as if aware of something in my voice.

'As far as I know, some papers. It is maddening. They are the kind that are really only of use to the owner.' He managed a wry smile. 'When I catch up with the thief, he won't kill any more dogs.'

The floor heaved gently under my feet. In the great gilded mirror on the wall behind him I saw the pale reflection of my face, the eyes huge with alarm.

'But I am frightening you.' He was the Al Scott I had known, polite and concerned. 'It *is* a frightening business. That is really why I am here. Susan and I must be free to make enquiries, but I don't want Vira around. Would you help us out by keeping her overnight? I would be very grateful. I could have asked the Nivens but she doesn't care much for Tina and she adores Mario.'

I was so taken aback that for a moment I could only stare at him. 'Of course, of course,' I said hastily. 'She won't be any trouble at all.'

'I thought you would say that.' For the first time he smiled. 'She is in the kitchen now with Mario and her case is in the hall. You see how I took you for granted!'

'Come and have your beer.' My thoughts were whirling, going round and round seeking the answer to the question, *Why?* Pia handed over to me! It seemed too good to be true.

Bruna was back, moving quietly from fridge to kitchen table with glasses of milk and plates of food for the children. She looked just as usual except for the bandaged hand.

Scott looked at it quickly and said rather sharply, 'How did that happen?'

103

'Bruna must have been hungry this morning.' I smiled. 'She cut herself rather badly when she was preparing her breakfast. I think she has found it a nuisance all day.'

'I believe Sylvana mentioned it. I had forgotten.' He spoke then in his rapid Sicilian and Bruna beamed. Moments later her eyes flickered uncertainly towards her basket, but almost immediately her face resumed its look of slightly stupid good nature.

He turned to me. 'I told her that Vira would be staying. I had forgotten that Mario could explain the position.' His eyes went to the tumblers on the draining-board. He finished his beer and handed the glass to Bruna. 'My car is on the highway. I've told her that when she has rinsed those glasses – provided you don't need her any more – I'll run her up to her house. Susan is waiting in the car now.'

For a moment he leaned heavily on the kitchen table, looking intently at the little girl. My heart contracted at the sight of the loving confidence in her gaze. 'Well, I'll get on with my detecting, though it is getting a bit late for it. I want to see the vet again.' He bent to kiss the child. Then Bruna and he left quickly by the back door.

I sat down hard on a kitchen chair and looked blankly at Mario, who was contentedly playing noughts and crosses with his friend.

Chapter 8

A pattern ought to have been emerging now out of the welter of facts, but to me the jigsaw pieces would not fit into any recognizable form. The sense of things being out of kilter worried me in the way that a sick person is troubled by an irregularity in the pattern of the wallpaper opposite his bed.

People, I thought furiously, should be what they seemed. Who was it who said that no man is a villain in his own story? Al Scott's worried face rose in my mind to mock me. Was it simply worry over the death of a dog?

Nothing, I decided wearily, made sense. Two people, famous, comfortably off, well educated, apparently sane, had arranged the kidnapping of their own child. A nursemaid who had looked after her for almost the whole of the girl's life was prepared to collaborate – albeit reluctantly – with a sophisticated gangster in order to conceal and shoot her charge. And he worried over the death of a savage dog!

Yet these were not inmates of Bedlam. They were the kind of people one met at parties; they were friendly neighbours; they were people whom one could *like*.

Keep calm, Stewart had said. Do nothing until I get to you.

But it would be about sixteen long hours before he could reach Taormina. Already the very prospect of waiting had aged me. I felt as taut as a violin string and afraid that I might snap just as readily.

Beyond the kitchen windows, the dim evening dusk deepened like a threat. I let out a sound like a sob and then looked guiltily towards the pair at the table, afraid that Mario had heard me. But he was engrossed in a long conversation with Pia, speaking slowly and distinctly in English while her eyes followed the shape of the words on his lips.

'You must go to bed soon,' he said in a scolding, grown-up

voice that carried faint echoes of a childhood scarred with nagging. 'We must be up early, because I want to take you snorkeling.'

Would Al Scott return when it was properly dark?

'We will play four games and then I will show you where you will sleep. Do not be afraid of the dark. I will be in the next room.'

She beamed at him, fully aware of his pleasure in her presence in the villa. Contentedly, her hand went out for the pencil and the feathery eyebrows went up in a movement that said as plainly as words, Shall I begin?

Perhaps I could have borne it if his words of comfort had sounded hollow and forced, but the serenity between them was almost tangible.

I was scared and sick and obstinate. Somehow, I thought desperately, I would find a way to keep the children safe until Stewart came.

Now I thought of them together, as though the danger that threatened the one threatened the other also. If the danger to Pia was physical, that to Mario was just as real. Should anything happen to his new friend, something in him would be irreparably broken. This I knew with absolute certainty.

I had a few wild ideas, but eventually I had to give them all up. No dramatic action of mine was going to get rid simultaneously of two sets of dangerous people. Self-protectively, I drifted into a sort of mindless wool-gathering, pointless and comforting. It took an effort to shake myself out of it.

It was warm in the kitchen, but I hugged myself as though I were cold, postponing the moment when I would have to leave its false security. I allowed myself to sit slumped in the chair for a few minutes, watching the quick darting of the supposed victim's hand as she added an X to the sheet of paper and drew a triumphant downward line.

She looked very small to be the focus of somebody's hate or greed.

Hunched over the wooden table, she was relaxed and happy, pulling at a dark curl in a vain attempt to nibble it. It kept springing back. Half of the mass of hair had been slotted through a ring of white elastic decorated with a crude pink plastic rose. It was the kind of ghastly hair ornament that little girls love. The rest of her hair was loose. I looked vaguely round for the missing pink atrocity and fished it up from under Mario's chair, then sat snapping the elastic gently back and forth while I thought about Al Scott.

The hall clock struck eight with a melodious finality and loudness that made me very conscious of our isolation in the villa. It had been a mistake to let Bruna leave. But had Scott left me any choice? Angrily I recognized that I had probably been out-manoeuvred.

Try as I would, I could not close my mind to the thought that, if Pia must meet with an accident, tonight, while she was in my charge, was the perfect time for it to happen.

I swallowed harshly, so that Mario looked across at me enquiringly. To escape those percipient eyes, I braced myself against the back of the chair, got up and went out of the kitchen like someone with a purpose.

In the hall I dropped the plastic hair-band on the table, wandered into the salon and studied the telephone distractedly, trying to summon the courage to call John Niven.

How do you tell a man that his friend, of some years' standing, is a kidnapper and a potential killer?

My thoughts shied away from the picture of John Niven's incredulous astonishment and angry disbelief. A man used to taking things at their face value would not be much help now.

My chin came up. Sourly I told myself that I could stand his contempt, just as long as he was prepared to keep vigil with me in the villa until morning. It would be difficult for Scott to attempt anything in broad daylight.

With a steady finger, I dialled the Niven number.

The bell rang nine times before the receiver was lifted. Against a background of party noises and music, John Niven's voice sounded impatient and slurred.

'Whosit? Whatja want? Whosit? Shpeak up!'

Gently I replaced the receiver.

An hotel for the night? I did not have Pia's passport, so that was no good. I cursed my moment of weak generosity in the Golden Dream.

I leaned heavily on the edge of the table like a sick person and tried to go over the small list of people I knew in Taormina.

The Fontana couple – the jolly artist and his mousey wife – lived, I recalled, well out on the road to Messina, probably too far away to be any good now. Scott's friend, Ciccio, who had been so blatantly attracted to Aurelia Schieria, was equally impossible. 'A favourite has no friends . . .' Nonsense!

The names of the other people at the party slid away from me. I began to feel the beginnings of panic. What use was Latin charm if it did not produce results? With sour insularity, I told myself, Give me a dour but helpful Scot any day. Fervently I hoped that the helpful Scot would not have to be me.

The old, wise voice of Don Michle, the man with the Vernis Martin fan, rang in my head like a marriage bell. He had liked me, I was sure of that. With a surge of hope, I reached for the telephone directory.

What was his name? Spino? No. Spiro? No. Spina! That was it. Michle Spina.

The letters on the directory page ran together, but finally I found the number. Thankfully I noted that his villa overlooked the Baia delle Sirene. Its opulent modernity had been pointed out to me.

Not too far away! I told myself exultantly.

The receiver was lifted as though someone at the other end had been waiting for the call. The spate of Sicilian confused me. I let it flow over me. When the torrent had ceased, I said as clearly as possible, 'Don Michle . . . Signorina Grant . . . Don Michle.'

I could hear heavy breathing. Then the receiver clattered, presumably against a table.

At least they haven't hung up, I comforted myself.

Presently another deep mellifluous voice said in halting English, 'What a pity, signorina! Don Michle Spina left this afternoon for Palermo. He will be desolated. Shall I give you his Palermo number? He will return in a few days.'

'No, thank you. I will call him some other time.' I cradled the receiver and looked at it with loathing.

There was nobody else.

I could hear Mario fiddling about in the kitchen, making coffee. I went in and leaned against the door jamb and watched his precise movements as he lifted down the pink lustre cup and saucer which he had decided was my favourite.

'It's for you,' he said in explanation.

Pia watched us both. If she had recognized me as the woman in the London park, she had given no sign. There was something oddly consoling about her acceptance of me.

'If ever I have to go on safari to Africa or find myself shouting *mush-mush* at the North Pole, I hope you are on my team,' I said warmly to him.

It was wonderful to watch the way the smile lit up his eyes. Nevertheless, they were a tired small boy's eyes and my heart contracted. Deliberately, I stopped looking at him.

'While I drink the coffee, will you take Pia upstairs? I'll come in a few minutes.'

'Have I to help her to get ready for bed?'

'No. Let her sit on your bed while you pack your case. Be as quick as you can.'

His eyes widened. 'We're *leaving*?'

'Yes. As soon as possible. I'll tell you about it when we are on our way. Try to keep Pia from asking any questions meanwhile.' Until I can think of a good reason, I thought wretchedly. 'I have to get some food together. We are going to Catania . . . to the Villa Casilda.'

He turned an astonished face to me.

'Have I done something wrong?' he said in a frightened voice. 'Is that why you are taking me back?'

'Oh, Mario, *no*.' I bent and hugged him. 'I wouldn't be without you for worlds. I need you.' I gave him a firm push towards the door. 'We must get Pia away as soon as possible.'

I saw the beginnings of comprehension in his eyes and a new kind of fear, quickly suppressed.

As they climbed the stairs together, he talked in a low, soothing voice to the child, aware that she could not hear him, but, like a good psychologist, aware also of the effectiveness of the radar system that operated between them.

Go on, I told myself, *go on. There is no one but you to look after them. Well . . . get on with it!*

As I rinsed the coffee cup, I began to plan and almost at once felt myself becoming calm.

It would be dangerous to stay in Taormina. Scott would look for us there. Besides, where could we go? But better not be too far away from the airport at Catania where Stewart would arrive. The empty Villa Casilda would be a godsend. I shrugged off the thought of the Biagottis' annoyance. There would be plenty of time for explanations and apologies later.

The great thing was to be calm now, to go methodically about filling the big shopping-bag with bottles of milk, butter, bread, a knife, tin-opener, cheese, fruit and tinned soup and meat. Remembering Melina's bulging parcels, the cupboards at the Villa Casilda would be bare. After a moment, I added the bottle of Marsala which Mario had sent away from the lunch table – not at all the act of a steady, sensible person. I went pensively round the kitchen, chewing a lump of cold sausage, while with the indifference of a practised thief I decided which of Arlene's possessions to appropriate.

I did not stop to analyse why I put Bruna's short utility knife, honed to razor sharpness, conveniently at a corner of the kitchen table.

There was no sound from the children above, though the house seemed to listen with me.

Remembering their tiredness, I thought it would be a good idea to have everything ready in the car so that when I brought them downstairs we could move off immediately. I fetched my handbag from the hall and found the ignition key at once.

When I reversed the Citroën on to the highway, I could smell the spring-flowering cherry, the almond and the Judas, and glimpse in the Nivens' garden cameos of oleander and palm, blacker than the surrounding darkness. Their visitors' cars lined the verge so that I had difficulty manoeuvring Arlene's great white monster out of the driveway, but at last I managed it.

Before I went upstairs, I locked the front door facing the beach and put the telephone pad and pencil beside the knife on the kitchen table.

Upstairs, Pia was sitting cross-legged on Mario's bed, reading one of the comics which I had bought a hundred years before at Heathrow.

By the time I had carried her unopened case back downstairs, Mario, very poised and serious, had finished his packing. Ostentatiously, he placed Tom Curzon's gift and his father's recorder at the top of the stairs before going back for his case. His face had a stubborn look as if he expected me to tell him to leave them behind.

I changed into my turquoise slacks and white sweater and draped over my shoulders Arlene's scarlet blazer which I had found in a bedroom cupboard. It was warmer than anything I possessed. The white silk headscarf which Stewart had bought for me in Engelberg went into a blazer pocket along with my dark glasses. I could feel my chin wobbling with self-pity when I looked at the scarf.

It took me three trips before the food, the children's possessions and my own were stowed in the boot. It was a very tight fit.

I tossed my jacket and handbag on the front seat of the car and went back into the house to get the children dressed for the journey.

They were not in the bedroom and their coats had gone from the bed. Presumably, Mario, the efficient, had attended to the dressing process.

Puzzled, I gathered a couple of pillows from the bed and blankets from the cupboard and deposited them at the head of the stairs.

When I went into my own room, the linen curtains over the french door swayed as though the door were open. I thought I heard a soft giggle from the balcony and the scuffle of feet.

I laughed, but my heart sank. It was not the best time for playing hide-and-seek.

They were not on the side facing the sea. The rush and suck of the waves had a lonely sound and the beach was blotted out in the blackness. Not a star burned, so that I had a momentary panicky feeling of claustrophobia.

They would be crouched between the hammock and the railings of the back balcony, directly above the kitchen door where a single light bulb illumined the back door step and cast deeper shadows on the balcony above.

I had reached the french door when the two shapes cannoned into me. Pia's hands closed like vices on my legs, digging into the flesh of my thighs with the desperation of a climber who feels the rock face sliding from his grasp. We were pushed into the bedroom and Mario closed the door as if all the devils of Hades were clamouring to get in.

The back door-bell rang.

Pia's trembling went on and on. Across the room, Mario and I stared at each other wordlessly. Gently I loosened her grasp and Mario moved over to hold her tightly. Her face was dark with a strangely adult grief.

The bell rang again.

'It's a man and a woman,' he whispered over her head. 'I don't know who they are, but Pia nearly had a fit when she saw them. Don't let them in.' His eyes were like saucers.

We could hear the feet on the crushed shells at the side of the house. They were moving round to the front door.

'I won't,' I said firmly, but my throat was dry and I found myself whispering. 'But maybe I'll speak to them. Keep Pia up here and don't make a sound.' I turned in the doorway and felt the hot anger flooding me when I saw the whiteness of his face.

'Mush-mush!' I said encouragingly and got a ghost of a smile in reply.

When I was half way down the stairs, the front door-bell rang. They must have seen the light in the bedroom, so it would be useless to pretend that there was nobody at home.

Had I locked the screen door as well as the inner door? I thought that I had.

Any self-respecting protector would have a gun at least, I told myself disgustedly, and thought fleetingly of Bruna's knife. The idea of my despatching two people in quick succession was so ridiculous that I think I was smiling when I switched on the porch light and unlocked the door.

It was silent in the softly-lit hall, but the music from the Niven villa came in a reassuring blare. Aurelia Schiera's high excited voice sounded very close, as though she was standing under the almond tree. There was a deep masculine cough, then a man's voice, urgent and persuasive. I wondered briefly if the pleading tones were Ciccio's. The sound was music in my ears. I decided to send Miss Schiera flowers before Stewart and I left for home.

So at first I was not really afraid when I looked at the couple on the doorstep.

They were the Daltons. There was no doubt about that. Probably they could be described as a splendid couple. The night air from the sea was chilly on my face. It may have been responsible for making the woman look cold and hard in spite of her smile. The wire mesh of the screen door cast blue shadows on her shining blonde head and along the firm line of her jaw. There were smudges like bruises under the magnificent eyes. I think I would have recognized her anywhere from Stewart's description. The perfection of her features evoked less response in me than a statue would have done.

The man stood far back in the shadows, but I had an impression of height and strength and a certain waiting quality that brought the goose pimples up on my arms. There was tenseness in his stillness.

The woman was so close up to the screen door that I took a protective step back into the hall before I reminded myself that, short of shooting their way in, they were safely marooned on the step. She had a beautiful speaking voice with a diction so clear that it was as if every word was carefully considered before it was delivered. In a detached fashion, I found myself listening with pleasure to her way of pronouncing each syllable with meticulous care. Had she cultivated the habit in attempting to communicate with Pia?

'Forgive us for disturbing you,' she said with a wide, actressy smile. 'I do hope you don't mind this intrusion.'

'Not at all.' I turned an amused glance in the direction of the staircase. 'I don't mind a bit, but I'm afraid that my husband is like a bear with a sore head when he is disturbed while he is working, so forgive *me* if I talk very quietly. Can I help you?'

Behind her in the darkness the man moved and Corinne Dalton looked over her shoulder impatiently.

'Do you have a little girl in the house? I was told you had.'

'A girl?' Even to my ears my laugh sounded forced. I would not earn an Oscar for acting, I decided. I went doggedly on. 'I have a little *boy*, who, I trust, is sound asleep by now. But the Nivens who live next door have a daughter called Tina. Perhaps she . . .'

I saw her eyes go past me to the hair-clasp on the hall table. Casually I raised both hands and swept my hair back into a pony tail. I groped for the plastic rose and slipped my hair through the elastic. I tried not to think how awful I must look. Corinne Dalton looked at me with acute dislike. The angry colour suffused her neck and crept upwards into her face. I sensed that like many beautiful women she was completely egocentric and could not bear to be baulked in any way.

Over her shoulder her husband said sharply, 'We are looking for our daughter, Pia Dalton. It's rather a serious matter. She has been missing for months. It's a long story. At any rate, a maid in a villa at the end of the beach told us that she had been left in your charge. At least, that's what we thought she said.' He took a step nearer. The pockmarked face looked vaguely threatening. 'Do you mind if we come in?' It was less a request than a demand. The voice was hard and taut.

I looked nervously towards the stair. 'Do you mind coming back tomorrow? Perhaps at about ten o'clock? I don't like to disturb my husband.' I tried to look browbeaten. 'But I really don't think I can be of any help. There are lots of children in

the villas along the beach, but I'm afraid I don't know them.
I'm very much of a newcomer. Your best plan would be to call
at the police station in the town,' I added helpfully. 'Good
night.'

Had I really succeeded in sounding a little impatient and
bored? Or had they sensed the underlying nervousness?

The man put a big hand on the screen just above the lock. He
seemed to lean on it and I saw the mesh bending. Hastily I
closed the front door, blotting out their furious faces, but
carrying the fear back with me into the recesses of the hall.

I listened until I heard the crunch of their feet on the shells
as they moved in the direction of the Nivens' villa.

As I switched off the porch light, my knees were shaking and
my reflection in the hall mirror looked unfamiliar with the
scraped back hair and the white, tense face.

I pulled off the silly hair-clasp and went quickly up the stairs.

The children stood close together on the far side of my bed,
as if for mutual comfort. Their eyes were fixed on mine in a
sort of desperate hope.

I went down on my knees before Pia and tilted her face up to
look at me. 'Don't be afraid,' I mouthed. 'They've gone.'

Her eyes were full of grief, but over-riding it was fear.

I had seen a similar terror in the eyes of colts who had been
badly handled. There was a thin beading of moisture along the
childish curve of her upper lip and the trembling had settled
into a series of violent tremors that shook her body like miniature explosions. She tugged suddenly at my hands, urging me
towards the bedroom door. Her fear that the Daltons would
come back communicated itself to me. She was not more
anxious to leave the Villa Noto than I was. Yet, never-racking
as it would be to wait, I knew that I must delay long enough to
make sure that the Daltons had left.

'Take the pillows,' I said crisply to Mario, as I gathered up
the blankets with the one hand which Pia had left free. We went
quietly downstairs.

I let the long seconds tick away. Somewhere above the house
a gull rose with a desolate, empty cry.

There was a bottle of aspirins in a kitchen cupboard. I swallowed a couple and, feeling rather guilty, gave each of the children a half. When I had wrapped Bruna's knife in an old tea-towel, it went into Mario's pocket with the pad and pencil.

He looked at me with an air of weary puzzlement that broke my heart. 'She says those people are her Mama and Papa. She has a special little tablet she writes on. How can that be? Isn't Mr Scott her Papa?'

I shook my head. 'I'll explain it to you later,' I said. 'Don't worry about it now. I'll take the pillows and blankets out first and come back for you.'

But he would not hear of that.

In the end, the three of us went hand in hand up the path, literally holding our breath until we got to the car.

I took the knife from Mario and put it in my handbag in the front seat, though I recognized that it was a poor weapon, in my hands at least.

The air was sweet with the smell of warm grass and the spicy tang of pinewood. Vaguely I remembered the coolness of the sea air at the front of the house. Away from the shore, a strange, hot wind seemed to blow. The children gasped with discomfort.

They lay down obediently on the back seat, burrowing among the pillows and blankets like young puppies. I vowed savagely that if the Daltons and Al Scott joined forces with the Mafia, the IRA and Hell's Angels combined, they would not get near them to harm them.

I felt reckless and strong when I slid into the front seat and turned the key in the ignition. Immediately I accelerated too much so that the car gave a great leap forward, but I calmed down almost at once. My solitary trip in daylight had been deceptively easy. The power-operated brakes had the well-known Citroën button-pedal, but I used heel and toe cautiously, taking no liberties with my great white lady. Yet I knew that I could handle her even in the dark, though, being short, I would have to be careful in judging widths, for it was a wide car and the scuttle was rather high. Gently I edged past the long line of cars strung out above the Nivens' villa. It was going to be all right.

Ahead, the lights of a passing car picked out two figures standing at the side of the road. Eric Dalton's tanned face, hidden by glasses, turned to watch as I swept past.

Chapter 9

A line of toy cars crawled up the Via Pirandello. Lights were blazing along the narrow length of the Corso Umberto and glowing like old rubbed amber from the windows of the fifteenth-century houses in the small belvederes.

Somewhere in a crowded street below the Greek Theatre, Bruna would be asleep in her one luxury, the bed with the wrought-iron volutes, while on the narrow pavements dark-clothed Sicilians strolled elbow to elbow or sat at café tables drinking the rough *retsina*.

But Andromachus's town which had been a place of refuge for the first Greek colonists who had settled in Sicily, at Naxos, would be no refuge for me. I looked up towards the patchwork of white, black and grey stone – limestone, lava and pumice – and recognized that this place of beautiful Gothic-blend arches, cornices and feudal façades could hold me like a trap. If the Daltons were following the Citroën, as I was convinced they must be, in moments I would be hemmed in on the single motorway that finished abruptly at the top of the Corso Umberto.

Quickly I abandoned my plan to leave a message for Stewart with Bruna. My foot went down hard as I passed the beginning of the Via Pirandello and the car leaped forward on the Strada Statale No. 114. Ahead was Catania and the sure refuge of the Villa Casilda.

I was in the region celebrated in the Odyssey. Somewhere ahead in the sea on my left, were the rocks with which Polyphemus had bombarded Odysseus's fleeing ship. Inland, in the darkness, Paterno dreamed high on its basalt cliff. Further off, above Catania, was Adrono, celebrated in classical times for its sacred dogs. Along its narrow streets had roamed the thousand dogs set to guard the temples against robbers. These they tore

118

to pieces, while they protected drunkards whom they led gently home. From the map, I recalled Bronte, still dominated by the descendants of Nelson . . . then over the Caronie range and the rich valley of Simeto . . . towards the Gothic complex of Randazzo . . . up the steep rise of the road to Linguaglossa with the country still trapped in the lava flow of 1923 . . . Make for Linguaglossa and retrace that route to circle Etna and drop down finally by the Via Etna and the Garibaldi Gate into Catania. In daylight, that would have been a sound plan. It was one I was sure that Scott would follow.

But I dared not risk the big car in such darkness on the superimposed layers of lava spewed up by the volcano over the years, by Pindar's 'heaven's column, father of eternal snows, whose chasm vomits forth the purest sources of inaccessible fire . . .' I must follow the fastest route to Catania, with the uneasy thought that the Daltons might be practically treading on my heels.

Above the purr of the engine and the hiss of the tyres on the road, I could hear the gentle breathing of the children as they slept the dream-haunted sleep of childhood.

I yawned widely and my mouth stayed open, my jaw slack with amazement at the scene ahead.

As if some unseen hand had turned on a thousand rosy lamps, the whole countryside was lit up by a pink glow. It showed, immediately in front, dozens of cars locked bumper to bumper along the road and occasionally moving languidly like tired flies.

I braked hurriedly. To be caught in a monster-sized traffic jam now!

Over my shoulder, Mario's sleepy voice said quietly with an undercurrent of fear, 'Etna is erupting. It looks bad. You know perhaps,' he continued with a return to his pedantic manner, 'that our island is supposed to rest on the body of the giant, Empedocles, when he was condemned by the gods. From time to time, whenever he feels crushed by the weight, he writhes. He is certainly doing it now!'

I could feel the tremors of the earth through the floorboards.

I got out of the car and stared helplessly at the great black wall, spiked with incandescent gleams, that was crawling down the sides of the cone of Etna. A burst of flame hurled a rain of black rocks at the sky. I had thought the cone as beautiful as Fujiyama in a Japanese painting, but now it was a surrealistic nightmare. The air was stifling and the horns of the cars ahead blared viciously in a cacophony of noise that made the night hideous. People stood at the sides of the road or leaned out of their cars and yelled at each other in fear and fury.

'*Cornuto!*' a man screamed in rage at the driver ahead.

Dozens of fishing boats had gathered, close enough to the shore for me to see that they had the eyes painted on their bows and the high stempiece that I had seen in the British Museum on fragments of Greek pottery.

Back towards Taormina the headlights of cars thrust golden swords of light towards us. In minutes, the Citroën would be a great white link in the chain that stretched apparently from here to Catania. I turned swiftly, threw myself into the driving seat and reversed so hard that Mario catapulted towards the back seat.

'Blimey!' he said, the classical scholarship of a moment ago forgotten. 'Look out! There's a hen's nest!'

My mind registered that he was using the French expression for a big pothole while I saw from a corner of my eye that the drivers in front had similar ideas about returning to Taormina. I had to move fast or be hemmed in. The Maserati engine responded like lightning, so that with only two turns of the sharp, taxi-like locks, the car was pointed towards Taormina. Recklessly I switched on all six headlamps in the hope that the Daltons would see only a great powerful shape without being able to distinguish colour or form.

I could make for Messina or stay overnight in Taormina and hope that Etna had settled down sufficiently to allow the road to Catania to be opened up.

Messina was out, I decided on reflection. It would be un-bearable to move further away from Catania and Stewart's arrival at the airport. We must take our chance in Taormina, though I remembered with a sinking heart that there we would be in double jeopardy – from the Daltons and from Al Scott.

Guiltily I muttered under my breath the swear-word most commonly used in Sicily and felt slightly better. At that moment I would willingly have traded Arlene's magnificent Citroën for the humblest Fiat with its blessed anonymity. Driving the white car was like wearing the Hope Diamond at an International Thieves' Ball.

The front seat folded up and slid forward in one movement, so that Mario was able to step from the rear of the car and sit beside me. In the glow from the dashboard his face looked pale and serious, but composed.

'Welcome, team mate!' I said softly.

In a few minutes we were forced into the side of the road by the volume of advancing traffic. The long column from Taormina slowed to a stop.

'Sightseers!' said Mario disgustedly.

'Some spectacle!' yelled a young Englishman, leaning far out of his car. 'The lava's moving on a three hundred and fifty yard front. Did you know that it has already engulfed ten houses, destroyed river bridges and set vineyards and orchards ablaze?'

He seemed to enjoy the ghoulish prospect.

'Are people in the villages in danger?' I called.

'Yes. They are evacuating the villages of Fornazzo, Sant' Alfio and Milo. I understand the lava stream is moving pretty close to them. I've been told that most of the red-hot lava has followed the course of a dry river bed between Fornazzo and Sant' Alfio. One fellow told me that the heat is so intense that it has burned trees a hundred feet away.'

'What about Taormina? Will it be dangerous there?' I was sick with fear for the children.

'Shouldn't think so. The official report is that the lava is moving down the mountain at about fifty yards an hour. Plenty of time to get clear. Besides, it could stop at any time.' He noticed Mario. 'Better than fireworks, sonny,' he said encouragingly as he drove off.

'Taormina for us then,' I said quietly to Mario. 'If the worst comes to the worst, we can always make for Castel Mola, the village at the top of Monte Tauro. We should be high enough there to be safe, but I'll eat your CASMS case if that should be necessary.'

He smiled at that. Presently he said uneasily, 'Are you thinking of spending the night at Bruna's house?'

'Yes. Why? Don't you like the idea?'

'We-e-ll . . . if I were Mr Scott, that's where I would expect you to go. And where would you put the car? It's pretty conspicuous.'

'You're right, but at the moment I don't seem to have any good ideas. Simply because the Citroën is so noticeable, I don't think it would be wise to sleep in the car. I don't fancy waking up to find either the Daltons or Mr Scott peering in at me.'

Somewhere along the road had been dropped any pretence between Mario and me that no danger threatened us. We were comrades in arms, though I could have wished for some effective weapons. Bruna's knife would probably be used for peeling an apple.

He was chewing his thumb reflectively. After a moment he said hesitantly, 'I know a super place where we could sleep and I think I know where you could put the car for the night.' In the lights of a passing car I thought I saw a mischievous smile on his face. 'Once I slept there for a bet. Aunt Arlene wanted to kill me when she found out.'

'Lead on, Macduff!' The lights of Giardini, the footstool of Taormina, swung up to meet us. I slowed in the narrow main street and swung the car carefully into a side street, then stopped. Tiredly, I arched my back to ease it. 'I'm bushed. Unfold the master-plan while I take a few minutes' rest and make sure that Pia is all right.'

She was lying on her back as contentedly as if she were asleep in her own bed. Her mouth was slightly open, so that I could see the perfection of the small, white teeth. Gently I eased the blanket over her shoulders. She stirred, but did not waken.

Instinctively and unnecessarily, Mario kept his voice low. 'We'll sleep in the cable-car,' he said.

I stared.

'You know that there is a *funivia* at the side of the BP service station above the Lido Mazzarò?'

'Yes.'

'The other end of the cable is on the Via Pirandello just above the Esso station, but on the other side of the road. At night the cable car is left up there. The car will be locked, of course, but I know how to get into it. I've done it before. We'll take the blankets and sleep on the seats. It won't start working until eight o'clock. We'll be away before then.'

I laughed. 'A cable-car! It's the last place in the world where anybody would think of looking for us. Mario, I love you!'

'Just above the Esso station there is a *pensione* called the Milano. It isn't much of a place, but the beauty of it is that there is a bit of wild ground behind the house where you could put the car. Actually I suppose it would be quite safe to sleep there. What do you think?' He sounded pleased with himself.

'No. The cable-car would be better. There is always the chance that someone might look into the car during the night and see us. Let's go!'

But across the street the lights of a *trattoria* winked invitingly. I scrabbled on the floor of the car for my handbag and sent Mario across to see what he could get. He came back with two enormous *prosciutto* sandwiches which we ate quickly.

I felt considerably better when we headed towards Taormina. The Citroën ate up the three zigzag miles of road to reach the ledge on which the old town was built.

When the car bumped over the rocky ground at the rear of the Pensione Milano, I felt like a criminal.

There was a thick screen of bushes almost encircling a saucer-shaped hollow. I doubted if the roof of the car could be seen even from the windows of the nearby house. For the first time since morning I began to feel safe. For a moment I hesitated about spending the night there, but decided against it.

As it turned out, Mario was almost responsible for our spending the night in a Sicilian jail.

Miraculously, Pia had slept through everything. I scrambled

into the back of the car and took her gently into my arms. She awoke at once, the large eyes snapping open as if on wires and the round mouth stretching in a soundless cry. Almost immediately the tremors began, but I rocked her gently and presently she was still.

When I gathered up the pillows and blankets and locked the car, she put her hand obediently in mine in the darkness and went quietly by my side, pressing close to me as if for reassurance.

Close to the Pensione Milano, Mario stumbled and went forward in a precipitous, headlong rush. His toe caught in an empty tin which went sailing through the night. There was an appalling crash of shattering glass from the direction of the house. An upper window flew open.

We froze.

'Drat that cat!' a guttural German voice bellowed. 'We leave in the morning. Some holiday!'

The window went down with a resounding bang.

'I'm sorry.' Mario's voice was a crestfallen whisper.

'Just be careful,' I breathed fiercely. I thought for a moment, feeling stupid with tiredness. 'Best if the three of us are not seen together. Go ahead and see what you can do about opening up the cable-car. We'll follow in five minutes.'

I stared into the darkness and thought about Stewart. He would be asleep now in one of Arlene's guest rooms, lying neatly on his side and breathing the long, deep, untroubled breaths of the trained athlete. Passport, money, flight tickets would be ranged on the dressing chest. The alarm of his wristwatch would be set for seven o'clock and his bag would be ready packed at the foot of the bed. Everything would be in order for his flight to Rome/Catania.

My breath came out in a long, whistling sigh of relief.

The phosphorescent hands of my watch gleamed greenly in the darkness. I did a rapid calculation. Keep the children hidden until this evening, I told myself. Then Stewart will be here to take over.

I squared my shoulders, trying not to think that the dangers

were not merely human ones. My back was turned on the
inexorable burning lava and the choking death of ash. Deliberately I pushed from my mind the thought of the earthquake
which had devastated part of western Sicily in December 1967.
This was no moment to dwell on the enormity of that disaster,
the number of victims and the stark misery of the survivors.

The elusive perfumes of oleanders and wild roses hung in
the air and at the side of the *pensione* the yellow ginestra
blossoms rose out of the rough, black ground, though the
bunches of golden bloom looked purplish-black in the darkness.

I pulled Pia close against my side and leaned tiredly against
the side wall of the *pensione*, letting the slow minutes tick away.

Nobody paid any attention when we crossed the road and
moved up to the cable-car. Mario moved out of the shadows
and we climbed quickly into the cabin. It was surprisingly
roomy, but before morning we would be cold. I cursed the
European emphasis on passports or identity cards. But for that,
we might have been comfortably asleep in a modest *pensione*
bedroom.

I had a bad night, haunted by dreams in which a pockmarked
face hung gloatingly above me before powerful hands plucked
me from the cable-car and hurled me down among the brown,
sun-dried rocks above Mazzarò.

The white sweater and turquoise slacks were damp with
perspiration when I fought my way back to wakefulness.

From the front of the car there was a breath-taking view over
the Ionian Sea. It was seven o'clock, but the night lights still
gleamed along the curve of the road. The air was so clear
that I could see the alley cats moving swiftly along the narrow
passages. A breeze full of the smell of dust and scorched earth
came in hot hard blasts from the direction of Etna. Far out on
the water a swordfish boat was riding the waves with a lift and
a swagger. A man was standing aloft on a small crow's-nest,
watching ahead of the boat's bows for the gliding shapes of the
swordfish. The water vapour in the air sent a rainbow of
dancing light flickering above the waves.

At my side, Mario said softly, 'It's very beautiful, isn't it?'

'Yes,' I said drily, feeling the knot of hunger in my stomach and conscious that I would never get the ache out of my bones. 'But I'll be glad to see the last of it.'

Mario's face closed up.

With a desire to propitiate him, I said gaily, 'Do you remember what Virgil wrote about your beloved Sicily?' I quoted softly, ' "But you could surely stay with me here for just a night with fresh leaves for a couch? I have ripe apples, soft sweet chestnuts and a good store of cheese. And look, already from those farmyard roofs the evening smoke is rising, and the shadows lengthen from the mountain tops." Mario, I forgive you for forgetting the fresh leaves for the couch, but the *morning* smoke is rising and I crave that good store of cheese. Let's move.'

He stood looking up at my face. 'You know, Miss Grant, you are the first lady I've known who is both pretty *and* clever. You know an awful lot.'

I laughed. 'I wish I knew how I could get breakfast and a wash-up without being seen.' My eyes followed the downward line of the cable. I pointed in the direction of the terminus. 'Mario, have a look at the building down there – just beside the entrance for the cable-car. Isn't that a hotel?'

'Yes, the Baia Azzurra.' He looked at me uneasily. 'Do you realize that Mr Scott's villa, the Golden Dream, is just across the road, though lower down on the Lido Mazzarò? Surely you are not thinking of going there?'

'Yes, Mario, I'm hungry. I don't care whether I eat chestnuts, apples or cheese, but eat I must. If you'll hide the blankets and pillows somewhere, we can wait and take the first *funivia* trip down to the hotel and have a wash and breakfast.' He looked forlorn. 'Don't worry so much. We can't go to the Pensione Milano,' I explained, 'for both the Daltons and Scott will expect us to go to some place up here in the town of Taormina, that is, if they know that we are back in the town, and I am sure they do. They won't expect us to do anything as bold as to go back to Mazzarò.'

He smiled uncertainly, but gathered up the blankets and

pillows and got quickly down from the car. I said to his disapproving back, 'Boldness, be my friend!'

He disappeared in the direction of the road.

Pia had been quietly watching us, turning her gentle, patient eyes from one face to the other as we spoke, following our lip movements. I had forgotten her. Now, as Mario moved off with his bundle, she began to write on the silver-framed tablet that hung from her waist. By pulling the bottom of the tablet, she could erase what had been written. Presently she held it up for my inspection. In small, neat writing was inscribed, *Mr Scott is good*.

Damn that man Scott, I thought savagely, but smiled broadly at her and mouthed like Ananias, 'He loves you,' and hoped that there was a special hell for people who needlessly hurt children.

In the end, it took three trips in the *funivia* to get us down to the Baia Azzurra. It would be safer, I decided, to travel separately. Nobody took any notice of the quiet little girl who stood at the front of the cable-car staring down at the tree-tops. Mario slipped into the car at the last minute when it was making its second downward trip. With my heart in my mouth, I watched it lurch out and down.

In the eternity until my turn came, I had the children seized, murdered and dumped in the sea many times over.

When a faultlessly groomed American in the cable-car drew fastidiously far back from me, I realized that my soiled slacks and sweater would stand out like a sore thumb in the sophisticated resort. I almost ran into the hotel.

Pia was already in the powder room, composedly washing her hands and face. She had created a lather that would have cleaned a battleship and she would obviously have been delighted to stay there for the rest of the morning. When I had washed her knees and combed her hair, she looked as fresh and normal as apple pie.

I was less sure about myself. I looked neither normal nor fresh. The mirror above the basin showed a young unhappy face with shadowed eyes and pale cheeks. I stretched to get a better view of myself in the mirror and wished I hadn't. I looked depressingly grubby.

Thank God for Elizabeth Arden, I thought as I went to work with my cosmetics. There was nothing I could do about my clothes, but when I had put the black wrap-round glasses in place and made a turban of Stewart's scarf to hide my hair, I looked like any smart young matron with a pretty little daughter.

The three of us ate like wolves and I did not discourage the children, for there was no knowing when and where our next meal would be. When the guests began to trickle into the dining-room, we left quickly.

It was scorching hot and I felt foolish with Arlene's scarlet blazer slung over my arm. I was alert for trouble, but there was none. We stood quietly just at the entrance to the hotel, waiting for the *funivia* to descend. The order of departure was to be the same as before. Scott and the Daltons might have been on another planet. Everyone and everything looked mundane and harmless. Consciously I relaxed.

'Have I time to buy two postcards?' Mario asked.

'Yes, but be quick. The cable-car should be down any minute now.'

Pia slipped her hand from mine and trotted after Mario. The boy at the reception desk took a lot of unnecessary trouble in spreading out his large stock for their selection.

A few yards away the cable-car thudded to a stop. Nobody got out. Two maids from the hotel, going off duty, got in. The car attendant looked casually around. He began to close the door.

In a panic I called into the reception hall, 'Come *on*! You'll miss the car.'

There was the unmistakable clang of a closing door. The cable-car lurched upwards. Infuriated, I watched it crawling away. For a moment I could not bring myself to look at Mario.

'No harm done!' said a cheerful English voice. 'I'll run you up. I was just going there, in any case.'

He was a tall young man with a pleasant, ordinary face which had had too much sun in the last few days. The stubbly brown hair was cut unfashionably short and looked damp, as if he had just returned from a swim. The hazel eyes were warm and friendly. 'Hold on a minute and I'll bring the car round.' He strode off confidently, as if the matter was settled.

Cautiously I considered the proposal and could see no harm in it. I gave him one of my special smiles as I settled into the front seat beside him.

The car was an old Bentley of uncertain vintage. I looked doubtfully at the unfashionable dark green coachwork, the tub seats so deep that I had difficulty in seeing the children and the complicated dashboard. There was a hint of a smile on the young owner's face, but I could not interpret it.

He was so normal, so unmistakably the sporting young Englishman that to my tired brain he was like a familiar stereotype. How well I knew his kind! Those weather-beaten, curiously innocent young men with their worn hacking jackets, stained anoraks and baggy whipcord pants, who haunt the steeple-chase race meetings, the motor-cycle hill climbing tests, the vintage car races!

I took a closer look at my companion. A modest hotel . . . a vintage Bentley . . . the eager, ingenuous expression . . . it all figured. Somewhere woven into the pattern that makes up the sporting young Englishman is a natural courtesy and helpfulness. This fresh-faced young man would respond instinctively to the dictates of that code. I was lucky.

He twisted round in the driving seat. 'I'm Jerry Mason. What's your name?'

I hesitated momentarily. 'Laurie Grant.'

'The children yours?'

'No.' I decided that after all it had been a mistake to accept the lift. I looked studiedly towards the black pall of smoke over Etna. The seat was so close to the floor that I had difficulty in seeing out.

He ignored my coolness.

'I'm an electronics engineer,' he continued, 'but archaeology is my hobby. That's what brought me to Sicily. I'm here for a month. I plan to spend most of my time at Enna, Syracuse and

Agrigento. I'm not the kind of archaeologist who goes around digging things up. I'm content just to look.'

'This is where I should say – "Its a small world." The person I know best in Sicily, an old friend, is an American archaeologist, but, unlike you, he likes to dig things up. He seems to be pretty successful at it. He's Professor Gregory Stein of Northwestern, Chicago. Do you know him?'

'*Know* him? Who doesn't? I've read everything he has ever written.' He turned his head to look at me.

The expression in the hazel eyes had changed. Now they were alert and curious, but I had a fleeting glimpse of something guarded in their depths. Apparently, until my calm, level-headed Stewart took over my worries, I was going to see something significant in the most innocent of actions or looks.

Fortunately, Jerry Mason had noticed nothing unusual about my expression. His eyes were fixed on the steep road ahead. 'Perhaps you can put me out of my misery,' he continued cheerfully. 'I've been dying to know why he stopped writing. He used to be a prolific writer, but he hasn't written as much as an article for any of the journals for at least four years. Why? Has he given up archaeology? A busted love-affair?'

'Oh, no. Archaeology is what brought him to Sicily just now. I can assure you, he is still very much involved.' This was a safe topic so I chatted on. 'I'll probably see him very soon. He is living at Trapani, on some old tub, called the *Più Tardi*.'

'An old tub!' He gave a long, astonished whistle. 'Lady, you just have to be joking!'

I opened my mouth to ask him to drop us at the Pensione Milano. Pia's hand came over the back of the seat and tugged frantically at the top of my turban. My eyes followed the direction of her pointing finger. I closed my mouth.

Al Scott was standing outside the cable-car terminus, in earnest conversation with the attendant. The Sicilian nodded vigorously and pointed down towards the beach.

With sickening clarity, I recalled the moment when the cable-car attendant's casual glance had swept over the three of us as we stood in the hotel entrance.

130

Chapter 10

Jerry Mason accelerated slightly. The car shot past the two men on the pavement.

He said mildly, 'You look as if you had made arrangements to blow that place up.' He gave me a quick, sidelong look. 'Is the good-looking fellow your husband? No. Don't answer that. It isn't any of my business.'

He pulled the car round the curve at the top of the road, so that the tyres juddered along the surface. There was a look of pain on his face.

He was, I decided, a very bad driver.

Just as the car was completing the bend, I was able to look back along the road. Scott was gazing after the car with the sort of slack, moony expression on his face that people have when their thoughts are far away.

Mason twisted his head again until his eyes met mine. He grinned. 'That was not my usual Jackie Stewart performance,' he said. 'Your good-looking friend – or husband – isn't interested in mug drivers. I was just giving you the chance to decide whether the divorce was on or off.'

He slid the car competently into the only vacant spot outside the tourist office.

My heart had left my throat and gone back to its usual position.

Pia tugged urgently at the top of my makeshift turban. Distractedly, I put my hand up and imprisoned hers.

Jerry Mason seemed to come to a decision. He slewed round in his seat and regarded me steadily. At first, I hardly heard him. I was busy calculating my chances of discovery if I went back at once to collect the Citroën. It did not seem to be a very good idea.

'Mrs Grant,' he said quietly, 'you don't seem to me the type that runs out on a husband. You would walk out in good order, if it was strictly necessary. Maybe you want to tell me to shut up and get on my way. That will be all right, but I suspect you could use a little help and if that is so, short of anything illegal, I'm willing to chip in with my contribution.'

He waited. 'You don't have much time.' His voice was gentle. 'My guess is that Good-Looking is on his way down to the Baia Azzurra. His car was parked at the side of the road – a Simca Aronde. Somebody is going to tell him that the three of you left in a green Bentley. I give him about ten minutes before he is offering to punch me on the jaw.'

One of my old teachers used to tell me that one ought to be able to write a summary of any story on a postcard. My account to Jerry Mason then of the Dalton affair was postcard size, but I was painfully aware of the expectant stillness in the back of the car and of how the bald recital must have sounded in Mario's ears.

While I was still talking, young Mason took a map of the town from the ledge under the dashboard and began to study it. When I had finished he pushed the map towards me, pulled a pencil from his pocket and, with the point, traced a route on the map. 'Here's where we are now,' he said. 'Walk down here along the Via di Giovanni. Soon after you pass the Villa Paradiso, which is on the corner of the Via Bagnoli Croce, turn left and that should take you to the entrance of the Giardino Publico. Wait in the gardens until I come. I'll find you, but I don't know how long I will be. You definitely won't consider going to the police?'

I shook my head. Mrs Mason, congratulations on your son! I said silently. 'They would hand Pia over to Scott, pending further enquiries. I'm not risking that.'

'Let me have your car keys.'

'What are you going to do?' The car was my lifeline, but I fished the keys from my bag at once.

'Find out what the news about Etna is – if the road to Catania is blocked or not. The tourist office should have some information. I'll buy a newspaper or a paperback and sit in the car and read while I wait for Good-Looking.' He grinned at my appalled expression. 'He's bigger than I am, but I'm younger and engineers have hard fists. Don't worry. I have a cousin – five times removed, I admit – in the Diplomatic Service. Maybe diplomacy runs in the family.'

I stretched up and kissed him on the cheek. He blushed scarlet.

As I walked off with the children, I could feel his eyes following me in a pleased way.

What explanation Mario gave to Pia, I do not know, but she came willingly enough, only occasionally dragging her feet when we passed a crowded ceramic shop. It was like walking end-lessly under a spotlight.

The old man at the entrance to the public gardens gave us a toothless amiable grin, but nobody else took any notice of us. It was too early in the morning for tourists and, from the brisk walk of the few people we met, I judged that they were hotel staff making their way to the Diodoro Jolly Hotel or the Bristol Park.

Under any other circumstances, the gardens would have been pure heaven. Shafts of sunlight lanced through tunnels of greenness, so that we walked on spears of gold to the top of flights of old worn, grey stone steps flanked by great solid walls of pink pelargonia. Between the yews, the dark blue of the sea had a purplish bloom.

I thought of the Visconti film, showing the 'Leopard's' summer journey in the bare desolation of the interior of Sicily. Here all was ripeness and rioting colour, Persephone's woody domain.

I sat on a bench and thought prosaically, I owe Arlene a couple of pillows and blankets. It will be appropriate if I have them sent out from Harrods!

Gradually, in the silence and solitude, my fears were stilled so that I could look with genuine pleasure over the vast and brilliant panorama of sea and sky and up to where the spring flowers crowded the lower slopes of Etna. I thought that the pall of smoke was denser than I had remembered and that the stream of lava glowed more strongly.

With shame, I admitted that I had given no further thought to the plight of the unfortunate people whose homes and orchards lay in the path of the destructive stream. Now I began to worry in case the authorities had closed the roads. It would be a cruel irony if Stewart were marooned in Catania, while we were cut off in Taormina.

After a time the silence made me nervous. Even the sound of the children's play was subdued.

I studied my scarlet-tipped fingers and told myself, unconvincingly, that there was nothing particularly irresponsible about handing over a valuable car to a complete stranger. Jerry Mason *would* be back. A little to my astonishment, the impulse to tears grew stronger and stronger.

At the end of an hour, the cold feeling inside me had spread. When a young boy, about twelve years old, came along the path kicking a stone in front of him, I looked at him with active dislike.

He stopped and spoke to Mario and they both came quickly towards me. Pia, her face alight with mischief, kicked the stone back along the path in the direction from which the boy had come.

'We must leave now,' Mario said breathlessly. 'A taxi-driver sent him to say that his cab is waiting for us outside the Bristol Park.'

The boy looked expectantly at me. I gave him one hundred lire and he ran off, whistling raucously.

We ran too. Anybody watching would have seen a young mother romping with her children.

The taxi was parked just inside the grounds of the Hotel Bristol Park, a little way up the steeply climbing drive to the left of the entrance. As soon as we were inside, the driver drove away without asking where I wanted to go.

He swung on to the Via Pirandello, dropped down to where the road joined the Strada Statale No. 114 and pointed the bonnet in the direction of Catania.

There was more traffic than usual on the road, I surmised, and Mario confirmed that impression. He spoke angrily to the driver and then explained to me that the man was driving too fast because he was anxious to get back to Taormina to pick up tourists who wanted to get a good view of Etna in eruption. Some people, Mario explained disgustedly, were walking as much as ten miles to get a grandstand view of the disaster.

The man switched from Sicilian to Italian, throwing the words at me over his shoulder in an almost insolent fashion.

'I would not advise you to stay in your villa, signora, although at Acireale you should get plenty of warning about the lava and time to clear out. But . . . one never knows.' He spat delicately out of the side window. 'That boiling mess has picked up speed during the night. I listened in on my transistor at eight o'clock and it is moving forward at the rate of sixty metres an hour. Mother of God! If it continues at that rate, in two days it will go right through the heart of Sant' Alfio. My friend, Giuseppe, went up to that village at dawn this morning and there were thousands of people there, all staring, staring, staring at a great wall of red embers, twenty-five metres high and four kilometres wide. Trees were bursting into flames from the heat.' He sketched a hasty cross on his forehead. 'Sant' Alfio defend us all!'

I was tempted to tell him to turn around and drive us to Messina so that we could catch the ferry that would take us to the mainland. But in a few hours, Stewart would be in Rome, on the last lap of his journey to Catania.

I said nothing.

When I looked at Mario, his eyes were tragic and opaque as though his thoughts were far away, remembering the story that I had told Jerry Mason. Probably he was telling himself that there were worse things than a mother with a phobia for counting calories. He gave me a nervous smile and began to talk with breathy emphasis to Pia, telling her the story of the giant, Empedocles.

Between Giarre and Acireale, the taxi crawled, edging slowly forward as the long queue of cars moved lazily, like a monstrous centipede. More than the stench of destruction was in the air. The atmosphere was electric with a combination of fear and morbid pleasure. Voices from the cars in front were high and excited, with overtones of anger. Somewhere ahead was one of the famous painted carts whose driver kept stolidly to the crown of the road, idly flicking a stick at his donkey and ignoring the enraged shouts and raucous hooting of horns. A thin grey pall of smoke hung above the orange and lemon groves and from the belching cone, almost four thousand metres above, the smell of death crept into the car.

Mario talked cheerfully to Pia of the Cyclops, the giants who ate the smaller human beings who ventured near them.

'They lived in caves in the mountains,' he explained carefully, as Homer did when he wrote his *Odyssey* from sailors' tales of the Sicilian shores. 'Etna was the chief Cyclop.'

Her eyes sparkled with pleasure, but I shivered and glanced at my watch and wondered rather desperately how long it would take us to reach the sanctuary of the Villa Casilda. As we inched forward, my impatience grew and for the first time I began to wonder if I would be in time to meet Stewart at the airport.

'Can't you hurry?' I asked the driver, while I recognized the stupidity of my own question.

He took his hands from the wheel to raise his shoulders in an expressive Latin gesture. He looked as disgruntled as I felt. 'Impossible! It is the fault of the crazy tourists.' His lip curled. 'The crafty peasants are encouraging them.' He threw an arm expansively in the direction of the side of the road where some enterprising villagers had hurriedly erected wooden stalls where they were selling fruit and soft drinks at exorbitant prices.

I sighed and reached for my purse as I saw the children's expectant looks. 'See what you can get, Mario. Go ahead, not back. We'll catch up with you.'

He ran off with the quick, purposeful step that was so familiar.

When he came back and scrambled into the taxi, both hands held the bottom of his cotton top like an apron in which was piled a golden mound of oranges.

His face was white and strained. He turned it carefully away from Pia before he said quietly to me, 'Signor and Signora Dalton are in a car, six ahead of us, just behind the Sicilian *carretto.*' He enunciated very clearly, as though reciting a lesson he had learned and was fearful of forgetting. 'It is small. I think it is a Fiat. The colour is robin's-egg blue. It is not new. I could not see the number.' He paused and added doubtfully, 'There was another man in the car. I think it was Signor Niven.'

Chapter 11

It was stifling hot in the taxi.

As I eased the damp edge of the white sweater away from my neck, I thought of my most recent and favourite daydream which I had enjoyed in Zürich. This was the one in which I had a small but perfect collection of Pucci resort clothes . . . my trousseau. Each morning, stunningly dressed, breathtakingly lovely, I breakfasted with Stewart on a sun-washed terrace overlooking the sea. Below us, regardless of the season, a grove of oranges or lemons sent up wafts of acrid perfume and the air danced with the blue mist from the oil of the ripening fruit. Stewart's arms went round me for a final adoring kiss before we stole down the hotel corridor, past the sleeping guests and went quietly out to the white Citroën. We followed the Golden Ribbon route round Sicily, stopping at will for *caffè latta*, for a lazy swim in turquoise seas, or to explore the honey-coloured ruins of the Graeco-Roman civilization. Before the lion-sun was high in the sky, we lunched in the coolness of another luxury hotel, then dreamed the golden afternoon away in the dimness of our shuttered bedroom . . .

I put my head down on my hands and sobbed. I was dirty, bewildered and alone, caught between Eric and Corinne Dalton ahead and Al Scott and Susan Bradford behind.

Where are you, Stewart? I asked fiercely.

I thought bitterly of John Niven. Five! Five was too much!

Pia's arms went gently round my neck. She had lost her handkerchief, so she lifted the hem of her frock and dabbed at a tear which was racing down my cheek. She had the absorbed, concerned air of a careful housewife.

I laughed and hugged her until her eyes danced and she gave the throaty gurgle which I had learned to recognize as her way of expressing happiness.

Mario gave me his uncertain smile and offered me an orange. I felt as powerful as an Amazon.

'Oranges have the smell of poverty,' said the driver disdainfully.

When we crept into Acireale, the dignified watering-place had an indescribable air of carnival, a feverish activity, as if by laughter and gaiety the dark heights of Etna could be blotted out. The white huddle of houses against the cliff face seemed small and vulnerable. Above them the land was green with vines.

Mario extended a thin arm to indicate one of the most famous of Sicily's remaining marionette theatres. 'That's where,' he said proudly, 'one can see performances of the traditional *Opera dei Pupi*, the old Norman romances.'

He kept giving me little furtive looks as if to reassure himself.

I smiled at him brilliantly and wondered if my face were clean. Nobody, I decided, was going to make me cry ever again.

The time at Taormina had taken on a dreamlike quality. I could scarcely remember the people I had met so briefly at the party and on the beach. Even Susan Bradford and Al Scott were like cardboard figures. I could no longer remember how they talked or imagine how they thought.

Only the faces of the Daltons stood out, like cameos against a background of jet.

In spite of my resolution, I almost wept again when Pia put a hand softly on mine and Mario said ruefully, 'She wants to stop here so that she can send a postcard to Signor Scott.'

Manuel, the mass murderer, I reminded myself, had stopped to feed a cat after he had brutally killed a mother and her young daughter. Children and dogs had adored him. I hardened my heart.

On the outskirts of Acireale the driver began to look carefully at the villas on the right side of the road. We were in the millionaire belt of pools and patios and barbecue parties. The poverty of a Sicily of meatless weeks and women who were regarded as breeding machines was an unpleasant dream, best forgotten.

'The villa with the red gates, isn't it?' the man called out, cheerful at the prospect that his job was almost over.

Mario and I exchanged puzzled glances and I shrugged helplessly.

I think we all saw the gates at once, startlingly scarlet in the brilliant light. They were open and led on to a steeply rising drive between great hedges of vivid pink geraniums. We took the drive in a rush, but I had an impression of extensive grounds, beautifully tended, where colour ebbed and flowed like a scene in a kaleidoscope.

Mr Mason has wealthy friends, I thought appreciatively.

The Citroën was parked at the front entrance.

The house was an impressive monument to wealth and modernity, in glass, chrome and redwood. An imposing terrace, wide enough and long enough to make a dance floor, jutted from the upper storey. It cast deep blue shadows over the front door and the long tiled patio that stretched across the entire front of the house.

Pia twittered with love for the white patio furniture and Mario cast a longing look at the heart-shaped pool at the side of the house. A white hammock, lined with green linen, swung gently in the shadows under the terrace. Jerry Mason was fast asleep in it.

It was ridiculous the way my heart lightened at the sight of his sprawling figure.

He came alertly to his feet at the sound of our steps on the tiles.

'*Fantastico!*' said Mario, looking around him with delight.

'*Ciao, mi' amico,*' said Jerry Mason cheerfully to him. Then to me, 'Got here all right?'

'*Grazie al Dio!*' I laughed.

He paid off the taxi-driver and came back to sit beside me on the hammock. It moved gently under our combined weights.

The children had run towards the back of the house. I looked after them uneasily, wondering where our host and hostess were. The house had an air of serene quiet.

'Who owns this?'

'I haven't the faintest idea.' His tone was pleasantly casual. 'Does it matter?'

'*Does it matter?* Do you mean that we are in the house of a perfect stranger?'

'Well, we are not exactly *in* the house,' he said reasonably.

I got to my feet in a panic.

'Now sit down,' he said quietly. 'Nobody is going to push you into jail for sitting on their front porch. I saw this place one day last week when I was in Acireale and liked the look of it. I wandered in to see the garden. There was only an elderly gardener about.' He pointed to the edge of the lawn beyond the pool. 'The lawn is the top of their house. He and his wife live there. The owners are in America until the end of the month. The gardener and his wife were going off on a holiday. He was delighted to chat and show me around. Nobody is going to disturb us. Calm down. It is better and safer than going to a hotel or café.'

I decided that compared with my crime of running off with somebody else's child, this was unimportant.

It was after three o'clock and the children were hungry. Jerry Mason gave me the car keys and I picked out the food basket from the pile of luggage in the boot. The milk was sour and had to be thrown away. The bread was slightly stale, but with the cheese and tinned meat it made an acceptable meal. The children ate theirs squatting by the side of the pool, accepting the strangeness of the situation as they had accepted all my previous eccentric actions, amiably and without question.

Jerry and I ate at one of the small tables with an ease between us as if we had known each other for years. Sometimes I caught him looking at me with a strange expression in his eyes. It was almost as if something about me had startled him. Yet, apart from Stewart, I had never met anyone more imperturbable.

I told him about the Daltons and John Niven and he frowned at that, but he simply said, 'It is better to have them in front than behind. Maybe they were making for the airport, to leave Sicily, having drawn a blank in Taormina.'

It was so wonderful to have somebody else to share the

responsibility that I scarcely bothered to think that through.

A cloud of butterflies flew upwards from a bed of snap-dragons so that it looked as if an unseen breeze had blown the petals skywards. Bees hummed in the lime trees and the peace of the garden acted on my stretched nerves like a narcotic.

At this moment, Stewart was over the Mediterranean, probably reckoning as I was doing that in less than four hours we would be together. I felt wonderful.

Jerry Mason said suddenly, 'I hope I find a girl like you some day. Your husband is a lucky fellow.'

I felt even better after that. 'I'm not married,' I said. His face brightened, though his eyes lingered on my ring. He went on slowly, 'I didn't think there *were* girls like you nowadays – spunky and prepared to wade in if somebody was in trouble. I haven't met that kind.' He bent forward and tapped the glass top of the table with a spatulate forefinger. 'My home town is Liverpool.' He smiled with a hint of pride in his expression. 'That place is a bit rough round the edges. Probably not more than any other port. I wouldn't know. But I do know that I'll be right beside you until your fiancé takes over and that won't be too long from now.' He paused. 'I expect you want to hear what was said by your friend Scott and me?'

'Word for word,' I said emphatically.

He grinned. 'That's exactly what you are going to get. I told you I was an electronics engineer. That means I am a sucker for gadgets.' He stretched out his left arm and rested his wrist on the table. He was wearing the usual modern outsize wristwatch with a broad leather strap.

I said flippantly, 'I see you have the kind of watch that has you saying, Half past full moon.'

'No . . . not exactly. It does tell the time, but it is really a portable dictaphone. It's very simple to operate. Needs only four small switches – on, off, rewind, playback. Reproduction is remarkably clear and faithful. You'll hear in a moment. It's been on the market for some time, but this is the latest model.'

I looked at it wistfully. 'Mario would love that,' I said.

Jerry Mason was delighted. 'Then he shall have it, as soon as this brouhaha is over.'

I was delighted too.

'Right. Now, about Scott . . . Incidentally, he is a very good-looking guy . . . lots of personality and charm, but I wouldn't like to meet him on a dark night, if he had it in for me. There's lots of muscle there and I could practically hear his brain ticking over. I wasn't much impressed by his fiancée . . . too insipid.'

'Was she there?' I was surprised.

'Yes, but she didn't open her mouth once. Scott did all the talking.'

'Was he aggressive?'

'Not at first. I was sitting reading in the car as I had said I would, with this wrist strategically draped over the edge of the window. Scott came strolling over as if he had all the time in the world. You can hear how it went. You are in for a few surprises.'

He touched a switch and Al Scott's voice came out, reedy and thin, but undeniably his. In spite of myself, I jumped.

'Sorry to disturb your reading, Mr Mason. My name's Scott . . . Al Scott. I learned your name at the Baia Azzurra. I came up here looking for you. I understand you gave a lift to a young woman with two children.'

'Yes.' The monosyllable was completely non-committal.

'I'm anxious to find them as soon as possible. Can you tell me where they went?'

'Sorry. Women don't usually talk about which shops they mean to visit.'

There was a short pause. When Scott spoke, there was steel in his voice. 'I don't imagine the lady was on a shopping expedition. And I don't think your encounter with her was quite as casual as you would like me to believe. I remember now – you drove this car up the Via Pirandello about twenty minutes ago. I remember thinking that it was probably some old guy behind the wheel – the original owner. That's what you wanted me to think. You wouldn't drive a £10,000 vintage Bentley as if you belonged to the era when a man with a flag went in front

... not unless you wanted to divert my attention.' There was a sharp slap as though he had brought his hand hard down on the car door. This was a Scott I did not know – a hard, angry, dangerous man. At least, he had not frightened Jerry Mason. 'Laurie Grant saw me and wanted to avoid me. She told you so. Why the hell would she do that?' There was genuine bewilderment in his voice. 'Mason, Miss Grant had my daughter with her – a deaf-mute child. It's important that I get in touch with my little girl immediately. I don't know what Miss Grant is up to, but it's in her best interests that I catch up with her as soon as possible. I would appreciate your help.'

'Sorry, but I'm afraid there is nothing I can add. I suggest you settle your private affairs without involving strangers. No hard feelings?' There was an unexpected maturity and ring of authority in Mason's voice.

There was a pause and I thought we had reached the end of the tape, but Scott went on in an altered voice. 'Mason, are you working for Dalton?'

'Dalton?'

'You're lying, Mason. That name means something to you. That innocent act won't work.' I could hear the harsh sound of his breathing. 'If I find out that you are working for the Daltons, I promise you that I'll break your neck. And I'm not sure that I won't break Laurie Grant's if she doesn't bring my little girl back soon. You are both meddling with something dangerous. I strongly advise you both to leave me to settle with the Daltons or you are liable to get hurt. Think it over, but don't take too long about it. I am not the most patient of characters.'

Jerry Mason switched off the dictaphone. 'There's another bit. Scott turned on his heel, took his fiancée's arm and made to walk away. He changed his mind, and came back. Listen to what he said.'

He switched on the dictaphone. 'Mason, the tape-recorder was a smart idea, but I knew about that type of dictaphone when you were still wet behind the ears. Here's a message for your friend – Laurie, I don't know what the hell you are up to. I only hope you do. I went to the Villa Noto this morning to warn you that a man and woman called Dalton were planning to kidnap Vira. These people are dangerous to you, but particularly to Vira. If anything happens to the child through your stupidity, you had better keep well clear of me. *And* take a good look at this fellow, Mason.'

Jerry Mason switched off the recorder. The hazel eyes were quiet and steady. Why had I thought him to be so young?

'I'll be sorry that I let you hear that tape if you are going to let it upset you,' he said. 'Don't look so stricken. Just keep reminding yourself that Scott is a phoney. He has no more right to the child than you have, so his talk is a lot of bluster. There will be no neck-breaking as long as your fiancé and I are around. In a short time, Mr Noble will be fastening his seat-belt for landing. We'd better be there to meet him. Get the children and we'll make for the airport. This Wednesday late flight may be a boon to travellers, but I prefer meeting planes in daylight.'

He began to gather up the remnants of our meal.

Deliberately I forced myself to look at him, casually but steadily. Surely this was no callow, transparent, good-natured extrovert? For the first time, I saw the competence of the swift movements and caught the subtle but unmistakable whiff of ruthlessness.

Were the hazel eyes just too open and innocent? Had the meeting at the Baia Azzurra been entirely fortuitous?

The special qualities of a nightmare are distortion and the sense of helplessness. The seeds of doubt had been sown, but it would be madness to let him sense my suspicions.

With chilling clarity, I saw what it would mean if the children and I handed ourselves over to the care of Jerry Mason . . . if he were in league with the Daltons. The danger was there, it was serious, but, I decided, it could not be avoided.

In the golden dusk, the garden became not a peaceful oasis, but a trap. Suddenly I was on fire to get away, to make for the airport, to be safe among a crowd of people. The thought of Stewart was like an amulet.

The shadows were lengthening across the pond like the dark

fingers of a giant hand. Mario's laugh startled me like a pistol-shot, so that I called out to him sharply and the children came running up to me, looking nervously at my face as though they confused my fear with anger.

Jerry Mason drove, handling the Citroën lovingly, while I huddled into Arlene's blazer and wondered what I could do if he failed to take the road beyond Catania leading to Fontana-rossa airport.

With elaborate casualness, I said to Mario, 'Perhaps you would call out directions for Mr Mason. We haven't time for mistakes. We don't want to be late for the plane.'

All the time I was aware of the dark menace of the mountains on our right and the oily glitter of the sea on our left. The lights of Catania shone out like beacons of hope. I don't think I breathed properly until we were in the crowded streets, with the homegoing Sicilians jostling each other on the pavements and the lights in the shop windows blinking cheerfully.

By the time we drove into the parking lot at Fontanarossa, I was in a state of nervous exhaustion and the children were ominously quiet.

Stewart could decide where we slept that night. Stewart could decide about Jerry Mason, and the Daltons, John Niven and Al Scott . . . in fact, about everything. I was too tired to care.

We stumbled out of the car and stood blinking in the over-head lights. Mario tugged at my hand and said miserably, 'That blue car has just come into the parking lot.'

That galvanized me into action. Jerry Mason swept Pia up into his arms and I hustled Mario towards the terminal build-ings. The concourse hall was packed to suffocation and for once I welcomed the milling crowd. Despairingly, I realized that my scarlet blazer probably made me as conspicuous as a search-light beam on a dark sea.

I said the Sicilian swear word forcefully under my breath and a respectable Sicilian farmer looked at me in scandalized horror. His plump wife laughed and there was a pleased twinkle in her eyes. I had a sudden hilarious picture of him looking at her doubtfully in the years ahead.

Near the announcement board, the crowd was thickest. Anxiously I scanned the list of incoming planes.

'The Rome plane is due in now and it is on time.' Jerry Mason squeezed my shoulder comfortingly. He laughed as I scrabbled in my handbag. 'Why does the sight of a plane make a woman dive for her lipstick? You are wasting your time, Laurie. It will be smudged in a few minutes.'

That earned him a blinding look of happiness.

The red light was extinguished. The plane had landed.

Wordlessly we made our way to the door from which the passengers would emerge. If I had been surrounded by a cohort of Daltons, I could not have been more indifferent.

For a moment I thought longingly of those Pucci resort clothes, but they did not really matter. The best hotel in Catania . . . a long, blissful soak in a bath . . . my pretty green chiffon cocktail frock . . . dinner with Stewart . . . I drew a long, happy breath.

The worry and the strain were over.

I knew he would not be among the first wave of travellers. Stewart hated that early, blind stampede towards the terminal buildings. I strained to look above the bobbing heads for my first sight of that well-shaped blond cap.

Jerry Mason murmured soothingly in my ear, 'You can relax about the Daltons. They won't trouble us here. My bet is that they are waiting to see which hotel you choose for tonight.'

My impatient shake of the head must have offended him for he said, rather stiffly, 'Would you prefer me to leave now?' I felt rather than saw the small sad wince.

There was only a trickle of passengers coming through the door. The pretty girl, who was a member of the ground staff, craned forward to look beyond them. She began to close the door.

Behind me was the sound of Jerry Mason's departing feet.

My grip on Pia's hand tightened so much that she whimpered softly. We went forward quickly to the uniformed girl. When she turned brightly from locking the door, I said unbelievingly, 'That can't be the last plane from Rome.'

'Yes, signorina. That is the last flight today.'

Jerry Mason said gently over my shoulder, 'I had a look at the notice board, Laurie. There's a message for you.'

When he handed me the folded blue paper, my fingers were so stiff that I had difficulty in opening it. I stared blankly at the writing: STEWART UNABLE TRAVEL FLU PLEASE PHONE ARLENE.

In a world grown suddenly dark and terrifying, I groped for the children, pressing them close to me, unaware then of how strange it was that I knew where to find comfort.

Music blared out from the espresso bar. The counter-girl picked at her teeth delicately and frowned at a bunch of young people who were indulging in a bit of horseplay. The chaos fitted my mood.

'Let's get organized,' said Jerry Mason. 'We can't stand here indefinitely. You'll want to make that telephone call, Laurie, but a cup of espresso first of all might help. Your fiancé will want to know your plans, so a little clear thinking is called for.'

I tried to smile but it must have been a ghastly performance. Plans? Was it really Jerry Mason who wanted to know them?

The music blared again.

Mechanically, I followed him, moving stiffly, as if at any moment I expected to fall apart.

Pia lagged, cocking a knee to support her writing tablet. She held the message up for my inspection.

Your hair is the colour of anger, she had printed.

That made me smile and the coffee did help.

An emotion, stronger and more bitter than disappointment, seemed to make my brain swell and contract, as if the angry thoughts inside could not be contained. My mood was hardening into a suspicious aloofness. Fate had dealt me one blow too many. Very well . . . I would depend on myself and devil take anyone who got in my way!

Chapter 12

At least the telephone call went through very quickly.

Some of the tension evaporated when I heard Arlene Curzon's slow drawl. '*So* glad you telephoned, Laurie! Stewart *will* be pleased. It has all been *frightfully* worrying. Tom chooses the most *awkward* times to be away.'

I sighed, recognizing the mood from the silly stressing of words. Carefully and clearly I said, 'I understand. May I speak to Stewart now?'

'*No*, dear. It was lucky you called *now*. I am just leaving for dinner with the Devereaux-Planters. *You* know . . . they have the lodge . . .'

'Arlene,' I said between clenched teeth, 'I do not care if you are dining with the Massington-Buffs, the Cholmondeley-Elliots or the King of Siam. I must talk to Stewart.' The sound of hysteria in my voice frightened me. I made an effort to be calm. 'Will you please step off Cloud Nine for five minutes and realize that several people seem to be seriously intent on injuring or killing a child and that I don't think my own neck is too safe. Let the caviare get warm or the canapés get cold or whatever other social disaster might finish the Buckingham-Browns, but *bring Stewart to the telephone.*'

'Yes, dear.' Her voice was crisp and cold. 'No need for hysterics. *But* . . . Stewart positively cannot come to the telephone. He has a very sharp attack of influenza. In fact, he was delirious this morning, *very* fevered. The doctor has stuffed him with antibiotics and he was so concerned about poor Stewart's general condition that he has given him a powerful sedative and swears he will keep him under, if possible, for several days. The doctor assured me that Stewart was at *breaking* point.'

Mentally I was being pigeon-holed: giddy young fiancée gads about the Mediterranean, flirts with attractive American gangster, careers round Sicily, while husband-to-be languishes on bed of sickness.

A revolting stain on the left knee of my turquoise slacks caught my eye. I could almost smell Arlene's perfume over the telephone. I got madder and madder.

'So . . . Stewart is dying and you are busy.' My voice was trembling, but icy. 'Well, Arlene, if you have a spare page in your social diary, please write this down. I will telephone again tomorrow night. We'll spend tonight in the Villa Casilda in Catania, then tomorrow I will join Professor Gregory Stein on his boat at Trapani. It is called the *Più Tardi*. I haven't worked out how long it will take me to get to Trapani, but perhaps my Sleeping Beauty of a fiancé will have emerged from his slumbers by then, and be prepared to do his own WMI work.'

There was a shocked silence from the other end.

'There is no need to be rude, Laurie. You sound hysterical. Perhaps it is just as well that Stewart can't speak to you. He would be extremely worried.' Her voice trailed off uncertainly. 'The Villa Casilda? How much weight did Casilda Biagotti lose? Does it *show?*'

I laughed. In a gentler tone, I said, 'Give Stewart my love if and when he surfaces. Enjoy your dinner, but first of all, please telephone Superintendent Lang of Scotland Yard. Ask him if he will be good enough to telephone me tonight at the Villa Casilda. Just a minute . . . I'll give you the number.' I added, 'If he isn't available, please leave word that I will try to get in touch with him tomorrow.'

She said good night very huffily and I had the feeling that the Devereaux-Planters would have a very dull dinner-guest.

While I talked, I had placed myself with my back to the wall so that I could watch Pia, Mario and Jerry Mason. They looked lonely in the emptying concourse hall.

Mario pivoted slowly round on one heel, grossly overacting the part of a bored young boy passing the time until a long-winded female finished her call. It was obvious that he was keeping a sharp look-out for any ill-intentioned creatures.

Dreamily Jerry Mason eyed the boisterous group of youngsters at the espresso bar as if he would not have minded joining them. Whether or not his sense of rejection had passed, I had no means of knowing.

But it was Pia who caught and held my attention. She was leaning back against the Englishman's knees, rocking gently on her heels, her hands clasped in his. The two restraining pink hair grips had long since disappeared, so that her mop of dark curls sprang up like a cloudy halo above her pale face. The big intelligent eyes met mine for an instant, then flickered away, almost furtively.

I would think about that look later, I decided.

Meanwhile, there were more important matters to be considered. The mood of reckless defiance was strong in me. The shock of knowing that I would probably have to depend on myself for the next three or four days at least had given me a curious, false feeling of elation, like a glass of champagne drunk on an empty stomach.

What was I to tell Jerry Mason? He was attracted to me. And I?

If he suspected that Stewart was not to be with me, he would, I was convinced, stay with me. I had accepted without question that the shortness of our acquaintance had nothing at all to do with the strength of the feeling between us. An impossible and perhaps a dangerous situation, I decided. Best to get rid of him, politely but firmly. Perhaps I was rushing upon the sword, but I had an almost feverish desire to be on my own. My feelings of relief when I had seen Jerry in the garden at Acireale were quite forgotten.

By the time I walked up to the group, I had made up my mind.

'*Men!*' I said with bright disdain. 'A bit of a cold! Stewart will be with me tomorrow.' I blushed for the lie. 'You and I can relax now, Jerry, and I'm most grateful. I intend to nominate you for the George Cross, the Nobel Prize for Most Helpful Man of the Year and any other bits and pieces like the Purple Heart, et cetera.'

He looked at me thoughtfully. There was a quizzical look in

his eyes as he hooked an arm through mine and we moved towards an exit door.

'Once you are settled for the night, this Boy Scout's mind will be at rest. Your Stewart sounds a pretty tough fellow. I wouldn't like to meet him if I let anything happen to you now.'

Suddenly the ice-chip coldness in his eyes was daunting. He no longer looked quite so young or so carefree. For the first time, I noticed the strong line of his jaw and the determined curve of the lips. The arm linked through mine had the hardness of iron.

Hastily, I freed myself, hoping that my uneasiness did not show, but I could see the knowledge in his eyes.

'Don't look at me as if I were a cockroach!' he said sharply.

I wheeled away from him, wondering how best to handle the situation. It would be dangerous to antagonize him and yet I had to get away.

I walked out of the concourse hall and stopped dead, staring at John Niven.

His surprise and shock was as great as mine. He was obviously nervous and did not appear to be enjoying the experience. A sense of shock froze his looks into immobility. How had I overlooked that stupid, owlish expression?

For a moment there was a heavy, unnatural silence.

His gaze went swiftly to the children, then behind me to rest on Jerry Mason. The big blond head came forward aggressively and the flush on his face deepened. He had the look of a man dangerously near to drunkenness. When he spoke, the pleasant English voice had coarsened and thickened.

'You've led us a merry dance, Miss Grant. What the devil do you think you are playing at? I've had my work cut out to persuade Mr and Mrs Dalton not to go to the police. I tell you – only my friendship with the Curzons has kept you out of a Sicilian jail. What the hell do you mean getting yourself mixed up with a kidnapper like Scott? You can't get away with it. That child is going back with me now to her parents.'

His face turned ugly with anger. 'You and Scott played a clever game, pretending that he was the father, pretending that

you two had just met . . . And to think you used my house as
your meeting place!' A vein throbbed in the middle of his forehead. There was a dangerous glitter in the blue eyes. 'We saw
Scott in Catania, but he is due for a disappointment, too. The
child goes with me.'

He looked vindictively at Jerry. 'Try to stop me, Noble, and
you'll be sorry that you ever got off that plane.'

Instinctively I moved back out of the reach of the forward-
swinging hands. Like a still in a film, there was a glimpse of the
frozen terror in Mario's face as he pushed Pia towards me, the
sound of the quick pad of John Niven's feet as they carried him
in a bull-like rush in my direction. Jerry Mason took one swift
step forward and, stupefied, I watched Niven's huge frame sail
over the young Englishman's head to land with a sickening
crash just inside the airport door.

Things happened quickly.

Two porters dropped the cases they were carrying and
pounded towards us.

'Judo!' Mario yelled delightedly.

Jerry Mason, breathing hard, pushed the car keys at me and
barked, 'Get to the car. I'll be with you in a minute. If Dalton
gets within touching distance, use the keys like a knuckleduster
and yell like mad. This is no time to be a lady!'

I had the children in the back seat and I was behind the
wheel when he raced up to the car, wrenched open the door
and slid into the passenger seat.

'As quick as you can, Laurie!' he gasped. 'I had to put the
big fellow to sleep, but he won't be out for long. My guess is
that we have about five minutes before the airport police will
want to have a word with us.'

Under my hands, the Maserati engine leaped like a tiger.
Above the surge of the engine and the crunch of the tyres, Jerry
Mason laughed apologetically. 'I'm sorry, but I'm afraid the
Sicilian police are going to be looking for Stewart Noble.
Certainly that fellow, whom I presume was Niven, will be
telling the Daltons that your fiancé gave him a haymaker. Just
before my fist connected with his jaw, he yelled at me, "Eric

Dalton will break you in two for this, Noble!" I didn't wait around to explain or hand him my visiting card.'

I was too busy handling the car to worry about what the Daltons or John Niven imagined. When I thought that the Citroën had finally reached its limit, it went on gathering speed. I accelerated to just over ninety miles an hour and, on a straight stretch, the needle swung round to one hundred. I was terrified. There was a bad moment when there was a sudden wheelspin as we tore over a carpet of water where a pipe had burst on the road.

'Aquaplaning!' groaned Jerry in alarm, but I lifted my foot to avoid traction and all was well.

Jerry let out his breath in a sigh of relief and the tension went out of his body. His faith in my ability to handle the car was flattering, but misplaced.

'Mario, see if anyone is following,' he commanded, but by the time we had reached the heart of the town, Mario had given up the task as hopeless.

In her corner of the car, Pia lay curled up in the foetal position, as if she had withdrawn completely from a situation that was beyond her comprehension. I ached to comfort her, but that must wait. It was vital to get off the streets at the earliest possible moment.

'Give me the route to the Villa Casilda, Mario,' I said crisply. 'Make it the shortest way and don't have second thoughts. The people behind us will be in a hurry.'

He was wonderful, swinging quickly back into his precise, pedantic manner, warning me in plenty of time when to turn left or right, so that not a moment was lost in retracing lost ground.

We swung past the Cathedral, made our way along the rebuilt Via del Cruciferi and finally left the Via Etnea to curve round into the district where I remembered that the Villa Casilda was situated.

One point worried me. I remembered also how the front door of the villa had opened directly on to the street and how conspicuous the great white car had been, standing on the op-

posite side of the road. It would be madness to park it there
for the night.

'Where is your garage, Mario?' I called out.

He understood at once and paused, thinking deeply. 'It is
off the road at the back of the house. The doors are broken,' he
said slowly. 'It would not be good to leave the car there, but
there is no problem.' He sounded more cheerful. 'If I can pick
the lock of a cable-car, I can pick the lock of a garage. It is not
impossible.' He was boasting, but I was careful not to smile.
'Three houses away from my home is the Villa Diane. The
owners have been gone for many months. They will not return
for many more. If they knew, they would be happy to offer you
the hospitality of their garage. The *capo* himself,' he finished
grandly, 'would not dare question me.'

Jerry and I exchanged amused smiles at the thought of the
chief of police interviewing the small boy. We had already
committed graver offences than using a neighbour's garage.
Jerry Mason was, at the very least, now wanted by the Sicilian
police for assault and battery and, if my suspicions were correct,
was probably an associate of Scott's in his crime of abduction. I
pushed the thought of the dictaphone out of my mind. As for
me, in suspecting me of kidnapping, the London police had
merely anticipated events!

As if he had read my thoughts, Jerry Mason said drily, 'I have
a feeling now that the very last people to hear about the
happenings of these few days will be the Sicilian police.' He put
a hand briefly and lightly on mine as it held the steering-wheel.
There was a new warmth in his voice that made me blush in the
darkness. 'My lovely accessory!'

The car swerved sharply, so that he exclaimed. 'Sorry,
Laurie,' he said apologetically, 'My fault. I shouldn't have
touched you. Sorry.'

The lights from the street lamps shone into the car and
touched my face. I was aware of his eyes searching my expression.

'What are you afraid of, Laurie?' He said suddenly. 'Of me?'

How could I say, I am afraid for my life?

Mario called urgently from the back of the car, 'Stop at the next villa. It is the Villa Diane.'

He and Jerry got out and swung the big door aside. I eased the car into the paved courtyard and sat, tense and nervous, until Jerry Mason came to my side of the car and said quietly, 'Get Pia out, then I'll run the car into the garage. It's huge – plenty of room for a couple of cars. I'll reverse, so that if we have to get out in a hurry, we're ready.'

Nervousness or fatigue made me stumble against him as I got out. He held me closely for a moment, so closely that I felt the steady thump of his heart quickening under my hand and the hard mass of the shoulder-holster almost under his left armpit. I laid my head gently against the gun and heard him draw in his breath sharply. He slid his hands down to my waist to steady me before he stepped back.

Quiet as a cat, he took my place at the wheel and the Citroën slid noiselessly into the black cavern of the garage.

Making a great convulsive effort, I swallowed my fear and stood motionless in the perfumed darkness, holding the children's hands firmly.

When he came back, he said softly in my ear, 'Better do without your suitcases for tonight. It will be easier to get in and out of the villa without them.' He pressed the car keys into my hand and I had the feeling that he was smiling. Yet, with a pang, I recognized how tired he was, how strained.

The Biagotti garden was a black jungle of trees and bushes. The hot breath of Etna moved through it like a sigh. Shapes, more solid than shadows, seemed to move secretly in the dimness with the vagueness of a threat. The children pressed close to my side, and comfort ran between us like an electric current.

There was a paved courtyard, echoing the one we had left, but here a path curved through the trees to end practically at the back door. I had an absurd memory of a fairy tale about a solitary house in the woods where the trees gradually moved in, like the tentacles of an animal, and choked it.

In the dimness Mario gave me a smile that made me ashamed of my thoughts.

'What's the matter?' he whispered. 'Are you scared? I'm not.'

Jerry Mason opened the back door and we slipped inside, standing patiently in the darkness until Mario found the light switch. We moved quickly through to the front of the house. The hall was full of the smell of trapped heat.

I had been wrong about Jerry Mason. He looked young and vital and happy. There was a light in his eyes as if he had had a sudden bright dream. Guiltily I recalled the treacherous moment when my head had rested on his heart.

'Wait here,' he said. 'I'll have a look around.'

One minute he was there and the next he was gone.

'Mr Mason can move quietly,' Mario said respectfully.

Pia yawned widely and, when I stopped it with a darting kiss, her eyes danced in the way that broke my heart. She looked slightly bedraggled, with the crispness gone from her frock and her little white socks faintly grey. I vowed to do something about it before the night was over. Some remote corner of my brain had registered the fact that I had no intention of sleeping.

Mario took Pia into the room where I had waited only a few days ago. I followed and sat in the same hard chair, looking with remembered dislike at the ugly discomfort of the furnishings.

'Everything is in order,' said Jerry Mason's voice and I started violently. He was leaning against the jamb of the door, tanned and smiling. 'I didn't mean to scare you,' he said.

'Everything scares me tonight,' I retorted bitterly, resenting the pounding of my heart in my throat. 'As soon as I get back to Zürich, I intend to make a date with a cardiologist.'

He laughed. 'A night's sleep will be cheaper and just as effective.' He hesitated, fingering his chin where a faint reddish shadow of a beard was beginning to show. 'I could sleep down here,' he offered. There was a quick wariness in his eyes, as if he was testing me.

'No.' My voice came out hard and firm. 'It wouldn't be proper.' I said primly. To my surprise, he blushed. Somehow I knew that Jerry Mason did not blush readily. I rushed on, filling the awkward moment with words. 'This house is like a fortress. We'll be perfectly all right – probably sleep like logs.

What about transport for you?' I added brightly, sounding like a polite hostess with an importunate guest.

He waved that aside. 'No difficulty. I'll walk into town and get a taxi. I just wanted to help, Laurie,' he said stiffly. He felt the rebuff.

He was looking at me with the same quizzical look that I had seen at the airport and once again I had the uncomfortable feeling that he knew all about those feelings of distrust. I felt badly about that, but I reminded myself stoutly that my first duty was to the children. The incident at the Villa Diane had been a momentary weakness because we were both tired. No more than that.

'You've been a wonderful help,' I said warmly. 'I can't thank you enough.' My voice sounded as false as a dud coin. It was sweet and relentless.

He looked at me quietly. 'Just to get things straight – I've got nothing to do with the Daltons or with Scott. Before to-night, I hadn't clapped eyes on Niven. I give you my word for that. I assure you that I am not a descendant of Al Capone in disguise. Well . . . good luck. You'll be all right once Mr Noble gets here. Make for the airport in daylight and sit in the lounge until he comes. You'll be safe there.'

He held out his hand, then after a moment he leaned down and kissed me on the cheek. Mario looked flustered and Pia watched him intently. I could see the struggle in her eyes. Her furtive look in the airport came back to me. She had been lip-reading when I told Arlene that she and I were in danger!

Probably Jerry Mason misinterpreted the pain and confusion in my face. He went quickly out and moved silently into the darkness.

I looked after him wretchedly. Jerry Mason . . . Al Scott . . . John Niven . . . I had rotten taste in men, I decided.

I shut and locked the door with the queer feeling that I was shutting danger in, instead of out.

Mario and Pia had already moved off, probably to his room.

The hall looked bleak and unfriendly. I hurried up the stairs, away from the closed doors that looked like deep-set eyes.

Chapter 13

Mario slept in the arid shabbiness of his bedroom with a pleased smile on his unconscious face as though he was savouring still the joy of having offered a friend a present.

Yes, Mario, I thought heavily, shelter from the enemy is no small gift.

Remembering the heavy doors and the barred and shuttered windows on the ground floor, I felt secure at last, though drained and spent and definitely unhappy about Jerry Mason. It was absurd to feel this residue of guilt about a relationship which had been ephemeral and innocently pleasant. Guilt persisted.

I bolstered my spirits with the thought that my charges were clean and comfortable and asleep and that by seven o'clock in the morning we would be out of the area and on our way to the opposite side of the island.

Arlene's car would remain in the garage at the Villa Diane until Stewart and Superintendent Lang sorted out the whole sorry mess.

At six o'clock, just before daylight, a taxi would pick us up with our cases from the back door of the Villa Diane. Mario had made the arrangement by telephone and had reserved three air-flights to Palermo. I would collect the tickets well before departure time and we would breakfast on the plane.

Nothing should, nothing *could*, go wrong. My mind moved gingerly towards the thought of my reunion with Stewart, wondering if he would sense a change in me. I felt changed. What had Jerry Mason done to me? *Of course* I loved Stewart.

I wondered vaguely when Superintendent Lang would telephone and hoped that the bell would not waken the children. We had a tiring day ahead of us, which would not be helped by the heat.

Some day, I thought ruefully, Stewart and I would investi-

gate the possibilities of my Zürich daydream, but at the moment
I had better concentrate on staying awake. If I overslept in the
morning and missed the Palermo plane, we might not get to
Trapani in daylight. I did not fancy looking for the *Più Tardi*
in the dark.

Perhaps, I thought, if I take a bath, this deep bone-tiredness
will ease. Mario had laughed when I said, 'I could sleep
standing up, like a horse.'

I looked at the ivory telephone on Casilda Biagotti's bedside
table and willed it to ring . . . anything to keep my eyelids from
drooping.

Anger came up in my throat like bile when I looked around
the room. Shabbiness stopped at the threshold. It was enormous,
running the whole depth of the house and divided with mathe-
matical precision into three parts – boudoir, bedroom area and
bathroom. The wall behind the bed was an antique mirror in
which the room was repeated like a half-remembered dream.

I leaned against the brocade door and looked at the dim,
beautiful tapestries on the walls, the pink and cream furniture,
the great brocaded bed shaped like a Venetian gondola. An
ivory *prie-dieu* with the kneeler upholstered in rose-coloured
velvet stood under a painting of a Madonna. From the arm-
rest hung a rosary of rose-quartz beads threaded on gold links.

Had Casilda Biagotti ever kneeled there and prayed for her
child? I asked fiercely.

From the top of the delicately painted desk under the front
window, her portrait looked back at me disdainfully. The eyes
hated me for being in her house, for using her room, for
touching her possessions. The patrician features were set in lines
of discontent acquired long ago. The White Queen in *Alice*
said, 'I have forgotten how to be glad.' It was an art which
Casilda Biagotti had never learned.

Almost cheerfully, I turned the photograph face downward
on the top of the desk and slid open the mirrored door of the
first of the long line of fitted wardrobes that occupied one wall.
Each garment hung on a padded hanger and was covered with
a transparent vinyl bag. It was an imposing array. I selected a

white silk dressing-gown with a broad sash weighty with gold embroidery. My conscience did not stir even briefly.

Pia lay on her back in the middle of the broad bed, her face calm and peaceful. Her writing tablet with its dangling pencil and Arlene's telephone pad and pencil lay ready on the bedside table, but I could see that she would not waken before dawn. Her eyelashes lay in dark crescents on her cheeks and, under the silky eyelids, her eyes looked sightlessly up at the elaborate curlicues, picked out in gilt, that decorated the high ceiling and whose ends were gathered carelessly into the plump hands of cherubim in the corners.

The temptation to lie down beside her was almost overwhelming.

I turned the crystal handle that marked where the door in the mirrored wall led into the bathroom.

Beside the light switch was an array of buttons. Experimentally, I pressed the first and the pink oiled silk curtains slid across the windows with a soft whisper of sound. Under the middle window, at the far end of the room, was a triangular bath of pink marble, mounted on a shallow dais of water-lily green tiles. Bottles of oils and perfumes were set out on the broad ledge. Pressure on the second button sent water spewing from the mouth of the gold dolphin tap. I heard a soft plonk and, when I investigated, found that the gold plug had closed automatically. I let the water run to see if it also cut off automatically.

I lost interest in the buttons when I caught sight of myself in the full-length mirror behind the door.

Angrily and softly I talked to my dishevelled image. Comb your hair. Your slacks are dirty. Take them off and wash them. They will be dry in a couple of hours. Must you be so stupid? Don't you know that it is bad for your morale to be dirty? Put that selfish creature's stuff to some practical use.

The sight of the glass shelves with their rows of expensive creams and lotions infuriated me. Suddenly it seemed intolerable that Casilda Biagotti should be serenely asleep in the comfort of the Clinic in Rome while we were being hunted like criminals.

I felt a small, mean satisfaction as I used her Eve of Rome soap to wash my slacks and underwear. Had she known, she would have hated that.

When I had rigged up my line of washing, the sybaritic bathroom looked faintly sordid. Nothing short of a purification ceremony would restore it in the eyes of its narcissistic owner.

Later, as I lay soaking in the perfumed water, I had difficulty in keeping awake. I had not slept in a bed for two nights and I was worn out with strain and worry.

Hastily, I dried myself on one of the big fluffy pink towels, slipped into Casilda Biagotti's dressing-gown and sent the curtains gliding back so that I could open one of the side windows overlooking the garden.

I put the light out and stood in the darkened room breathing in the scented night air and staring at the angry glow in the sky where Etna's hot breath was still spitting out death and destruction.

Jerry Mason had told me of the pitiful religious procession organized by the villagers of Sant' Alfio in which the chanted prayers rose in agonized waves of entreaty for the intercession of their patron saint.

I wondered how they had fared.

I wondered how *he* was faring now. My discomfort about him was beginning to be tedious. I put the thoughts aside.

Dreamily I leaned on the window-sill and contemplated the sooty tangle of trees and bushes below.

Somewhere in the darkness a man cleared his throat!

Under my feet, the floor of the bathroom tilted crazily. The starless sky spun in dizzy widening arcs and my fingers closed on the edge of the window-sill as if safety lay there. Spine and neck muscles were rigid with a fear so profound that I felt I had literally been turned to stone.

My straining eyes found the spot where the darkness deepened, where the wavering shadows took on a menacing solidity.

A man was standing motionless under the tree nearest to the house.

I had the illusion that a pale blur of face was tilted upwards to look at the black outline of the window where I stood. Stiffly I moved backwards into the room, swinging the window outwards with nervous haste to shut out the threat. I stumbled to the door and found the button that closed the curtains.

Behind me, in the bedroom, the telephone rang angrily. I rushed to grab the receiver, feeling almost witless with fear. Before my locked throat could open, Al Scott's voice said angrily, 'Laurie, is that you? Damn it, answer! I know you are in the Villa Casilda. Put Noble on. He's there with you. By the living God . . .'

Gently I put the receiver back on the hook.

Under the white robe my body trembled as if I had an ague. Pia stirred in her sleep and burrowed deeper into the pillows.

I pushed myself up from the edge of the gondola bed and made myself go out through the brocade door into the blackness of the corridor. I dared not put on a light which would have shone like a beacon above the garden. I groped my way to Mario's room and found the bundle of his clothes and sandals.

He grumbled sleepily as I roused him and he went with me like a sleepwalker along the corridor and into the deceptive security of the softly lit bedroom. I turned the key in the flimsy lock and stood for a moment with my back pressed against the silk of the door, my eyes shut and Mario's head heavy against my breast.

'Is it morning?' he asked drowsily. 'Is it time to get up?'

'Not yet.' I found I was whispering. 'But I want you here, so that we won't waste time when we have to go.' I pulled back the covers of the bed. 'Get in,' I urged, 'and go back to sleep.'

He gave a tired, puzzled sigh: his eyelids drooped and soon the soft, snoring breaths told that he was fast asleep.

I forced myself to look calmly round the room. There was not a single article of furniture that I could move and which, at the same time, was heavy enough to be an effective barricade. I tilted one of the ivory chairs under the handle of the door. It would not keep an intruder out, but it would give me warning of his approach.

I dressed hastily, feeling defenceless in the silk robe. The hot, sub-tropical air, and the synthetic nature of the fabric had ensured very rapid drying. My clothes were still slightly damp and clung unpleasantly to my skin, but I donned them like armour.

I tucked Bruna's knife into the top of my slacks and felt like an *apache*. My mind slid away from the thought of using it. I longed to blank out all thought, but especially the memory of the silent figure in the garden and the menacing anger in Al Scott's voice.

Belatedly I began to reason. It was madness to wait tamely until Scott or the man in the garden forced a way into the house. There were at least two hours of darkness left. It was morally indefensible to rely solely on my own resources. I had to summon police assistance.

When I had made the decision, it was as if a weight had rolled from my shoulders. While I waited for them, I would figure out what precisely to tell them. Meanwhile, it would be enough to report that I had had a threatening telephone call and that an intruder was trying to force his way into the house.

Casilda Biagotti's list of emergency numbers was beside the ivory telephone. I found the number for the nearest police-station and dialled carefully. There was no sound at all. I stared at the instrument and jiggled the receiver frantically. In my ear was the 'nothing' sound of a dead telephone. Stiffly I replaced the receiver and faced the truth.

The wires had obviously been cut.

Without the telephone, I was like the last survivor in a be-leaguered city. Perhaps the house was secure enough to keep people out, but we could not stay there indefinitely and starve.

At least, I thought thankfully, we had been able to make the call for the taxi.

That set me worrying about how we were going to get out at daylight.

Was the watcher in the garden still there?

He could scarcely deal with three of us simultaneously.

From the mirrored wardrobe wall, my face looked back at me,

the eyes huge with worry, but the features calm as if they were too frozen with anxiety to register the tumult within.

The reflection showed the peacefully sleeping children, the sumptuousness of the rosy brocade cover which I had felt too weary to fold back; the magnificence of the gondola bed with its soaring, gilt-decorated prow. Like a child whistling in the dark to keep his courage up, now I had all the lights blazing behind the closely drawn curtains. The pink glow from the table lamps picked out a knight on a wall tapestry, accentuating the haughty curve of lip and nostril as he hefted a lance with deadly purpose. From the centre of the ceiling hung a Venetian glass chandelier composed of delicately tinted flowers and leaves. In the mirror, it was as if all the blossoms of spring had been frozen in mid-air in the act of floating down to the ivory carpet.

As if in response to a noiseless clap, the whole scene was extinguished. The room was plunged into darkness.

For me, it was the worst moment of all. Groping in the blackness of the corridor to Mario's room had been bad, but endurable, because I had known I had only to put out my hand and press a switch to get light. I had been in control of the situation. This was different.

My heart pounded in my throat, so that I could scarcely breathe.

First the telephone, now the lights!

Was the man inside the villa?

I crouched on the bed and practically gibbered with fear, my brain paralysed with a terror that had its roots centuries ago when my ancestors had cowered close to a small fire that was their total protection against the wild animals and the more fearsome evil spirits that ranged in the darkness beyond the light of the flames.

It was moments before I realized that I was behaving exactly as the Daltons or Scott wanted me to behave. I was utterly demoralized.

With the curtains closely drawn, there was not a vestige of light in the room. It was like being closed up in an airless tomb, but I forced myself to smile at the thought that the mere absence of light had the power to terrify me.

I talked softly and scoffingly to myself as cautiously I fumbled my way towards the bathroom where I had left my handbag with my pocket torch.

Call yourself an adult! I accused myself furiously. It's probably nothing but a blown fuse. A blind person could find his way out of a darkened house, so you can do it. And if it is difficult for you to move around, it won't be any easier for whoever may be playing ducks and drakes with the Villa Casilda.

I talked bitterly and angrily to Stewart. What was it you told me you would say to that minister? You would promise to cherish me. Cherish! While I am practically having a heart attack in this horrible woman's horrible villa, what are you doing? Sleeping comfortably in the lap of luxury while I have positively to steal the soap to get a bath! And who found Pia Dalton? And who snatched her practically from under the noses of Al Scott and the Daltons? I did! And who'll collect a big, fat salary from WMI for saving them a big, fat claim? You will!

Oh Stewart, I need you!

My face was wet with tears. That seemed to me the worst thing of all. Sicily is turning me into a cry-baby! I thought furiously. For one ghastly, treacherous moment, I wished that I was marrying somebody safe and dull, like a schoolmaster or a grocer.

But it was amazing how my courage came back when I was able to switch on the small beam of the torch.

I pressed the button that controlled the curtains in the bathroom, but nothing happened. There was no sound of running water from the bath when I pressed the second button. Obviously, this was no case of a blown fuse. Everything electric in the villa was out of commission.

When I pulled back a corner of the curtain and peered into the garden, nothing stirred in the darkness. Strain as I might, I could not tell if the watcher was there or not. I shrugged as if it did not matter, and went back to take my place between the door and the bed.

166

I cursed my folly in sending Jerry Mason away. Better the
devil you know . . . !

When the illuminated hands on my watch had crept round to
five o'clock, I wakened Mario, speaking as reassuringly as I
could.

'There has been a cut in the electricity. We'll have to depend
on this torch. Wash and dress as quietly as you can. We won't
waken Pia until the last possible moment.'

When he was ready, we sat side by side on the edge of the
pink marble bath and made our plans. Plans! My lonely vigil
in the darkness had brought no brilliant flashes of insight, no
ingenious method of outwitting our pursuers. No matter how
long we stayed in the villa, nobody was going to come to our
aid. We had to get ourselves out and, though I racked my
brains, I could think of no method other than making a bold
dash for the back of the Villa Diane in time to get our cases on to
the road and wait for the taxi.

I hated to do it, but I had to give Mario some idea of what we
were up against.

'There is a chance that Mr Dalton may be in the garden. The
important thing is to make sure that Pia gets away safely.' His
eyes were enormous and unblinking in the reflection from the
torch. 'Do you have a whistle?'

He nodded. 'In my room . . . I will fetch it before we leave.'

'Well, I want you and Pia to leave by the front door . . .
before me. When you get out, run to the top of the street and
wait until I come along in the taxi with the cases. If anybody
tries to stop you, blow the whistle like mad, make for the
nearest house and ask the people to telephone for the police.
Got it?'

He nodded again.

I hesitated. 'Supposing I'm . . . well, delayed . . . You must
get to Professor Stein at Trapani. Tell him the whole story and
you'll be safe with him.'

'How will I get to Trapani?' he asked practically.

'Collect the flight tickets. Get on the plane and, at Palermo,
hire a taxi to take you to Trapani.' Carefully, I divided the

money in two. 'Take care of it. That's all I've got meanwhile.'

He put it into his money-belt with the grown-up, responsible air that wrenched my heart.

He looked thoughtfully at me. 'If my CASMS really worked,' he said regretfully, 'I'm sure the BO "bug" would label Signor Dalton and Signor Scott as a couple of stinkers.'

'Mario!' I tried to hide my laughter, but in the end we both giggled helplessly for several minutes.

It was he who wakened Pia and, by his own special radar magic, conveyed to her that it was inconvenient, but not frightening, that she would have to get ready in the dark.

By the beam of the torch I watched him fastening her writing tablet to her waistband and saw him putting the telephone pad and pencil in his own pocket.

It was a bad moment when I took the chair away and unlocked the brocade door.

My heart was in my mouth when we went along to Mario's room to collect the whistle. It was on a chain which he hung round his neck.

'It would wake the dead,' he whispered gleefully.

I had a sudden thought.

'Mario,' I said quietly and as casually as I could, 'if you wanted to put the electricity and the telephone out of commission, how would you do it?'

His eyes sparkled in the light of the torch. 'Do you want me to do that, Miss Grant? That will be easy. Papa has a small workshed on the left as you come in the back gate. It's beside the garage. All the electronic equipment, gas and electric meters are there. Shall I do it now?'

'No. I simply wanted to know.'

That is a danger spot, I thought coldly. Maybe somebody is waiting there now.

I fingered the handle of Bruna's knife and hoped that the blade would not cut my abdomen. Awkward if the scar comes above the bikini line! I thought, with a macabre attempt at humour.

Before opening the front door, as we stood in the darkness of the hall, I was shaken by a rage and fear so great that I thought I must die of it. It seemed to me monstrous that I should thrust the children out into the blackness to dangers at which I could only guess.

Pia put her fingers up to feel my face and I forced myself to smile, to give her the rabbit kisses that brought the delighted gurgle to her locked throat and, finally, to put her hand gently into Mario's and to send them out.

The darkness swallowed them up and I could not hear even the soft shuffle of their sandals on the pavement.

Rather tardily, my weary brain registered the thought that if I had worked out the plan earlier, I could have gone with them. Now it was too late to make the long detour to reach the back of the Villa Diane and our cases.

In the short time that I stood tense and motionless at the front door of the Villa Casilda, the quality of the light changed, moving imperceptibly through a spectrum of colour from plummy blackness to a soft, dovelike grey. The true dawn was only minutes away. Here it would in fact come up like thunder. The pavement had been barely visible, but now I found myself looking dreamily down at the dark veining of soil between the stones.

It was an effort to jerk myself out of my trancelike state and go back through the silent house, holding my breath in anticipation of the sudden blow from a dark corner or the feel of a man's fingers on my throat.

It was even worse when I closed the back door softly behind me and stood braced against the coldness of the wood until my eyes grew accustomed to the gloom.

Automatically my eyes swivelled to the tree where the man had kept his lonely vigil, watching the house.

The leaves rustled with a dry secret whisper and the shadows drifted under the arching branches. Wisps of thin grey mist rose from the damp earth, so that the garden seemed to float eerily above the ground. The smokelike veils swirled and reformed so that at first I thought that there was only a deeper patch of shadow beneath the tree.

My throat dried.

My original intention had been to avoid the dark tunnel of the garden and make a dash for the cobbled courtyard and the dubious safety of its open space. Now, like a sleepwalker, I went on stiff legs towards the awkward, sprawling bundle under the tree.

He lay on his back with one leg drawn up under him as if he had been pulled backward so swiftly that there had been no time to brace himself on those strong legs. Pain and surprise were in the widely staring eyes.

As if I had been pole-axed, I dropped on my knees and took the lolling head on to my lap. Under my fingers the broken neck was quite cold. He had been dead for some time.

Sightlessly, Jerry Mason looked up at me in pained wonder.

Chapter 14

At school, the scene from *Treasure Island* which terrified me most was when Jim's mother knelt by the dead body of her lodger and, in spite of the imminent approach of his murderers, insisted on counting out the money due to her, stubbornly determined to take no more and no less. It had seemed to me then foolhardiness carried to the point of lunacy.

Something of the same madness possessed me as I knelt cradling Jerry Mason's poor broken head. My body curved above him in a useless agony of remorse and grief.

Now I knew beyond any shadow of doubt that he had left me only to go on guard, patiently watching the back of the house from where danger might come.

My treacherous imagination spared me no detail. As if I had been present, I saw Scott or Dalton going quietly into the out-house, then, seeing the switches, proceed to put telephone and lights out of commission before trying to get into the villa. Silently they had come on Jerry Mason . . . *which one, oh which one?* . . . and the sudden snap of the neck had ended his life.

I rocked in agony.

Oh God. Oh God.

But both had thought that Jerry was Stewart!

It seemed incredible that throughout an endless night that thought had not penetrated; that I had not worked out that, if both Eric Dalton and Al Scott believed that Stewart had arrived at Catania by plane, had believed that it was Stewart who had struck John Niven, that it was Stewart who was with me in the Villa Casilda, then Jerry Mason could not possibly be an associate of either of them.

One of them had murdered the wrong man!

The first wave of shock had passed and fear, corrosive and paralysing, gripped me. I was deeply, terribly afraid and I was alone.

Was the murderer still in the garden?

Only if he was mad, reason told me.

Obviously the killing had not been planned. It had been the quick reaction of one man coming unexpectedly upon the watcher in the darkness. Surely he would get away as quickly as possible, but how could I be sure?

My teeth began to chatter.

Take the gun, Laurie, said the dead voice of Jerry Mason. *Take the gun.*

My hand fumbled under the thin cotton jacket and pulled the vicious-looking automatic from the shoulder-holster. Fear made me clumsy, so that the barrel of the gun caught on the inside pocket and dragged out a bulging black pinseal wallet. It fell with a soft plop into my lap.

I was on the point of stuffing it back into the jacket pocket when I hesitated. There would be letters in the wallet and at least one card giving his address. Somewhere there would be, perhaps, a mother or a sister or someone who would want to know how he had come to die. I owed them that at least.

Gently I eased the burden of the head back to the ground.

Vividly the scene in the garden at Acireale came back to me with the reedy voice of Al Scott issuing from the tape and warning Jerry Mason that he would break his neck.

That small tape must still be in the murdered man's pocket. There were seven tiny boxes. I tried to steady my hands to fish them out and push them into the big white leather handbag which, suddenly and illogically, brought back a vivid memory of Dukes' Hotel, London.

I had to force myself to take the watch/dictaphone from his wrist. It would be necessary for replaying the tapes.

Besides, I told myself insanely, he did promise it to Mario.

Probably I was more than half mad when I left him . . . sleeping the big sleep, as Chandler had vividly expressed it. The phrase burned in my brain as I went through the silent garden, holding the gun stiffly before me and straining to hear the first telltale crack of a twig or to feel that almost imperceptible change in the air that warns that another human being is close at hand.

But nobody stopped me and I was at the Villa Diane before I noticed that the safety-catch on the gun was still on. I put the gun into my handbag.

As I closed the garage door and carried the cases out, I wondered how long it would be before the Citroën went back to the Villa Noto.

The taxi-driver was prompt and sleepy and seemed to see nothing unusual in picking up two children at the top of the next street.

Mario took one scared look at my white face and chattered feverishly in Sicilian to him.

I leaned back and closed my eyes and decided that I couldn't possibly go on any longer. Probably, if either Dalton or Scott had poked a head into the cab at that moment, I would have handed Pia over without a murmur. Maybe . . .

But my spine had stiffened by the time we reached Fontana-rossa.

Only a few people were strolling in the concourse hall and there was no difficulty about the air tickets. The girl at the desk was pleasant and helpful. She apologized prettily for yawning twice while she was talking to me. She gave me a sharp, shrewdly assessing look.

'There's a marvellous new lipstick on the market, signora – just the shade of your blazer. You may be able to get it on the 'plane.'

'Italian or French?'

'Italian . . . made by Arcari of Rome . . . the shade is called Great Expectations.' She laughed, as if the implication had just dawned on her.

I grinned back. '*Arrivederci, signora.*'

'The *imbattu* is dying.' She used the Sicilian word for the sea breeze. 'You should have a good flight. *Arrivederci, signora!*'

Woodenly I did all the things that might be expected of me – bought newspapers for myself, comics and sweets for the children. Sourly I bought a highly coloured picture-postcard of the airport buildings for Arlene Curzon and wrote on it, 'Wish you were here.'

The thought of her lying sound asleep in her comfortable bed in Surrey gave me such a pang of envy that it was like a physical pain.

'If there is such a thing as reincarnation,' I said to Mario, 'next time round, I'm going to be a nun in a contemplative order. I won't go anywhere,' I added firmly.

'You mean an enclosed order.' There was a gratifying return to his old-man style. 'I'm going to be a QC.'

Pia was watching us both.

'I'm going to have red hair like yours,' she wrote on her tablet.

I seized her round the waist and whirled her round and round until we were both breathless.

She's worth it all! I decided.

Probably neither Mario nor I relaxed until we were airborne and the Mediterranean was a sheet of wrinkled blue enamel far below.

I did not mean to sleep, but I did sleep, briefly and agonizingly, with Jerry Mason cradling me gently in strong young arms. *'Don't cry, Laurie,'* he said, *'don't ever cry.'* He took my hand and Stewart's ring had gone. He turned up the palm and kissed it, then laid it down. *'I love you, Laurie Grant,'* he said sadly and everything was aureoled in golden light. The hazel eyes laughed into mine and we were floating, floating . . .

'Please fasten your seat belt, signora. There is a little turbulence.'

Dazedly I made the long, slow journey back to reality.

The air hostess stared at the tears running down my face as if she did not understand weeping.

'Is something wrong, signora?' Her voice was a shocked whisper.

No, I wanted to say. For him, everything is right. He had his golden dream . . . only briefly, but he had it. I'll weep no more for Jerry.

While I drank the strong Sicilian coffee, I examined the black pinseal wallet. The bulkiness was because of a bundle of clippings from newspapers and journals. All of them referred to places in Sicily. The papers were secured by a rubber band and, at the front of the bundle, was a quarto-sized typed sheet, listing places on the islands with notes about the archaeological discoveries. The notes were scrappy, like information culled from travel folders.

I frowned over the sheet and took a closer look at the clippings. They were up to my standard, but no more. They would have given someone like myself a quick *Reader's Digest* type of rundown on the special archaeological features of Agrigento, Syracuse, the 'Mango' district of Segesta, Selinunte, the Aeolian Islands and the Milazzo region. Most of them dealt with the Aeolian Islands.

Defensively I reminded myself that Jerry Mason had not claimed to be an expert. I had simply assumed that he was, so that this deflated feeling was unfair and rather ridiculous.

When I had put the clippings aside, the wallet was very slim. There was no money in it, so he must have had a separate bill-fold. I felt relieved about that. There was a receipt for the hire of the vintage Bentley from a firm in London. That surprised me. My mental picture of a young car-mad Englishman had been built around that particular car. My confusion grew. Didn't the appeal of a vintage car come in *owning* one? I let the thought go.

His interest in archaeology, however shaky it might have been in knowledgeable foundation, was obviously real. A small typewritten sheet of paper had a concise outline of Professor Stein's origins and background, with a list of his publications. Jerry's hero! What luck it must have seemed for him that he was then in Sicily and that, through me, he had a chance of meeting him! That bright dream, like so many others, was over.

Get rid of the clippings, said the dead voice.

I screwed them up, shredded the typewritten lists and dropped them into a paper bag in the holder of the seat in front.

At first I did not recognize the thin green book as an American passport. Jerry Mason looked serenely out from the page, a younger, but a harder, Jerry than I had known. He had been born in Tallahassee, Florida; had brown hair, hazel eyes; was 6 ft 3 ins; and was thirty years old. So old?

175

I looked at the pictured face for a long time and talked to him softly.

Why did you do it, Jerry? Didn't you trust me? Why? Why? I don't believe that you were one of those crazy anglophiles who wear English clothes, smoke English cigarettes, buy English furniture . . . You would be proud of being an American. Why did you deceive me? A Liverpudlian . . .

He looked blandly back at me.

There was an up-to-date student's record card, made out to Jerry Mason, aged twenty-one, taking a liberal arts course at Duke University, North Carolina. He was majoring in archaeology.

With rigid fingers I drew out the last document, a double folded card which identified Jerry Mason as an FBI agent.

The gun in the white leather bag was heavy on my knees. It belonged, not to Jerry Mason, private citizen; not to Jerry Mason, student; but to Jerry Mason of the FBI who moved like a cat and who had been trained in judo.

How could you let them kill you? I accused him, furious that he had been guilty of that final carelessness.

Al Scott's civilized features swam hazily before me, the planes of the face shifting gently upwards as the mouth curved in the familiar, lazy, sexy smile. How bright and intelligent the eyes were! How slim and powerful the hands! How gently he had kissed Pia! Would he kill?

All tall men, I thought drearily, Scott . . . Niven . . . Dalton . . . Any one was tall enough, strong enough, to snap a neck like a twig. But wasn't there a trick to it? Which of them would know how to do it?

Would the hands of a man who earned his living by his pen have the quick, acquired skill?

The brilliant turquoise eyes of Eric Dalton told me nothing.

John Niven? Those powerful fists might smash a man in the heat of a quarrel, but was he the type to nurse his anger, to hide in the darkness and kill treacherously? Wouldn't he have gone back last night to Taormina in angry frustration?

Mentally I scored Niven's name off my list. From what I

176

knew of him, he lacked the temperament to take a man from the rear and the skill to approach an FBI agent so silently that Jerry had had no time to put his training into effect. Besides, John Niven would never have lurked in the garden. He would have come storming up to the front door, demanding Pia and roaring imprecations like a maddened bull.

Jerry mocked me silently. *Get rid of the wallet*, he told me.

There was a folder in the pocket of the seat in front. It held a map of Sicily, a combined letter and envelope where passengers were invited to list any complaints against the company, a wine list and some notepaper and envelopes.

For a moment I nibbled the end of my pen and wondered what to do. Finally I slipped the wallet between two sheets of paper and edged it into the flimsy envelope. I addressed it to Superintendent Lang, CID, New Scotland Yard, Whitehall, London, England. It was the first solid piece of information I had to give him.

When I pressed the button to summon the stewardess, she came with alacrity, flashing her bright, meaningless smile defensively against the weeping signora. She was so relieved to see my calm face that she almost ran to fetch me Sellotape and stamps.

When I had strengthened the edges and the flap of the envelope, I over-stamped it liberally, marking it hopefully Special Delivery.

The girl was happy to undertake to post it.

Pia came from her seat across the aisle to lean on my knee and look gravely up into my face. I cupped her cheeks between my hands. Her skin felt silky and slightly damp and the brown of her eyes had little golden flecks.

She pushed her tablet towards me.

When shall I go home? she had written.

I mouthed, 'Where is home?' and then felt conscience-stricken. What a question to ask this particular little girl!

She thought for a minute, then balanced her writing tablet on my knee and wrote in her careful, small script, 'Where Mr Scott is.'

She looked at me hopefully.

The pain must have shown in my face, for she put a small finger gently against my lips as if apologizing for having asked the question.

Susan Bradford had tended her carefully since she was a baby, yet where Al Scott was . . . that was home!

The order to *Fasten seat-belts* flashed on. The stewardess clipped smartly down the aisle, checking belts. She lifted Pia into her seat and snapped the clasp of the belt into position. There was a hint of reproach in her look at me. Obviously ATI personnel considered that they had an exclusive right to a display of emotion.

A part of my brain registered that there had been a tiny discrepancy in the saga of events, but I could not pin it down.

Fatigue is dulling my wits, I decided.

Things were beginning to look slightly muzzy round the edges as if something had happened to my eyesight. Murder before breakfast isn't the most tranquil start to the day! I told myself bitterly.

There was a blinding flash. I turned my head sharply. The stewardess was crouched in the aisle, with a camera pointed in my direction. Ignoring my angry exclamation, she swung the camera round towards the children. The two flashes were like gun-fire.

There was a puzzled spate of Sicilian from Mario. Some of the passengers craned to look.

'*Bello puppone!*' she said placatingly and went swiftly down the aisle.

My fingers tore at my seat-belt, clumsy with haste and fear.

The girl was in the small galley, whispering urgently to the wine steward. My letter was propped on top of the aluminium cupboard which, presumably, held the breakfast trays.

As I reached forward to take it, a part of my brain registered with a sense of shock that Bruna's knife was no longer in my waistband.

The pair turned quickly, open-mouthed, and there was a flicker of fear in the girl's eyes. Her hands tightened on the camera. My eyes went beyond her.

The man kept his head, though I sensed his anger as he glanced at the letter. He said expressionlessly, 'Did the signora require something? We will be landing soon. It is forbidden to leave the seat.'

I grabbed the camera and dived for the toilet, slamming the door as his foot went out to wedge it open.

'Cornuto!' he said furiously. 'Signora, it is forbidden!'

The floor vibrated gently under my feet. I braced myself against the tiny wash-hand basin and pushed the letter deep into a pocket of my slacks. When I opened the camera, the film clicked out. Roughly, I wrenched it free, opened it up to let the light at it, then flushed it down the toilet.

When I looked at myself in the mirror, flags of pink were flying in my cheeks.

It gave me a tiny, foolish satisfaction that both the Sicilians were bigger than I.

There was no sign of the steward when I emerged. The girl was pushing a coffee pot angrily into one of the aluminium cupboards.

'I've been admiring your camera,' I said sweetly. 'Oh, and I've decided to post my own letter. Thank you so much.'

I put the camera down on the top of the cupboard.

She did not turn her head.

Mario looked tense and anxious, so I gave him a quick reassuring wink. 'Everything is under control, partner,' I said quietly and fastened myself into my seat.

The plane streaked across the *Conca d'Oro*, the Shell of Gold, skirting the circle of mountains behind Palermo, Sicily's queen of cities. Almost remotely, I wondered how many of its half a million inhabitants had already been alerted by the Mafia that Laurie Grant was aboard the plane with Vira Scott/Pia Dalton. Francesco Picciotto, Al Scott's powerful friend, had moved swiftly on his behalf, but wasn't he out of his territory now?

Could the cabin crew telephone the ground staff or could only the Captain do that? I did not know.

My head swam as if I had drunk a glass of wine before a dinner that was too long delayed.

Below loomed the tremendous mass of Monte Pellegrino, which Goethe called the finest headland in the world. Beyond the barrier of mountains was the less spectacular Monte Catalfano. The outlines of the city were still shrouded in the glittering light of morning, though presently I could distinguish the thin thread of the city's principal artery, the long main street that ran parallel to the sea. It began as the Via della Libertà, became the Via Rùggero Settimo and finally the Via Maqueda.

Somewhere below there must be at least one friend.

'*Mi' amico*,' I whispered, 'where are you?'

Over the sea, the horizon was pearly with mist. It would be a fine day.

'That is the fishing village of Mondello,' said Mario, pointing from his seat across the aisle to a white huddle of houses far below. 'I have watched the fishermen sitting in the sun, holding the tarred ropes of their nets between their toes while they mended them. It is a fine sight.' All the pride of Italy was in his voice. 'Once Papa took me to the church in the square to let me see how the fishermen leave their nets and their gear on the steps of the church for a blessing. They collect them at four o'clock in the morning before they go out to sea.'

I knew what I would do. Spina! Only let him be *Capo dei Capi*! A mere *Capo-mafia* would have to take orders!

The green arm of the fruit trees that embraced the city looked secure and protective. The long, low foothills of the Madonie Mountains were coming up fast now and, further off, the city spread itself, matt-gold in the sun.

The darkness of the orange and lemon groves slid behind us. The plane struck the ground angrily; stuttered towards the air terminal buildings; then, with a last mighty roar of the engines, stopped.

On the tarmac the stewardess waited, blinking her eyes in the hot sunshine. She had the air of an impatient schoolteacher waiting for her pupils to form a procession. Her eyes slid over me to the people behind.

Grasping the children's hands, I stood quietly beside her,

waiting for the moment when she would shepherd her flock to the building.

Timing was important. I had to find out if I was right about Picciotto's Mafia connections.

The tiny muscles around her mouth firmed in preparation for speech.

I said swiftly, 'Was it Signor Francesco Picciotto who passed the word about the child?'

The shock in her eyes was frightening. I wanted to shout gleefully, but I breathed a quick prayer and took the big gamble. 'Don Michle will not be pleased,' I said severely.

Her face was like putty. She tried to speak, but only a strangled gurgle came out.

When she walked stiffly ahead, I got myself comfortably into the middle of the procession where I could watch her.

Al Scott's friend had done his best for him, but it had not been quite good enough. It was a splendid moment for me and Mario sensed my pleasure and took a few dancing steps ahead much to Pia's amusement.

The girl spoke to a man who was standing just beyond the glass doors. His eyes flickered uncertainly in my direction. He said something quickly to the stewardess. She shrugged and shook her head angrily. Her attitude said quite plainly that she was washing her hands of the entire matter.

How far did Picciotto's Mafia chain of observers stretch? Would they be merely observers, like runners in a marathon race passing on to the next Mafioso the task of plotting the course of a Scotswoman and two children? At what point would mere observation stop and Al Scott overtake us to give the word that now was the moment to snatch Pia back?

Stewart, I cried furiously, why aren't you here?

At least there was a chance that Superintendent Lang was on his way, but I did not want the wallet longer in my possession than I could help. Some deeply ingrained sense of caution warned me to keep to myself the puzzling fact of Jerry Mason's FBI connection. That information should go only to Stewart and to Superintendent Lang. Fortunately London was only six hours away from Palermo, but it would probably be safer not to wait for their arrival, but to post the envelope as I had originally intended. After my experience with the cabin crew, I would not risk posting it unless at the main post office.

We boarded the airport bus and I willed myself to relax.

Pia kept her eyes glued to Mario's face as he talked to her in his pedantic fashion. He was repeating some of his school lessons.

'The Ancient Phoenicians called Palermo, Ziz, which means flower, but the Greeks renamed her Panoramus, which means all port. At one time, there were fifteen ancient gates to the city.' He glanced at me. 'Perhaps we will walk down to the sea to the very old Porta Felice. It used to lead to the Arabs' Cassaro, but that is now called Corso Vittorio Emanuele. I know it well,' he continued grandly. 'I have been in Palermo many times.'

Pia looked bored, so I mouthed hastily, 'You can have a lovely dessert, called *cassata*, which is not at all like what is served outside Italy. It is a delicious pastry which is a mixture of sponge-cake, almond paste and cream cheese, blended with a lot of sugar and candied fruit.'

Their eyes brightened and I thought, Poor children! They have been dragged from pillar to post and yet there has not been a single grumble. I vowed fiercely to make it up to them.

When we left the bus I stood for a moment letting the sun beat down upon my head, then chose the second taxi from the rank.

It was a relief when I deposited the letter at the post office. In the coolness of the hall I looked for Michle Spina's address in the telephone directory. He lived in the old town, beyond Quattro Canti Square.

The taxi took us along the Via Maqueda, past the fountain of Piazza Pretoria, and soon another world exploded.

'The sea!' yelled Mario when we reached La Cala, the old harbour. It was cluttered with fishing-boats, gleaming with oil.

The closely packed houses were peeling with age and the corroding Mediterranean sun. Dozens of children spilled from the shadowy doorways and alleys. Gossiping women cuffed them and yelled at them. They were harridans, quite unlike the Taormina women who sat in the open doorways of their homes, with their backs to the road in Arab fashion, lest passers-by should see their faces or legs. Stalls piled with fruits and vegetables ran along one side of the street. Jostling sailors bargained with the merchants.

The taxi turned quickly into what at first looked like a dark alley, pointing at right angles to the Via Roma. The street widened and lightened and the crumbling buildings gave way to a row of beautiful old baroque houses with lacy balconies of wrought iron. I could still smell the pitch from the fishing-boats which were being tarred and caulked on the foreshore opposite the entrance to the old street.

Michle Spina's house had a shabby splendour that must have made his lovely modern villa at the Bay of Sirens seem vulgar and ornate.

The driver shook his head vigorously when I asked him to wait. 'No, signora,' he said emphatically, 'not at this house. The signor does not like people to linger.'

I shrugged and paid him off. If I were right, transport would not be a problem.

The quietness of the street, in such odd contrast to the teeming, rumbustious life so close at hand, seemed to intimidate the children.

'Rum spot,' said Mario with forced cheerfulness, and silently I agreed with him.

The elderly servant who admitted us wore a green baize waistcoat, a snowy shirt with a frilled collar and cuffs and close-fitting strawberry-coloured breeches. He looked like somebody out of a Ruritanian musical.

Pia was obviously impressed. She touched one of his shining silver buttons, and he bent and kissed her forehead with simple dignity.

When I asked to see Don Michle, he looked at me doubtfully. 'Don Michle is very ill,' he said soberly. 'Perhaps it will not be possible for him to see you. He is old and very tired, but he does not always obey his doctor. Be so good as to wait. I will see.'

We waited in a side room and it was a long time before he came back.

He beckoned from the doorway and we followed him up the flight of shallow marble steps to the floor above. The withdrawn quality which the Spanish invaders had brought to their architecture had been very evident on the outside of the house, with its narrow grille windows and towering, blank walls. Here and at the back of the house, there was no sense of that inward-looking feeling.

Through a window at the end of a broad corridor could be seen the cool elegance of a paved courtyard fringed with trees and a tumble of brightly coloured flowers. The splash of water nearby had a refreshing clarity.

The marble of the corridor had a clean, damp smell. The light crept soft and diffused along the vaulted shadows of the walls, picking out the colours in a collection of fine Japanese prints. A gilt lacquer display cabinet stood under a David Cox hunting picture and beneath the window was an eighteenth-century Dutch marquetry bureau. I was almost certain that the aloof figure of the dog on top was a Wei.

With a lift of the heart, I saw that one shelf of the display cabinet was devoted to what I thought were three examples of K'ang-Hai lacquerwork. I had not over-estimated Spina's interest at the Niven party in the Vernis Martin fan.

I went confidently into the bedroom.

The old servant led the children to a long brocaded stool near the window, then drew a chair for me close to the four-poster bed.

The high ceiling was like gold lace and the bright sheen of gold was repeated in the ivory brocade of the bed hangings.

The voice of an almond-seller drifted up from the street, startling me with its unexpectedness. 'How beautiful are these almonds! The children weep to taste these almonds!'

The man in the bed frowned. He was like a picture of one of the *pupi* that I had seen outside the Acireale theatre. The nose was more hooked than I had remembered, the nostrils more pinched and the spry, birdlike figure of the man at the party had become a very old, sick man. Could such a feeble old man really be the head of the Mafia?

I felt a stab of compunction.

'I am sorry to intrude, Don Michle, when you are not well. I will be brief, since you have been good enough to see me. Believe me, if it were not important I would not trouble you.'

His eyes watched me steadily. 'It is a pleasure to welcome you to my home, Signorina Grant, but I apologize that I am not able to entertain you as I would like. You see, I have a terminal illness – old age.' The eyes twinkled. 'I understand there is no cure for it.' He gave a dry cackle as if he had told the joke many times. 'How can I help you?'

'Very simply, but I must give you some explanations. Are you familiar with the story of the kidnapping of the Dalton child?' He nodded and his eyes went briefly to the children sitting quietly at the other end of the room. 'I have good reason to believe that Signor Scott, the American, whom you know, kidnapped Pia, the little girl who is with me this morning. Her parents arranged the original kidnapping and Scott appears to have taken advantage of the situation to abduct her himself. I am trying to look after her until my fiancé arrives from England. That should be in, I hope, a couple of days. Meanwhile, it is clear that we are in physical danger from both Dalton and Scott.'

His face was quite expressionless. I ploughed on. 'Scott is very friendly with Signor Francesco Picciotto of Taormina and I think he appealed to him for assistance.' I paused.

'Did he get it?' There was a note of gentle irony in the voice.

'Signor Picciotto tried to give it. Fortunately I was able to upset his plans, but I can scarcely hope to out-manoeuvre a man who seems to have as many friends as Signor Picciotto. The staff on the plane and at least one man here in Palermo have taken an unusual interest in my movements.' I drew a deep breath and forced a note of amusement into my voice. 'One would almost think that a branch of the Mafia had become interested in my actions. Isn't it remarkable how one becomes imaginative?'

'Quite . . . quite . . .' The hooded eyes closed wearily. 'Everyone talks about the Mafia, and *omertà* and abductions and
killings. Everything is blamed on the Mafia. Early this morning
a young Englishman was found murdered in the garden of a villa
in Catania and already the crime has been laid at the door of
the Mafia, on no more grounds than that a Sicilian knife was
found beside the body. Poor Ciccio! He tries to help a friend and
now he is a member of the Mafia!'

The eyes opened widely. 'I am glad that you are taking a
sensible view of the matter, Signorina Grant. It is never wise to
stir up trouble. Presumably, you have come to enlist my help,
but what can an old, sick man do?' The eyelids drooped.

'If it were not something very simple, I would not ask you,
when you are ill, to do it. It entails no more than a telephone
call.' I made my tone as bland as possible. 'Surely you have a
good deal of influence in this area and in Taormina? Surely, if
you consider the matter, you will be able to think of a man
sufficiently influential to persuade Signor Picciotto's over-
zealous friends to leave me alone?'

I waited, then sent up a quick, fervent prayer. 'No doubt it
would be, to say the least, embarrassing if I were to submit some
names to the anti-Mafia commission. I understand that soon the
regional elections will take place. The murder by the Mafia of
the Chief Public Prosecutor must have made the general public
very sensitive about the names of public figures being associated
with the Mafia. As a public figure and a possible candidate for
election, you must be aware of that. Am I wrong?'

'You are foolhardy, Signorina Grant. This is not a conversation that members of the Mafia would like to hear. Obviously
you fear the power of this society. Don't you think that you are
inviting disaster by this conversation, even with me? Who knows
what dangers lurk in the very street?' His bright glance was
sardonic.

'I am not entirely a fool. This morning, I posted to myself . . .
out of Sicily . . . a report which would spark off a good deal of
trouble here, if anything happened to me or to the children.

Your powerful friend – I am conjecturing, of course – must guess this.'

'In effect, what you are saying to me is, "Tell your friend to call off his dogs, or his chances of becoming a Senator are threatened." But my dear young lady, what if my friend – and I do not admit that such a friend can be found – says that he has grown old listening to threats? What then?'

'Bribe him!'

'You have something to offer?' The hooded lids rose in the first real surprise.

'Yes. I imagine that you would associate with a man with tastes similar to your own; a man, for example, who would share your enthusiasm for antique lacquerwork; who would love that Vernis Martin fan as much as you do.'

The figure in the bed was very still. 'You have *another* Vernis Martin fan to offer?'

'No . . . something much better. Be so good as to tell your friend this. As he will know, the Japanese were the supreme experts in the field of lacquerwork, but unfortunately the secret was lost for centuries. At the beginning of the eighteenth century there were four young Frenchmen, brothers, who were coach-painters. They envied the Japanese skill and spent thirty years trying to recapture their secret. Shortly before 1760 they succeeded – hence, your lovely fan.'

'Go on . . . go on.'

'For thirty years the youngest brother kept a diary in which he recorded every detail of their aspirations, their attempts and their formulae. It is a voluminous account, not only of their own work, of their final success and of the pieces they created, but it gives details of the great examples of Japanese lacquerwork that they studied. The manuscript is a collector's dream.'

I sat back and prayed.

He had pulled himself high on the pillows while I was talking. There was a hectic spot on each cheek which alarmed me. He said thickly, 'Mother of God! I would give a fortune for that. Where is it?'

'In Glasgow. I can't afford to make a present of it to your

friend, but I think I can guarantee that he will be able to acquire it. Is it a deal?'

'*Is it a deal?* Signorina Grant, I would trade with the devil for that.' He tugged violently at a bell-pull at the side of his bed. 'I must get up. When can I get it?'

'As soon as Pia Dalton and I are safely back in London.'

He struck his hands together with a flat, ineffectual slap. 'Done!'

He hauled the telephone towards him and dialled rapidly. The stream of Sicilian sounded cold and authoritative. He replaced the receiver with a satisfied bang.

'Signorina Grant, I am grateful to you. You have given me the best tonic I have had for years. I will await your next prescription. I think I can promise you at least that it will be more difficult now for Signor Scott or Signor Dalton to be dangerous.' He peered at me. 'Difficult, but not impossible, so do not be foolhardy. I will help you further, if I can.'

The old servant came quietly into the room.

'Gaspare, I must get up.' He waved away the man's objections. 'First, my guests must eat.' He turned to me. 'What are your plans? Do you stay in Palermo?'

'No. I would like to hire a car and drive to Trapani. An American friend has a boat there. I will stay with him until my fiancé arrives.' He was scarcely listening.

'Eat now. The car will be waiting for you when you are ready to leave.'

I almost floated down the marble staircase. At last my luck had turned.

The children and I had a gay lunch, punctuated by endless questions about the boat. I waved my wineglass and improvised shockingly, drunk with happiness at the sight of their excited faces.

Tonight, perhaps, I would be able to talk to Stewart. Tonight I would sleep soundly on the *Più Tardi*, knowing that the members of the Mafia were no longer my enemies, but my friends. Tonight Gregory and I would talk about the happy days at Northwestern University. I would not talk to him of Jerry Mason, for tonight was to be a happy night.

There was no sign of life as we left the house, but a car was already at the front door. The driver was dozing at the wheel, but he got out alertly as soon as we were on the pavement. He was a distinguished man of about forty-five with dark hair already going grey at the temples. He had the typically saturnine face of the southern Sicilian, but there was humour in the dark glance and a reassuring solidity about the muscular body. He had the air of a successful businessman.

Mario, in his *grand seigneur* mood, ignored him, but Pia flirted with him shamelessly, giving him great melting glances that obviously enslaved him.

Not even a cat stirred in the street. The walls still gave off the noonday heat, but it was not yet the siesta time, so I could not make the excuse of closed shops. My rash promise of *cassata* had to be kept so, basking in my new-found feeling of security, we left behind the dirty and neglected streets beside the harbour.

As they licked their dessert spoons blissfully, I sat back, feeling like the character in the old fairy tale who wore a suit of invisible armour. It was the first time since I had set foot in Sicily that I did not feel entirely alone, for, helpful as Jerry Mason had been, there had always been an elusive feeling that he had a divided mind.

I pushed that thought away, as I pushed away any others that seemed to threaten my new-found serenity. Two major ones kept intruding. What was to become of Pia when Stewart arrived to take over? What was to become of Mario? *You will be like a superannuated Nanny!* Arlene's voice mocked me.

Meanwhile, at least one telephone call had to be made as soon as possible. It went through quickly. The girl found the number for the antique dealers in Glasgow with commendable speed and Rose's deep, musical voice, calm and soothing as ever, sounded in my ears. After the first excited exchange of greetings, she said, 'Natie will speak,' as though telephone calls from Sicily were commonplace.

'Natie, I have made arrangements for the sale of your Vernis

Martin manuscript.' Thank God, Natie was a listener! There
was silence from the other end. 'I know you will say that it is
quite impossible to part with it. Please, for my sake, don't say
that. You simply must be prepared to negotiate.' I allowed some
of the desperation to creep into my voice. 'Please, Natie . . . I
know how you hate to part with your treasures, but in return for
the information that the manuscript would be available for sale,
a Sicilian friend is prepared to do me a very big favour. Without your co-operation, I will have lost my bargaining power.'
My false laughter tinkled out.

'I understand. Why do you get excited, Laurie? Always you
get excited. I understand.' The chuckling tones were blessedly
reassuring. 'I must think about the price. Such a valuable
manuscript . . . Shall I be approached or do I wait until I hear
from you?'

'Oh, Natie, you *are* good! You may be approached. You know
how eager collectors are! But please be non-committal until I get
to London and speak to you again . . . in a few days. My friend
drives a hard bargain, I warn you.' I laughed again. 'I want this
sale to come to a *very* satisfactory conclusion.'

When I replaced the receiver, I felt as if the weight of the
world had been removed from my shoulders.

While I sat in the powder room, combing my hair over and
over again, I wondered where Spina had placed the bug.

It had to be on something that I had with me always.
Thoughtfully, I regarded the white leather handbag standing
innocently on the top of the Vanitory.

The ends of the double handles were secured by four
lozenges of silver, each held by two studs with heads the size
of a pea. Now there were, apparently, three studs on each of the
silver plates.

Clever! I thought, with real appreciation. Michle Spina, I
give you full marks for ingenuity. I would probably have
noticed an extra stud, but four . . . no!

For a moment I thought of warning Mario, but remembering
his ghastly over-acting at Fontanarossa airport, I decided against
it. What could he possibly give away that Spina did not already

know? Mario knew nothing of Jerry Mason's connection with the FBI, nor of Superintendent Lang's probable arrival.

Once we were aboard the *Più Tardi*, we would be out of range of the recorder which was probably somewhere in the car. Till then, I would be careful.

But at least Spina had given me an idea.

I scribbled a note to Mario: *Don't say a word, either now or when you come back. As quickly as possible, buy a set of new batteries for your father's recorder.*

If I had enrolled him as a member of the CIA, he could not have been happier.

When we got into the car, Pia was clutching a Sicilian doll and Mario a fat pencil-torch. Both were wriggling with pleasure. The driver gave them his gay, flashing smile as he opened the door for us.

Tucked in the inner pocket of my bag, like a scroll for the Freedom of Sicily, was Michle Spina's card. Written on the back, in Italian, in his spidery writing, was the message: *Any courtesy or favour shown to Signorina Laurie Grant, the bearer of this card, will be greatly appreciated by Michle Spina.*

I made a bundle of Arlene's sadly abused blazer, propped it in a corner of the window and prepared, thankfully, to doze until we reached Trapani.

Hazily, I saw the windy stretches of the airport of Punta Raisi, then, below the bare mountain slopes, the jade green of meadows alternating with the silvery flash of olive groves and small copses. I was dimly conscious of the children straining to see the long stretches of lonely, shining sands cradling the great bay of the Golfo di Castellammare. The town looked small and dirty.

From Palermo to Trapani was only sixty-eight miles, but the driver made it a leisurely journey, especially when the road swung away from the sea and cut across a wide valley, fertile with olive trees and vines.

Now that I had the time and the peace of mind for thought, I could not concentrate. With my face almost smothered in the red blazer, I had only two objectives – to get aboard the *Più*

Tardi and, after I had made arrangements with Gregory Stein, to telephone Stewart and, probably, Superintendent Lang.

But above all I yearned, I lusted for sleep, for long, dreamless hours when Greg would hold the fort against any attack from the Daltons or Scott.

The blinding hours of heat were almost over when we slid into Trapani, a cramped grey town built on a long, narrow promontory. The sirocco had swept the streets clean and the silence emphasized the Middle Eastern impression of the houses built directly on to the water of the north-facing shore. 'A sickle,' *Drepanon*, the Greeks had called Trapani. Here Anchises, the father of Aeneas, died, having survived the burning of Troy, and was carried on his son's shoulders to live to see this flower-strewn corner of Sicily.

The flowers were everywhere, bee orchids, gladioli, rosy snapdragons, wild cyclamen and the small perfect blue irises that bloomed only for a day. They starred the fields between the pine trees and the emerald sweep of sea and pointed up the bleaker aspect of the southern shore with its docks and mudbanks and steely glitter of salt marshes.

Unmistakably we were in a port, a place of the sea. The tall ochre-coloured houses, set in the narrow, winding streets, were salt-rimed and sea-faded. At one end of the harbour, where the fields came right down to the water, fishing-boats were already strung out in an undulating brown line. At the other end of the harbour there was a bewildering mixture of moored boats.

'I can't see the *Più Tardi*,' said Mario, craning his neck.

'Scarcely – since you don't know what you are looking for.'

'It will be a converted fishing-boat, maybe a swordfish boat,' he asserted confidently. 'I know what to look for.'

Pia pressed her doll's face against the window of the car to give her a view of the glitter from the sea and the misty outline of the distant Aegadian Islands.

I felt tranquil and almost happy.

A lemony glow slid along the rooftops of Trapani and the wind boomed against the harbour walls. Spray flickered against the car windows and when I rolled them down, all at once the car was full of the sound and smell of the water. Beyond the breakwater, sea and sky were piercingly blue all the way to Africa.

The driver brought the car to a crunching stop.

'*Per favore, signorina,*' he said with his gleaming smile. 'Stay in the car and I will seek the boat. *Capisce?*'

Behind was the cry of a salesman extolling his wares, '*Bello! bello!*'

I called after the driver, 'Please go to the Capitaneria del Porto. The documents for the *Più Tardi* will be there. Perhaps they will know where she is moored.'

But Pia and Mario were too excited to remain in the car. I held on to them as they stood perilously near the edge of the harbour wall, with Mario chanting the names of the boats like a litany.

'*Dove andate?*' Mario would call to the leather-faced seamen.

'Levanzo . . . Formica . . .' The names drifted sweetly on the breeze.

The driver came clumping back over the cobblestones. Before he was quite up to us, he called out, 'The *Più Tardi* has gone!'

Chapter 15

A fisherman was brooming some fine sand from behind the capstan on a fifty-ton fishing-boat. A scent of coffee was in the air. An old man carrying an oar walked past, heading for the main harbour.

'*Buon giorno, Capitano!*' he called merrily to Mario. Shyly he ducked his head at me. An empty demijohn, suspended by string from his leather belt, banged gently against his thigh as he walked.

The Customs officer, strolling over the cobblestones behind him, had an air of languid elegance. He saluted smartly, white teeth flashing in an olive face. He had the insatiably amorous look of the Sicilian male.

'*Buon giorno, signora!* Can I assist you?'

The little finger of his left hand was about two inches long, the caste mark which showed that he did not belong to the labouring classes. He spoke the melodious Italian of the well-educated. The disappointment in my face made him lift his shoulders slightly and spread his hands in a tiny gesture of sympathy. He waited, the bright eyes inquisitive and inviting.

'We were hoping to join a friend on the *Più Tardi*, but evidently the boat has gone.'

'But only temporarily. She will be back some time tomorrow evening. I would think at about the hour of the *passeggiata*. That is usually when the Capitano Stein returns.'

'Oh.' I felt the sweet flooding of relief. 'He is certain to return?'

'Oh yes. Since early spring he has been sailing regularly to the Aeolian Islands. Some new archaeological diggings on Filicudi, I understand. A scholar and a sailor . . . it is a fine combination of gifts. He has much manliness. Not a landlubber like me.' The white teeth flashed. 'But I looked at the documents just now. They say that he was to be in Filicudi two days ago. Tomorrow, if the Madonna of Trapani is kind to him, he will bring back some treasures. Not the "bikini girls" of Casale perhaps.' He roared with laughter. 'But, after all, there are better mosaics. But something . . . he will bring something.'

A few hours ago his talk would have filled me with the blackest despair, but Michle Spina's card in my handbag was my talisman. Greg Stein's absence overnight was an inconvenience, but no more. I felt stronger now, less liable to think that the unexpected was necessarily a disaster. There were, indeed, the poet's cohorts about me to left and to right. I gave the officer my brightest, most winning smile. The keenness of his gaze was flattering. Mario scowled at him.

With the children's hands in mine, I eased the straps of my handbag on to my forearm and pivoted on a heel, smiling into the lean, dark face.

'It will then indeed be *più tardi* when I see my friend, but no matter. It will be a pleasant surprise for him. The children will love sleeping on board tomorrow night. *Grazie tanto.*'

He laughed. 'Do not be late then . . . *non troppo* . . . not too much, or the others may be before you.'

I stood perfectly still. 'The *others*? What others?'

'They are not friends of yours also? Only of Capitano Stein? Today there have been four people who asked about the *Più Tardi*. First, there was an Americano and a blonde girl who said nothing, so I do not know if she was American or English. Then, perhaps an hour ago, a man and woman, both very tall, both big, asked also.' His gaze sharpened. 'Both looked for a girl with two children, so you see, signora, they are your friends.'

My tongue crept along my lips.

'Did they say that they would be back tomorrow night?' The bleakness of my smile was making him uneasy.

'*Scusi*, signora, but I made a mistake. I was at the *taverna* beside the harbour when they asked. The documents are in the Customs house and I did not remember. I thought it is my saint's name day in two days and then Capitano Stein comes back, but I am wrong. It is tomorrow.' He shrugged. 'It is not important. They will come back.'

He glanced down at the children. 'Trapani is good for you, signora. There is much to interest you in the town – the della Robbia Madonna of enamelled terra-cotta in the Church of Santa Maria del Gesù and that lady who came one day direct from the studio of Giovanni Pisano, the Madonna of Trapani. There is the Town Hall, the Cathedral . . . oh, much . . . but for the children . . . no.'

'I see.' I was scarcely listening. Slowly the old terrors were creeping back. For a moment Jerry Mason's dead face seemed to float before my eyes. The driver, lounging against the car, was all at once a comparatively small man physically compared with Scott and Dalton. One of them had managed to kill an FBI agent. Would that smiling Sicilian be a serious threat to either . . . an effective guard for us?

There was a ketch almost immediately opposite us. Up the mainmast, in a bosun's chair, a man was hand-sanding the mast. Outside a hut on the left an old watchman swung gently back and forth on a kitchen chair, half dozing in the heat. His newspaper had dropped to his feet. Two fishermen in faded blue jerseys with black trousers rolled above their knees were mending their nets. To be hunted in broad daylight in a busy, peaceful harbour was weird and unreal. What made it terrifying was that there seemed to be nothing I could do about it.

Suppose I were to call the police? Arrest that man: he wants to get back his own child. By the way, I think, but I can't prove that he murdered a man. Arrest that other man: he wants to shoot this little girl. Who says so? This little boy.

The dark, clever eyes of the Customs officer were watching me curiously.

'I see.' Tears came into my eyes, perhaps because I was confused and tired. I looked blankly at the dark blue waters of the port, streaked with moving light.

There were a host of questions in the officer's eyes.

'What do you suggest? Can you recommend a place? It would

be only for tonight and tomorrow. I am very tired. The hotel need not be de luxe, only restful.'

He swung an arm in a graceful arc towards the sea. 'The islands would be best, the Isole Egadi. Perhaps the island of Marettimo would be best of all. It is, as you will know, the island described as Ithaca, in the Odyssey. Perhaps Capitano Stein will take you there.'

'Meanwhile, no boat.' I smiled. 'We would have to depend on him.'

'No. It is not practical. Then let it be Erice.'

'Where is that?'

'By car, an hour from here, along the coast road. It is very mysterious, very beautiful, an Elymian city of mythical origin, built on top of a mountain.'

'It sounds wonderful, but can we be sure of hotel accommodation?'

I thought that his eyes went briefly to the driver. 'You can be sure,' he said. 'Tourists go there, but not too many stay. People are losing the ability to cope with solitude. Some call it the silent town.'

He saluted and went away with a gracious show of reluctance.

Mario scowled after his retreating back. 'He would like to be familiar,' he said accusingly.

I laughed and got back into the car with a sense of relief.

As we were leaving Trapani, there were tantalizing glimpses of mazes of alleys; beautiful old baroque houses, elaborately decorated with swathes of fruit, garlands of flowers and fat-bottomed cherubs; a garden of tropical trees and a handsome marble edifice decorated with statues. I stared at the scimitar-shaped promontory between the open sea and the land-locked harbour and wished that I could wake up from this dream and find myself back in Zürich. It seemed a million weary years since I had left London.

'How is it possible for people to have got to Trapani from Palermo before us? Is there a shorter way than we took?' I asked the driver.

'Of course! It is only twenty minutes by plane.' He shrugged.

'For people in a hurry there are always ways. For example, you could go up to Erice from Trapani by cable-car, but is time so precious? Better to climb up by road, as we will do. Possibly we will go through the clouds. It is interesting, though the land below Mount Eryx is not. From the mountain, you will see Mount Cofano which changes colour endlessly in the light. It goes sheer into the sea. You will see the Egadi Islands like three great ships riding the waves. Perhaps if the light is good, to-morrow you will see Tunis.' He glanced in the mirror at the children. 'Later,' he said delicately, 'I will tell you the in-teresting history of the famous shrine of Venus, on top of Mount Eryx.'

Mario was pink with annoyance. He glared at the driver's broad back and said furiously, 'I am not a baby. All Sicilians know the story, but it is not for the signorina.' He was back in his lordly rôle, but the mood did not last.

He said miserably to me, 'It seems as if only Pia is to be trusted. I did not mean to do wrong, but I remember that, when we were on the *Golden Eye*, I spoke to the boys of Professor Stein's boat. Mr Scott must have heard and that is probably why he was able to come today to Trapani. I am sorry.'

'Well, he won't know about Erice,' I said comfortingly, hoping that I was right. 'Let's relax and enjoy ourselves.'

But as we crawled through Trapani, I looked with lacklustre eyes at the fascinating warren of winding alleys, with their crowd-ed stalls piled high with plaited loaves and rolls thick with car-away seed; at the glistening heaps of silvery *dendici*, gar-fish, mullet and octopus, still smelling of the moving sea; at the golden pyramids of mandarins; and, bedded in papyrus reeds, the pale-green mounds of *zibbibbu*, those kidney-shaped grapes that taste of honey and the sun-warmed vineyards of the west.

Somewhere behind the dark doorways or in one of the grace-ful old squares, at this moment death waited for us. I knew it, as surely as I knew that the blood was pounding in my veins. The sun was all about us, flooding the car, but the cold that wrapped Jerry Mason round now, touched me also.

Pia's weight against my knees was a sweet and terrible

burden. For a moment I considered going back to Palermo, to the quiet street by the harbour, and begging Michle Spina for the shelter of his house until Stewart arrived.

My adrenals, I decided, had stopped functioning. There was no more fight in me.

Mario said timidly, 'You look sad,' and put his arms in a curiously protective gesture round Pia, as if he knew that, emotionally, I had withdrawn from them.

Reluctantly I faced up to the fact that I was dangerously tired, with a weariness that was more than physical. Probably I was no longer capable of making sensible judgments. The exhilaration following my talk with Michle Spina had worn off, leaving me vaguely depressed and uneasy. I wondered why I felt obscurely wrong, as if somewhere, at some point in the headlong flight from Taormina, I had made a bad error.

Involuntarily, as though I had a stomach ache, I doubled up and put my head down on my knees. Despairingly I told myself that I was sick of running, sick of being caught up in a situation which I did not understand, sick of feeling afraid. I ached for the comfort of Stewart's arms.

Until this morning, buried deep in consciousness, had been a tiny doubt that the danger was in fact real. Jerry Mason's murder had changed that.

Impatiently I pushed the hair back from my eyes and rolled my head to lean it against the door of the car. Lazily my gaze travelled along the narrow channel of light between the front seat and the side of the vehicle. Far back, under the dashboard, a tiny aerial seemed to grow out of the floor-boards.

All at once, I wanted to laugh joyously. Of course I was not alone! My cohorts might not be as reputable as Chesterton's angels, but they were powerful flesh-and-blood allies, with an ancient history of resourcefulness and cunning. Dalton's murdering hands might find their match in a short length of Sicilian rope or in a wickedly effective Sicilian knife.

Of course every man had his price! Like Spina, for a collector's dream item, I too, for the sake of the children, was prepared to deal with Lucifer himself.

Pia's fingers tugged at my hair. She put her face close to mine, so close that I could see the amber flecks in her eyes and, for a moment, there was something familiar and loved in the searching, intelligent scrutiny.

My kiss on the tip of her nose drew forth her wonderful smile. I tilted her face up and sang softly, ' "Do you want the stars to play with? Or the moon to run away with?" '

The driver's eyes met mine in the mirror. He was grinning widely.

I said apologetically, 'In future, I'll leave the singing to Miss Callas.'

Now was the time to put Spina's card to a small test. If he were only a driver, it was best to find out.

I leaned forward. 'We will spend tonight and tomorrow in Erice, then go back in the evening to Trapani to board the *Più Tardi*. All of us are very tired. Do you think that we can really relax in Erice?'

The eyes in the mirror were suddenly cold and flat.

'Assuredly, signorina. It is my task to make sure that you do. My orders from Don Michle are clear. I might as well throw myself into the sea, if any harm befalls you. If possible, those who trouble you have not to be harmed, but they have to be stopped. They will be stopped.'

He fumbled in an inside pocket and drew out an envelope which he passed back to me.

'These are the men I must watch,' he said in matter-of-fact tones.

They were poor prints, but the features were unmistakable.

'But how on earth . . . ?' I spluttered.

He shrugged. 'Not difficult. The main newspaper office in Palermo had many of the writing man. The other came by wire from Taormina. Signor Spina has many resources. My task is not difficult. Tonight you will sleep well with the little girl in your room, and perhaps a maid to see that you are not disturbed. It can be arranged. The boy will share my room.'

' "Do you want the stars to play with? Or the moon to run

away with?'" Mario bellowed off-key, and all at once the car
was full of laughter.

The sun was a ball of fire low on the horizon and the sea,
streaked with gold, had never looked so beautiful. The great, flat,
fertile plain fell away as we climbed higher and higher. In the
slackening light the salt-pans gleamed with the soft pallor of
thin silver made gentle by age. The windmills looked like toys
from a child's collection. The pinewoods crept closer until
we were looking down on a dense dark-green carpet that appeared to go right to the water's edge.

'Crikey!' said Mario, looking at the sheer drops at the side of
the road. My stomach heaved. Unperturbed, Pia pressed her
nose against the window and looked serenely down.

It was a relief when we swept between the trees and saw the
entrance to the medieval town, which I understood was, in fact,
more like a village. The air was cold with the spicy aroma of
woods that had dreamed all day in the sun.

The car edged carefully through the Porta Trapani along the
Cyclopean walls. It was like entering a pool of quietness and
serenity. There was a good deal of restoration of the Norman
and Gothic porticoes, but a detached campanile built as an
Aragonese look-out tower was indubitably early fourteenth-
century and was in an excellent state of preservation.

We crawled slowly along the Via Vittorio Emanuele, catching
glimpses of tall dignified houses of simple grey stonework of
exquisite proportions. Wind and sun had weathered them to a
smoky softness that emphasized their Norman origins. History
pushed up through the cobblestones which were separated by
slabs of white marble. Streets and houses looked almost artificial
in their perfection, like a carefully constructed film set. Nobody
walked along the cobblestones; nobody peered from the
windows. There was the eerie feeling that long ago time had
stopped here, imprisoning the people in their houses or at their
pursuits, as it had done nearly nineteen hundred years ago at
Pompeii.

'Where are the people?' I asked in a puzzled whisper.

'Ah!' said the driver. 'You feel the difference? Here the

people are not at all like Sicilians. They are remote; they do not smile much and they have a courtesy which alas! the rest of us have forgotten. It is not their custom to walk in the streets. We Sicilians like to loiter and talk with our neighbours, but not these mountain people. Perhaps it is the Arab influence. Who knows?' He shrugged. 'At any rate, it is completely unspoiled by tourism. You will not want to leave.'

The street widened into a little town square, the Piazza Umberto I, and there was just time to see that there was a tiny bar in one corner before the car turned left along the Via D. Vultaggio which took us to the Porta Carmine, the second of the three town gates.

Presently we drove between pine forests that looked gloomy and oddly threatening in the gathering dusk.

'This is the Via Addolorata,' the driver announced. 'To-morrow you will see how beautiful and how peaceful it is here. The road turns round to the back of the Hotel La Piñeta where you will spend the night. You will be comfortable.'

But matters did not go quite as smoothly as he had inferred. After a few minutes, he emerged from the hotel looking grim.

As he got back into the car, he said abruptly, 'It is better, after all, that we spend the night at the Jolly Hotel. It is near the *funivia*. You will like it. It is set among the pines and looks right down to Trapani and the sea.'

A look at his thunderous expression told me that it was best to ask no questions.

Mario said rebelliously, 'Why can't we stay here?' but I quelled him with a warning look. Pia was half asleep in her corner of the seat.

The car sped along the Viale delle Piñete as though the driver was suddenly in a hurry and, when we got to the hotel, instead of going in alone as before, he hurried us into the reception hall, not pausing to lock the car doors or to remove our luggage.

At the reception desk he had a brief, quiet-spoken conversation with the clerk, who reached behind him to take four passports from a pigeonhole. The driver inspected them carefully, then, apparently satisfied, nodded abruptly to the clerk.

Mario raised his eyebrows enquiringly, 'Man in a hurry,' he said.

'Probably hungry,' I replied equably and we exchanged smiles.

Shortly after we had gone to our rooms, and while Pia was washing blissfully in the adjoining bathroom, there was a soft knock at the door.

'Come in!'

'Don't ever do that again,' the driver said angrily. 'You must lock your door whenever we are separated. I cannot be in two places at once.'

'I didn't think.' I was crestfallen, lulled, I realized, into a false sense of security by the remoteness of the place. 'Is something wrong?'

'No. It is not really important, only a nuisance. No more than that, but it is better that I tell you about it. The Daltons arrived this afternoon at the Hotel La Piñeta. They have booked in for two days. It is a nuisance,' he repeated, 'but it changes nothing. Relax. They will not harm any of you here. The place is too small and they could not get away quickly enough, if they attempted anything. Relax.' His expression softened. 'Do you have any questions?'

Momentarily I gazed at him stupidly, trying to evaluate the news. 'Yes,' I said. 'What is your name? I can't go on behaving as if you didn't have one.'

He grinned. 'Benito. That is sufficient.' His glance became mocking. 'I am sorry that I cannot change for dinner, but I assure you that I shall use the correct forks, signorina. Do not be surprised if you learn that Signor and Signora Capocci are staying here for a week with their children. Mario has no objection to his temporary papa and I promise to be a model husband.' He bowed formally, a gesture oddly at variance with the mischievous, dancing light in his eyes.

Too many fathers! I thought inanely. That's what got me into this mess. Too many fathers!

On an impulse, I took a carnation from the bowl of flowers on the dressing-table and threaded it into the left lapel of his jacket. He looked jaunty and happy and very competent. I decided that it was foolish to worry about the Daltons while he was around.

He paused in the doorway. 'I know nothing of the man Scott,' he said, 'but I would be willing to wager that he is not in Erice. What the mathematicians call the law of averages is against it, but it can be checked. There are only three small hotels and three *pensioni*. I scarcely think that he will be leading the simple life at the Camp Polisportivo. I am told that he is a sophisticate.' The white teeth flashed in the dark face. 'Tonight we will drink to perdition to your enemies. May the fish eat them!'

With my hand on the door knob, I said demurely, 'My husbands usually call me Laurie' and shut the door before he had time to reply.

Reluctantly I put Stewart's photograph back into my case, but I talked to him softly while I bathed and dressed, telling him endlessly how tired I was and how much I missed him.

Finally, when I stood before the dressing-table mirror smoothing down the skirt of the green chiffon, my reflection looked back at me with a sparkle and a freshness that I had not seen since the night of the Nivens' party.

I bent while Pia dabbed perfume behind my ears and on my wrists. Solemnly I did the same for her and for her Sicilian doll, and we exchanged the secret, understanding looks of the daughters of Eve.

For a wretched moment she looked small and lonely in the middle of the bedroom and that horrible thought came back: What *is* to become of her when Stewart claims her?

Gaily I swept her up and deposited her on her back in the centre of one of the beds, indicating that I intended to telephone. She watched me with bright, happy eyes, but when I sat on the edge of the other bed, I was careful to keep my back to her.

The call to London went through quickly. As if she were in the room beside me, Arlene's sweet, fluting voice came clearly over the wires. She sounded brisk and happy, quite unlike the weary socialite of our last call.

'You sound unusually bushy-tailed,' I said suspiciously. 'Is Tom home?'

'Not yet, but he will be tomorrow. Marvellous news. The Masouri case isn't even coming to trial. Thanks to Tom, it has been decided that there is no case to bring against Masouri. Mind you, Laurie, no case does *not* mean no guilt. Do you follow?'

She sounded like a provincial Mata Hari. I beat back my irritation, feeling guilty about my vast disinterest in the affairs of Tom Curzon and Masouri. After all, she *was* looking after my sick Stewart.

'Masouri is terribly grateful to Tom,' she babbled, while I gritted my teeth and wondered how soon I could decently cut across her prattlings to ask about Stewart. Her voice dropped an octave, so that I had to strain to listen. 'Tom never accepts anything for himself . . . just *never* . . . but Masouri is very, very influential. Do you follow me, Laurie?'

She might just as well have yelled Mafia across the wires. In spite of myself, I smiled.

'Yes. I think I do.'

'Well, Tom told him something of *your* problem.' Her voice brightened. 'You don't have to worry any more. His *friends* will be taking care of you until Stewart gets to Sicily.'

I had a sudden hilarious picture of members of the Mafia zooming in from all directions on a *Rescue Laurie* campaign.

'*And* Stewart has promised to bring both the children back to Sunnycrest.' A fretful note came into her voice. 'What Stewart has not explained is how Mario came to be with you. Didn't you say that Casilda Biagotti is back at her villa?'

'Never mind that just now, Arlene.' I tried to control the impatience in my voice. 'What about Stewart? Is he better? Can I talk to him?'

Suddenly she sounded contrite and sensible.

'Oh, Laurie, I *am* sorry. I should have put your mind at rest *at once*. Stewart is much better. The doctor said this afternoon that he must have the constitution of a dozen horses. He is to be allowed up tomorrow and, if he is as well as the doctor thinks he is, he will be allowed to travel to Sicily on the following day.' Her voice dropped conspiratorially. 'I understand he will have a *travelling companion* from a well-known yard.'

Endure it for a few minutes longer, I told myself.

'I'll switch your call through to the extension in his bedroom,' she said brightly. 'Look after yourself, Laurie.'

Hearing his deep, calm voice was even better than I had dreamed. I closed my eyes, my old trick to bring him closer. Suddenly I trembled, shaken by a wave of love that left me breathless. Wildly I clutched at control.

'You don't sound at all ill,' I said accusingly.

He laughed. 'Sorry about that. Where did I get the silly notion that you would be glad to have me once more among the quick rather than the dead?' Nobody had his deep, pleasant voice.

'Oh, but I am! It's just . . .' I made a stronger effort at control. 'I'm tired, worried, and confused. The sooner you are back in charge of affairs, the better. There's simply too much to tell you now, Stewart, but there are some things you really must know before you come to Sicily. The children and I are in Erice.'

'*Erice?*' He was startled out of his usual calm. 'What the devil are you doing there? I thought you were joining Professor Stein at Trapani?'

'When I got there today his boat had left for Filicudi where he has been doing something about the "diggings" there. He'll be back tomorrow evening, so we'll join him there, sleep on the *Più Tardi* and probably have a sail in the Mediterranean while we wait for you. I suppose that will mean a change of plans for you. I mean, you'll fly to Palermo, not Catania. Then there's a twenty-minute flight to Chinisia which is about eight miles south-east of Trapani. The airport is called Birgi. Have you got that, Stewart?'

'Yes.' There was a pause. 'Filicudi, did you say?'

'Yes, but that's not important.' I gave the receiver an impatient shake. 'Listen, Stewart. When I telephoned from the airport at Catania and talked to Arlene, I thought it discreet not to tell her that I was with a young man called Jerry Mason, who drove us from Taormina to Catania and who was a self-appointed watch-dog.'

'An Englishman?'

'Ostensibly, but . . . no. He spent the night in the garden of the Villa Casilda keeping an eye on us because we knew that both Scott and the Daltons were in the vicinity.' My voice broke, but I hurried on. 'I found his body early this morning in the garden. Someone had broken his neck.'

There was a long silence at the other end of the telephone. 'Any idea of his background?' Stewart's voice was cold and flat.

'Yes. FBI. I took his papers and posted them to New Scotland Yard, to Superintendent Lang. I couldn't think of anything else to do. The newspapers are suggesting that it was a Mafia killing.' I paused. 'Stewart, whoever killed him thought he was you.'

There was a pause. I thought that we had been cut off.

'You did very well, darling. You've done very well all along. It sounds as if the wrong member of the team is drawing the salary. The documents won't have reached Lang before we leave, so tell me all you can remember about them.'

As factually as possible, I described my examination of the contents of the wallet, but omitting the memo dealing with Gregory Stein and the newspaper clippings. That was not important.

I thought Stewart swore when I described the surveillance on the plane. I said hastily, 'I cooked their goose. It's all right, Stewart. I enlisted the aid of the *head* of the Mafia.'

'*You did what?*'

I had never heard such a stunned note in his voice.

I hesitated and decided that it would be very unwise to pursue this particular topic. Hurriedly I said, 'Don't ask any questions now, Stewart. The final thing I want to tell you is that the Daltons are here in Erice, but it doesn't worry me. My Sicilian friend has provided me with a bodyguard who won't leave me until Gregory Stein takes over. Satisfied?'

'No.' His voice was urgent. 'Darling, don't take any chances.

I still don't know very much more about Scott, but Dalton was in the Special Forces of the American Army in Vietnam . . . in the commandos. Tell your present escort that. An expert in unarmed combat isn't to be fooled with. Get aboard that boat as soon as you possibly can and don't get off it, even for a swim, until I get there. Don't try to find me. I'll find you. Unpleasant though it may be, keep reminding yourself of a few facts. First of all, there is a matter of $600,000 at stake and only one small child between the Daltons and that fortune. She'll be very dead indeed if Dalton can get within touching distance of her. He'll probably argue that you and Mario would make dangerous witnesses, so . . . need I urge you to be careful?'

I swallowed painfully.

'The next point is that if Lang and/or I take Pia back to Britain, not only will Dalton lose the money, but he and his wife will be ruined professionally and will certainly be charged with attempted fraud . . . not to mention the prospect of the gas chamber or the electric chair for Dalton. American opinion seems to be swinging back in favour of capital punishment. Mason's murder seems to carry Dalton's hallmark. He'll know that if the FBI tie him up with that through you, they'll never give up. *Be careful, darling.*'

My head was whirling. I tried to collect my wits.

'If,' I said unsteadily, 'anything were to happen to the three of us – and it won't,' I said fiercely. 'I promise you that it won't – but if something did happen to us, wouldn't it be awkward for the Daltons that they were in Sicily at the time?'

'No, not necessarily.' Stewart's tone was cruelly uncompromising.

Our talk was not turning out at all as I had imagined. 'Dalton can point to Scott, the girl Bradford/Rice or to a very dead you. Just don't give him the chance to make it you. He would be the anguished parent who failed to catch up with his child in time. Now, darling, don't panic. You've kept your head very well up till now. Lang and I will be with you soon. Meanwhile, don't overlook the danger from Scott. I suspect that, intellectually, he is a million light years ahead of Dalton. The playwright is, from all the evidence so far, a stupid crook, but Scott is a different breed. Watch out for him.'

'Pia loves him,' I said miserably.

'No doubt.' His tone was dry. 'I believe quite a few people loved Bluebeard, the Brides in the Bath murderer, Crippen and Neville Heath. Charm in a man should be viewed with suspicion.' His tone lightened, 'You are better off with a roughneck like me, darling. Now bring that bodyguard of yours here. I want to talk to him.' He seemed to ponder for a minute. 'And don't tell Stein more than you have to. He may not want to get mixed up in murder.'

'Very well, Stewart, but there is just one more thing that you should know.' Hastily, I told him about the death of the Dobermann; about the packages I had taken from Al Scott's villa –

'Where are they now?' he interrupted sharply.

'With Bruna, but she won't hand them over to anybody but me. The Inquisition couldn't make her.'

'Then *you* must make her,' he said crisply. 'I want those packages as soon as I arrive. I'll talk about that to your friend. Bring him now.'

I grabbed Pia and practically ran along the corridor to the bedroom that Benito Capocci was sharing with Mario.

He listened intently. 'Stay here with the children,' he said. 'I will not be long.'

He was back within a few minutes. 'Signor Noble is reliable,' he said. I knew that that was the highest praise in Sicily. He glanced quickly at his watch. 'Will the maid go to your villa even if you are not there?'

'Yes.' Mario's tone was definite. 'She told me she would, otherwise it would look as if she knew something about our movements. She will be there now. Shall I telephone her?'

He had lifted the telephone almost before Capocci could answer. We stood awkwardly around while he waited.

Pia wrote enquiringly on her tablet, 'Mr Scott?' I shook my head gently and mouthed, 'Bruna,' trying not to see the disappointment in the gentle eyes.

When Mario's face lit up and the first spate of Sicilian poured into the mouthpiece, Benito Capocci grinned, tapped him on the shoulder and gave him what seemed like a series of short, clear instructions. These Mario passed on to Bruna.

I took the telephone from him and said slowly, '*Buona sera, Bruna. Capisce?*'

I heard the tiny gasp of pleasure. '*Si, si, si, signorina. Capisco.*'

'*Arrivederci, Bruna.*'

'*Arrivederci, signorina.*'

I replaced the receiver with the feeling that something positive had been accomplished.

The Sicilian touched me gently on the arm. 'Let's go down to dinner, signorina. That matter will be taken care of. Let us enjoy Erice.' With an attempt at lightness, he added, 'Do you think that the goddess Venus will allow hate to conquer in her territory? To make sure she is on our side, tomorrow we will visit her temple and make her an offering. Perhaps we will sacrifice Mario.' He laughed and put an arm affectionately across the boy's shoulders. 'A father may sacrifice a son, may he not?'

For a moment Mario stiffened, struggling with his pride. Then he put his hand into Capocci's and we went downstairs like a united, happy family.

I remember very little of that evening. What remains is an impression of the darkness of the night; of the winking lights of Trapani far below to the south-east; of the amber glow of the lamps on the big tunny-fishing boats making for Favignana; and, above all, the aroma of balsam that drifted in through the open bedroom windows, washing the air in perfume.

The sense of history was all around, as if the peoples of long ago sought to give me some message – perhaps a reminder of the transience of life . . . *tout passe* . . . Many had looked, as I did, over the dark waters of the Mediterranean and feared. That elusive race, the Elymi; then the Phoenicians who had built the old, protective walls; then the Romans who had restored the ancient temple of Venus of which Virgil wrote. Standing in the darkness, I seemed to feel the comforting presences, restoring my equilibrium, giving me serenity.

With Pia almost within touching distance, I slept the deep, dreamless, refreshing sleep of a mind at ease. Towards dawn, I was dimly aware of the bedclothes being pulled back and of Pia's small body fitting warmly into the curve of mine.

The clarity of the early morning light woke me. A silvery radiance pervaded the room, sending bright fingers along the ceiling and turning the mirror into a pool of glittering light. Pia was already dressed and was standing quietly at the middle window looking out. She looked comical, for she had wrapped herself in a bath towel which trailed untidily round her feet.

The air had a knife edge and I realized with a sense of shock that Pia, unlike Mario and me, had only an overnight case, with no warm clothing. That would have to be remedied this morning.

In the end, Benito Capocci took care of that and, by mid-morning, Mario, Pia and I looked like members of a performing troupe with our matching navy slacks, thick white pullovers and dark anoraks. Thankfully I recognized that now I had an excellent excuse for burying the white handbag in the depths of my case and for substituting for it a navy shoulder-strap handbag. When I snapped the locks of the case shut, I experienced a heady sense of freedom.

The feeling was short-lived. At the reception desk, there were a number of guide books and picture-postcards showing the highlights of Erice. I picked out a book and several cards.

Mario giggled over the description in one pamphlet. 'Look at that,' he said.

'A feeling of the sweetest peace in a superhuman silence is given by the neat medieval sinuous lanes intersecting Erice in all directions, by the small flowery courtyards inside the houses, by the century-old arcades covered with moss and grey time-overlay and by the woody precipice glens. Surrounded by an almost monastic silence, just as if living out of time, Erice appears with its towers, its millenary walls, its numerous churches a suggestive and fascinating dream-town.'

'Let's have some of that superhuman silence and those

sinuous lanes,' I said cheerfully. 'But most of all I want to see the collection of Phoenician glass scent-bottles in the small town museum and also the Well of Venus.'

'No.' Benito Capocci's voice was blunt and firm. 'Sight-seeing is not possible. The last thing the Daltons want is to walk into you in a public street. That would force them to claim the child, invoke the law, make a public fuss. That would not suit them at all. As far as they are concerned, you can walk about the main streets of Erice in perfect safety. They want to make a great fuss about searching for their child, but not of finding her. Do you understand?'

'Yes, but . . .'

'The danger here is from the man Scott. I do not know where he is or what his connection with the Daltons may be. I cannot protect you against a shadow. Since he is a kidnapper, probably he will not kill. That is unlikely, but not impossible. Certainly he will not kill Pia.'

I thought of the gun and of the blood-stained handkerchief, but said nothing.

'I think his object is to get Pia back. You and Mario will be hurt only if you come in the way when he tries to snatch Pia back. Today I think I can afford to disregard the Daltons and concentrate on finding Scott. I have a helper here who is doing that. My job is to stay close to you, but we will not ask for trouble by going out into the town.'

'Do you mean,' said Mario explosively, 'that we have to stay in *all day*?'

'There isn't too much of the day left. Soon it will be time for lunch, then a siesta and then, before the evening light has begun to fade, we will go slowly down the mountainside. For you and Pia, I have bought the English game Scrabble. You will see, it will not be too bad.'

My sense of anger and frustration was almost as great as Mario's. Certainly, from the windows of the hotel, we could see as far south as Marsala and the great sweep of the coast; the vast western plain of Sicily and as far as Castellammare. We were not cut off from the tingling needle scent of the pines, nor from the fascination of watching the slow drift of cumulus on the foothills below us.

Already long grey streamers of mist were driving through the streets of the town. I wanted to feel what it was like to walk through the clouds. The thought of the golden lacework of the ceiling of the cathedral which I would never see enraged me. Was there, as the books claimed, a feeling of love in the air of Erice? I would never know.

Inwardly I cursed the Daltons and Al Scott who were responsible for the deprivation, but I turned a smiling face to the children and set them to their game, warning Mario to remember how limited Pia's vocabulary would be.

After lunch I saw what was meant by the famous mists of Erice. They settled like gauzy veils of muslin over the town, swirling along the streets and veiling the tops of the pines. The drifting nimbus gathered, scattered and reformed in endless patterns until, by late afternoon, a downy quilt hung suspended between the scarred mountain top and the sickle of Trapani.

Beneath the thickness of the white wool sweater, I shivered and saw Mario and Pia hunch themselves up against the penetrating dampness.

Benito Capocci looked worried and his conversation became monosyllabic.

'Let's have something to heat us.' I pressed the bell for the waiter. 'The children ought to have hot milk. Will you join me in a brandy, or do you prefer something else?'

'No . . . nothing. I must keep my wits about me for the road. It is bad enough in good weather. Even then it terrifies many people. But in this weather, it is more than terrifying. It is very dangerous.'

He got up abruptly, turning his collar up, as if he intended to go outside.

Almost immediately, the door opened and four Italians, the only other guests, erupted into the room, talking volubly and excitedly. Their noses were pink and drops of water glistened in their hair like diamonds.

'Mother of God!' said the younger woman explosively. 'Erice

is a ghost town, not a dream town.' She laughed heartily as though she had thoroughly enjoyed the experience. She shook herself, as if to rid herself of the dampness.

The older woman sat on a chair opposite me, drying her face with a tiny lace handkerchief. She looked cheerful and placid.

'You did well, signora, to stay indoors. We are from Livorno. It cost our poor husbands a fortune to bring us here, but it will cost them more to cure us of rheumatism.' She smiled expansively. 'Down below, there will be bright sunshine.' She looked at her damp handkerchief. 'Down below they will be wiping the sweat from their necks. Here there is only one thing to do today – drink much *liquore Ericino*.'

The men exchanged tolerant smiles and rang the bell.

One of them who had merry brown eyes and a humorous mouth almost lost in folds of fat said in tones of mock terror, 'I am a prisoner here until that mist lifts. Fortunately I am a coward, so we are all safe. I would not drive down for all the treasures of the Vatican. And you, signora? Do you stay long?'

'No. I think we leave today, but I must leave that decision to my husband. The affairs of business will not always wait.'

Before there was time for further questions, Benito Capocci came back. He beckoned imperiously from the doorway and I got up like an obedient wife, followed reluctantly by the children who had now completely succumbed to the charms of Scrabble.

I thought that he looked harassed and that his cheerfulness was forced.

'Maybe we'll fall over the cliff-edge,' Mario said apprehensively. 'It is not unusual. I have read of this danger.'

'Well, it won't happen to us. We will leave a little later than I had planned.'

'*Later?* You mean earlier. It will take longer to get down.' There was a hint of scorn in Mario's voice.

'Mario,' I said crisply, 'leave the arrangements to Signor Capocci. He knows more about this than we do.'

'Good.' Capocci sounded pleased. 'Now I want you to pack

and get ready for leaving. I will go downstairs and pay the bill. Will twenty minutes be enough?'

I nodded.

'Then I will order sandwiches and coffee which, with your permission, we will eat here. There is no great hurry. My assistant, Pietru, will take the car down to Trapani and meet us at Raganzili, where the cableway ends. He is native to Erice and knows the road well. We will go down by the *funivia*. That is why we leave later. It will take us only ten minutes.'

He saw the apprehension in my face and said mockingly, 'Perhaps, signorina, you would prefer to walk down by the mule-track. On a good day that would take you only three hours.'

I did not bother to answer that.

He halted in the doorway. 'The Daltons have already left. They checked out of the Villaggio Turistico Hotel La Piñeta immediately after lunch. I had a telephone call from the hotel to inform me. So, enjoy your sandwiches. Probably they have decided that you have shaken them off.'

We did enjoy the sandwiches and when I commented on their unusual and delicious flavour, Benito explained. 'The bread is from the old town and has that taste because it is baked in ovens heated with burning orange wood. It is traditional.'

As we boarded the *funivia*, I promised myself that Stewart and I would come back to Erice, the place of love. But not by cable-car, I decided, as I felt the sway of the car in the wind and looked down into the cotton-wool depths below. I shut my eyes and pulled my anorak close about my throat.

The scent of the land came up to meet me and I thought that I could hear the mumbling of the sea.

'You can open them now,' said Benito's amused voice after an endless interval. 'We are just moving out of the clouds. Look over to your left. That is our car. Pietru has made good time. We will not have long to wait for him at Raganzili.'

We seemed to burst into the brilliance of the evening sun, as if a mighty torch had been shone suddenly into our eyes. I turned my head away from the harsh glitter of the sea to watch

Pietru's steady progress along the grey ribbon of road. Soon he would reach the last curve which would bring him to the final stretch leading into the square below.

Then an ear-splitting explosion rocked the cable-car dangerously, so that the people next to me screamed and clung to each other. My eyes were fixed incredulously on the spot where the car had been. Part of the road itself and bits of the car were spewed upward and outward like a macabre firework. The noise struck the mountainside and was flung back at us, making our ears ring. An immense spiral of grey smoke with a heart of flame shot up towards the sky.

A woman beside me screamed again and again. A man said dully, 'That car was blown up. How can a car be blown up?'

Chapter 16

As the cable-car hurtled towards the terminus, I saw the auto-mobile exploding again and again. Like a section of a horrific film being run continuously, the road fountained upwards its rain of rock and metal and human flesh.

One part of my brain registered Benito Capocci's rigid features, carved in walnut; Pia's convulsive shudder and the glassy staring of her eyes before she pressed her head against my legs; Mario's white, drained face and the way his grip tightened on Tom Curzon's gift and his father's recorder.

The cable-car was the Tower of Babel, full of strange cries and words that meant nothing.

Round and round in my brain went the words: *Not Pietru. Not Pietru. You, Pia, Mario were to die* . . .

There was a grey cloud gathering round me. I put my face in my hands but I could not blot out the picture or the words. For days I had been running away from this violence. It would go on and on until the three of us were dead.

Benito's arm around me was a band of iron.

My head cleared. It was not that I stopped being afraid, but now I knew with crystal-clear certainty that I had reason to be afraid. A known fear is never as terrible as an unknown fear. I was no longer panic-stricken. The vagueness was gone and, with it, the sense of loneliness, of being one girl against a nameless terror.

Take what you want, said God, and pay for it.

In the seconds before the cable-car thudded to a stop, I knew that I must make a choice and perhaps pay for it through-out the rest of my life in terms of conscience. For the children's lives, I was prepared to sacrifice my peace of mind for as long as I lived.

We emerged from the cable-car into a wide square where

people had stopped to stand motionless as statues, staring up towards the mountain road. Two vehicles were already racing towards the scene of the tragedy. Nobody paid any attention to us as we walked smartly towards a *taverna* on the left. Benito hesitated for a moment before pushing the glazed door.

It was a poor place, smelling of garlic, fish and rough wine. The walls were covered with fishnets and sea shells. The scrubbed wooden tables were occupied by dark, leathery-skinned men eating bowls of pasta and beans, or spearing slices of mortadella sausages or *ricotta*, the sugar-sweetened local cheese, to lay on thick chunks of bread. There was so much noise in the room that the sound of the explosion had not penetrated. There was no unoccupied table, but two men at a table against a wall got up to make room for us.

Benito Capocci spoke briefly to them and they laughed, looking at me in shy deference.

'They are from Alcamo, a village in the hills at the back of the town.' Benito said. 'I asked them to choose a wine for you, knowing that they will send over their own. Most of the men here are down from the hills to sell their wine. It is not the new wine, so they do not get very much.'

When it came, I relaxed my grip on Pia to lift the greenish-yellow liquid to a throat so dry that I could not have uttered a syllable. Faint tremors from Mario's body as he huddled against me communicated themselves to me.

Benito watched us closely. All the laughter had gone from his eyes, but otherwise he seemed his usual self, though a colder, more controlled self.

'I have ordered hot milk for the children with a dash of brandy,' he said evenly. 'It is not a child's drink, but that was not a child's experience.' To make himself heard above the din, he was practically shouting. It gave the illusion of anger.

'I must telephone,' I said. There was no phone booth. My eyes went to the instrument on the wall beside the counter. 'I must speak to Don Michle. Is it possible to telephone Palermo from here?'

'No . . . I mean, do not telephone. I must do that. There is nothing for you to do now and nothing for you to say. It is no longer a question of an arrangement between you and Don Michle.'

How had he known that? Who was he?

'But you don't understand. My fiancé told me that Eric Dalton had been a member of the American Special Forces in Vietnam. As a commando, he knew how to rig the car so that it would blow up when we were in it. He was responsible for Pietru's death.'

I thought that the men in the *taverna* were staring at me secretly.

Benito's eyes darkened.

'I understand perfectly that Pietru was an innocent victim, but,' I went on steadily, 'my duty is to the children. Now I must use every possible means to see that Dalton is stopped. I simply cannot afford to wait until Mr Noble comes.' I closed my eyes. 'I am prepared to beg Don Michle to do something about it immediately.'

At another time I am sure Benito Capocci would have laughed at the sight of a girl stamping on her conscience in order to hit back at a murderer.

When he spoke, his voice was gentle. 'You will not need to tremble before the judgment seat on account of Dalton's death. You will not need to use the gun in your handbag.' I raised startled eyes to him. 'Sleep deeply tonight. Pietru's friends stretch like the strands of a fowler's net over Sicily. Beneath it, Dalton is like a trapped bird. He will not escape.'

When he left to telephone from a more private place than the bar, I pressed Pia's head gently against my breast and spoke softly and urgently to Mario. His eyes were enormous in his pallid face.

'I have not been fair to you. I am very sorry indeed that I have got you involved in this mess. If I had had my wits about me, I would have left you with the Nivens. You would have been safe with them. But I gave you no choice. That was unforgivable of me.'

He shook his head, but I hurried on. 'Now I think it would

be better for you if we split up. Scott and Dalton are both looking for a girl with *two* children. If I have only Pia, they may be misled, but, more than that, they will certainly not take time to go after you. Signor Capocci will look after you. I will arrange it.'

'No.' He jerked upright. 'I will not leave Pia and you. I am a Sicilian. Many bad things have been said about Sicilians, but we do not desert our friends. That is our strength. If I have been a trouble to you, I am sorry. I will try not to be, but I will not leave you.' He managed a small, tight smile. '*Mush, mush . . .* you promised.' A hectic spot of colour stained each cheek. 'Perhaps I will offend you, but I must say this. Many newspapers write as if Italy was made up of gangsters, but my race was old and civilized when the people of Britain were savages and the Indians squatted in their hovels in what is now America. Uncle Tom told me that never have the Mafia, anywhere, been involved in the kidnapping of a child.'

'Oh, Mario.' I sensed his outraged pride. 'Of course no Italian is to blame. Please don't feel hurt. It is a shame that this has happened in your lovely country, but it will soon be over. And of *course* I want you with me.' I drew him forward and stroked a finger gently down his cheek. 'We'll stay together to the end.'

Benito Capocci made his way between the tables to where we waited.

'It is arranged,' he said flatly. 'The *Più Tardi* came in more than three hours ago. Your troubles, I assure you, are over. Once you are aboard, only Professor Stein and the two members of his crew will be allowed to board. I have other plans for the Daltons.' The calm voice embraced hatred.

'No!' The word came out in an explosion of horror. I was behaving like a weather-cock, but I was steadier now. No matter what the provocation, one does not condone the use of violence. With shame, I recalled my first reactions to Pietru's death.

Benito gave me a troubled glance and continued evenly. 'Even such people as the Daltons do not sleep well after such a

day. They will be afraid. A thousand times they will ask themselves if they are safe. A quick death tonight would be merciful,
but we do not feel merciful. Put the matter out of your head
now. Such talk is not suitable for you.' His tone was flat and
matter-of-fact.

We went outside, and found that a cool breeze was gusting
along the square, blowing from the Mediterranean. It was full
of the clean tang of the sea. None of us looked towards the
mountains. The people on the street walked slowly with their
heads down, moving in the time-honoured ritual of the *passeggiata*. The street lights were dim, accentuating the blackness
of the night. The children walked between us, clinging to our
hands. Incongruously, Benito Capocci carried Pia's doll.

It was a strange feeling to have only the clothes on my back
and the contents of my handbag. My debts to Arlene were
mounting.

Things had gone completely beyond me. I was grateful for
Benito's cold assurance. He made a slight soothing gesture in
my direction as if he sensed my blankness.

Half way along the street, we halted at the edge of the pavement while he went into a shop. When he emerged, he was
carrying a white plastic shopping-bag.

'This will keep you going until tomorrow,' he said. 'Tooth-
brushes, toothpaste, soap, newspapers, some sweets for Pia and
Mario . . . It is rather late to find sleeping wear. Does it matter?'

'No. You are very thoughtful.' Suddenly I was afraid to be
without his support. 'Shall I see you tomorrow?'

'It is unlikely. There is much to be organized, and it is not
good to trouble Don Michle with details. He is old and sick. The
man Scott is a difficulty.' He looked at me oddly. 'He is a true
son of Machiavelli.'

Two tears slid down my cheeks.

'Benito, what makes people do such bad things?'

'Money or power.' He shrugged philosophically. 'You have
a bad impression of the island, but it is not different from any
other place in the world. Where there are men, there will
always be the good, the bad and those in between who are

sometimes one and sometimes the other. It is the law of nature.
The priests try to change it, but they are wasting their time.
The important thing is to be strong.'

In the light from a street lamp he looked like a hawk. Absently one hand cradled Pia's head.

I sighed. 'I wish people fitted into neat little pigeonholes. It
would make life so much easier.'

In the taxi he took out a packet of cigarettes and smoked with
a preoccupied air, as if suddenly weary.

What a strange life he leads! The thought was startling and,
for the first time, I wondered if he had a wife and children. He
had been unfailingly kind and yet I hoped desperately that after
tomorrow I need never see him again.

'Let me see you smiling,' he said, out of the shadows. I made
a big effort, concentrating on the thought that each minute that
ticked away was bringing Stewart nearer.

He leaned forward and kissed me very softly on the cheek and
smiled, as if he were laughing at himself.

Gradually the sounds of the town receded. Towards the
south-east the blackness of the sky was tinged with pink and I
remembered Etna. Suddenly, I was full of a confused anger
that, in the face of what nature could do, man persisted in
inflicting pain on his fellow man. Homer's tales of the Cyclops
who devoured the smaller humans was still true today. Would
man never learn?

Uncharacteristically, Benito Capocci talked endlessly about
Trapani, about the market, about Italian film stars, about Italian
music, but never about himself.

When the taxi stopped, there was a deafening chorus of
grasshoppers and the hard slap of the waves against the harbour
wall. The perfume of the flowers was everywhere.

When he had paid off the driver and we stood uncertainly in
the light outside the harbour café, Benito said suddenly to
Mario, 'Can you imitate a sea-gull?'

The harsh, mournful sound soared in the darkness and came
back like an echo, repeated over and over again.

But Mario was not listening. His gaze was fastened in stunned disbelief on the great white shape rising and falling gently on the swell of the waters.

'You did not tell me that Professor Stein was so rich,' he said. 'Are all Americans millionaires?'

'It is a rich man's boat.' Benito's voice was unconcerned. 'In English money, it would cost – let me think – about £50,000, at least. It is a Baglietto 16.50.'

My mental picture of a converted fishing-boat faded rapidly. Did even an American professor's salary rise to such luxury?

Out of the past, Jerry Mason's voice came mockingly. *An old tub! You have to be joking!*

He had known about the *Più Tardi*! Probably he had seen the boat. I would think about the implications later.

Benito Capocci seemed to sense my confusion. 'What matters is that you will be comfortable.'

'I've never seen anything like it.'

'No. It would not be suitable for the waters around Britain. It is ideal for the Mediterranean. It is an Italian boat, the best of its kind.'

I could not tear my eyes away from the overwhelming size of the *Più Tardi*.

Pia tugged impatiently at my hand. Come on! her hands were saying.

Mario was clamouring for details.

Length? About fifty-four feet. Diesel-powered, of course. Maximum speed? Twenty-two knots. Cruising range? At least, thirty-two hours. That? Oh, the flying bridge. Benito's explanations were patient, but weary.

Outside the harbour the wind was still gusty and the sound of breaking water carried clearly in the salty air. The boat began to buck and dance and Mario let out a yell of delight when the sea-swirl changed into countless explosions of water and spray.

A light went on in the saloon, ringing the boat in a bracelet of gold. When a sailor stepped on to the deck, Benito hailed him and there was a quick volley of question and answer.

Benito cursed briefly. He lit another cigarette and walked up and down on the cobblestones, four steps one way, four steps back.

Disinterestedly, I wondered what complication had arisen.

Finally he came close to me and spoke softly so that Mario would not hear. 'I must go to Catania tonight. The police have identified the man murdered in a garden there as an Englishman, Mason, who was staying in Taormina. He was the cat that walked by itself, so they are very interested, because he was seen with a girl and two children. It would be inconvenient if they found it necessary to talk with you.' He lifted his shoulders in a shrug. 'It may be possible to get them to sniff after another scent. I do not know, but I can try. Professor Stein is in the town dining and perhaps getting a little drunk.' He smiled tolerantly. 'It is the habit of men when they have been at sea. Perhaps it would be best if you went on board and went straight to bed. In the morning the captain will have a clear head.'

He gave me the plastic bag. 'The sailor is reliable, a little stupid, but reliable. He is from the mainland, from the north, so you will be able to talk to him. Tomorrow evening, without fail, I will be back.' He bent his head to look deeply into my eyes. 'You are not afraid?'

'No.'

'Listen.' He gave the melancholy sea-gull call. The answers came back, drifting on the wind, sombre and peaceful, with undertones of ancient grief.

'Stay aboard until your fiancé comes or until I come. Already there is much police activity in the town. There may be shreds of women's clothing from your luggage in the wreckage. Maybe the people from Livorno will enquire if you and the children are safe. It can happen.'

I had a superstitious impulse to tell him to stay away from me, that I was not lucky for men, but I pushed my anxiety into a silent corner of my mind and thanked him for his help. We smiled at each other stiffly and he waited until the sailor had lowered the tiny gang-plank and each of us had negotiated the swaying steepness at a run.

I did not look back. I tried to think of something reassuring: Stewart; my apartment in Zürich; Tom Curzon's calm mind. Still I felt a slight twinge of anxiety.

The children went almost crazy when they walked into the saloon. Their excitement pleased the sailor. He beamed at them, showing every white tooth in his head. He was a man in his early fifties with a pleasant, rosy face; thick dark hair which fell in a black comma across his forehead; a stocky body with an ovoid paunch straining out of a pink cotton shirt. He padded about happily on stockinged feet, showing the children his small kingdom.

I put the plastic bag down on one of the black leather seats and wondered where the devil Greg Stein had got the money to pay for all this luxury.

The saloon was spacious, with teak-lined walls; a pale honey-coloured carpet with a pile that went on and on; a gleaming expanse of coffee table which, I discovered later, at the touch of a button, rose silently upwards to dining-table height and opened to accommodate eight people. Along one wall was a four-seater black leather banquette with a pair of matching armchairs set at right angles to it. My gaze travelled from the beautiful teak and leather drinks-container to the television set on the opposite wall and the startling compact stereo equipment. On another wall a small engraved copper plate announced facetiously that the captain of the ship was authorized to conduct marriages for the duration of the voyage.

I was impressed and worried.

Mario called urgently from the doorway. 'Come and see. It's *super*! There's a kitchen and chart-room and three double cabins and two toilets and showers and quarters for the crew and . . .'

'Slow up!' I begged and took the single step up out of the saloon. The galley on the left was a model of shining chrome and walnut Formica, with telephone, twin steel basins, a stove with two gas and two electric burner jets. It looked like a setting from a glossy magazine.

Illogically, the telephone impressed me most.

'There are nine telephones on board,' Giuseppe, as he was called, announced proudly.

Beyond was the bridge, a compact room dominated by the

flat chart table and the light six-spoked chrome wheel. On the left of the table was a padded black leather container for a whisky glass and ashtray. Beyond the curved glass window impenetrable darkness stared back at us.

Mario ran ahead down the narrow carpeted stairway, not a ladder, with its padded grab-rail on the left.

The sense of luxury was repeated in the cabins. The first one at the foot of the stairs was obviously Greg's. A book on archaeology lay on the ledge alongside the bed. There was water in the carafe and a packet of American cigarettes on an empty ashtray. Otherwise, everything personal was stowed out of sight.

The other two cabins were immaculate, with gay matching pink bedcovers and curtains. There was no sign of occupation.

I checked with Giuseppe.

'No. There are only Captain Stein, Alberto and myself. Alberto and I have cabins forward.' He waved a hand.

'Then Mario can have this cabin and Pia and I will sleep in the other one.'

An expression of extreme alarm crossed his face. 'No, no, no. It is impossible. The boy cannot have this cabin. It is forbidden. He must sleep in the big cabin with you.'

I stared at him blankly, then shrugged. Why a cabin should remain empty was beyond me, but the important thing was to get the children to bed as soon as possible. I refused the offer of coffee, said that I would see Captain Stein in the morning and smiled a grateful good night to him.

He padded softly along the corridor, switching off the light as he went.

It was almost midnight by the time I had showered and washed my hair. When I went back into the cabin, Pia and Mario were sound asleep and did not stir when I switched on the light. I glanced at the papers, but could see nothing about Jerry's murder and I realized that there had not been time for a report on the car incident.

My horoscope caught my eye. 'You have been living dangerously. It suits your ebullient temperament, but caution is required in the adventurous days ahead. Prepare for greater surprises.'

As I curled myself round Pia, I smiled in the darkness at the absurdity of imagining that anything could possibly equal the unexpectedness of the last few days. I'll settle for a little dullness, I thought sleepily, yielding to the soporific rolling of the boat.

I seemed to be wakened suddenly by a sound or a feeling. I did not know which and, when my eyes opened in the darkness of the cabin, I felt disorientated. Under the blankets I was cold and pulled Pia closer into the curve of my body and away from the chill of the side of the boat.

There was a dull, steady pounding which made the carafe on the ledge dance lightly in its stand. The wind's note had changed, and instead of the gentle roll, there was a hard Slap! as water crashed somewhere ahead of the cabin. I shot upright in the darkness, yanking at the curtain cord. Spears of water threaded the glass, silvery against the blackness.

Stunned and incredulous, I peered at the hands of my watch. Five minutes to five and we were moving at a great clip through the waters! The sea was running powerfully and I knew, from some source of primitive wisdom, that we were well away from the marsh people who tended the salt-pans and who fished for oysters and crustaceans of many varieties. Here was the place of the big boat fishers, hunting for sword-fish, tunny-fish; the place of the nobbly, tousled men whose every day began with the shadows slowly stirring above the dark line of the waters. We were on the living sea.

Where could Gregory possibly be making for during the night?

If I had found myself unexpectedly on the trans-Siberian express, hurtling non-stop towards Vladivostok, I could not have been more startled or more dismayed.

Today Stewart and Superintendent Lang were due to arrive in Trapani. I simply *had* to be there to meet them.

I was half way out of the bed before reason prevailed. Gregory Stein was certainly not going to turn back to satisfy me. Something more than a whim had brought him to port and out to sea again within the space of a few hours. I lay and listened to the night noises and thought about it.

Was he smuggling archaeological finds out of Sicily? Vague memories of newspaper accounts of laws to ensure that national treasures and finds were retained tugged at consciousness, but refused to surface. Remembering the steadiness of Greg Stein's eyes and his shrewd, alert mind, I could not picture him involving himself in such petty theft. Momentarily, I felt ashamed of my suspicions.

Rather uneasily, I considered how little I really knew of the man beyond the handsome, bluff exterior. During my one year at Northwestern, Chicago, I had enjoyed many privileges as an overseas student – the opportunity of joining the small groups that Professor Stein occasionally took on trips to the museums at Washington, Cincinnati and New York; the intimate, jovial parties that he held for a favoured few in his bachelor apart-ment overlooking Lake Michigan; the few, heady occasions when he had taken me, alone, for dinner at the Sheraton Hotel. Suddenly, I was appalled at how little it amounted to and the extent of my effrontery in imagining that he would welcome the presence of a young woman burdened with two children.

The longer I postpone meeting him, the better, I decided.

But where were we headed for?

Geography had never been my strong point, but now I lay and tried to conjure up a picture of the map of Sicily.

He could be making for Messina or for any of the places of archaeological significance before that port – Agrigento or Syracuse. On the other hand, we might be speeding in the opposite direction – to Palermo, to Cefalu . . .

I do not know at what point I became convinced that we were making for the Aeolian Islands, but the idea took root in my brain and refused to be banished.

The thought was alarming. The map of Sicily seemed to float before my eyes with the Liparis strung out across the broad expanse of the Tyrrhenian Sea. Volcano . . . Lipari . . . Salina . . . Filicudi . . . Alicudi . . . The longer I thought, the stronger was the impression of remoteness and inaccessibility.

Filicudi . . . Hadn't that been where Gregory had done the 'diggings' lately? Hadn't that been the name that had seemed to interest Stewart? Another thought tugged at my memory, but it slid away before I could capture it.

Lovely she goes! I thought, with an involuntary thrill of pleasure as I felt the boat behave well under wheel, rising to meet the seas with impeccable good manners. If only I had known how far Filicudi was from the mainland of Sicily, I might have been happy, but the thought of Stewart hunting vainly for me in Trapani was torture. It took me a long time to work out that there was nothing I could do about it.

What was of immediate importance was how I was to explain to Greg Stein the fact that I had now two children in tow and that all of us had only the clothes we stood up in.

In Dukes' Hotel in London I had preened myself on my ability to hold my tongue, but my path across Sicily had been starred with people who had listened to the saga of my woes. Grimly I told myself that my garrulousness would stop right on this boat. At the very least, I owed it to Gregory not to allow him, knowingly, to involve himself in an affair of murder and kidnapping. That, I knew quite certainly, would be anathema to the conservative and law-abiding professor.

Beyond the porthole, the quality of the light was changing slowly, from pearly grey through a lemony yellow to pale rose-madder. Shortly it would be full dawn. Light was gradually filling the cabin. There was no sign of land, but when I craned my neck, straining carefully above Pia so as not to wake her, I could see great golden blobs of light where half a dozen fishing-boats were coming out of the west. Above them, clouds pierced by shafts of light were gilded like summer apricots.

Curiosity and hunger were gnawing at me. It seemed a very long time since we had lunched in the hotel in Erice.

Cautiously I slid my legs out of the bed and eased a pillow against Pia's back to keep her warm.

I peered anxiously at Mario, but the frightening pallor had gone and his dreaming face had a look of deep contentment. For a moment I hesitated, wondering if I should leave Jerry Mason's watch/dictaphone on the ledge beside him, knowing how it would delight him. In the end I strapped it on my own wrist and, with my thick jersey and workmanlike slacks, it did not look at all incongruous.

When I closed the cabin door quietly behind me, I had to steel myself to climb the narrow stairs to the chart-room. It was a few minutes after six o'clock and the smell of coffee and bacon made me almost faint with desire.

When my head was practically level with the top step, Greg Stein's voice boomed cheerfully, 'Good morning, little Laurie! Welcome aboard! I took the liberty of looking in at you during the night, but you were sound asleep. Giuseppe told me that all of you went to bed supperless, so let's do something about that now. I'm just handing over to Alberto. I'm getting old. Two hours on the bridge is enough for me.'

The man at the wheel ignored me completely, looking steadily through the curved window, with the dour, unsmiling concentration that I had seen often in the faces of Sicilians from the south-east.

In the saloon the table was set for two, with an attractive sapphire blue tablecloth and napkins and a colourful Susie Cooper breakfast set. The room was full of a gentle sunshine which deepened perceptibly, moment by moment.

I closed my eyes and sniffed luxuriously. 'That is the best sight and the best smell I have experienced for a long time. Down with dieting.'

He laughed. 'I still remember your ability to deal with a Knickerbocker Glory. Thank God, you're not obsessed with slimming. Sailing means big appetites and we are well stocked up. I have even taught Giuseppe how to make brownies.'

The meal was unalloyed bliss. Greg was gay and put me completely at ease. Giuseppe served us huge helpings of bacon and eggs, toast and coffee.

At the end of the meal I leaned back against the leather banquette and sighed with contentment. 'Marry me, Greg,' I said lightly, 'and we'll do this all the time. I'm sure Stewart will see reason. In any case, I never seem to see the blighter.'

The silence lasted a little too long. When I turned my head lazily, he was watching me with great intentness. His gaze flickered away.

His smile broadened. 'Under the circumstances, it is very bad taste to mention a fiancé, just as I had decided that you are very pretty, even when you are not smiling.'

He lit his pipe. 'You are paler than when I saw you in Catania. Other people's children, no matter how well-behaved they are, can be very trying. A day at sea will do you good – bring the roses back to your cheeks.'

'A day? Are we bound for somewhere special or are we just cruising around? Do you mean that we are going back to Trapani tonight?'

'What a lot of questions! We are bound for the Aeolian Islands . . . for Filicudi, to be exact. I've been practically living there since I dug up some interesting fragments. I won't be doing any digging today. In the first place, it will be too hot when we arrive. We should probably make landfall at about eleven o'clock. The island is too small for a decent hotel, so it might be fun for the children if we had a picnic.'

He drew contentedly on his pipe, a big, quiet man who made no attempt to keep the admiration out of his eyes. I remembered that in Chicago he always seemed to be making fun of things; but there was nothing superior or cynical in his eyes now.

He refilled my coffee cup.

'The second thing is that I found I needed a piece of equipment before I dared proceed any further with the excavations. All archaeologists are a bit cracked, so when I found that it had arrived at Trapani, I decided to head for Filicudi again and let my labourers get on with setting it up. *But* I must be back in Trapani again tonight. We'll probably make landfall by eight o'clock this evening. I promise you a slap-up dinner, if you aren't sick to death of my company by then.'

'Greg,' I said impulsively, 'why haven't you married? You are *so* attractive.' I'll swear that he blushed.

'Perhaps I haven't found the right girl.' He pointed the stem of his pipe at me. 'Get rid of that man of yours and I'll take you up on your offer.' He glanced at my ring. 'You're not the emerald type. I'll give you a diamond like a headlamp.'

Now it was my turn to blush. I pushed myself up from the banquette.

'Do you sleep now?' I asked him lightly.

'Yes. I take over from Alberto at eight o'clock. He and I do two-hour watches. Actually, I could stay at the wheel quite happily for the entire voyage, but it is better for Alberto to get plenty of experience.' He yawned and smiled. 'I've boasted too soon. Join me on the bridge for morning coffee and don't fall overboard in the meantime.' His expression sobered. 'Put life-lines on the children. Giuseppe will show you where they are and how to manipulate them. It isn't at all the weather for them – the sea is practically like a ballroom floor – but since they are not used to a boat . . .'

He stretched, smiled and went aft, looking suddenly tired or preoccupied.

For a moment I stood uncertainly in the middle of the pleasant, sun-filled room. Giuseppe came in to clear the table and re-set it for the children, though I warned him that it would probably be hours before they awakened. He gave me his good-natured grin and went on with his task. He was still wearing the pink cotton shirt and the faded blue trousers, but the shirt had lost a button and the oval paunch was more than ever in evidence.

While I fumbled in my handbag for my sunglasses, I had a disquieting thought which made me stop abruptly before stepping out of the saloon on to the deck.

Surely Greg Stein had asked surprisingly few questions? Had he no curiosity about my stay at the Villa Noto? None about Mario or Pia? None about my sudden, unheralded appearance late at night? Did he know that we had no luggage?

There had been a kind of relief in his look when I had accepted the sailing arrangements without question. Had he imagined that I was going to yell hysterically, Take me back now, straightaway? That made me smile. He's a confirmed bachelor, I told myself comfortably. Doesn't like a woman upsetting his plans. I had better keep the children as much as possible from under his feet.

For the first time for days, I was enjoying myself. Looking back, I could see the Conca d'Oro blazing under the morning light and wondered how it was with Don Michle lying small and still under the ivory and gold hangings.

The light from the sea dappled the surface of the deck. I thought I could hear the clank of sheep bells from the land and smell on the breeze the scented shrubs and the acrid pungency of the lemon groves. The sun was setting fire to the headlands where the land was already beginning to shake with heat. Presently the outline of Sicily rolled away, the sea was vivid below me, clear as crystal and warm as new milk.

Ahead the water was dotted with sailing craft – small fishing-boats and caïques that beat up towards us with a fussy urgency.

This is what Ulysses saw, I thought with a lift of the heart.

The distant sound of singing drifted over the air from a sailing boat. Presently we were close enough to see a fat, heavy-jowled man handling the sails and a young, smiling boy standing ankle deep in fish which were still palpitating gently.

As I watched, bright silver showers of flying-fish flashed from the sea. *Angeletti* (little angels) the fishermen called them.

Giuseppe came to stand beside me at the rail.

'You'll see many more when we get near Lipari,' he said, 'and many dolphins. But I hope we do not see the Sea Maiden.' He moved away before I could ask him what he meant.

My mind washed clear of worry. Indeed it was difficult to remember what had brought me here. The puzzles and the violence of the past few days were mist-wrapped, dream-wrapped, like a child's vague fears before waking. The sun was hot on my face and head and my lips tasted of the sea. I was mindlessly, drowsily happy. I wanted everything to be silent and peaceful and never to waken out of this torpor.

It was barely seven o'clock. Above me on the flying bridge, Giuseppe sang quietly to himself. I was too hot in the white wool sweater, so I moved to the part of the deck shadowed by the doorway to the saloon, where Giuseppe had already set up a blue-topped chrome table and four chairs.

I fell asleep thinking of the Aeolians and the God of Winds. For a frightening moment before my mind yielded to the dark, I could not recall Stewart's face; but the great fangs of the dog reached for my throat; the dog's face became the pockmarked face of Eric Dalton; Pia said hoarsely, 'I've lost my handkerchief,' and Al Scott sneered, 'Give her the blood-stained one' . . .

Mario's giggle wakened me, floating down from the flying bridge with the hiccoughing gasp that was the sign that he was supremely happy. Suddenly I had a longing to believe that nothing that had happened to us was true; that I had never gone to the Green Park and tossed a red ball to a happy, laughing child . . .

The string tickled the tip of my nose and I was satisfactorily puzzled, frightened and annoyed. Mario's and Pia's faces beamed down at me and presently they thundered down the stairs to lean on my knees, their eyes shining, mouths curved in pleasure.

'Have you had breakfast?' I wanted to know.

'Yes, about half a kilo of sausages!' That sent Pia into her silent paroxysm of laughter and Mario looked delighted with his own wit.

Thank God they are resilient! I thought thankfully.

Each was dressed only in underpants and looked cool and comfortable.

When Giuseppe came to take them down the narrow ladder to the engine-room, I watched them go with the feeling that a weight had been rolled from my shoulders.

Quite deliberately I pushed all thoughts of the Daltons and Al Scott into the deepest recesses of my mind. I would think about them, I decided, when we returned to Trapani.

I lost track of time. Behind me, Greg's amused voice said, 'She died of modesty! Laurie, that outfit will be ideal when we are going back this evening, but it must be murdering you now.' He held out a pair of navy bathing trunks and a turquoise cotton shirt. 'You are not the girl I think you are if you can't manage to look ravishing in these.' He grinned widely. 'I can't claim that we'll look like twins.' He was wearing an identical outfit with not even the addition of a pair of espadrilles. He looked sleepy and content and I felt the warm rush of affection that had marked our relationship at Northwestern.

Impulsively I said, 'Oh, Greg, I do love you! You are so *good*.'

A shade seemed to come down over his face. Almost abruptly he turned away. 'Coffee on the bridge in fifteen minutes. That's an order.'

'Aye, aye, sir!' I went quickly past him and down the stairs to the cabin, wondering what devils were plaguing my old friend.

When I looked in the long mirror behind the door in the cabin, I wanted to giggle like Mario. Stewart would definitely not have approved.

I would have been a fool if I had not recognized that I looked very attractive. My hair was like burnished copper above the turquoise of the shirt. I had tied the ends of the garment in a loose bow high under my bosom and even my worst enemy would have admitted that waist and legs were *good* . . . probably more than good. Satisfied, I went up to join Greg.

A man does not need to tell a woman when he thinks she is beautiful. Greg and I smiled at each other above the thick coffee mugs and I recognized that we were back again on the old sweet relationship.

He slid back the teak doors on the right-hand side of the room and showed me the bewildering array of switches. Their complexity terrified me. He showed me also the collection of charts, explained how the radar system worked, the gale warning system . . . and I said dreamily, 'Yes, Greg' . . . 'No, Greg' . . . and didn't understand a word of it . . . and was blissfully happy.

Shortly before ten o'clock, I padded into the kitchen and helped Giuseppe to assemble our picnic lunch.

'We'll buy fresh mullet in Filicudi and smoke them on sticks over a little fire,' he explained, as he packed anchovies and lettuce, cold chicken legs, hard-boiled eggs and bottles of wine.

He glanced down at my bare feet. 'Shoes,' he said firmly.

'There are no smooth pavements in Filicudi. It is a harsh, wild island, very bleak, like all the Liparis. At school we were told that the Roman emperors and then the man Mussolini used to banish political prisoners there.'

A light broke. 'Didn't the present Italian government send sixteen of the Mafia bosses there . . . deport them, to live there under police surveillance?'

His face closed up and he was very busy, easing into the basket one of the white, sausage-shaped cheeses with the salty flavour called Provoletta, made around Ragusa. Evidently, any discussion of the Mafia was taboo.

Feeling a little rebuffed, I went to join Greg on the bridge.

'How far are we from the mainland of Sicily?' I asked.

'About forty kilometres. I've been here oftener than I can remember, but I still get excited when I see that beautiful rugged coastline. Have you ever seen more luscious, rioting vegetation? Filicudi's ancient name was Phoenicusa, because of its fern vegetation.' He pointed ahead. 'Just look at the colour of that sea.'

I had never seen anything more beautiful in my life. Sometimes the water burned green as emeralds, but close to the rocky shore it deepened from a cloudy azure to a blue so intense, so brilliant, that the arching sky above the cone of the island seemed pale by comparison.

Close to the water, above a tiny suggestion of a harbour, was a small cluster of white and pink flat-topped buildings. Directly behind them, the land climbed the hill in a series of shallow, man-made terraces, so that our approach to Filicudi was like coming to the foot of a vast green stairway.

'I can't understand why the guide books dismiss Filicudi as uninteresting,' I protested.

Greg looked pleased. 'It certainly isn't uninteresting. For the average tourist, there is the wonderful legendary grotto, called the Sea Ox. There's the lighthouse, if you like that sort of thing, and excursions to the two small islands called the Elephant and the Rock of Fortune. What interests me and I imagine would interest you is the prehistoric Bronze Age village at Capo

Graziano.' He smiled. 'What interests Giuseppe is that it is famous for its lobsters.'

He spun the wheel.

'Aren't we landing there?'

'No. I brought you in close simply to have a look at the place, but we'll go ashore close to where I've been carrying out the excavations.' I had an impression that he looked down at me swiftly. 'We will be near a magnificent seventeenth-century Tuscan-style farmhouse, an architect's dream, but don't raise your hopes. We are not on visiting terms. It houses the Mafia bad boys, the big bosses from Italy and America. I've often talked to them. They can wander around freely, but there are some pretty tough carabinieri around, whose sole job is to see that their guests don't go on a voyage.' He looked grim. 'We don't want to tangle with them.'

Mario tugged at my hand. 'Would you mind putting some oil on my back before we go ashore?' he asked.

'Of course!' I hurried after him to our cabin, anxious not to miss the approach to the island.

Almost roughly, Mario pushed me into the head and locked the door. We stood squeezed up in the narrow space, staring at each other.

The flicker of excitement in his eyes showed up clearly in the shadowy light.

'There's something funny going on,' he whispered. 'I found a bug in the cabin, on the top of the lamp at the head of your bed. But that's not all. Fitted into the chart table behind those teak doors is a CASMS computer.' His eyes bulged. 'It must have cost a *fortune*.'

My blood was hammering in my veins. I swallowed nervously.

'Besides, I looked in the picnic baskets. There's food in one all right, but the other has men's clothes and laser beam equipment. *Laser beam!*'

Chapter 17

'I haven't the faintest idea what you are talking about.' I edged him round in the confined space and reached over his head for the tube of sun-tan cream. 'Haven't laser beams something to do with painless dentistry?'

He wriggled impatiently under my hands. 'That's enough. I don't burn. I simply wanted to talk to you. Yes, they do have a connection with dentistry, but they are used for lots of other purposes.'

He twisted round to face me and his face was troubled. 'I know you were a bit amused about my CASMS case, but that manual is *super*. I've learned a lot from it and studied all the diagrams and the apparatus. There's a bit about recent discoveries – really an advertisement put in by the makers.'

'Mario – ' I tried to keep my voice calm and patient – 'this is *not* the moment to discuss your one true love. Please let's go. Professor Stein will be furious if we keep him waiting.'

His face set in determined lines. Rather to my amusement, he backed against the door, as if he meant to hold it like a fort.

'Miss Grant,' he said earnestly, 'you simply must listen to me. When I was staying with Aunt Arlene at Sunningdale, I remembered reading that an English electronics firm had made experiments with laser beams at Wormwood Scrubs jail. By directing a beam on to a chimney or tower, a man outside was able to speak to a man in a cell inside. It caused a fuss because it was a big security leak. They were able to send messages to contacts inside the prison and, since the laser beam was only half an inch in diameter, there wasn't much risk that it would be seen.'

I stared, feeling completely out of my depth.

Greg Stein's voice bellowed from the top of the stair, 'Hurry it up, Laurie! Bring the oil with you.'

Distractedly I looked at Mario and wondered desperately what it all meant.

'But wouldn't it be dangerous? And wouldn't it need very elaborate equipment? And what on earth could Professor Stein possibly want with laser beam equipment? Something to do with the "diggings"?'

'No ... nothing to do with the "diggings". Yes, it's dangerous, particularly to eyesight. That is why I am sure that it has nothing to do with the "diggings". It *does* need elaborate equipment, but I am sure that is already there.'

'*There?* Where?'

'Where the Mafia bosses are being kept . . . at the Tuscan farmhouse. Some prisoner in there already has the equipment he needs – it is very simple – and he can speak along the beam to Professor Stein.'

'*Professor Stein!*' I sat down abruptly on the toilet seat. 'You think he is going to take one of the members of the Mafia off Filicudi today?'

'Yes. But what I am wondering is – *what is to happen to us?*'

Now the empty cabin made sense and I remembered the hollow ring which I had fancied I had detected in Greg's welcome to me. My hands went distractedly through my hair. Mario watched me anxiously.

'I can't believe it,' I whispered. 'Professor Stein *can't* be a member of the Mafia. Why would he become involved when he is so wrapped up in archaeology?'

But I was remembering the opulence of the *Più Tardi* and that an FBI agent had carried in his wallet a brief history of Greg Stein's career and publications.

Remember the gun, said the dead voice of Jerry Mason.

Why had Jerry carried a gun on a peaceful archaeological holiday? He had to be investigating Greg Stein!

I got unsteadily to my feet, gave Mario a wan smile and said with more bravado than conviction, 'Let's go, partner! Forewarned is forearmed. We'll keep our eyes open. I don't think my friend is planning to *shoot* us. If he is, I have a little piece of cardboard that may cut him down to size.' I hesitated with my hand on the door. 'I haven't the faintest idea about what is going to happen, but one thing you must promise me – if I tell you to do something, don't argue, but do it at once. Agreed?'

'Agreed!' His eyes were dancing with excitement. Obviously he had already lost sight of the danger, and now the adventure of the situation was in the forefront of his mind.

'Just a minute, Einstein!' The dark eyes laughed up at me. 'Does this laser beam work in daylight or does it have to be dark?'

His face fell. 'I don't know,' he said reluctantly, like an Honours graduate who had just been told that he had failed his final examination. 'I think, but I don't know, that it would be better to use the equipment in daylight. There would be less chance of the beam being seen.' His face crinkled in a smile. 'Isn't it *exciting*?'

I swallowed and said 'Yes,' rather drily.

When we got on deck Greg Stein scarcely glanced in our direction. He smiled absently at me. 'Like a cigarette?' he enquired, obviously forgetting that I had never smoked. He did not wait for a reply, but hustled around, yelling directives to Alberto, who was at the wheel, and to Giuseppe who, looking as amiable and untidy as ever, was holding on to Pia with one hand and steadying the two baskets between his widespread feet.

Three rush hats, such as the country people wore, lay on the deck just beyond the entrance to the saloon. Greg Stein waved a hand imperatively towards them. 'They are not Mr John models, but they'll protect you from this fiendish heat. Put them on, Laurie,' he commanded.

In the end, I had to carry Pia's and Mario's headgear until we got ashore, as they were almost eclipsed by them.

Landing was surprisingly easy. We had gone, Greg informed me, about one-eighth of the way round the island, hugging the shore. I was alarmed until I was told that the water was very deep and that we would be able to anchor close to the land.

Further out, a big fishing-boat went chugging past, heading towards Lipari. Several of the men leaned over the side and called to us, but the wind carried the sound away.

When the chugging of the fishing-boat had died away, the silence was profound, broken only by the lapping of the waves against the rocks and by the dry rustling of the ferns which seemed to grow everywhere. I could make out a coarse type of grass, patches of clover and wild sea fern and, opposite where Greg obviously intended that we should land, billowing lines of foliage which crept upwards towards what was too small to be called a forest and yet was more than a large clump of trees.

'I'll get the anchor ready,' yelled Giuseppe, and the children scampered after him.

Greg seemed to be everywhere at once, but, almost effort-lessly, Alberto berthed the boat close in, where the rock shelved and the water was so clear that we could see the silver darting of tiny fish far below.

There was a faint bloom over the sea towards Sicily, but here the stillness of the morning heat was a blinding, golden veil.

'This is where the old Greek traders came,' said Greg contentedly in my ear. He put an arm affectionately around my shoulders and I told myself that I must be sun-crazed to imagine that he had any part in Michle Spina's set-up.

We went ashore in the rubber dinghy, an experience which I found alarming but which the children enjoyed hugely. Looking at Mario's happy face, I asked myself rather dazedly if I had imagined our talk in the head.

The yellow eyes of a goat followed our progress up the narrow strip of stony beach. Alberto had remained on board, but Giuseppe strode ahead carrying the baskets and was greatly hindered by Pia's clinging hands.

We threw ourselves down on a stretch of dry, sweet-smelling herbs. Somewhere behind us frogs shouted at us and the solitary goat peered at us from behind a bush. Under the shadow of the rocks, the water was almost purple, but back towards Ali-cudi the bloom on the sea was changing until it looked like mist.

'I hope we don't see the Sea Maiden on the way back,' said Greg uneasily. 'But if we do, Giuseppe knows the words.'

The two men laughed.

'Explain,' I said drowsily, my feet on fire, but my shoulders cool against the herbs.

Giuseppe went off to try to buy mullet or sea-perch.

'She's a woman who appears out of the water, alongside your boat. It's really a Greek legend. According to the fisher folk, she leans towards you, her hair streaming down over her shoulders and she always calls out the same question. 'How is it with the great Alexander?' It is equally fatal not to reply or to say that he has been dead for thousands of years. If you do either, her grief is terrible and she is said to stir up the sea against you and wreck your boat.'

'Good grief! What's the password?'

Greg grinned. 'Just say "He lives and reigns still." Got it? Then she'll be quite content, give you a beaming smile, sink back into the sea and you can be sure of a fair wind until you get to port.'

I came out of my reverie, sat up and said, 'I'm slacking. Do you want me to set out the vittles?'

One corner of my mind registered that there was now only one basket beside the bush.

Greg glanced at his watch and down to where Pia and Mario were splashing in the waters creaming along the rocks. 'Leave it for a bit. By the time Giuseppe does his bargaining, it will take him fully twenty-five minutes to get back here.' He appeared to hesitate. 'Leave the children here. They'll be perfectly safe.'

He put two fingers in his mouth and gave a piercing whistle which brought Alberto to the side of the *Più Tardi*. 'I'll fetch him and he can make sure that they don't drown each other. You and I can stroll up and have a look at the "diggings". Incidentally, you'll be one of the very few to get a look at that famous pleasure house for the élite of the Mafia. Scared?'

He was laughing at me.

While he was gone, I tried to collect my thoughts. If Mario was completely wrong about Greg Stein, then I was wasting a beautiful day in foolish imaginings. If, on the other hand, the American really was a member of the Mafia and really was engaged in a rescue operation, had I anything to fear?

Now it looked to me as if Benito Capocci had passed the word to Greg that he had to take us to Filicudi and to ask no questions. However high up he was in the echelon, he could scarcely ignore Michle Spina's card. Better to take no chances. I would show it to him at once.

I stood up as he approached, looking alarmingly big and confident. Behind him, Mario waved to me rather uncertainly.

Fumbling in my bag, I drew out a Kleenex and let Michle Spina's card float to the ground. Greg bent to retrive it. Carelessly, I handed it back to him.

'That practically gives me the freedom of Sicily,' I said lightly. 'I met that old boy at a party in Taormina. A case of mutual attraction, I think. Pity he's so old! I got that whiff of wealth and authority about him that women adore. I know I fell for it and he came up trumps by giving me his card.' I took the slip of cardboard back and studied it wistfully. 'Maybe it will come in useful, who knows?'

Did I imagine a controlled anger beneath that smiling face?

He laughed with a good deal of affection in the sound and put a hand under my elbow to help me over the uneven ground. 'You don't need anybody's card, Laurie. One look at that dear little face of yours and any man would be tumbling over himself to help you. I know that I'm just one of the many suckers. What was that old song? "If you're ever up a tree, send for me!" '

' "Friendship!" ' I chanted. ' "It's friendship!" '

He had his arm round my shoulders as we climbed the slow incline of the hill among the trees and we sang the famous Judy Garland song together. The path was rough and stony, but it was cool and peaceful under the tall pines. Greg strode along confidently although there was no path or crosstracks, only an occasional scuffing of the dusty surface to suggest that the way had been used on other occasions.

He had become quite verbose, as if his brimming good humour had to be expressed in words. Shafts of sunlight slanted across his close-cropped brown hair and showed up the rich tan of his big, jovial face. He looked exactly as he had looked that day in Washington when he had pointed out to me the fine points in Dali's *Last Supper*. Now, as then, he was excited and voluble, full of his subject.

'Tread carefully, Laurie,' he boomed, 'for you are treading on history. This place is a good example of how each of us may have our little day and then fade away.' Once again he was the professor trying to light a fire in the hearts of his students. 'We know a great deal about Capo Graziano culture during the Early Bronze Age. You've seen enough of Filicudi to realize that there are now very few inhabitants, not many more than two hundred and most of them are leaving because they don't like the presence of the Mafia deportees. Well, during the prosperous Early Bronze Age, just think how favourably placed the Aeolian Islands were when trade was focused on the Mediterranean. Lipari, Filicudi, Salina and Panarea probably monopolized the trade that linked east and west at that time. Here at Filicudi was the furthest point reached by the Aegean navigators. Here they would take on the raw materials brought by the Aeolian ships and leave in exchange the refined products of their arts and craftsmanship.'

'Yes, Professor,' I said meekly, ashamed that I was not more interested.

He swept on as if I had not spoken. 'How do we know this? And why has the entire Aeolian civilization of the Late Helladic period been called the Capo Graziano culture after the village over there?' His arm swept vaguely to the left. 'Because,' he continued triumphantly, 'of the large amounts of fragments of Aegean pottery found in the villages. Aegean products simply had to be widely diffused in the Aeolian villages.' My silence communicated itself to him. 'Here endeth the lesson,' he finished penitently. Almost apologetically, he added hurriedly, 'Do read an authoritative work. I'll recommend one.'

While he had been talking, my confusion had grown. Only a fool would have doubted the genuineness of his enthusiasm and knowledge. His academic background was, I knew, impeccable. Historically and scientifically, there seemed to be excellent reasons why his studies should be concentrated in

Filicudi. It would have been tragic if he had not been allowed to pursue them here freely. Had this been part of the Mafia bait?

Had Mario and I lived in such an atmosphere of intrigue and suspicion during the last days that we saw menace in every shadow and threat in every harmless gesture? Was I imagining that Greg could be corrupted by the offer of the freedom of Filicudi?

I sighed. He was the kind of enthusiast who would stop at nothing to achieve his ends. Had this been his Achilles' heel for the Mafia?

He looked anxiously down at me. 'Have I bored you? Never mind. We'll have a quick look at the outside of the house – pity we cannot see more of it than that – then back for our picnic lunch.'

I watched him carefully. I would know, I told myself confidently, the minute he did something at all unusual or out of character.

Detective Grant hasn't done too well up till now, I reminded myself bitterly. I've stumbled from one ghastly situation to another. Not much control on my part.

I made a small mental vow that this time it would be different. I was intrigued rather than alarmed. Mario was correct in thinking that it was exciting to be in any way involved in a jail-break, which, if it succeeded, would certainly be the most sensational since the Germans had snatched Mussolini from the Mediterranean island under the very noses of the Allies.

For the first time I wondered which of the Mafia deportees would be in the cabin next to mine on the return voyage. Was there any special reason for the timing of the attempt? Any special reason why he and not one of the fifteen others had been chosen for release?

A memory of the frailty of the figure in the high canopied bed in Palermo came unbidden into my mind. I stumbled and Greg put out a hand to steady me. The blood began to pound in my veins.

Would I travel back with Michle Spina's heir-apparent?

'What are you scowling over, Laurie?' He knitted his brow

at me, setting me a very bad example. 'I love watching your face – it is so mobile – but at times you worry me. You look so grim and it is an expression that doesn't suit you.'

I let that one pass. 'Are we nearly there?'

'Just about. Normally, the men would be in the tents out of the sun but you can bet your bottom dollar that today they will all be very busy doing nothing. When the boss is due . . . It's an old custom, not confined to Sicily.' He laughed tolerantly. 'They are good fellows who work hard and *carefully*. In archaeology, the patient plodders are worth their weight in gold. And that's just about how I pay them,' he added philosophically.

We came upon the house suddenly. The trees ended abruptly at a rough but fairly wide road that stretched in the direction of the little hamlet of Filicudi on the one hand and, on the other, curved round an extensive clearing to disappear somewhere behind the house.

The silence was intense and the house sat serenely in its rustic setting as if it had grown out of the soil. Beyond the delicate tracery of wrought-iron gates, at least twelve feet high, could be seen an enclosed courtyard where two dogs were asleep twitching gently in the heat. The right wall of the house ended in a piazza with a terrace, where pots of massed flowers made a river of colour against the grey stonework. On the left was a ninth-century basilica and a bell-tower.

I turned a bewildered face to Greg who had followed the direction of my gaze. A Florentine building!

'The bell-tower is intriguing. It is said to have been built at various times between AD 1000 and 1645. I am told that there is a replica of this place somewhere in Florence but I expect it was the other way round. This is a replica of the Tuscany farmhouse. Intriguing, isn't it? I keep promising myself to go and have a look at the Florentine one, but I've never got around to it.'

I just bet you have, I told myself exultantly. That gave you the blueprint for this one and helped you to carry out this particular plan. I was full of a reluctant admiration.

'Have you seen inside this one?'

'No. I believe it is quite magnificent, all oak beams and ancient vaulted stone arches. The place is a warren of cellars. I understand that there are twenty-six rooms in use now and about ten more are being restored. All mod. cons., of course.' He smiled.

'So the deportees are not exactly roughing it?'

'No, scarcely. It's an odd set-up. Remember that they *are* deportees. They have a fair amount of freedom, but are under constant police surveillance. They are on Filicudi for the rest of their lives and don't forget that Adam and Eve got fed up with the Garden of Eden.'

He glanced at his watch. 'I want to have a word with the men. They will be sour if I keep them from their siesta. I expect Pia and Mario will be equally sour if we don't eat soon. Besides, I promised you a dinner in Trapani tonight, so we must not be too late in leaving. The *Più Tardi* must feel like a ferry-boat these days. We'll be heading back for Filicudi again at about four o'clock in the morning. After that, the poor old girl will get a rest. I'll probably stay here for at least a couple of weeks.'

My jaw dropped. Without thinking too deeply about the matter, I had assumed that if Greg snatched the Mafia boss from the farmhouse today, he would be getting back to Sicily as quickly as possible and finding some excuse for getting away from the area immediately.

Instead, he was behaving exactly as I would have expected an innocent Professor of archaeology to behave – courteously taking the children and me back to Trapani and then returning to pursue his own interests.

I gave up.

We sauntered along the edge of the road to the corner of the clearing almost directly opposite the west wing of the house. Three small khaki-coloured tents were set well back from the edge of what looked like an over-sized shallow grave. Two men, burned the colour of teak, were crouched in the hollow. They were brushing the surface of the soil gently with what looked like miniature brooms. One man was in the act of entering the nearest tent. He gave us a blank look and let the flap of the tent drop behind him. A fourth man was fiddling with an instrument, squinting along it into the darkness of the trees. There were several other instruments around, looking to my uninstructed eyes like theodolites, or surveyors' instruments.

Keep your wits about you, said the dead voice of Jerry Mason.

I switched on the wrist dictaphone. It was exactly one o'clock.

Greg Stein clicked his tongue in exasperation. He strode forward, gave the man a slight, friendly push out of the way and said irritably, 'Not that way! How can you possibly see anything against the dark background of the trees? You need light. Swing the instrument round and take a bead on . . . say . . . the house would do.' He was amazingly quick and deft for a man of his size. 'Make it one of those upper windows. That reflects the light beautifully.'

Presumably the window in question was the one just below one of the chimney stacks.

He squinted into the instrument, his big hands moving as lightly as butterflies over the mechanism. He had quite regained his good humour.

'Everything's fine now,' he announced with marked satisfaction. 'By two o'clock, it should be perfect. It's a pity that I am planning to leave by three o'clock at the latest, so I will have to leave you to carry out instructions on your own. But you know what to do.' He shot the man a winning smile. 'As well as my friend, Signorina Grant, I have two children aboard, so I simply must let them sail round Filicudi before we leave. Please carry on.'

The man looked stolidly back at him.

Casually I had followed the line from the instrument to the chimney. Between the bell tower and the house a single tree broke the smoothness of the lawn. The laser beam cut across the topmost branches and for about six inches could be faintly seen against the darkness of the foliage. Happily, Greg Stein was quite unaware of this.

Indifferently I scrabbled in my shoulder bag, eased Jerry's gun out of the way and pulled out my powder compact.

'Heavens! Is there a good hairdresser in Trapani? Put a dozen brass rings round my neck and I would look like one of those native women from the Fiji Islands.'

He ruffled my hair a bit more, grinned and said, 'You look beautiful, but hungry. I don't need to ask the men about any world-shaking discoveries. If there had been any, they would have announced them as soon as we stepped out of the woods.' He pretended to look doleful.

As we walked away, he called back over his shoulder, 'See you at the same time tomorrow. Better get that instrument packed away out of the sun. It won't do it any good to be left standing there.'

I switched off the dictaphone.

At least, I did not have to make any pretence about my enjoyment of our picnic. The sea smell was heavy around us, mingling with the sweet scent of the land and the acrid perfume of the orange-wood fire that Alberto had built on the shore. He brought us grilled mullet, spitting and crackling from the heat, and white wine which he had cooled by suspending the bottles from strings till they lay in the cold depths of the shadowy pools under the rocks.

He was a dour, unsmiling man who had shown no special interest in the children, but now he brought an enormous conch shell, the nacreous interior flushed with pink and the faint jade of summer seas. Holding it carefully in both hands, he lifted it to Mario's ear to let him hear the eternal surging and pounding of the sea.

The boy listened dreamily, his head cocked to one side and his eyes fixed gravely on Pia's face.

Alberto turned and placed the shell to Pia's left ear. Her eyes were fixed questioningly on his calm face. I saw their expression change. The eyes darkened until they seemed to be all dilated pupil. The feathery eyebrows lifted as if in deepest wonder and incredulity. Like a shadow passing across the sun, fear grew and grew in the gentle eyes until finally she jerked her head back and hurled herself away from the shell and into my arms.

My heart was jerking like a trip-hammer. Pia burrowed

against my neck and I crooned inanely, 'Silly baby! Silly baby! It was only an old shell.'

Alberto looked alarmed and Greg Stein said impatiently, 'What on earth triggered that off? Did the shell have a sharp edge that hurt her?' He took the conch shell from the sailor and ran a finger experimentally along it. 'I can't feel anything.'

He drew his arm back as if to hurl the shell into the sea.

'No! No! Please let me have it.' I passed it to Mario. 'Please take good care of it for me,' I said, wondering what kind of imaginative fool I was.

To change the atmosphere, I said brightly to Greg, 'Where's Giuseppe?'

'On board, I hope. It's his turn to keep watch. Conditions are ideal here. No reason why anything should go wrong, but that is precisely when it pays to be extra vigilant.'

He lay flat on his back on the herb-strewn grass at the edge of the beach, puffing contentedly at his pipe though I warned him that in that position, it was liable to choke him. 'I think poor Giuseppe is a bit off colour. He wasn't his usual, chatty self this morning.' He rolled over and looked up into my face, smiling impishly. 'I'm a selfish devil. As long as Giuseppe's vapours allow him to remain on his feet till we get the *Più Tardi* back to Trapani, I'll willingly pay for a witch doctor for him. I warn you, Laurie, I'm a hard man.' He hesitated and an unexpectedly sombre look darkened his expression. 'Maybe if I were completely honest, I would say that I am a bad man.'

It was a dangerous moment. I was swept by a wave of warm affection for this man who had been unfailingly kind and helpful to me. The grey eyes had an odd look of appeal.

'Well,' I said briskly, 'it's never too late to mend your ways. Remember what St Augustine wrote: "Do not despair: one of the thieves was saved. Do not presume: one of the thieves was damned." Now you know!'

'Laurie, you delight me! You've got a salty word for every occasion. Thank the Lord you are about to be happily married, or bang would go my bachelor status.' He turned to Alberto.

'Better get aboard now. I'll take you out and we'll leave at three o'clock.'

When he came back, he brought two plastic water carriers with him. He flung one to Mario. 'We are going to take a walk,' he announced cheerily. The sunlight showed up the warm gold of his skin and the crisp hair, silvery grey at the temples. The eyes were clear and candid but there was a flicker of excitement in their dancing glance. He moved like a great golden cat over the stones of the beach, picking his way fastidiously.

'Is there a well?' I asked.

'No . . . a couple of springs, with water as sweet as a grape, as Giuseppe puts it. A local legend has it that if you drink from one of the springs, you will always return to Sicily.' His great laugh boomed out. 'I've drunk so much of the stuff by now that I think I must be destined to become a permanent resident.'

'Not at the farmhouse, I hope.' I could have bitten my tongue out the moment the words were over my lips.

'There could be worse fates,' he said lightly, but I thought that his glance lingered on me longer than was strictly necessary.

My recklessness was not quite under control. When he pulled me to my feet I hesitated, looking doubtfully towards the *Più Tardi*. 'Maybe I shouldn't go,' I suggested. 'I'm very hot and sticky. Maybe I should have a swim. The water looks heavenly. Between them, Giuseppe and Alberto can haul me aboard.'

How could I ever have imagined that his face was open and friendly? The eyes were cold as northern seas and the smiling lips had thinned, making his features seem all at once coarse and forbidding. He looked silently down at me.

To steady myself, I put my hands against the strong barrel of his chest and felt his heart beating steadily against the rib cage. With forced provocativeness, I said, 'Do I go or stay? You make the decision.'

Unmistakably, his features relaxed.

'Beware the anger of a patient man,' he quoted with mock sternness. 'Come on! Of course, I want you with me. I hate to admit it, but being a bachelor can be a pretty lonely business at times. I have no intention of letting you out of my sight until I have to, so resign yourself.'

We began to wade through the ferns walking in single file behind the American who was obviously making for an easier path among the trees.

By Jerry Mason's wristwatch, it was five minutes past two. Operation Jailbreak had begun.

Pia was close behind Greg Stein, with Mario a few paces ahead of me. The ferns brushed against our legs, making Mario protest that they tickled, but it was obvious that he enjoyed the sensation.

I did not. 'Look!' I said to Mario, pointing to the thick viscous drops hanging from the underleaves of the ferns. 'We used to call those "the devil's spittle". Ugh!'

It was a relief when we reached the clearer ground beneath the trees. From the dreamy coolness of their shade, we could see the waters dimpling and flashing in the sun. A small boat crept along the line of the horizon, looking lonely and frail against the great sweep of the sea.

An explosion of sound brought my head up alertly. There was a silvery flash above the sea and a great tail of white foam stretching like a broad ribbon towards Palermo.

'The weekly hydrofoil!' Greg boomed over his shoulder. 'It is making for the hamlet. It usually brings a few tourists, but most of them feel they are uncomfortably close to nature and are glad when it is time to leave.' His tone was pleasantly contemptuous, but I had the feeling that the glimpse of the hydrofoil had pleased him.

Would the presence of the tourists on the island and their wanderings muddy the picture for Alberto who was, I was convinced, at that moment manipulating the CASMS computer?

'Do you ever get helicopters here?' I called to Greg.

'Oh yes! Regularly once a week, but quite often well-heeled tourists who are too lazy to see Sicily on their own two feet hire one to give them a bird's-eye view of the islands. We had one a few days ago . . . yesterday, as a matter of fact . . . yes, it was yesterday. I believe that it flew so low over the island that every bird must have had a heart attack. It will be weeks before the fish come close inshore again.'

Who told you that, Greg? I asked him silently. *You were heading back to Trapani then. Of course you could not drop the bugging devices before yesterday. Or rather, your fellow conspirators could not. They did it from the helicopter.*

A hilarious picture of one of the metal sensors dropping on the head of a *carabiniero* drowsing in the heat, floated before my eyes.

As I placed one foot automatically before the other, my brain was wrestling with vague memories of my talk with Mario as we had left London behind en route for Rome. Distastefully I recalled his explanations of the research carried out at the American Combat Development Command outpost at the tightly guarded United States Army's experimental station at the Hunter Ligget military reservation. Mario had talked with an embarrassed smile of sensors disguised as animal droppings and of the Acousdid, a sensor which picked up human speech. These were dropped in trees.

Involuntarily my eyes swept upwards.

I had no longer any doubts that the approaches to the *Più Tardi* were seeded with sensors which would accurately predict the movements of carabinieri. My mind boggled at the probable cost of today's manoeuvres, but the prize was also great.

For the first time I began to feel afraid. Like an ostrich, I had buried my head in the sand, refusing to acknowledge that the snatching of an important member of the Mafia could possibly have anything to do with me. My mind had been blinkered by my sense of responsibility to the children against any thought that I might have a moral responsibility in the matter.

Now I was less worried by that than by the thought that a group of powerful men who had obviously spent a fortune planning, financing, executing such a daring exploit as was taking place at this moment, would have no scruples about crushing like a fly anyone who stood in the way of its successful completion.

I swallowed and cursed the impulse that had led to our acceptance of the Curzons' offer of the Villa Noto.

Stewart, I told him fiercely, if anything happens to these children, I'll . . . I'll . . . I'll divorce you!

Let's get married first! he seemed to say mockingly.

The stretch of water between us and the distant outline of Sicily had the high glitter of beaten gold. Beyond the tree-tops there were no clouds at all and the warm chuckle of the waves against the rocks had a homely, reassuring sound.

Lightly I touched Jerry Mason's wristwatch and reminded myself that by now Stewart and Superintendent Lang had left Fontanarossa Airport and even now might have Stromboli in their sights.

I squared my shoulders and began to sing 'When the Saints Go Marching In'.

It was twenty-five past two.

Ahead, the children were convulsed at Greg Stein's antics. The tinkle of water, falling from a series of rocky steps, sounded like the swaying music of tiny bells. Greg clowned like a thirst-crazed man crawling to an oasis in the desert. The children loved it and, in their excitement, poured more water over themselves than went into the plastic containers.

The smell of damp, mossy earth, thyme and lemon was exquisite. I drew long, refreshing draughts of the air. 'Bottle that,' I breathed, 'and the women of the world will make you as rich as Midas.'

'What a materialist you are!' He grinned and tilted my face up. 'I'm going to miss you, Laurie. Any chance of your getting tired of your Zürich businessman? Remember what I said to you in Catania? Come loaf with me! The offer still holds . . . now and always.'

His eyes were serious and compelling. Behind him, Mario was scowling fiercely.

'It wouldn't work, Greg.' I strove to keep my tone light. 'I get sore feet on islands and in the country. They are only comfortable on city pavements, but then, a lady can always change her mind.' I glanced down at my wrist. 'Isn't it time we went back, if you want to sail by three o'clock?'

'Time?' His tone was bitter. 'That's the story of my life . . . a story of mistiming. Well, let's get this one right at least.' He swung a carrier into each hand. 'Too heavy for you now, Mario. Look over there at the dragonflies.'

My throat was thick with tears. I was dangerously disarmed by pity for this big, likeable man who now felt cheated. Steadily, I looked towards the little pool. Above it, dozens of dragonflies hovered, their delicate wings glittering like mica in the quivering air. The insects were like tiny lamps, bobbing and lifting in the drifting heat. Pia put a finger up tentatively to touch them and they were gone in a whirr of iridescent wings.

The walk back to the dinghy was pleasant, with companionable silences, laced with brief references to mutual friends at Northwestern. It was a subtly demoralizing experience, with Greg once again the honoured Professor and me the gauche student, fresh from Britain and unsure of herself in an exotic culture. He was too shrewd not to be aware of the change of mood between us, though to give him credit, I do not think that he had consciously striven for that effect.

As he helped me on to the *Più Tardi*, he said briskly, 'I don't know what your chances are, Laurie, of returning to the Aeolian Islands. Just in case you are not back in the near future, I want to let you see a little more of Filicudi. You can have another look at its great metropolis and, even if there isn't time to sail right round the island, you can at least see part of it. Take the children forward. It should be comfortable there. Watch out for the Sea Maiden!'

Evidently we were to be kept on deck while we were within sight of Filicudi. The children and I were not entirely nuisances. What could be more innocent than a couple of adults and two children enjoying a sail?

Greg came to stand beside me and look into the water as Alberto took the *Più Tardi* carefully away from the rocky shelf.

It was exactly three o'clock. Operation Jailbreak should have been completed.

Chapter 18

The deep thrust of the boat through the sea threw up great snowy cascades of water that curled and feathered into droplets of light. Behind us the Tyrrhenian sea was a mass of foam. A long saffron-coloured cloud began to lift over the rocky cone of the island and the land palpitated gently in the heat, like a great heart throbbing with life. As the light slid along the rosy edges of the rocks, the island became girdled with fire.

The buck and bounce of the boat and the silence of the sea set peace like a seal on the bright afternoon.

Greg Stein drew deep lungfuls of pipe smoke and held me close in a gesture of such warm companionship that I felt the quick sting of tears behind my eyes.

As he gestured to the green arm of trees that embraced the lower edges of the hills, a silver shower of angel-fish fountained upwards almost against our faces. We were so close inland that we could make out the thyme and wild grasses clinging to the rocks.

'It is deep water all the way,' said Greg. 'We can go in close.'

For the first time, I noticed the long eyelashes and the firm, contented lines of his mouth. He looked like an advertisement for a member of the English aristocracy smoking a Dunhill pipe. The modern pirate, I decided, was difficult to recognize.

Behind us, from the flying bridge, Mario's voice came clear and untroubled, in one of his endless, soothing conversations with Pia.

Probably only the man in the cabin and I had anxious thoughts.

I stirred, pulled away from the rails and said lazily, 'I hate to leave this even for ten minutes, but I *am* sticky. I must shower. Tell me what I miss.'

He was watching the drift and eddy of the grey thread of

smoke from his pipe and gave only a meaningless grunt, but I thought that the hand holding the bowl tightened involuntarily.

'Alberto thinks I'm mad,' I continued chattily. 'I hate to be reminded that this boat depends on man-made instruments. I'm a human ostrich. I avert my eyes from that awesome array of gadgets and pretend that, in an emergency, we could row back.'

'Idiot! Your trouble is that you may have to *swim* back. Here I go, arranging to circle the island for your special benefit and you decide to spend the afternoon in the head! What's being sticky compared to this?' His arm went out in a broad sweep that embraced the perfection of sea, sky and land. His voice deepened. 'This moment, little Laurie, may never come again.'

But he made no attempt to detain me and turned back to his placid survey of the flickering patterns of light along the prow.

If for a moment the thought had crossed his mind that I was aware of the presence of a guest below, he knew that I would work out for myself the danger of such knowledge. The last thing either of us wanted was a direct confrontation with either the man or the situation. 'Where ignorance is bliss, 'tis folly to be wise,' jingled in my head as I padded across the sun-warmed boards of the deck.

Under my feet, the carpet of the saloon felt cool and slightly damp. Almost directly below the black leather banquette, the stranger would be lying on the pink-linen-covered bed, staring up at the ceiling and wondering how soon it would be before he was missed.

Conviction grew in me then that Giuseppe had taken his place and was now in the farmhouse waiting for two o'clock tomorrow when today's manoeuvre would be quietly repeated. Giuseppe's fake indisposition would be acted out in the lofty bedroom under the chimney stack, with fifteen razor-sharp brains to ensure that no guard went inconveniently close to him.

I felt intrigued, but remote from the situation, studiously averting my eyes from a problem which I knew I could not solve.

Four steps took me from the beginning of the chart-room to the head of the narrow stairway. Alberto looked up briefly from the CASMS computer to give me a grave, unsmiling greeting. The wheel, I noticed, was locked in position.

I left my sandals on the top step and went blithely down the stairs. With a small shock of surprise, I realized that I had not thought of the Daltons nor of Al Scott since we had boarded the *Più Tardi* the night before, but all of a sudden my mind was full of them.

My hand slid along the grab-rail on my left without the smallest whisper of sound. Where the stair curved at the bottom on the right was the slender black leather-covered column split to provide a final grabrail. I transferred my weight to it on the bottom step and swung round into the beginning of the narrow corridor between the cabins.

A man came out of the first head and stood facing me, his face drained of expression, but I noticed the slow curling of the powerful hands.

Giuseppe's pink shirt was as crumpled as ever and the shabby, faded trousers were snug against the curving outline of the paunch. The stocky figure and the stockinged feet were familiar, but the comma of black hair fell carelessly above the brow of a stranger.

Remember the children, said Jerry Mason and, in an icy moment of clarity I made my choice. Fear for the children made my mouth dry. I could almost hear the disapproving whirr of the wings of the Recording Angel.

My eyes went casually to the stranger's midriff. 'I see you haven't sewn on that button yet, Giuseppe,' I said pleasantly. My gaze sharpened. 'You don't look yourself at all. Why don't you lie down in the spare cabin? It isn't being used. Lock your door and I'll guarantee not to let the children disturb you.'

Something moved briefly behind the cold eyes. The weight of Jerry's gun was a comfort against my side. Unbidden, a newspaper photograph came briefly to memory. From some obscure corner of my mind erupted the knowledge that the man who had moved quietly to one side to let me pass was Giulio Moro, Mafia boss of Chicago, deported from the United States to Italy, then deported from the mainland to Filicudi.

He had his back against the cabin door and for a moment Jerry's gun swung between us.

I made myself pause to say through dry lips, 'Don't move until we get to Trapani. When Professor Stein samples my cooking, he'll probably raise your wages.'

There was a flicker of amusement and of something else in the dark eyes. I could feel them following me until I closed the door of our cabin behind me.

Knowledge lay between us with a weight heavy as death.

As I stood with my back pressed against the coldness of the white-painted metal, my chest tightened as though I would never be able to breathe again. Gradually I realized that it was the full-length mirror and not the door itself that was chilling me. I swung round and was suddenly angry at the reflection of the white face beneath the halo of coppery hair. There was something in my stance that reminded me of a small angry Yorkshire terrier that had faced up to an Alsatian.

I was obliged to swallow several times before I could manage to whistle shrilly 'Love is a many-splendoured thing . . .'

All the time I was saying fiercely, Stewart Noble, you should be here!

Under the shower, with the needles of cool water pricking my shoulders and back, I had a long, earnest talk with myself in an effort to bolster up my flagging courage. The rivulets coursing down my cheeks were like the despairing, futile tears of the Sea Maiden.

Call yourself a Scot! I said contemptuously. The Romans couldn't beat your forebears, when all the Picts had against their sophisticated weapons were a few rough staves and their native wits. Robert Burns said 'Hae faith and ye'll win through!' Well, hae faith in your own brains. This man isn't the flower of Italian breeding and intelligence. He's a jumped-up peasant with the mentality of a thug, and with as much in common with the Italian people as a louse on the flank of a thoroughbred.

The soap slithered out of my angry grip.

Every man has his price. Drive a wedge between Moro and Gregory Stein and you and the children may yet win home.

I turned off the water and whistled defiantly, 'Scotland the Brave.' After all, I still had Michle Spina's card.

The sweets Benito Capocci had given the children the night before lay neglected on the ledge in the cabin. I peeled the wrappings from three sticks of Spearmint and chewed vigorously.

When I was dressed in my navy slacks and white sweater, I carried Jerry Mason's watch back into the head and, under cover of the rushing water, played the tape over until the setting was correct.

Take the boxes, he told me. I fished the seven of them out from where I had hidden them behind Tom Curzon's case.

Outside the door of the locked cabin I halted, literally holding my breath while, as gently as if I were handling an explosive, I plugged the keyhole with the sticky mass of chewing-gum. In the intense heat, within moments, it would harden like cement.

I drew a deep breath. I was ready.

When I stepped from the top of the stairs into the chart-room, Alberto was still busy with the computer and I had an insane impulse to smash the instrument that was reassuring him that the movements of the *carabinieri* were the heat-drugged, normal movements of any uneventful day. Beyond the curved glass, Filicudi slipped past like a green island seen in a dream.

In the saloon I lifted the padded lid of the drinks-holder and pushed the gun inside, wedging it between a bottle of Chivas Regal and one of Gordon's gin. I gave them an experimental push, but there was no rattle.

Remember the safety-catch, said Jerry Mason.

Gregory Stein had not moved. I recognized the mood of almost mindless enjoyment, when the swift darting of a shoal of tiny fish or the precise, lovely angle of the rising spray was the most important thing in the world.

Fill him now, I prayed, with thoughts of Homer and of the dear, dead past. Blot out the present for him for just a little longer.

I climbed to the flying bridge where the children played

contentedly, almost submerged under the rush hats. The heat
struck up from the boards like a blow.

'Siesta time,' I said lightly. 'Mario, take Pia down to the
cabin. Lie on your beds and sleep. Remember, no talking.' My
eyes were fixed on his in desperate appeal.

'Mush-mush?' he said on a rising note of enquiry.

'Mush-mush. Lock yourselves in,' I whispered, 'and don't
open the door till I come. Promise?'

'Promise.'

When I joined Greg Stein at the rail, he bent to sniff at the
top of my head. 'You smell of sugar and spice and all things
nice. What did you use in that shower? Attar of lemon groves?
Pot-pourri of orange blossom? The sweet wind off the
sea?'

'Carbolic soap,' I said flatly, 'my unimaginative host.' I
breathed deeply, closing my eyes against the sight of the per-
ceptive grey eyes, as if I could blot out too the treacherous
memories of his kindness to me in Chicago. He, as much as the
man in the cabin, stood between the children and safety. I
hardened my heart.

There were many watery miles between Filicudi and Trapani.
No one, if I could help it, was going to make coral of our bones.
Once we were away from the island, Greg Stein, I felt sure,
would visit the cabin to reassure his guest. When he learned
that I had seen the Mafia boss, there was no doubt at all about
where his loyalties would lie. Michle Spina himself would not
have spared me. Moro would give a quiet order which Greg
Stein would ignore at his peril.

We were, I knew, not very far from the hamlet where I had
seen for the first time this morning the sweep of the great
stairway behind the cluster of white and rosy buildings. Against
three hefty males my chances of survival were slim. Once the
boat headed away from the hamlet for Trapani, Greg would go
below and I might as well jump overboard with a child in each
arm. I perspired gently.

'Hell's bells!' I exclaimed with great vigour.

He was standing on my right with his folded arms resting

lightly on the polished wood of the top rail. His body was slack with ease.

He turned his head to look at me in amazement. '*What* did you say, Laurie?'

He was as astonished and as shocked as if the Madonna in one of the little wayside shrines had leaned forward and spat at him.

'I have a problem which only you can solve.' To my horror, my voice wobbled. That made me mad. My chin came up. With apparent lightness I said, 'I've had a word with my friend, St Augustine. He really *is* worried about you, Greg.' The big frame stiffened perceptibly. The jocular heartiness of a clubman had quite gone. 'As a Protestant, I am not up in saints, but this razzamatazz character has always been a favourite of mine. He is great on reminding people that they have choices.'

'Well?' His voice was a hard, steely whip.

I touched the tiny nob of the wristwatch. Greg Stein's voice came out, reedy but unmistakable.

Everything's fine now. By two o'clock, it should be perfect. It's a pity that I am planning to leave by three o'clock at the latest, so I will have to leave you to carry out instructions on your own. But you know what to do. As well as my friend, Signorina Grant, I have two children aboard, so I simply must let them sail round Filicudi before we leave. Please carry on.

I looked up at him. The wry gaiety of eyes and mouth had been completely obliterated. He knew that I knew of his Mafia involvement.

He looked stunned. 'Where did you get that?' he asked in a terrible voice. 'How could you possibly . . . ? It doesn't mean anything.' He sounded desperate.

'I got it when you were operating the laser beam at the Tuscan farmhouse . . . when you were signalling to Moro. I got this dictaphone/recorder from a member of the FBI. It would have been only a matter of days before you were picked up.'

'I can explain . . .'

'Can you explain the sensors that will be found on Filicudi? Can you explain why a Professor of Archaeology has a CASMS set on a suspiciously expensive boat? Or where the money came from? Or why you just happened to be on Filicudi when Moro escaped? Face facts, Greg. You are finished.'

In a flat, unemotional voice, I told him about Jerry Mason. 'He is dead, Greg,' I concluded, 'so you do have a choice, but you must make it soon.'

The big, leonine head was like a stone carving I had seen once in the Arizona desert.

'FBI agents always keep records,' he said tightly.

'I have them.'

Nothing appeared to surprise him more than that.

I touched my bag. 'I have them here.'

'What do you want?'

'Safe conduct for the children and myself back to Trapani. No communication between you and Moro until we reach Trapani. That is for your sake as much as for mine. If you don't talk to Moro, he can't give you any instructions about me.' That brought a wintry smile to his lips. 'Is it a bargain?'

'Agreed.' I thought that there was relief in his voice. 'How do I know that you will not hand Mason's records to the FBI?'

'Hold that, please.' I handed him my handbag, took off the wristwatch and extracted the tiny tape. It seemed to dance for a moment on the surface of the water before it disappeared.

'There are seven tapes in my handbag. You can throw them in the sea, or keep them. It's up to you.'

His expression was unreadable. 'When I knew you in Chicago, you were such a baby, Laurie . . . a pert, pretty little baby.' There was a grim wonder in his voice. 'How could you grow up so quickly?'

As he was dropping the seventh box over the side, I said lightly, 'Don't drop my compact, Greg.'

I took my handbag from him, swung the strap over my shoulder and leaned my head wearily against his arm. 'Thank goodness that's over! Get yourself out of this mess, Greg, as soon as we get to Trapani. I won't have a happy moment until I know that you are safe. Oh, Greg, why did you do it? Surely a man of your education . . . ?

He laughed at that. 'Obviously you've forgotten Disraeli's adage that nature is more powerful than education.' He waved in the direction of the island. 'Do you think that the men in that farmhouse are illiterates? They are men like myself, who take a gamble for the sake of power and money.' He looked at me thoughtfully. 'You've set me a problem, Laurie. Provided Moro makes it, perhaps I do have a choice.'

A tiny rivulet of perspiration dripped from the point of my nose and landed on the polished rail. His choice had been made too easily, too quickly. Power and money? No. Freedom to pursue archaeology had tempted him. Filicudi had seduced him.

'For heaven's sake, let's go inside, Greg, before I melt.' Walking ahead of him was the bravest thing I have ever done. I half-turned towards him, but he was walking with his head hunched between his shoulders as though he had forgotten me. Was he thinking that his usefulness to the Mafia was probably over?

It was wonderfully cool and pleasant in the saloon. Alberto did not look up when we went in, but Greg called out 'Everything all right?'

'Perfect,' was the answer.

I threw myself down on the banquette and Greg Stein slumped in the black leather armchair just inside the door and sat looking at me with lacklustre eyes.

I lifted off the padded top of the drinks-container. 'We both need a drink,' I said wearily. 'What will it be, Greg?'

I remembered to release the safety-catch as I pulled the gun out and pointed the muzzle just above the line of his swimming trunks.

His astonishment almost made me laugh. Suddenly he was quite, quite sure that this was no game of pretence. The big hands tightened on his knees and there was a curious stiffness about the set of his neck.

Very softly I said, 'Tell Alberto to take the boat to the hamlet. I like you, Greg, but I like the children more. These bullets are their insurance. Don't make me prove that I take my responsibilities seriously.'

His face was stiff with horror. 'Don't be mad, Laurie! Think what you are doing. If you put Moro back on Filicudi, neither you nor I have a ghost of a chance. The Mafiosi are fanatically loyal to each other. We'll never leave Sicily alive.'

'There's no question of Moro going back. I made an agreement with you. I mean to keep it. Besides, I have a debt to Don Michle. I won't interfere with his plans. He saved the children's lives and mine. He can manage his own affairs. Alberto goes ashore.'

'Alberto!'

'Yes. I can't spend the voyage watching two men. If you are busy navigating, you won't have much time to get up to tricks.' I slipped the gun into my bag and said crisply, 'This is vinyl, not bullet-proof glass, so don't let out of sight be out of mind.' I glanced quickly through the window. 'We are almost there. Give Alberto his orders and they had better have the right ring of authority.' I felt no sense of victory, no satisfaction even.

Surprisingly, he laughed. 'Divide and conquer! What a fool I've been! You were right under my nose in Chicago and I was so busy trotting you round museums to look at chunks of ancient pottery that I didn't take a good look at you. I've never really seen you until this last half-hour. I could have married you . . . I believe I could have married you. But this is hardly the moment for psychological reflections or regrets.' He raised his head and called to Alberto, 'Change of plans! This will only delay us by about fifteen minutes, but we must put in to the hamlet.' He sounded good-natured and relaxed.

What worried me was that Alberto was outside my range of vision, but Greg Stein was not even looking in his direction, so I had to assume that there had been no time for the passing of any signal.

My heels were beginning to drum on the floor with nervousness, but I reminded myself that I had at least six hours of surveillance before me. It was much too soon to crack up.

The *Più Tardi* sidled up to the tiny spit of rocky landing. Greg and I stood on the deck and watched the channel of water grow narrower and narrower. An open fishing-boat came bucketing alongside to let the men stare up at us. The current pushed us steadily backwards, but Alberto controlled the boat so that we came gently to rest less than the gangway's length away from the small pier.

Alberto came to stand beside us on the deck. If he was puzzled, he gave no sign.

Greg Stein said, 'Ashore with you, Alberto! There's nothing wrong. I'll see you as arranged tomorrow. Giuseppe and I will take the boat back to Trapani.'

We watched the sailor run quickly down the gangway and elbow his way through the half a dozen people who had appeared miraculously from nowhere.

My grip on the gun in my bag tightened. I had no possible means of knowing if the people on the narrow landing were friends or enemies.

'Move aside, Laurie.' Greg Stein's tone was impatient. 'I must get the gangway up.'

'Not yet,' I said in a strangled voice. Three figures had emerged from behind a small building at the end of the pier.

Stewart, Al Scott and Superintendent Lang were coming quickly towards me.

Chapter 19

Superintendent Lang was the first to come bounding up the tiny gangway, skilfully accommodating his weight to the disconcerting swing of the frail structure. He looked very British against the flamboyant background of Filicudi. The impeccably tailored dark suit, white shirt and conservative tie reinforced the impression of authority.

How well I knew that bland expression!

Greg Stein was obviously hypnotized by the clipped British accent and the firm, courteous handshake. Lang's expression, too, gave very little away.

Al Scott came close behind him, moving confidently with the air of a man boarding his own yacht. His eyes were fixed curiously on Greg and, even in the moment that my eyes were on him, I was aware of the total good looks, the devastating charm that shone through the anxiety that had thinned his face shockingly in the days since I had seen him and robbed the eyes of some of their merriment. Much of the jauntiness had gone, but he did not look as if Superintendent Lang, or anybody else for that matter, had arrested him. A cool customer, if ever there was one!

My eyes went in puzzled query to Stewart, but, blotting out my sense of astonishment that he and the others had appeared in Filicudi, apparently out of the blue, was a great wave of love and happiness.

It was enough that Stewart was here.

The air between us danced in great golden waves that dazzled my eyes and had the odd effect of making his tall, well-knit figure seem insubstantial, like the hazy outline of a blond Viking in an ancient Norse story-book.

My heart pounded in my throat until I thought I would choke from mingled love and pride. The light gilded the down-bent head and slid along the strong, calm features.

Look as remote as you like, I thought happily, but I know that you are no story-book figure. You need human contact and you are as impatient to put your arms around me as I am to feel them.

Dizzy with happiness, I closed my eyes momentarily in anticipation of the joy of our meeting.

He inched around the group at the head of the gangway and it registered with me that somehow my observant Stewart, who missed nothing, had failed to see Greg's outstretched hand.

In three strides he was before me. 'For heaven's sake,' he said sharply, 'give me the gun. Do you want to kill somebody?'

Somehow it was out of my handbag and into his pocket before I was even aware that I had loosened my finger from the trigger.

'Everything all right?' He was glaring at me balefully – if anyone as handsome as Stewart could be said to look baleful. There was an icy alertness in his eyes. If he had any tender feelings for me at that moment, they were carefully hidden.

I stared at him, wondering what had gone wrong. There was a tightness in my chest which I was horribly afraid was the forerunner of tears. Nervously I swallowed and rubbed one bare foot distractedly against the other.

'Where are your shoes?'

I had not mistaken the irritation in his voice. My speechlessness seemed to infuriate him further. The waves of hostility were almost tangible.

Behind him, Superintendent Lang said warmly, 'That's very civil of you, Professor Stein. As you probably guessed, we came by hydrofoil, but there would not be room for Miss Grant and the children on the return trip. We are indebted to you for your hospitality. How long will it take to sail to Trapani?'

The expression of Al Scott's eyes was hidden behind his dark glasses, but the face turned in my direction was cold and disapproving.

The nerve! I thought, furiously . . .

'Are the children all right, Miss Grant?' The policeman's English voice was pleasantly unemphatic.

Not 'Are you all right?' I thought, sick with rage. These men seem to think I've been on a picnic.

During the long, tormented days and nights that I had spent in Sicily, I had not doubted for a moment that as soon as Stewart appeared, all the worry and confusion would be over. That was what love was for, wasn't it? That was what fiancés were for, weren't they?

Mine had turned away and was talking quietly to Al Scott, while Lang was taking a keen interest in Greg Stein's raising of the gangway.

Nobody seemed to be paying any attention to me.

The tightness in my chest got worse. Very forcefully, under my breath, I said the Sicilian swear word and immediately felt better.

I was very, very tired, I decided, of being pushed around. I had been harried for days, terrified almost out of my wits, had narrowly escaped death and, of the five men aboard the *Più Tardi*, not one seemed to be prepared to give me a kind look.

To hell with them! said the dead voice of Jerry Mason. *Are you a redhead or a mouse?*

I went blindly through the saloon and into the galley, slamming the door and sliding the bolt into position to lock myself in. Mechanically, I plugged in the coffee percolator and listened absently to the snoring thuds as the water heated.

What did I do wrong? I asked myself fiercely. Were Stewart and Lang angry because Al Scott had followed me to Filicudi and they had been obliged to pursue him there? No, that wouldn't do. They had implied that Scott had travelled with them in the hydrofoil.

The rolling of the boat had changed to a steady surge and dip. We were under way.

Mechanically I sipped the coffee, leaning against the cool rim of the steel sink, nursing my anger.

In moments of stress, I tend to touch up my lipstick. I did it now, noting that I would soon require a new lipstick.

Someone rattled the handle of the door. Greg Stein said urgently, 'Come out, Laurie. I want to talk to you. I don't want to leave the wheel.'

Deliberately I finished the coffee, lingering to see if Stewart would seek me out, but the minutes ticked away and finally I had to accept that he would not come.

When I stepped into the passage, I could hear the pleasant hum of voices from the saloon. At the wheel, Greg Stein was whistling quietly under his breath. The whisky glass on the stand at his elbow was half full and I thought I heard the clink of glasses from the saloon.

Suddenly I wanted to laugh. It was all so desperately normal, like any pleasant voyage on an opulent boat. There seemed something ridiculous in the thought that little more than ten minutes ago I had pointed a gun at our host's stomach with every intention of pulling the trigger, if I had had to.

He turned his head to look at me. The whistling had been a piece of bravado. His face was taut with anxiety. For a moment he watched me bleakly. I knew that he was willing me to say nothing.

Jauntily I swung my shoulder-bag and hoped that he had not seen Stewart take the gun away from me. I was reckless and unhappy, but stubbornly determined to finish the affair as I thought best.

The trio in the saloon had scarcely overwhelmed me with anxious questions. So far, the assistance they had given me had been exactly nil. My anger mounted.

'What are you going to do, Laurie?'

The one thing I had been certain of was that Stewart would bound joyously towards me as soon as we met.

'Do, Greg? Why, nothing. We made our agreement – safe conduct to Trapani for the children and myself and you and Moro could settle your differences with the Italian government in whatever way you pleased. I agreed that that was not my affair. Nothing has happened to change that. I certainly don't want Moro arrested and I don't want you arrested. That may smack of sophistry on my part, but that was the agreement.'

He was gazing at me with owlish bewilderment, as if he could not quite believe his ears. How could I have forgotten that at times he could look heavy and almost coarse?

'Maybe I am not doing you such a big favour, Greg. It looks

as if St Augustine is still pushing you to make a choice. Well – '
I glanced at my watch – 'you have about four and a half hours
to decide if you want to reject both despair and presumption.
It's up to you.'

I was turning away when he stopped me with a light touch
on my arm and a quick look towards the saloon. Only a tight
rein was keeping his panic in check.

'What are we going to do about Moro meanwhile?' he asked.
'It isn't as simple as you make out, Laurie. If I betray him to the
Sicilian police, I'll be signing my death warrant and your own
position won't be too comfortable.'

I thought about that. 'Well, he can't stay in that cabin.
Stewart Noble is an inquisitive man. A locked cabin is going to
start him asking questions.' I came to a decision. 'This has
nothing to do with the men in the saloon – nothing at all.'

Greg Stein turned back to the wheel and sucked at his pipe,
screwing up his eyes against the glitter from the water. He
looked all at once relaxed and almost happy. St Augustine was
going to have a struggle with this one, I thought sourly.

'I think it is time Giuseppe recovered and got on with his
duties,' I said. 'I'll go down and rout him out.'

I moved quietly, so as not to waken the children. Already the
chewing-gum had hardened in the lock. Whether it would have
kept Moro imprisoned in the cabin, I was unlikely to find out
now. It took a long time to clear the keyhole with my nail file.
As I worked, I was quite sure that the man in the cabin was
standing motionless on the other side of the door. It was an
eerie feeling and I had to suppress a panicky impulse to run
upstairs to the saloon.

Ironically, I found Greg's whistling reassuring.

Finally I put my lips to the keyhole and whispered, 'Signor
Moro, it's Signorina Grant. Please open the door.'

The silence seemed to stretch endlessly, then all at once the
door was sliding open and I slipped into the cabin. It closed
quickly behind me.

Giulio Moro was facing me, feet planted apart to steady
himself against the motion of the boat. On a level with his chest,

he gripped between his hands the ends of a guest towel which he had twisted into a rope.

In one horrified glance, I recognized the substitute for the short rope, the traditional Sicilian instrument of execution.

It was too much. My hand shot forward in a push that ended up as a violent punch in his chest. He staggered backwards against the bed, his face almost stupid in its astonishment.

'*Diavolessa!*' he gritted at me.

I stormed over him, 'What the devil do you think you are up to? I'm doing my best to help you and all you can think about is behaving like Al Capone! Do you realize that there are three men upstairs who will be down here like lightning at the merest whisper of trouble? Use your head! One of the men is a Chief Detective Superintendent of Scotland Yard. Unless you have discovered the secret of walking on the waters, you had better behave yourself.' I paused for breath. The dark eyes were fixed on my face. 'You are supposed to be Giuseppe. Get upstairs and start acting like him. Prepare coffee and sandwiches for five.'

'The English policeman will recognize me.' His tone was flat and matter-of-fact. The hooded eyes studied me intently.

'I'll carry the tray into the saloon. You prepare it and keep out of sight as much as possible. If you keep your wits about you, the presence of a high-ranking English detective is a help, not a hindrance to you. No one would dream that you could travel back in his company.'

He looked at me in a puzzled way. 'Why are you doing this?'

'Because I owe Michle Spina a favour.'

But in my heart I knew that my motives were not quite as simple as that. My last illusions about the gay, extroverted professor had quite gone. The heady mixture of jovial charm, bonhomie and scholarship still had some appeal, although I recognized that he would have got rid of the children and of me, regretfully no doubt, but firmly. His own interests came first and, I suspected, always would. Bringing Moro down would mean bringing him down also. Much as he deserved it, I wanted no part of it. Much also as I loved Italy, she must, I decided, set her own house in order.

But deeper than any dread of personal involvement was a fear of involving Stewart and Superintendent Lang. It would be, at the very least, a matter of great embarrassment to them to have to deal with the situation. Stewart's rigid code could have international repercussions. For Lang, it would be a delicate matter of protocol, which might well jeopardize future relations with the Sicilian and Italian police. He would not thank me for thrusting under his fastidious English nose an example of Sicilian corruption. Besides, I was coward enough to dread drawing down upon our heads the vengeance of the Mafia.

Tell a bit and keep a bit, had been the advice of my Scottish grandmother. It was, I decided, excellent advice in this situation.

I halted with my hand on the door handle. 'Waken the children,' I said grimly, 'and *I'll* throttle *you*.'

He gave a quickly suppressed laugh. 'You're some girl,' he said and followed me quietly.

At the head of the stairs, Greg Stein was smoking his pipe placidly as he stood at the wheel, his eyes fixed on the dimpling mass of turquoise waters. He looked as far removed from complicity in crime as he was at that moment physically distant from Mars.

I gave him a sour look. Mario had been a better judge of character than I had been. How could I have allowed myself to be stirred by his kiss in Catania? My cheeks grew hot at the recollection.

When I was busy doing nothing in the galley, Stewart poked his head round the door to say pleasantly, 'Your presence, madam, is requested in the saloon. There are things to tell and things to hear.' His glance slid over Moro. 'Be as stubborn as you like about the shoes, but take it from me "a sweet disorder in the dress" simply isn't your style.'

I could cheerfully have killed him. For a moment, I wondered how long it took to get a divorce. After we got married, of course! A man who lost taste for his girl simply because she was not wearing the cream of the Pucci collection deserved an . . . an . . . *Arlene!*

Perhaps it had been a mistake not to verify Benito Capocci's marital situation. And, I concluded airily, it seemed the okay thing nowadays to be part of the Mafia set-up.

'It's a pity you have such a bad temper,' said Moro regretfully, carefully arranging sandwiches on a plate. 'Many women in the north of Italy have your colour of hair, very beautiful, but always they have bad tempers. Pity!'

I glared and took the tray from him. 'Take the wheel,' I said curtly, 'and let Professor Stein have his coffee.'

In the saloon the three men sat side by side on the black leather banquette, like members of an interviewing committee.

Al Scott got automatically to his feet to relieve me of the tray. If his position between Stewart and Lang had been a precautionary measure, it was having no restraining effect on him. He reminded me of one of those rubber figures which bounce back as soon as they have been knocked down. Almost before my eyes a metamorphosis was taking place, the worried lines on the forehead smoothing out, the mouth taking its familiar, upward, humorous quirk and the fun-sparkle coming back into the tired eyes. Even his scrutiny of me was less jaundiced than when he had first come aboard.

From the armchair nearest to the deck, I dispensed coffee and artificial smiles until my jaws ached.

Greg Stein swallowed his coffee in a gulp and got quickly to his feet, very much the big, reliable man whose place was at the wheel.

He cast an uneasy glance in Stewart's direction. 'Sorry, folks,' he said genially. 'It's like driving a car. I make a bad passenger. I'm never really happy unless I'm in complete control of my baby. Must go now, but please help yourself to drinks.' He gestured in the direction of the padded drinks-container.

I could not restrain an ironic smile.

'Not yet, Greg!' My tone was molasses-sweet. 'Not before Stewart thanks you for saving my life.'

I had forgotten how deeply, wonderfully blue my beloved's eyes were. They opened wide now and became steely points.

I had the attention of all four.

'If Greg had not allowed us aboard the *Più Tardi* last night, I am quite sure that by now Pia, Mario and I would have been dead – probably blown to bits, as was attempted earlier in the day. Each of us now has only what we stand up in.'

Carefully, I did not look in Stewart's direction.

'Miss Grant!'

The horror and sympathy in Superintendent Lang's voice was my undoing. I put my head between my hands and sobbed loudly, all the fear and tension finding release in a great, childish, angry bellow. Dimly through the misery I was aware of Stewart's arms going strongly round me, cradling my head against his chest and rubbing the tears away with fingers that even I could feel were shaking in a most uncharacteristic fashion.

Everything was so beautifully, gloriously right again that I took a long time to recover. Greg gave me his handkerchief. Lang put a small glass of brandy into my hand and Al Scott surveyed me quizzically.

There was just *nothing* that man did not know about women.

Greg said tensely, 'It is true. The man who brought Laurie to the *Più Tardi* last night told me what a narrow escape all of them had had. A home-made bomb had been planted in their car. The man who drove the car down from Erice to Trapani was blown to pieces. I was asked to take Laurie and the children right away from the town in case the mistake in identity was discovered and a fresh attempt made.'

The propitiatory note in his voice revolted me.

The others were exchanging rather odd glances.

Somehow, in the midst of my emotional cloudburst, a game of musical chairs had taken place. I was beside Stewart, close beside him, on the banquette. Al Scott had taken my seat and Superintendent Lang was in the armchair facing him.

The boat gave a sudden sickening lurch.

Greg Stein said frantically, 'Pardon me, but Giuseppe is not good at the wheel.'

He disappeared in the direction of the chart-room.

There was an awkward silence which I endured happily from the circle of Stewart's arms.

Reflections from the sea dappled the roof of the saloon and the contented chuckle of water under the stern almost obliterated the angry mutter of voices from the chart-room.

Moro stumped through the saloon and out on to the deck without as much as a glance at any of us.

'Godammit,' Greg Stein yelled, 'that's as good as mutiny. Stay in your quarters and I'll see that you lose your ticket.'

I thought that his performance merited an Oscar at least.

'Laurie,' said Al Scott, in a voice of exaggerated patience, 'we have now been on this boat for more than an hour and a half. I want to see Pia.'

'*You do!*' I sat bolt upright in my indignation, almost spluttering in surprise at his effrontery. 'I've gone to a great deal of trouble to ensure that you *don't* see her and I can think of no good reason why I should change my tactics.'

He was gazing at me with that mixture of quizzical good humour and tolerant exasperation which I had found so appealing in the past. Then I had suspected that it was part of his armoury of tricks, but now, when it had worn threadbare, it seemed real.

Stewart said hastily, 'Laurie, Mr Scott is showing a very natural concern . . .'

'*Concern!*' I shook off Stewart's restraining hand and glared at Scott. 'What kind of concern did you show when you took Pia from those rotten parents of hers and pretended that you were her father? Oh, I don't mean the kidnapping. That wasn't the real cruelty. I suppose, technically, I was a kidnapper, too.' I waved that airily aside, stabbing a finger angrily in his direction. 'Have you the faintest idea how slowly and painfully a deaf child builds up vocabulary, adding one word to another, like acquiring bricks of gold? Have you any idea how puzzling human relationships and quite ordinary situations are to such a child? What the devil do you think Pia understands now by the word *father*?'

His eyes were fixed on me as if he were seeing me for the first time.

Stewart and Lang were very still.

I rushed on. 'You brought a killer dog into the house where Pia was, a dog you had had for only a matter of *days*. I don't care whether it was meant to protect Pia or scare off the Daltons or the Brigade of Guards. The point was that neither you nor anybody else in your household really knew how that dog might behave in any given situation. You didn't know and yet you exposed Pia to the risk of being mauled by it.'

'Laurie . . .'

'I haven't finished. Let me tell you – I'm glad that dog is dead. *Glad!* I've never seen a more vicious-looking animal in my life and yet you let it run around loose where Pia was!'

He was looking at me with a kind of awe. 'You killed the dog! You! But it's just not possible! How could a little girl like you kill a Dobermann?'

Caution halted me for a moment. Bruna, I reminded myself quickly, must not be involved. I made an expansive gesture and hoped that I looked tough enough to have dealt with a black mamba.

'Obviously, you still have *something* to learn about women, Mr Scott. Your principal crime,' I gritted at him, 'is that you have played a sort of yo-yo game with Pia's emotions and fears. What kind of conduct was it for you and Susan Bradford to take her on the *Golden Eye*, among a bunch of extroverted, muscle-bound children? Have you the least inkling of how confused and afraid she was?' The treacherous tears welled up. I brushed them angrily away.

'You love her,' he said in a strange voice.

'Of course I do, but it looks to me as if in all the eight years of her life nobody else has. Nobody seems to have investigated the reason for her deafness. Nobody seems to have wondered if it is a hysterical condition.' My voice rose and I tried to control it. 'Do you know that there are indications that she can hear something? If, as I suspect, yesterday's explosion triggered off something, then she can be taught to speak.'

277

There was a silence in the saloon so profound, so charged with electricity that for a moment I was afraid. I hurried on.

'Did anyone take the trouble to find out if there is indeed nothing organically wrong? Did nobody suspect that she suffers from a long-standing trauma? Somebody subjected that poor baby to a shock so great that she cut herself off from all the sounds in the world. *Were you responsible, Mr Clever Scott?*'

He buried his face in his hands and, to my utter horror, a tear seemed to spurt between his fingers and plopped on to the floor.

Superintendent Lang's calm voice halted me. The dark, tip-tilted eyes were wise and kind. 'Obviously the situation is in need of clarification. I suggest that we take advantage of Professor Stein's hospitality and that I pour a brandy for each of us.' He busied himself at the drinks-container. 'Wasn't it Petronius Arbiter who wrote of this very area . . . "this place demands the reckoning of my days"? That is what we must do now – give a reckoning of our days and get at the truth.'

Stewart was watching me impassively, though he kept one of my hands imprisoned in his.

'I can cap that,' I said bitterly, my eyes on Scott's down-bent head. 'When I went to school that passage started . . . *i nunc et vitae fugientis tempora vende divitibus cenis.* If you did not have the benefit of a classical education, Mr Scott, that means . . . "Go now, and sell your life, your fleeting life, for feasts and riches." Isn't that what you have done?'

His head shot up, the swimming eyes blazing with anger. 'Of course not! You've got it all wrong.'

Stewart said equably, 'Swallow the brandy, both of you, and leave the talking for a few minutes to Superintendent Lang and myself. All of us have been involved in a sorry tale of cupidity, stupidity, tragedy, with at times the elements of a comedy of errors. Both evil and foolish mistakes have been made. Let us try and get the record straight now.'

He got his pipe going and above the flame of the match his eyes met mine with the look of tender humour which always left me defenceless. 'Do put your shoes on, darling,' he suggested, sliding a hand under my elbow to help me up.

By the time I had rescued them from the head of the stairway and had taken my place on the banquette, Al Scott's face was back to normal.

Stewart said evenly, 'Laurie, Superintendent Lang and Mr Scott already know of my involvement in the case of the kidnapping of Pia and of my discoveries later at Exton. There is no longer any doubt that the Daltons planned the disappearance of nurse and child, planned to collect the insurance money and duped Emma Rice or Susan Bradford, whatever you choose to call her, into believing that they would allow her to adopt the child quietly and would finance Pia's support and education.' He looked levelly at Al Scott. 'Your fiancée appears to be dangerously gullible.'

Scott stiffened and his face flushed angrily.

'Yes,' Lang interposed. 'The significance of the payment of *three* months' salary appears to have escaped the young lady. Mr Noble and I established that, legally, the Daltons' responsibility for the child ended then.'

I opened my mouth, but he put up a minatory hand.

'We cannot prove it, but my friend Stewart and I are convinced that they planned to kill the child early in May. Isn't it correct, Stewart, that Mrs Dalton lodged her claim, timed to ensure that settlement would take place at the beginning of May or at any rate some time during that month?'

'Yes. Quite clearly, the nurse was destined to depart this life at the same time as the child.'

'But how could parents plan anything as diabolical as the death of their own child? It's unnatural.'

'Stewart has been of immense assistance to us in answering that and other vital questions.' Lang's eyes twinkled. 'Between you, you have given some of my fellows several good lessons in the art of detection. No wonder I cultivate Stewart's friendship!'

'I had help,' Stewart stated baldly. 'Let me answer your question, Laurie, and then I suggest you give us your side of the story.' He tamped down the tobacco in his pipe and seemed to be at pains to look at nobody in particular.

'I started with three facts – Mrs Dalton's age, her Christian names and that she was of English nationality. I handed those three solitary pieces of information to Tom Curzon, who passed them on to his clerk, Thompson. He went to work on the records at Somerset House and came up with three very illuminating certificates. The first, a birth certificate, told me that Deborah Corinne Peat had been born in Bristol. It was not difficult to follow her career there. When she was ten years old, she was sent to what was then called an Approved School. It was in Fishponds, which is a suburb of Bristol.

'At the age of eighteen, she was transferred to a Borstal Institution, near Clifton, where she remained until she was twenty-three – an unusually long period. But then the circumstances were unusual.'

It was very quiet in the saloon.

'At the age of ten, Deborah Peat had murdered her six-year-old sister – not, I may add, in a fit of temper, but coldly, sadistically, remorselessly. While she was at Fishponds she almost succeeded in killing a fellow inmate. She was an unfortunate child in that nobody seems to have pointed out or indeed to have realized that she was a psychopath, in desperate need of treatment and that it was criminally irresponsible to turn her out at the age of twenty-three on an unsuspecting world.'

Lang's face was a stern mask and Scott seemed to be having difficulty with his breathing.

'As you will have guessed, Deborah Corinne Peat became, in spite of that calamitous start, the wonderful soprano who thrilled two continents and, also in the fullness of time, became the glamorous Mrs Eric Dalton.' He paused. 'Suppose you take the story from there, Laurie.'

I was so sickened by what I had heard that I hurried over my part in the affair, omitting only Jerry Mason's connection with Gregory Stein and what I knew about the Moro affair.

I looked accusingly at Al Scott. 'You sicked the Mafia on to me at Catania. That was a horrible thing to do.'

Instead of looking penitent, he merely looked interested. 'How the devil did you shake them off?' he enquired. 'I would have taken a bet that nobody could have done that.'

'I went to the head of the Mafia in Palermo, and asked for his protection. After that it was easy.'

Lang looked stunned. Obviously this was news to him. 'And he gave it to you? How did you manage that?'

'It wasn't difficult. He is besotted with antique lacquerwork. I made a bargain with him – the only possible bargain – promised him, in return for our safety, access to a valuable Vernis Martin manuscript. I knew that he couldn't possibly resist that.' I sounded suitably airy, as though making a deal with the head of the Mafia was just one of those little, unimportant things. 'Of course I took the precaution of telephoning my antique-dealer friend in Glasgow to make sure that Spina didn't try any under-the-counter arrangements. Natie understood perfectly.'

Stewart said evenly, 'But what happens if your antique dealer decides not to sell?'

I stared at him blankly. 'But how could Natie sell what he hasn't got? There is no Vernis Martin manuscript. I made it up.'

Stewart's expression was unreadable. 'I suspected as much.'

'You mean, Miss Grant, that you *tricked* the head of the Mafia?' Lang's voice had a strangled sound.

Al Scott was looking at me with such an expression of horror that I wanted to laugh. 'Do you realize, Laurie, what he'll do to you when he finds out?'

Suddenly it did not seem funny at all. I turned blindly to Stewart.

'There must be an angel looking after you,' he said with a comforting smile. 'Michle Spina died early this morning. In future, don't push your luck too far.'

On a wave of nausea, I was remembering the hefty punch I had administered to Giulio Moro. My capacity for irritating those in high places seemed to be unlimited.

Stewart gave me a reassuring pat on that accursed red hair that is always getting me into trouble. 'Don't look so stricken, darling. There's a roar in the British lion yet. Nothing is going to happen to you.'

I gulped and went on with the saga.

When I described the blowing up of the car, Al Scott's handsome face became almost ugly with anger. 'Mario's CASMS saved all our lives,' he stated flatly. 'When I found that bug he had placed, I had a good look around. There was a time-bomb in the cockpit of the *Golden Eye*. I heaved it into the Mediterranean and knew that Dalton was somewhere on the island and would not leave until he had got rid of Pia, Susan and me. I went almost mad with worry when it dawned on me that you had taken off with Pia. I didn't know what to think. Besides, I couldn't figure out where that cocky young American fitted into the picture.'

Carefully I avoided his eyes. The less said about Jerry Mason the better.

'Well,' said Lang in his clipped British voice, 'no one will have to worry any more about the Daltons. Eric Dalton had the ingredients for his bomb-making in his luggage, probably in a small case. We'll never know for certain, for Corinne and Eric Dalton disappeared last night in an unexplained explosion on the road between Taormina and Messina.'

A picture of Benito Capocci's hawklike face came vividly before my mind. There had not, after all, been time to allow the Daltons to wonder and fear. Vengeance had been swift and, in their case, merciful.

The saloon was full of the hot Italian sunshine, but I shivered and moved closer to Stewart.

He said gently, 'Have you told us everything, Laurie?'

I looked at Al Scott's face, drained now of all its humour and smiling charm and somehow the words about the pistol, the blood-stained handkerchief and the letter stuck in my throat. All my anger and hatred had drained away, purged perhaps by the violent, pointless deaths of two people, rich in talents, but apparently cursed by the gods from birth.

I buried my head in Stewart's shoulder – Laurie, the ostrich, who could not bear to look any longer at the ugliness of man.

Scott's threat? Mario could have been mistaken, I told myself.

Lang stirred in his chair and said quietly to Stewart, 'I think you have something to add?'

'Yes. Those other certificates . . .' He pushed me upright. 'One was the certificate of a marriage which had taken place in London nine years ago between an English woman called Deborah Corinne Peat and an American called August Scoffone. The other certificate was the birth certificate of their daughter, Elvira Pia Scoffone, born one year later. I have been looking for a man called August.' He paused. 'An American of Italian extraction who had probably Americanized his name by deed poll.' He looked at Al Scott. 'You are the man called August.'

I gave Al Scott such a look of blinding happiness that it seemed to dazzle him. 'You are Pia's father! Oh, how wonderful!' My eyes filled with tears. All I could think about then was Pia's coming happiness. I said earnestly to him, 'Never for a moment did she lose her love for you or her faith in you. That's pretty wonderful.'

A gun, a letter, a blood-stained handkerchief . . . fiddle-de-dee!

I leaned forward. 'Do you know what she wrote when I asked her where home was? She wrote, "Where Mr Scott is!" '

The other two might not have existed.

Al Scott said urgently, 'When she was a baby, her mother tried to kill her. Pia has the scar of the bullet wound on her right arm yet. I kept the gun and the bullet and made Corinne write an account of what she had done. I kept them as a sort of insurance that she would treat Pia properly.'

He swallowed convulsively, 'What a fool I've been! I thought Corinne had a fiendish temper, uncontrolled because she was spoiled, but never for a moment did it cross my mind that she was psychopathic.'

His face was dark with remembered grief. 'At our divorce, I had a court order giving me access to the child from the first of May each year until the end of July – three months. I didn't ever exercise that right until this year. My child was too young to be in my care. But this year I guessed from Susan's story that

Corinne and Eric Dalton had planned something bad. It didn't take me too long to work out what it was.'

He glanced briefly in Stewart's direction. 'That means that I had a perfect right to take Pia wherever I wanted, from the first of May. I had made up my mind to put pressure on Corinne through the gun and the letter, to force her to relinquish all rights to my child. I had finally come to realize just what danger Pia was in, but a man doesn't readily admit to himself that a woman he once married could be guilty of infanticide. You keep pushing that thought away.'

He looked guiltily at me. 'Susan and I are not completely stupid. We guessed what it might do to Pia if she found out that her own mother had tried to kill her. We were feeling our way.'

A desperate hope came into his face. 'Do you really think that she may be able to hear again?'

I nodded vigorously, with all the authority of an eminent audiologist. I felt like turning handsprings because a little lost girl had finally found the way home.

Quickly I described the moment on the cable-car when the ear-shattering explosion of the automobile had rocked the cable-car violently and Pia had buried her face in my lap against the noise. The explosion of a gun eight years ago had locked ears and throat. Now, ironically, Corinne Dalton, who had made her child a deaf-mute, had, in another shattering report, set her free.

I said swiftly, 'The person who has helped her most has been Mario Biagotti. The rapport between them is wonderful. You will have to find the way to keep them together. They really need each other.'

At that moment Al Scott would probably have promised me the Kingdom of Heaven.

Stewart said mildly, 'Don't you think he might see his little daughter?'

I flew to the galley with the man called August close behind me. I could hear the telephone ringing briefly in the cabin below. Happily I said, 'Mario, open the door! Tell Pia her father is coming down to take her home and I suspect that you are going with them!'

There was a short silence. He said plaintively, 'Do you think he could bring down some grub? Pia and I are starving. We've been sitting here for over five hours. We've eaten all the sweets, but somebody stole the chewing-gum.'

I pushed the sandwiches into Al's hands and prodded him gently towards the stairway. I was impatient to get back to the saloon and Stewart.

From his post behind the wheel, Greg Stein twisted to look at me and smiled broadly, but there was the sheen of perspiration on his forehead. 'We should be in Trapani in about twenty minutes. Look! Aren't the lights beautiful?' He was attempting to mask his nervousness with a joviality that had a hollow ring. He would never, I was sure, go back to Filicudi. For him, it was finished.

Beyond the curve of the glass, the town was outlined by a string of softly glowing amber that crept up the hill in a fading thread of light. There was a burst of music from a harbour café and the anguished notes of a love song trembled on the air.

It *was* beautiful. Everything was beautiful!

The big American hesitated, then said uncertainly, 'Don't you think you should have a word with your fiancé, Laurie? I mean . . . his jealousy is so ridiculous. He might get awkward if he doesn't understand how it has been with you and me.'

Jealous! So that was what had been wrong!

I flew into the saloon, colliding with Superintendent Lang.

'I'm going to watch Professor Stein taking this boat in,' he said. 'For a landlubber like me, it's fascinating.' I thought there was a twinkle in his eye.

Stewart was outside at the prow, hands thrust deep in his pockets, eyes fixed steadily on the fast approaching shore.

I slipped between him and the rails and felt his arms go strongly around me.

Like Pia, I had come home.

The wind off the sea was almost unbearably fresh and sweet, with the tang of seaweed and lemons on its breath.

I snuggled close against Stewart, shivering suddenly with exhaustion and the release of tension.

He opened his jacket and pulled me against his chest. Comfort flowed from its warmth and solidity. Presently, under my hands, the steady beat of his heart quickened and I could feel the savage leap of his blood as if in response to mine.

Weariness fell away. As I raised my face blindly for his kiss, the dark vault of the sky seemed to spin dizzily above us. A solitary star streaked in a silvery, fading arc across the blackness.

'Catch a falling star and all your dreams will come true,' I quoted softly.

He laughed low in his throat then, the deep, triumphant note of the male who knows that he is supreme. 'The only star I need to imprison is you, my darling. And I know how to do it, my little flirt. Within a wedding band.'

'*Flirt!*' Indignation made my voice squeak.

'Yes . . . flirt. My darling, can you put your hand on your heart and swear that you ever thought very long or very lovingly about me while you were with that Casanova, Scott, or that pompous ass, Stein? Tell the truth! And what about young Mason? You've been suspiciously quiet about him.'

I buried my nose deeper in his chest and wriggled impatiently.

His lips brushed gently across my hair, but his hands on my body were suddenly urgent. 'You're susceptible, Laurie, very susceptible and it took this case to show me the danger.' There was no accusation in his voice. 'You're my girl. Let them kidnap the Queen of Siam, the President of the United States and the Sultan of Johore! Let them rifle Fort Knox, steal the Honours of Scotland and make off with the Mint! I won't be there to care. I'll be off on my honeymoon. Care to join me, Miss Grant?'

There was a long, long interval in which there was no deck under our feet, no sound of the moving waters in our ears and no gold-girt shore easing gently towards us. Slowly, reluctantly, we came back from a world of singing silences and of a joy that seemed endlessly fresh and was born anew with each shared breath.

While I strove to get back to normality, Stewart murmured in my ear, 'Wasn't that sailor, Giuseppe, remarkably like the Mafia boss, Moro?' There was a hint of laughter behind the words.

Hastily I closed his lips in the quickest possible way. 'And,' he mumbled, 'what's a CASMS?'

'Oh,' I said airily, 'just child's play.'